"What if you knew that for the rest of your life
you never again had to worry what someone thought
of you, because you knew you were totally loved?
Every thought. Every gesture.
Every laugh. Every curve of your body."

D0483257

Dear Reader,

Perhaps within all of us is a spark of something we call destiny, some inner yearning that enables us to bravely push forward each day, sure that something wondrous awaits. Casey O'Reilly has been waiting thirty-one years for hers to make an appearance, and when destiny finally calls she's unprepared.

Heaven on Earth *is the story of a very reluctant heroine, an ordinary woman who experiences an extraordinary love. It began with my own visit to one of my favorite cities, Santa Fe. There is a reason it is known as "The City Different," for there is magic in the air and in the land. Steeped in an ancient culture, it seemed to call to me to write about it, and one day, while sitting on a rock and looking out to the breathtaking mountains as lightning flashed in the distance, I imagined the beginning of the book you are now holding. All I saw was the scene where the hero and heroine meet, yet I was filled with excitement, for I felt I was about to push the boundaries of time travel once again by having not one, but two travelers journeying through time to discover their heroic nature and the magic of love.*

These two characters captured my imagination in Santa Fe, and in the following months, while I wrote, they also entered my heart. I hope you will invite them into yours for a short while and watch as they each discover it's true . . . there is such a thing as destiny. Maybe we only have to be open to it.

Kindest regards,

Constance O'Day

Other Avon Books by
Constance O'Day-Flannery

ANYWHERE YOU ARE
ONCE AND FOREVER

ATTENTION: ORGANIZATIONS AND CORPORATIONS
Most Avon Books paperbacks are available at special quantity
discounts for bulk purchases for sales promotions, premiums, or
fund-raising. For information, please call or write:

**Special Markets Department, HarperCollins Publishers, Inc.,
10 East 53rd Street, New York, N.Y. 10022-5299.
Telephone: (212) 207-7528. Fax: (212) 207-7222.**

Constance O'Day-Flannery

Heaven On Earth

AVON BOOKS
An Imprint of HarperCollinsPublishers

This is a work of fiction. Names, characters, places, and incidents are products of the author's imagination or are used fictitiously and are not to be construed as real. Any resemblance to actual events, locales, organizations, or persons, living or dead, is entirely coincidental.

AVON BOOKS
An Imprint of HarperCollins*Publishers*
10 East 53rd Street
New York, New York 10022-5299

Copyright © 2000 by Constance O'Day-Flannery
Excerpt from *Here Comes the Bride* copyright © 2000 by Pamela Morsi; excerpt from *Heaven on Earth* copyright © 2000 by Constance O'Day-Flannery; excerpt from *His Wicked Promise* copyright © 2000 by Sandra Kleinschmidt; excerpt from *Rules of Engagement* copyright © 2000 by Christina Dodd; excerpt from *Just the Way You Are* copyright © 2000 by Barbara Freethy; excerpt from *The Viscount Who Loved Me* copyright © 2000 by Julie Cotler Pottinger
ISBN: 0-380-80805-6
www.avonromance.com

All rights reserved. No part of this book may be used or reproduced in any manner whatsoever without written permission, except in the case of brief quotations embodied in critical articles and reviews. For information address Avon Books, an Imprint of HarperCollins Publishers.

First Avon Books paperback printing: August 2000

Avon Trademark Reg. U.S. Pat. Off. and in Other Countries, Marca Registrada, Hecho en U.S.A.
HarperCollins® is a trademark of HarperCollins Publishers Inc.

Printed in the U.S.A.

WCD   10   9   8   7   6   5   4   3   2   1

If you purchased this book without a cover, you should be aware that this book is stolen property. It was reported as "unsold and destroyed" to the publisher, and neither the author nor the publisher has received any payment for this "stripped book."

This one is for the readers,
those wonderful time travelers
. . . You know who you are.

Prologue

*S*omehow, even though everything in her life seemed at times to point to the opposite, she believed a greater destiny awaited her. She really believed it, yet truthfully, that eternal hope was becoming more difficult to hold on to amid the incessant routine of daily living. She just knew *something* awaited her, something that would point to her purpose, alter her life, 'cause this just couldn't be all there was . . . and if this *was* it . . . well, she was gonna be pissed.

Okay, so she was probably working the dullest job in America, in the accounting department of a major soap manufacturer . . . not exactly excitement and glamour. In her mind's eye she saw what she had left yesterday . . . the rows upon rows of gray desks, the beige computers sitting precisely at right angles, the stooped shoulders of the workers, mostly women, punching in numbers of cases of soap. Like their very lives depended on how many cases of

Sundrifty were ordered that day, increasing the coffers of one of the biggest corporations in the world. She suddenly realized that in the last eight years she had worked her way up to be the head soap drone and number cruncher, and where had it gotten her? Really? A sinking feeling grabbed hold of her stomach. Had she sold her soul for soap? *Soap?*

She suddenly found that she couldn't care any longer whether Sundrifty was closing the gap with Tide, or if Mrs. Buttery was beating I Can't Believe It's Butter. It all seemed beyond ridiculous in the greater scheme of things. Sundrifty. Mrs. Buttery. What genius thought up those product names anyway? Was it because she was finally on vacation, away from the office, or was it something more serious than a career slump? What had she done to herself? she wondered as she drove into the setting sun and took a serious inventory of her life.

She was thirty-one, didn't even own a cat, and had to admit the image of sinking in quicksand crossed her mind at least once a day . . . and far more on weekends since all her friends were now married and busy. They seemed to look at her as if she was either competition or pathetically left behind, and, quite frankly, acted as though she had some unknown disease. It was called being single, and there were no vaccines or miracle cures in the new millennium for that one. She was out there, drifting aimlessly, on a lonely sea of uncoupled madness. Sheesh, it did sound pathetic, yet how was a woman to meet men in today's crazy world?

There were on-the-job flirtations that never worked out, and then, feeling rejected, the guy wouldn't talk to you until he found someone else to date. Accountants weren't exactly known for their joie de vivre, and she yearned for someone *alive,* or at least breathing with some vitality.

Forget the club scene. It was beyond depressing, especially since she was beginning to feel like a chaperone at a frat party. It all seemed so mindless . . . but it had been the appearance of the Macarena that had convinced her her club days were definitely finished. As soon as that phenomenon had hit, she'd taken it as a divine sign that her time of being cool was over, way over. Plus, it just took too damn long to pull her act together in front of the mirror now . . . another sign of aging, she supposed. She adjusted the sunglasses she'd bought at the airport before she began this journey west. Is that what happens when one ages? You just get tired?

She thought of her home in Pennsylvania. There weren't that many supermarkets to meander through in a town of under twenty thousand, and anyway, it was only the married men who tried to hit on her in the vegetable aisle. There was also only one art gallery in her hometown, and her venture into the creative arts hadn't provided her with a single prospective heterosexual male. What was an intelligent woman to do? How long before her family started fixing her up with strangers, promoting her with that dreaded kiss of death . . . *she's got a great personality*?

Whine, whine, whine, she mentally berated herself, and then thought she was justified as long as she did it silently. She was just about at the end of her rope as far as finding a partner was concerned, and she was tired, tired of looking. She'd quit browsing the mega bookstores when one genius attempted to draw her into conversation by swearing that Noel Coward had been a professional wrestler. She'd almost spit out her mocha cappuccino as she'd disengaged from Mr. Intelligence and vowed to stay home and rent a video before again attempting to find a decent man. Wherever he was, whoever he was, if he even existed at all . . . he would have to find her. She was through seeking the impossible.

Casey O'Reilly had surrendered.

Mountain ranges on both sides of her were illuminated by the setting sun in hues of yellow and brown. Shrubs of white and purple sagebrush, varieties of yucca trees and piñon and juniper, whisked by her view. It was an aromatic warm evening in June and she found relief in the dry air rather than the humid conditions she was used to on the East Coast. There was no need for air-conditioning in the car as she rested her arm out the open window and felt the desert energy enter her pores. A sense of freedom began to invite her onward and she found herself settling comfortably into it.

Funny the way life turns out, she thought as she drove on. Once upon a time, in a mental land far, far away, she'd actually thought that by the time she had turned twenty-seven she would be happily married, preparing for her first child, and carrying on the societal torch of family values. She almost laughed at herself now. She was four years late and had thrown out the damn schedule.

Maybe she would spend the rest of her life alone. It really wouldn't be so terrible, she thought as what looked to be a bolt of lightning flashed in the dimming skyline. She wanted a child, though. Really wanted one. That was all she knew, all she'd known ever since she was a little girl. Growing up, she'd gone along with the tenets of the liberated woman, believing she was equal to any male even if he didn't acknowledge it yet. She'd gone on to college and a career and was independent and all that . . . but the one thing she had always known was that she wanted to be a mother, that her child would be precious and somehow make a difference in the world.

Probably all women thought that, she surmised as she drove toward the fading sunset and again thought of being a single mother. Somehow, even though she had given up looking for a mate, she still didn't have the courage to walk into a sperm bank. It seemed too clinical, too cold, and her family would never understand, but she hadn't ruled it out. If being a mother was the only thing she knew for certain that she wanted to do with her life, why should she have to explain to anyone? It wasn't like she was hung up on romance and desperately seeking her hero! Now was the time to be practical.

The sun had disappeared entirely from its spectacular setting, engulfed by edgeless clouds of ominous blues, grays, and purple. She removed her sunglasses, tossing them onto the passenger seat as her mind continued to wander and she blankly stared into the approaching darkness.

Where were the heros today, anyway? Seemed to her that all the men who were admired by society were either making billions or shooting baskets, neither of which she considered heroic. She started to think of mythical heros and realized she didn't want a warrior either, too much testosterone. Wasn't a man who remained faithful to his wife, provided for his family, and helped raise his children heroic? In her book he was . . . he was just already married. Maybe a sperm bank was the way to go after all. Maybe that was why she was making this trip across the country.

Watching a spectacular light show begin, she suddenly realized she was racing right down the middle of this valley as the lightning slashed at the mountains around her. She mentally began counting . . . two one thousand, three . . . yet she found herself wincing at the distant rumble anyway. She began wondering if she was soon going to be driving through rain. Maybe not. Her sister had told her that electrical-heat storms in the desert were common.

Forcing her mind from the storm and her own life, Casey imagined her sister waiting for her in Santa Fe. She still couldn't believe her younger sister had relocated to the desert from the Northeast, yet Amy had sounded so happy that when she'd invited her to visit, Casey had decided to see for herself what her sister was raving about.

She kept her eyes riveted on the black highway but sensed the flashes were charging increasingly closer to her. She wished she'd paid closer attention to the weather report on the plane before landing. She didn't recall hearing about any storm. She'd flown into Albuquerque, rented this small car, and headed out into the picturesque desert. Relax, she reminded herself. In less than an hour she would be at her sister's home. She thought at rush hour there would be more cars on the interstate, but she'd only seen a few. Probably everyone knew to wait out the storm and only tourists were crazy enough to venture out into it.

Thank goodness she was in a car. She had always heard it was safe to be in a car during a storm like this. Just keep driving, her mind encouraged as she rolled the window up and pressed her foot down on the accelerator. She gripped the plastic steering wheel with both hands and glanced into the rearview mirror. She could see a car approaching and noticed the sky was lighter behind her. Great, she was driving into the storm, not outrunning it. She took a deep breath and turned on the radio for some news, maybe a weather report, but all she heard was static and garbled words. She flipped the radio to AM, and it was worse. Okay, music. She needed some music to calm her nerves and fumbled in her purse for the Walkman she'd used on the long plane ride. Her fingers found the case and pulled out the tape. Popping it into the tape player, she settled back and tried to relax as the smooth voice of Jackson Browne filled the interior of the tiny vehicle.

She knew the words by heart and started singing along. Great lyrics about trusting yourself rang true within her and her voice sang out as the other car passed on her left.

"Next voice you hear will be your own . . ."

She didn't care if she looked like an idiot, all alone and

singing her heart out. It always helped when she was nervous. And she was beginning to get really nervous as the lightning increased. It wasn't just one or two streaks, but seven or eight simultaneously exploding all around the desert floor. Noticing the red running lights of the car speeding in front of her, Casey turned on her headlights and was glad that she could follow someone into the darkness. She could barely make out the distant mountains on either side of her now.

At once, a streak of brilliant white light exploded almost on top of her and Casey jerked in fright as the road and everything around her seemed to reverberate in response.

"Next voice you hear," she sang louder with emotion, as her head bobbed in time to the music, "next voice you hear, the next voice you hear will be your own . . . *Shit!*"

A loud thump suddenly hit the front of the car, and instantly she began fighting the violent shaking of the steering wheel as the car swerved sharply to the right. Automatically releasing the accelerator and using both hands to counteract the motion, she pulled and pulled to the left until her arms ached. A rhythmic thudding became louder as the car slowed and she was reminded of a flat tire. With much effort, she managed to pull the car to the side of the road. Once off the highway, she let go of the wheel, slammed the transmission into park, and pulled up on the emergency brake lever.

Stunned, she collapsed against the seat and stared out the front windshield. What the hell was she going to do now? She didn't have a cell phone to call for help and there wasn't another car in sight. Rubbing her hands to get circulation back into them, she figured she would just sit in the car and wait until someone came. She fumbled around with the steering column until she found the hazard lights and then sat back and finally allowed the tension to leave her body.

"The next voice you hear will be your own . . ."

"Oh, shut up," she snapped at the tape, and turned off the car. Really, what could she do? This was a rental car and she hadn't a clue how to change the tire and she certainly wasn't about to get out in the middle of a lightning storm to try and figure it out. Looking into the rearview mirror again, Casey caught her bottom lip between her teeth and wondered whether another car would come by soon—and how she would flag it down.

Damn, maybe she should get out and check the car. What if she hit something? She couldn't see anything in the road behind her, but it was getting dark and if she was going to help herself, she ought to begin before total darkness descended. Opening the tiny glove compartment, she pulled out the car's manual and turned on the overhead lights. She flipped through the pages until she saw the illustration for inserting the jack. Okay, she could do this, she thought . . . when another assault of lightning torched the sky, and thunder roared in its wake.

Shaking with fright, Casey didn't know how long she could just sit alone in the little car. How long did these electrical storms last? What if no one came? She couldn't remain out here in the desert alone. She didn't even have a flashlight, so if she was going to attempt to change the tire, maybe she'd better do it soon. But she was scared.

Be brave, she told herself. It would only take a second . . . She could run out and check the damage. Maybe it wasn't a flat tire at all. Maybe she had struck something and all she needed to do was clear it away . . . and maybe she was grasping at straws. Perhaps patience wasn't one of her strong suits, but just sitting around didn't seem to be helping anything.

Every time she worked up the courage to open the car door, another intense round of body-pounding sound and blinding light surrounded the vehicle, as though warning her to stay within its shelter. Okay, she was safe here because the tires were rubber, so even if the car were hit by lightning, she should be all right as long as she wasn't touching anything metal. That was what she'd heard anyway. Plus, staying in the car right now seemed the smartest move.

Again she looked in the rearview mirror and sighed with disappointment at the darkness behind her. She felt the beginnings of despair descend upon her like a heavy, sodden blanket, and her eyes were stinging. No sense in crying now. It wouldn't help. Damn, she should have just spent the extra money and rented a midsize car. At least she wouldn't be in this stupid plastic model that had fallen apart less than twenty minutes after she'd left the airport! Amy was going to be worried, and she had no way to reassure her sister that she was okay, just stranded in the desert in the most incredible lightning storm she had ever seen in her life.

Breathe, she told herself. Let go of the stress. She could only sit and wait it out . . . be entertained by the spectacular show of nature. If she weren't so frightened, it would be awesome. How she wished she were with someone, anyone, right now. Five streaks exploded in quick succession around the car, and the ground rolled in retaliation beneath her. She held on to the steering wheel, twisting her fingers around it tightly, as though the action might stop her mounting fear. It didn't, and the hair on her body seemed to rise of its own will as a weird energy entered her body. It was the storm. It had to be.

A light caught her eye and she looked with hope once more into the rearview mirror. Two lights! A car! Someone was coming! Relief swept through her while at the same time her mind seemed to yell at her to get out and stand in front of the car to wave the driver down. Now terrified of the lightning directly above her, Casey admitted to herself she was even more scared of being alone, so she gripped the door handle and whispered aloud, "You can do this. You *have* to do this. Do it!"

In one swift act of courage, Casey O'Reilly opened the car door and stepped into the unknown, into the dark and terrifying night, just as a most brilliant, powerful streak of light enveloped her in a blinding, searing heat that swept through her body with incredible force, taking her beyond the car, beyond the road . . . beyond anything she had ever imagined.

He cautiously eased his pickup truck behind the red compact that had just been encircled with a blazing iridescent crash of lightning. Letting out his breath, he slowly opened the door, stepped to the ground, and made his way to the vehicle. In the illumination from the truck's lights, he saw the open car door and a blue leather shoe on the ground, and he heard the rhythmic ping signaling that the keys were still in the ignition. No one was inside.

In a flash of light, he saw a purse and the car's manual opened on the passenger seat. Looking around again, as though for signs of life, he reached in and unzipped the purse. Bringing out a woman's small wallet, he flipped it open as another bolt of lightning illuminated the driver's-license picture of a woman named Casey O'Reilly, a woman from Pennsylvania. He held it up against the truck's lights. In seconds his mind memorized the statistics . . . five foot four, 130 pounds, birth date, blonde hair, blue eyes.

He stood for several moments, staring at the picture, and then squinted around into the surrounding desert. There was nothing moving anywhere. He slipped the wallet into his pocket and picked up the woman's shoe, noticing a burn mark on the heel. Tensing his shoulders, he made a decision, despite the great reluctance he felt, and a single word escaped his lips.

"Damn . . ."

One

*E*very muscle in her body ached and it was all she could do to remain curled in a tight fetal position to protect herself from the sand whipping her body and the deafening roar that was overwhelming her. She could barely breathe and didn't know if she had the energy to move at all. Her brain felt fried, and reasoning was beyond her as pain continued to assault her from every direction, like pins thrust into her exposed skin. She spit sand out of her mouth, and groaned as she forced her hand to her lips to wipe it away. It took such an effort that she wanted to cry out her anguish, yet couldn't expend the energy ... yet survival impulse kicked in and she labored to open her eyes.

Immediately she closed them in response to the torrential wind that forced particles of sand into them. Her eyes now watering in retaliation, she blinked furiously, and mentally commanded herself to move again, hiding her face under her arm as the sandstorm lashed relentlessly and charges of lightning crashed all around her.

Had she died? Was this hell? Purgatory? Never in her life had she faced such an intense, terrible force of nature. Her chest throbbed with every intake of breath, as though someone had punched her, and her body began to shake violently, as if the ground rumbling beneath her were demanding she comply with its motion.

Somehow her brain sent the message that if she were dead, she wouldn't feel this pain, and she must move, find shelter, any protection. Weary, more exhausted than she had ever been, and frightened, Casey again tried to summon the energy to lift her head from the ground even slightly. Slowly, sending signals to each muscle in her arm, she again managed to bring her hand to her face. Sheltering her eyes, she tried once more to see where she was as sand pelted her hand and lightning illuminated the desolate landscape. She was in the desert.

A desert? Her brain couldn't compute it and she closed her eyes as she allowed her hand to fall back to the sand. Why . . . ? How had she gotten here? Another flash of lightning streaked before her closed lids and Casey shuddered in fright from the crack of thunder as she tried to pull her legs closer to her chest. Her left foot burned with a horrible pain. She had to get up, find shelter. If she stayed here, she would be hit and . . .

Move, her brain commanded, and for the first time in her life Casey felt removed from her body. It was as though her body weren't *hers*! In her mind's eye she saw herself observing the whole situation, making decisions, like she was trying to find a way to fix a broken piece of machinery.

Was this death, this feeling of separation from her body? She wasn't ready to die! She wanted . . . She wasn't sure what she wanted, yet just the thought brought her back and she felt the pain again.

Then the images came to her . . . a storm . . . getting out of a car . . . and then heat . . . unbearable heat . . . nearly suffocating . . . and a light so bright she felt she had melted into it.

Shaking her head in confusion, she focused on getting away from the stinging sand and the terrifying electrical storm. Pushing herself up onto her elbows, she kept her face close to her chest as her straight, short hair snapped against her cheeks. Cupping her hand to her eyes, she again peeked out to the desert while lightning flashed, yet she couldn't make out anything large enough to protect her, and the mountains were too far away.

Dear God, if she wasn't dead, she would be soon if she stayed out here!

And then it happened . . .

Casey thought it might be rain or perhaps thunder when she heard the crackle begin, yet it grew increasingly louder . . . and it wasn't stopping. As every hair on her body rose, she knew static was filling the air. She looked up to the sky and her impulse to cringe was suddenly replaced by awe. It was as though heaven itself split open to thrust out an immense beam of light impaling the desert floor. The earth vibrated with a repetitive hum all around her, like nothing she had ever felt in her life . . . She held her breath, yet there was no sound of explosion on impact. This wasn't mere lightning, her mind whispered, as she stayed riveted to the wide swath of silver, white, blue, and gold light which was now rebounding from the ground and spreading out like fantastic wings across the blackened sky.

Then, sounding above the blasting of wind and sand, an ear-piercing squeal flooded her ears as she watched the solid beam begin to contract, falling into a spiral that appeared to be swallowed up by the earth. All that remained was the impression of opaque wings slowly dissipating into the sandstorm. She blinked rapidly, not so much to shield her eyes as to ensure they were open . . . for a solid, dark figure was emerging from the ghostly mist. The earth had stopped shaking and the ringing in her ears subsided as she gasped for breath. It was now beginning to move in her direction.

She was making this up. Whatever was happening was all in her mind. *It had to be!*

Desperately Casey rubbed at her eyes and then cupped her hands around them to shelter her face as more lightning, familiar narrow streaks, flashed around her and thunder rumbled. When she again looked, the silhouetted figure, with what appeared to be sails flapping at each side, approached steadily. Was it a man or . . . what, a beast? As it moved closer toward her, she could begin to make out a long dark coat and a wide cowboy hat. It was a man. Her heart pounded against her chest as he came closer. She didn't know whether to be frightened or relieved by his presence . . .

She was paralyzed by the entire bizarre display.

Wherever she was, whoever he was . . . somehow, none of it could be real. Could she have died and this really was hell? Had she been such a horrid person to deserve this?

There was no more time for questions as the man slowly, deliberately, walked closer, as though he had no fear of the lightning or the sandstorm. Her voice was strangled in her throat. She wanted to ask him who he was, but only garbled noises emerged from her mouth as she watched him unbutton his dark coat above her. His face was hidden by a wide turned-up collar and the cowboy hat pulled low over his brow, but somehow the closer he came, the less she feared him. And what could she do, anyway? Scream? Ask for help? She was barely able to breathe!

He knelt before her and, without a word, wrapped the edges of the raincoat around her, pulling her to his chest and sheltering her from the sandstorm. She could feel the strength of his arms around her back, and immediately sensed peace as she was gathered into the sanctuary of his body. Concealed from the attacking sand, she could finally breathe, and the lightning seemed to dim beneath the barrier of his coat. She felt the strong beat of his heart reverberating against her face. She smelled something citrusy, very earthy, about him, and lifted her hand to cling to his soft shirt.

"You are all right, Casey O'Reilly."

She almost jumped at the close proximity of his voice resonating from his chest and into her ear. The low soothing tone sent shivers throughout her body and she found herself clinging even more tightly to his shirt.

"Who . . . ? Who are you?" she managed to mutter.

"I've come to help," he answered, holding her tighter as another crash of thunder made the ground shake violently beneath them.

"Thank heavens," she sobbed. Tears came into her eyes as relief spread like warm honey down her body. She felt so protected in this stranger's embrace. A part of her was denying that any of this could be taking place at all, and yet she was very aware that the man holding her, sheltering her from the elements of nature, felt mighty real.

"Yes," he replied gently.

Somehow she felt incredibly safe, more so than she had ever felt in her life. Her body was tingling with some strange and powerful energy that was unfamiliar and yet . . . so perfectly wonderful. She felt a renewed strength welling up in her muscles, spreading through her body down to her burning foot. Her chest stopped aching and her headache eased as this man, who had just walked out of a bolt of lightning and into her life, continued to hold her patiently.

"Can you move?" he asked, shifting his head slightly.

She felt the movement, yet was afraid to lift her head to

look at him. What if he disappeared? What if this was all a dream, or she was hallucinating, and she found herself alone again, in pain, dying in a sandstorm?

"Can you move?" he repeated.

She nodded. Not only had the pain in her body eased, but the thunder seemed farther away now. "I . . . I think so," she answered in a voice that sounded, even to her ears, like a child's.

"Try," he encouraged, lifting her slightly as he rose. "I'll help you."

She gathered all her courage and commanded her muscles to obey as she pushed off the sand and stumbled against the hard muscles of his chest.

He caught her and held her tighter as she regained her balance.

"I . . . I'm sorry," she whispered with embarrassment, as she allowed herself to be pressed against him even tighter. She inhaled deeply as a wild surge of sexual energy raced through her at the contact, and again her brain felt fried. How *could* she be thinking such thoughts at this moment? What was wrong with her?

Almost of its own accord, her head lifted slightly and her gaze slowly rose from his chest. She could make out an open collar and a lean neck beneath a strong square chin. Staring at it, Casey felt the area around her heart heating up as though trying to protect and expand at the same time. Her breath felt ragged as she tried to pull more courage from some untapped well within her, forcing air to her lungs and giving her the endurance to continue what she knew she must . . . She had to see his face . . . to make sure he was real.

Lips, round and sensual, were held in a relaxed way, as if he was comfortable with her inspection. His cheekbones were cradled by lean muscles that spoke of strength. Slowly her gaze traveled up beyond a straight, almost perfect nose. She really couldn't see more as the brim of his cowboy hat hid his eyes from her.

Her stomach clenched with regret and then, suddenly, a more distant flash of white illuminated his entire face. Astounded, she gaped at him.

"Ohmygod . . ."

Barely a trace of amusement was reflected in his soulful dark eyes. "Not quite," he said with a friendly grin.

Casey experienced a moment of intense pleasure that her moan was thankfully disguised by the distant thunder. Damn. She simply must pull herself together and decide if she had truly lost her mind, or was still unconscious from the lightning that hit her when she left the car and was imagining all this and . . .

She remembered now. Flashes of memories raced across her mental screen. The flat tire. The horrid electrical storm. Her hand holding the metal door as she stepped into the darkness and was enveloped in the most intense light she could have ever imagined existing in any color spectrum. Deafening sound. And then heat, more than her body could handle, then a searing pain in her left foot as she left the earth and soared into oblivion.

"It's over now, Casey O'Reilly, you're okay," he reassured, as though he were reading her mind. "The earth and sky are no longer pulling at each other."

"Who . . . who are you?" she asked, noticing that since he began holding her, the sand and electrical storm had subsided.

He lifted his hand from her back and tipped the brim of his hat slightly, before smiling with open friendliness. "Luke d'Séraphin."

"You . . . you're Spanish?" she asked stupidly, responding to his accent, not knowing what else to say to this incredible man who stood so close to her.

He smiled and her heart again expanded before melting. What the hell was happening to her? *Pull your act together,* she mentally scolded herself. She instinctively knew she would need every ounce of wit, intelligence, courage, and *common sense* to find logic in any of this! None of it could possibly be real. It couldn't . . . !

He again held her as she swayed against him. It wasn't the wind either, but she would be very grateful if he thought that was the cause.

"I have visited Spain . . . yes."

"But you're not Spanish?" He certainly must carry some of those genes. Why was she asking these stupid questions!

"My name is French and Spanish. Does that matter to you?" He seemed genuinely interested in her answer.

She was stunned by his question, for it caused her mind to focus. "Well, no . . ." she mumbled. "I asked because of your . . . unusual name. Of course it doesn't matter." She was embarrassed for herself. Whoever he was, she wasn't making a great first impression. Then she thought about how she must look. She had just gone through God knew what, after traveling for seven hours, and she was only wearing one shoe! She felt the sand beneath her toes, reminding her that she was human after all even if she looked like a nightmare.

"Of course it doesn't," he answered, repeating her words. He allowed her to stand on her own as he reached into his pocket. "It's just a name. Like yours . . . Casey. A man's name for a lovely woman . . . intriguing. What does it mean?" She found his slight accent to be very pleasing.

"It's a family name," she said quickly in defense as she stood alone and pulled her sweater down. "Gaelic," she added. She could shake off his raincoat now, since the wind had died down and the electrical storm was moving off toward the direction of Albuquerque. But she really

didn't want to move away . . . yet. Dusk was rapidly beginning to envelop them in the vast desert, adding to the
bizarre scene, and she lifted her chin. Kind of a weird conversation to be having, considering the situation.

"Ahh," he murmured as he brought something dark out
of his pocket. "And in Gaelic what does it mean?"

She stared at him as he held it out to her. Fear raced
through her body when she recognized her missing blue
shoe. "Brave," she whispered dumbly. "It means . . .
brave."

"Your shoe, señorita?" he asked with a challenging grin.

Her lips barely moved. "Yes . . ."

She swore his eyes sparkled with something more than
friendliness, something making her reach out and hold on
to his shoulder as he lowered his body to squat before her.
Knocking sand out of the flat, he held the shoe invitingly in
front of her foot.

Oh, this isn't happening . . . Her mind struggled to find a
balance amid the chaos of thoughts and feelings. How
could he have her shoe? How could he have survived that
lightning? How could he be this handsome? How could she
stop mentally rambling and stick her foot into the damn
shoe! Jeez, she was beyond rattled!

She pushed her tousled hair back off her face and
clutched his shoulder even tighter as she lifted her foot and
brushed the sole against her right calf, sensing a tenderness
at her heel. The pain, though, was gone. She then slipped
her foot, rather awkwardly, into the soft leather. He looked
up at her and smiled briefly before rising.

"We must seek shelter for the night," he said, standing
beside her as he gently enveloped her in the wide material
of his long raincoat again. The coat reminded her of one of
those they wear in Australia, a heavy oiled sailcloth protecting them both now from the cool night air.

He was at least a good foot taller than she, and she fit

quite snugly under his arm as she joined him to look out over the surrounding desert. "Where's my car?"

He didn't say anything for a few moments. "I would imagine it is still on the road."

She peeked around the edge of his raincoat, not seeing anything but desert. "Where is the road? How far did I get thrown?"

She felt his deep intake of breath, as he hesitated again.

Silence seemed to surround them until Casey heard a faint rumble of thunder, as if warning her she wasn't going to like his answer.

Lowering his gaze, he looked directly into her eyes and said, "You were thrown back about a hundred and twenty years, as far as I can tell right now."

She merely blinked.

"What . . . ?" she finally was able to mumble. She couldn't have heard him correctly.

He answered her unspoken question. "Yes, you did."

She instinctively pushed him away and pulled herself together. She didn't care if he'd saved her life, or whether he'd come out of a blazing light, or if he was freakin' Starman himself . . . that couldn't be real!

"Look, where's the road?" she demanded, thinking of how Amy would worry about her and how she would reach her sister.

"I am attempting to help you realize you have just traveled back in time, Casey O'Reilly. It is imperative that you accept what has happened," he added in a serious voice.

Okay, she didn't care if he thought he was the reincarnation of Zorro, or some other western fantasy, he was obviously nuts. Again she pushed strands of sandy hair away from her face before stating flatly, "Look, I need to find my car. I appreciate everything you've done, Luke d' whatever . . . but I'm not about to play this game." She spit out some sand. "I know I was struck by lightning and my brain is a bit rattled, but I'm walking away from all of this . . . all right?" She pointed out to the desert. "Let's find the road . . . *now!*"

He smiled. Smiled!

"You do live up to your name, Casey O'Reilly. You are brave."

"Yeah . . . well . . ." She fumbled for an answer, while nodding her head like an idiot as she backed away from him. How did he know her name? Right! How *did* he know that?

"How do you know my name?" she demanded in what she thought was a semi-intelligent voice while poking her finger at him. "Tell me that, huh?"

He seemed amused as he reached into an inside pocket of the raincoat and withdrew something. "Your wallet, señorita."

"You went in my purse?" Why that shocked her, she had no idea, considering her situation. Anything was possible now.

"How else was I to know whom I was seeking? Casey O'Reilly. One seventy-four Beacon Street. Langhorne, Pennsylvania. One nine zero four seven. Hair color, blond. Eyes, blue. Weight—"

She grabbed her wallet from him and held it to her stomach. "That's enough!" she interrupted him before she heard *those* numbers. She had lost ten pounds since that lousy picture was taken nearly two years ago. "Okay, so you saw my license. Thank you . . ." she added when she realized what she had done. "Thank you for bringing me my wallet . . . and my shoe, but this proves you know where my car is!" she added with a defiant tone.

He smiled at her again. "Yes, I know where your car is, but you must believe me when I tell you it is not within your reach now. We will not be able to walk to it this night."

"Tsk." Casey clucked her tongue in frustration. She

couldn't believe he was continuing with this time-travel story. "Would you please drop the sci-fi, adventure act? It can't be eighteen . . ." She mentally subtracted 120 years from 2000. "Eighteen eighty-something! It's physically impossible."

He simply nodded and then pushed the hat back on his head, revealing a few strands of tiny black curls that fell onto his forehead. "Yes, of course."

She sensed he might be mocking her again as he turned and looked out into the desert, then repeated, "Now we must find shelter and perhaps some food."

"Well, I need to find some sanity, cause this is madness!" Casey blurted in disgust, turning quickly away and peering into the darkness. "Please . . . where's my car, the road? I have a sister who is expecting me and will be worried. I must get to her."

"And that is why I am here. I will do everything I can to insure you are returned safely to your family."

"When?" she pleaded, turning back to him.

"When the time . . . is right. Please, come along with me now. I know of a place in the mountains where we can find shelter."

She didn't move. Terror was racing through her system.

"It is your choice, Casey O'Reilly. I cannot force you to do anything, but I would advise you to trust me, and if you would not trust me . . . at least trust yourself."

The words of the Jackson Browne song seemed to reverberate inside her head. *The next voice you hear will be your own.*

Could she trust him? Could she trust herself?

She needed help.

None of it made sense. The car was gone. The road was gone. There was nothing but her and this . . . this incredible-looking man, who was obviously a little crazy, but had been, for the most part, helpful.

"Well?"

"Wait a minute," she said, looking out to the mountains. They were so far away! Could she walk to them? And what if she did? Would she ever see her sister again?

"Perhaps your decision has been made for you," he murmured, looking away from her.

She followed his line of vision and couldn't see anything, but she did hear something. It sounded like . . . like metal clanging against wood. "What is it?" she asked.

"I believe a wagon is approaching. Here," he said, removing his coat. "Put this on."

She stared at him, at his soft chambray shirt tucked into tight black trousers; a large belt buckle with a chunk of turquoise captured her attention briefly. "Why do I have to put on your coat? It's way too big. I won't be able to walk in it." She needed to say something to cover up her blatant inspection of him.

He winked at her. "Hopefully, señorita, we won't be walking. However, you are dressed inappropriately for a woman of this time. Accept my direction in this."

"Inappropriate . . . ?" She tried not to sound offended and glanced down at her own attire. She knew she must look a sight, with sand stuck everywhere, but—

"Your jeans would not be explained easily," he continued as though she hadn't interrupted. "A sophisticated woman of this era would be wearing a skirt to cover her legs, so we must improvise as best we can. Quickly, slip your arms into this now," he said, holding out his coat to her, "and trust me," he insisted.

His "sophisticated lady" remark made her turn back to his face. She stared directly into his eyes and was certain she saw another twinkle. Angel or Devil . . . ? The mental debate continued.

"*Por favor.* Covered up, you will stir fewer questions,

and I assure you we can find you something proper to wear in Santa Fe."

Shaking her head in disbelief at her own submission, Casey turned around and slipped her arms into the huge, heavy coat. It felt like armor around her and weighed her down, the sleeves dangling far beyond her hands.

"Well, when I get to Santa Fe, I can find my sister and then straighten out everything," she asserted, and turned toward the sound of the wagon. She stepped forward, nearly stumbling on the long hem of the coat. Grabbing the bulky fabric up into her hands, she attempted again to walk. "Amy will help me," she added, then began to tramp off in the direction of the approaching vehicle.

She felt his strong hand gently grip her arm, motioning her to stop. "You must wait here, señorita. I shall greet whoever is traveling north at this hour and find out if they are able to assist us." In a fluid motion, he tipped his hat, smiled grandly at her, then brushed ever so slightly against her as he passed.

She watched him stride away, while still feeling the heat of his body inside the coat. Part of her wanted to run after him and make sure he wasn't trying to trick her. Time travel indeed! Like this was some hokey movie of the week, and she was supposed to just blindly follow the big handsome cowboy into the unknown?

Yeah, right!

Seeing the flatbed wagon nearing, she could make out two figures seated upon it in the light of the small lantern they carried. Why didn't they have a car? Then she remembered Amy telling her that although Santa Fe was beautiful, the Indian and Hispanic populations, for the most part, were still impoverished. Casey yanked up the tails of the heavy coat and disobediently followed him. Maybe she could get some sane answers from these people.

She came up beside him as he waited for the wagon to stop. Without turning around, he said in a firm voice, "Do not speak a word, Casey O'Reilly."

"What d'ya mean *don't speak*?" she demanded.

He turned his head and stared at her. Although it was just after sunset, she could see the seriousness in his expression through the dusk. "These people may not speak any English, and that will only add to your confusion."

"*M-my*—" she stuttered as she watched him turn with a grin back to the oncoming travelers. Her mouth gaped at his insinuation, leaving her to obey his command. *I'm confused*? Her mental rant continued. *You're the one who thinks he's H. G. Wells, Master Time Traveler. And I'm confused!*

"Shh . . ." he whispered as though he had heard her thoughts, and then began waving at the driver. "*Hola! Buenas noches.*"

She listened as another man's voice answered with the same words. She couldn't help but look in fascination as Luke spoke in rapid Spanish to a man and a woman. In the dim glow of an oil lantern attached to a pole on the wagon, she could see they appeared to be poor, dressed in crude clothing . . . the man with a tattered jacket, and a long black shawl covering the woman's head and shoulders. Yet they seemed very friendly as they happily conversed with Luke. She had no idea what any of them were saying, and she meekly smiled when they all glanced in her direction. She could only imagine what Luke might be telling them.

He turned to her with a reassuring grin. "We have been offered a ride to town by this most gracious family, Señorita O'Reilly."

Casey smiled again as best she could. "Thank you."

"In their language," he whispered, then tutored, "*Muchas gracias . . .*"

She smiled again, wishing she had paid more attention

in her high school Spanish class. *"Muchas gracias, señor y señora."* She remembered that much!

The man and woman smiled back to her and motioned them both to get aboard.

Luke's eyes sparkled again with pleasure. *"Muy bien."*

Oh, that was a compliment . . . It meant she had done well. He certainly was taking on the tutor role with gusto. Speak when spoken to, huh? She hesitated briefly in her thoughts when he held out his hand, inviting her into the back of the wagon. Rather than make her point now, Casey merely smiled again to the family, who nodded back to her. But she wasn't about to be silent for the rest of the trip.

Just as she was wondering how in the world she was going to climb into the wagon with such a heavy coat, Luke lifted her off the ground as though she were as light as a feather.

"Oooph—" She wished she'd been able to stop the sound of surprise that burst from her throat when she experienced that moment of wonder . . . and then found herself promptly deposited in the cluttered back of the crude wagon.

She stood, making more room while he climbed in, and noticed his fancy black cowboy boots. Well, he certainly dressed the part, she thought as she awkwardly lowered herself to the wooden planks. Suddenly she noticed something small moving toward her and she jumped in fright, nearly yelping as two big brown eyes stared directly at her.

Luke laughed along with the couple and spoke again rapidly in Spanish as he settled in across from her. "Their daughter, Elena," he translated. "She is only a babe, and a bit shy of strangers." He tugged on the front of his hat in a show of courtesy to the child huddled in a colorful blanket, then began in a soothing tone, *"Mucho gusto, Elena. Soy* Luke d'Séraphin, *y esta es mi amiga,* Señorita Casey

O'Reilly. *La dama tiene mucha hambre, pero no va a morder una angelita como tú."*

Everyone laughed again, except Casey, as they began to rock in a comfortable rhythm with the donkeys' pulling. Now that she could make out her features, Casey saw the child grinning back at Luke.

"What did you say to her?" she asked, wanting to know what was so funny and also wanting to make friends with the child.

"I merely told the little angel it was my pleasure to meet her and there was no need to be afraid as you are a friend of mine." He paused and she watched as a smirk grew on his face.

"That's not all you said to her. I heard 'hungry' in there somewhere."

A boyish look of confession came over his rugged face as he admitted, "I told her, although you were very hungry, you would not bite her."

There was a moment of silence as Casey tried to decide if this man's sense of humor was harmless, then she couldn't help but erupt into a chuckle, which made the small girl giggle in response.

She smiled back, delighted she could make up for the startling meeting when she'd first noticed the child.

"Ven aquí, angelita," he said to the child, and held out his hand. Very hesitantly the girl placed her tiny hand inside his large one and he pulled her onto his lap. Grabbing the blanket, he wrapped it once more around her and grinned down at Elena. "Such a lovely creation," he murmured, and playfully touched the child's nose. *"Sí, tú eres muy bonita."*

Elena's smile widened with pleasure at the compliment. Shyly she reached up for his wide hat. Luke gave it over and placed it on her tiny head, and the child seemed to disappear.

Without looking up, he spoke again in English. "Esperanza and Sergio are traveling to Esperanza's sister's home to assist in the birth of this little one's cousin. Have you ever witnessed birth, Casey?"

"I saw my dog have puppies once," she muttered, trying very hard not to chuckle as she watched Elena push back the large hat she was practically lost inside and start climbing up on Luke to play with his curly hair. It amazed her the way the man allowed this child to have free rein with him. It was as though he was . . . well, enchanted or something. She noticed the way he held the child, making sure she was still protected from the night air by the blanket. He must be a father.

That thought stopped all others.

Here she was, being completely rattled by a man she'd just met, and he was probably married. Not likely a guy like *him* would be single. Silently Casey thought the woman very fortunate . . . even if he was a tad nuts.

His attention remained on the child as he began speaking. "I have never married, and I am not a father, yet surely I am now holding a miracle . . . no?" He then turned slightly and stared right into Casey's wide eyes.

Holy shit . . . this guy must be reading her mind!

She wasn't sure which bit of information stunned her more. That he seemed to read her mind or that he was unmarried. *Say nothing*, she advised herself, and quickly turned to gaze at the incredible display above them. The stars were so bright, appearing closer than she'd ever known before . . . and she felt she could almost reach out to grab one. A thought crept into her brain, making her wince. Could the fates be so cruel as to have this man turn out to be uninterested in women? It wouldn't be the first time she'd been fooled.

Casey closed her eyes briefly and whispered a small prayer that she find her sister as quickly as possible and end this craziness, for none of this could be *real*!

But then . . . ever since that flat tire, nothing was exactly ordinary.

She heard him laugh lowly, and when she reluctantly opened her eyes, he was still smiling at her as Elena ran her tiny fingers through his curls and giggled with delight.

This time she stifled the groan.

Two

"Tell me about yourself, Casey O'Reilly."

Startled, Casey mentally slapped away her paranoid pondering and blinked a few times. She had been trying to steady herself for the past few minutes. Though, if truthful, she was also trying not to stare at the man and the way he seemed to entertain the child without doing anything. It was as if tiny Elena, no longer shy, was quite happy just to be around him. Furthermore, it was a powerful scene for a woman whose biological clock was nagging the hell out of her. Well, she wouldn't tell him *that*!

"Uhhhhhmmmm . . ." She drew out the sound, trying to buy time. What could she tell him and how safe would it be? The image of him coming up to her when she was terrified and wrapping his coat around her for protection flooded her mind. She could trust him. Call it female intuition. "Well, you know that I'm from Pennsylvania," she began, and then not wanting him to think of her license again and all those statistics, she quickly added, "I was on my way to visit my sister in Santa Fe when I got a flat tire. I guess I was hit by lightning or something, and then woke up in that sandstorm."

She could see him nod even as the darkness grew around them.

"The forces of nature are unpredictable," he answered, grinning as Elena, still wearing his hat, bumped his face with the wide brim. The child giggled at the game and did it again. This time Luke tilted his head and Elena missed. They both chuckled, like old friends enjoying each other. "You are fortunate, Casey O'Reilly to be here. That was a powerful charge you received."

Her mind tried to focus, yet she felt almost mesmerized by the picture of this large, strong man and this tiny, dark child playing together. "Ahh . . . yes. It was powerful and I know I am lucky."

"You believe in luck?" he asked, again dodging Elena's attempt to prod him with his own hat.

"Well, sure. I'm alive, right? I was never struck by lightning before, so I must be lucky. Don't you . . . believe in luck?"

He shrugged. "I don't believe in chance myself."

She found that interesting and decided to probe further. Might as well pass the time in conversation until they reached Santa Fe. Wait until she told Amy about this guy! "So you think I was meant to be hit by lightning? That it was my . . . my destiny to be blown outta my shoe and nearly killed?" Who's he kidding!

He again chuckled, this time at her words. "I really don't know. Only you could answer that question. I am merely saying I don't believe it was a coincidence that I came upon your car . . . but I can only answer for myself, Casey O'Reilly."

"Why do you keep calling me by my full name? Just

Casey is fine." The formality was beginning to annoy her. She refused to delve further to find out why. Maybe it was just a form of respect, 'cause his speech and manners were a bit too elegant for the middle of the desert. Later. She'd figure this all out later, or maybe she'd be fortunate enough to forget it.

Again he nodded. "You have all your answers, Casey. Patience."

Now, *that* annoyed her. "Patience? Do you realize how . . . how weird you sound? First you tell me I've"— she lowered her voice—"*time-traveled!* And then you tell me I'm back in like eighteen seventy-something and, oh . . . let's not forget you came right out of a lightning bolt, the likes of which I've never seen in my life and—"

He was chuckling, and she knew it was at her and not the child.

"This isn't funny," she scolded. Somehow it felt much better to challenge him than surrender to a powerful attraction that made her feel just like Elena!

"You don't have to hide your words," he said with a chuckle. "No one can fully understand you right now. English is not their language. And yes, Casey. You have time-traveled. It is best that you accept this as quickly as possible."

She blew her breath out, and her lips vibrated against each other. "Yeah, right! Time travel! Now, see . . . that's when you sound weird. You want me to believe a bolt of lightning threw me back in time and *that* is my destiny?" She couldn't stop her laugh of disbelief.

Grinning even more widely, he looked up from the child and said, "See, Casey? You do have the answers after all."

Incredulous, she stared at him. Leaning forward, she said through clenched teeth, "I have *not* time-traveled, got it? I am going to find my sister and explain how *lucky* I am to have survived all this."

He didn't say anything for a few moments, and then, as

if by mutual agreement, Elena and Luke stopped their game and the little girl put his hat back on his head and sat down in his lap. He left the cowboy hat sitting way back, and wrapped the blanket once more around the child. Elena sat quietly and stared across the small space at Casey. The wide-eyed interest only added to her charm, and Casey smiled.

Elena shyly smiled back as Luke said, "It is but a word, is it not? You call it luck, pure chance, that you are alive in this time. I merely happen to think there is a pattern unfolding, perhaps even one that hit you like a bolt of lightning to get your attention. I respect the pattern, Casey, that's all."

She looked around her. "What pattern?" she demanded.

"The pattern of all these events . . ." he said with a hint of a smile. "They are unfolding, are they not? Did you expect to be riding in a wagon to reach Santa Fe?"

"No." Even though it really didn't require an answer, she wanted to say the word with emphasis to let him know how crazy all of this sounded.

"And here we are. Did not this wagon appear just when it was needed?"

She shrugged. She wasn't about to give him anything. "I could have found my car."

He laughed and shook his head. "Not in this time, you wouldn't. It is dark and you are surrounded now by only miles of barren desert. You will see when we reach town." He held the child more closely to him and continued, "Your senses say you can believe this precious child and her parents are simply poor people, too poor to own an automobile, yet you can't imagine they could be living over a hundred years ago. When we come closer to Santa Fe, then your beliefs will be challenged. It is good you are brave, Casey O'Reilly."

"Who *are* you?"

Smiling, he said, "I have already told you my name, Luke—"

"I don't mean your name," she interrupted. "And you know that. Who are you? *What* are you? How do you know what I'm thinking? And just how did you walk out of that lightning? Answer me that. Was that your destiny?" Yeah . . . let's get some answers, she thought with righteous anger.

"You seem to have so many answers already. Are you sure you want mine?"

Tricky, but she wasn't about to be put off. "Yes. I want yours."

"It is my destiny in this moment to be of service to you."

"Be of service?" How was he about to service her? The thoughts rushing through her brain were sudden and shameful, and she pushed them out. "Oh, you mean like helping me in the storm . . . bringing me my shoe and wallet. That kind of thing."

He looked down at the child, and Casey saw that Elena's lids were getting heavy. She was also grateful not to see the expression on his face after her last desperate attempt to save some dignity.

"Yes," he said, shifting his arm so the child would be more comfortable. Elena sighed and snuggled into his chest.

Casey watched as he wrapped the blanket more firmly around the young girl and flipped the edge of it over his shoulder to provide himself some warmth. She felt a twinge of guilt for wearing his coat, which was keeping out the night chill. "Well, I do thank you for that," she said, "but what about the lightning? How could you have walked right out of it? It doesn't make any sense."

He glanced up and grinned. "It doesn't, does it?"

She shook her head. "How did you do it? Why weren't you hurt?"

"Do you have a good imagination, Casey?"

It wasn't a direct answer, but she'd play along. "I think so."

"What do you do for employment? Are you creative at all?"

"I . . . I'm an accountant," she fumbled. "But I can sing . . . well, I've been told I can sing fairly well. I don't paint or do sculpture or anything really creative, but—"

"Good enough," he interrupted before she could again challenge him. "Can you imagine what it was like only five hundred years ago when almost everyone believed the earth was flat? That if you walked far enough, you would fall off it?"

"Well, I can't imagine that," she said impatiently. "I mean, everyone knows the earth is round."

"You know that now, but try to imagine what it would be like for you to speak to someone from that time and try to explain something new, when they hold a very strong belief that everything you are saying is . . . how did you word it? Weird. Would it not be difficult to communicate your experience, your knowledge? Even though you know your truth to be real for you, that the earth is round and they will not fall off the edge of it?"

She thought about it for a few seconds. Why was she even getting into this maddening conversation with this man? She did not have a swell feeling about where it was leading. "I guess it would be difficult," she conceded.

He nodded his head slightly. "Thank you." He tilted his hat back into place, now that Elena seemed to be sleeping, and added, "Perhaps you will be patient with me, as I, too, find a way to communicate with more clarity."

She wasn't sure if he was saying she was backward, or what. "You certainly have perfected the fine art of evading a direct question, haven't you?"

He chuckled. "I am not evading. I am remaining patient, as should you."

"Why? Just tell me. Do you think I'm too stupid to comprehend your explanation? You're not speaking to a simpleton . . ." she said defensively. "I know the earth is round and I do have an imagination, but rationally, time travel is freakin' impossible!"

"Even though your words are not understood by the others, your tone is. *Por favor,* lower your voice. Elena is sleeping," he said quietly as he tenderly stroked her small head.

Feeling guilty, Casey cleared her throat. "Okay," she said in a near whisper, "so talk to me . . . I would really appreciate it if you answered my questions."

He paused for a moment, as though hesitant to continue. Finally he said, "Time is not linear, as you have been taught by others and have accepted in your rational, accountant's mind. It is circular, like a spiral, and travel within the spiral *is* possible."

Her brain, on overdrive, refused to comprehend his words. "Okay, forget it," she said with a wave of dismissal. "Let's just allow Elena to sleep the rest of the way and not disturb anyone with any conversation at all! Time travel . . . jeez, must be the millennium madness!"

"You can now see this dilemma," he answered in a soft voice. "Patience, Señorita O'Reilly. We will both need it to follow the pattern of events yet to come."

She refused to answer him and give credence to the insanity coming out of his mouth. They sat in silence for what seemed like an hour. Luke appeared very comfortable with it, yet Casey had a dozen questions racing around her mind. He still hadn't told her anything. Not who he was or where he came from or why he was able to walk out of the bolt of lightning without even so much as a blister. If she hadn't seen it with her own eyes, she wouldn't have believed anyone could survive that kind of powerful force. Not only had he survived it, he seemed unaffected by it, and literally unaffected by everything else!

He didn't seem to be surprised to have found her . . . or these people . . . nor did he seem concerned that she didn't believe his crazy notions. He seemed perfectly happy just to go along with whatever happened and he was overly patient with it all. She glanced at him and could make out the outline of a man with his head bent, his hat now pulled down to create a shield for himself and the child he embraced in his arms. It was quite a scene, and she had to admit that unlike Luke d'something, she was definitely . . . affected.

She heard Elena's parents speaking in low voices, and Luke lifted his head and squinted out to the night. "A rider is approaching," he murmured, sitting up straighter and handing the child to Casey. "Take her and keep her close to your body."

Casey was stunned. "What do you mean? Look, you're waking her." Elena was making tiny whimpering noises.

"Take her," he insisted, and placed the child gently into Casey's arms. "Wrap the coat around her and remain silent," he finished. In one fluid motion, he was on his knees behind the adults in the front of the wagon.

Something told her to follow his directive and she drew Elena to her while wrapping the heavy oilcloth coat around them both.

"Buenas noches, compadre!" Elena's father shouted out into the darkness.

Another rapid-fire burst of Spanish followed, and Casey was completely lost again as Luke sat back down and released his breath. "The rider is Esperanza's brother-in-law. He has come to find them as it appears his wife's time to deliver has arrived and she is in dire need of assistance."

With his words, the reins were flicked and the wagon jerked. Casey held tighter to Elena as they picked up a rough speed. They must have hit every single rut in the ground, and she found herself crooning to the child, who was being jostled with each bump.

"It will not be long now," Luke said, while touching the outline of Elena's head under the blanket. "I do not think Esperanza's sister lives in town."

Casey didn't answer. She thought she saw something in the distance. A small fire, perhaps, and the outline of a tiny shack, but the wagon was moving so fast that it was lost in a jumble from her view. Another fire was sighted, and then another and another. Houses, small ones, became clearer on the open plain. She could make out occasional groups of trees in the valley. They had to be approaching a town or a settlement of some kind. Amy was right, these people must be very poor to live like this, she thought, as they lurched forward. She held Elena tighter with compassion. How she wished she could help the child.

They began to slow and Casey saw the houses were built closer together, almost like a town. Turning down one street, she was able to distinguish people and faces, all staring at them as they passed the adobe homes that were now attached, like row houses. Someone was playing a Spanish guitar, making it all seem surreal to her. Turning onto another street, the wagon finally came to a slow stop.

Letting out her breath, Casey looked at Luke. "Are we here? Is this Santa Fe?"

He nodded. She watched Sergio leap off the seat and hurry around the wagon to his wife as his brother-in-law slid off a huge horse. She heard them all speaking in Spanish as Luke reached for Elena.

"I will bring the child into the house."

Just as he took Elena, another woman came up to the back of the wagon and spoke in a pleading voice. Luke handed her the child and then answered her. It was frustrating not to know what was going on, but she didn't want to interrupt what seemed like a very tense time for a translation. She was definitely the outsider here.

The woman appeared to be Hispanic and said something quickly to Casey before rushing back into the tiny adobe house. Luke looked down and said, "We have been invited inside and—"

Sergio hurried back to the wagon and pulled a large cloth bag from the front seat, while saying something in Spanish and waving them inside.

"It would be an insult to refuse their gracious offer of hospitality," Luke finished, as he reached down to help her stand.

Casey rose on stiff legs and had to hold on to his arm to steady herself. "Well, that's really nice of them, but I have to find my sister."

He didn't answer her, just led her to the back of the wagon. After jumping down, he held out his arms to her. She only hesitated a few moments before allowing herself to fall into them. It was quite a rush after all the jostling in the wagon to be held in his arms again, but Casey wasn't about to allow him to work any more magic on her. She straightened herself and stepped out of his arms. "Thanks," she muttered. "Now, which way to Santa Fe? Do you think we can hitch another ride?"

A smile played at his lips. "You *are* in Santa Fe, Señorita O'Reilly. Welcome to The Royal City of the Holy Faith, as Don Pedro de Peralto has so christened it. Ironic name, is it not?"

She found nothing amusing in his words, though she knew he must think himself very witty that she would be in a city named for faith when she had very little at the moment.

"This is it?" she asked in disbelief, jumping as she heard a woman's scream from inside the small home.

"Yes, this is it, Casey. Now, come. We will not insult our very generous benefactors. Perhaps we can be of some help."

She backed away when he attempted to take her upper arm as though to lead her inside. Taking off his coat, she handed the heavy thing back to him and fought off a chill as the night air entered the tiny knit of her sweater. "I don't know anything about assisting in a birth," she said in a firm voice. "I will leave you now and find my sister, and then—"

"Oh, do stop your rambling, Casey," he said, taking his coat and again holding her upper arm. "I am not about to allow you to wander off into the night. We shall rest here and see if we can be of any help, to reciprocate the assistance we have received."

She was led toward the house, feeling like a selfish child. When they entered the small dwelling, she could see in a bright amber glow of lanterns that Sergio was holding Elena and talking to a very worried looking man. There was a rough wooden table and several chairs. A bottle of something was on the surface, and four small glasses looked as though they had been left in a hurry.

Another scream of pain was heard beyond a wall of colorful material that acted as a divider in the small room, and Casey again stiffened with apprehension. The man next to Sergio shook his head with worry and muttered something.

Luke left her side, dropped his coat and hat onto a chair, and walked up to the man. He held out his hand and whispered something in Spanish. The man nodded, smiled briefly, and accepted Luke's hand before speaking again, this time so fast that to Casey it was all a blur of sounds.

Turning, Luke translated over his shoulder. "His wife, Maria, is having a troubled birth. It may be breeched." He listened again to the man, nodding in sympathy, and then walked back to where she stood, rooted to the dirt beneath her feet.

"We must help, Casey," he pronounced. "The woman is suffering and the child may be lost if not turned quickly."

She felt like Butterfly McQueen as she blurted, "I don't know anything about birth." Fear raced through her that this crazy man would suggest she did! "Where's the doctor?"

"There is no doctor. None that would come here to the home of a Mexican peasant," he added with a trace of irritation in his voice. "Come with me and we shall see what we can do. I have already obtained the father's permission to assist."

"*You're* going to help?" she asked in a stunned voice. "Are you a doctor?"

He looked her directly in the eyes and said, "No, I am a traveler, just as you, but I will be of service if I can." He left her in the room with the men and walked behind the curtain.

Casey felt both men staring at her, the way she was dressed, and as Elena whined in fright when the woman again yelled out, she instinctively hurried to the child and held out her arms. "I can hold her," she said to Sergio.

The man seemed to understand her words, or maybe it was her body language, yet when he tried to hand Elena over, the child cried out and held tighter to her father's neck.

Even the child didn't want to be around her. Feeling even more guilty, she wrapped her arms around her waist and wondered if there was anything at all that she could do to be of help. Certainly she wasn't about to go beyond that curtain . . . was she? She had never seen a live human birth and, even though she desperately wanted a child herself, she was really scared of the process. She'd heard too many horror stories from the women she worked with, even her own friends who'd had children, to think it was anything more than the term implied . . . *labor.*

Maybe she could clean up their house or—

"Casey, bring me my coat."

She heard the words and saw the men staring at her, knowing that even if they didn't understand the English, it was obvious that Luke was directing her. Reluctantly she walked back to the wooden chair and picked up the heavy coat. Earlier, in the wagon, she had replaced her wallet in one of the huge pockets. What in the world could he want with it now? Surely the woman in labor didn't need it.

"Casey!"

"I'm coming," she yelled back, and walked over to the curtain. Not wanting to invade the woman's privacy, she merely handed the coat past the curtain.

"What are you doing? Bring it in, Casey," Luke demanded.

Slowly she pushed the curtain aside and gasped when she saw Luke holding the hands of a dark woman who appeared to be in agonizing pain. Esmerelda had her hand inside her sister's body. Casey felt the blood drain from her face as she clutched the coat and squeezed her eyes shut.

"In the pocket, the inside pocket, you will find a small stone. Get it quickly," Luke whispered gruffly.

Glad for something to do, Casey began fumbling blindly through his coat. She felt the stone with her fingers and pulled it out. She opened her eyes to see a crystal of some kind, and when she held it in her hand it rapidly began to get warm.

"Give it to her."

She tried to smile at the terrified woman while reaching across the low, simple bed and handing the stone to Luke. He released the woman's right hand and clutched Casey's wrist. Instantly the woman flailed her loose hand and grabbed on to Casey's sweater, pulling her to her knees. Luke held Casey's hand up in front of the woman's face. He spoke to the woman gently, in soothing tones in Spanish, and then whispered in English, "Place the stone in Maria's hand, Casey, and then hold it closed. Do not let go."

The woman looked up at her with huge brown eyes that spoke of hours of agony. She eased the woman's grip from her sweater and tenderly wrapped their hands around the stone. Casey's heart seemed to melt at the tragic expression and she smiled encouragingly as Maria seemed engulfed in pain. No longer was she afraid for herself. It was the woman who was in trouble. The yelling had become whimpers. Casey needed no translator to know the woman was begging for someone to end her misery.

Luke spoke to Esmerelda, still working between Maria's legs, and when the older woman finally withdrew her hand and nodded, Luke looked at Casey and said, "Do not let go. No matter what happens . . . keep holding her hand. She will need your courage now."

Casey nodded dumbly, not knowing what he was talking about. She listened as he then spoke to Maria in a coaxing voice. The woman moaned loudly and then grabbed hold of Casey's hand with such strength, she swore the stone pressed between their palms would surely cut them both. But she didn't let go. Instead, she found herself pushing with Maria, willing her to give birth.

Luke called out, *"Siga adelante! El bebé quiere venir ahora mismo, Maria!"*

Sweat broke out all over Casey's body as she felt the pain in her hand, the heat of the stone, the strange urge she had within her to push along with Maria . . . anything to help. Casey stared at Luke, who merely nodded for her to continue as Maria screamed once more and he spoke to her in Spanish, again soothing her. She noticed that his right hand was now braced on the outside wall, as though he, too, needed to lean on something for strength. Soon Maria tightened her grip again and started pushing as another contraction demanded action.

The grunt of labor made Casey tremble as beads of sweat dripped down her spine beneath her sweater. Why in the world would any woman willingly go through this torture? she wondered, trying not to look at her own mangled hand. It had little feeling left in it. How could there be an overpopulation problem? Her mind was scattered and she felt herself feeling faint with fatigue. How could Maria, or any human being, survive this . . . ?

Esperanza spoke excitedly, and Maria licked the moisture from her lips and tried to smile in response, right before another contraction took her prisoner and the blood-curdling scream this time brought Casey back to her knees.

Everything was happening as if suspended in time . . . Maria's wail of misery, the searing pain in her own clasped hand as Maria seemed possessed of superhuman strength, the sound of Luke's heavy breathing . . . all of it being painted with brushstrokes of memories onto her rattled mind. Now very close to the woman's hips, Casey turned her face slightly and saw the most amazing sight . . .

A tiny head, with wet black hair, and a shoulder.

She watched as Esperanza twisted the baby and then quickly, as though propelled, the body slipped out into the waiting woman's hands. Casey couldn't breathe. She could barely think as a tiny sound was heard, and then a stronger one as Esperanza wiped the child with a rough cloth and it cried out in protest.

Maria released her hand and started crying and laughing at the same time. Luke stood up and let his breath out, and Casey cradled her numb hand at her chest as she stared at the incredible scene. The baby, still attached by the umbilical cord, was placed on Maria's chest, and Casey had to blink away the rapid flow of tears. She couldn't believe it. She had witnessed a birth!

"A son," Casey whispered, as she watched mother and child bond.

Luke came up behind her and helped her up. Her legs were unsteady, and she stumbled. Luke caught her in his arms and hugged her slightly. She didn't want to turn away from Maria and the miracle in the woman's arms, but she didn't want to be rude either. Casey smiled reassuringly at the woman as Luke turned her to the curtain. "Esperanza can finish here."

She nearly collapsed against him as he held the fabric aside and Sergio and Maria's husband stood with expectation. Luke waited until the others rushed past and then dropped the material into place. He walked Casey to the table and picked up the bottle. He sniffed, wiped the crown with his shirtsleeve, and held it out to her.

"Here. Drink," he said with a grin. "I think we have earned it."

Her one good hand was shaking as she tilted the bottle to her mouth and gulped. Immediately she gasped and coughed as the fiery liquor burned her throat. Tequila. Luke patted her back and then drew the bottle to his own lips. After swallowing, he, too, expelled his breath with a gasp.

Grinning at her, he said in soft husky voice, "Tonight you lived up to your name, Casey."

She sighed with exhaustion as the tequila spread through her bloodstream and a surge of heat raced through her veins. Luke put his arm around her shoulders and squeezed lightly.

"You were very brave."

She couldn't even smile as she rubbed her right hand, trying to bring circulation back into it. Had she really just seen that? Even participated in it?

Stuff like this just didn't happen in her life . . .

Three

"*W*hat happened with that stone in there?" she whispered in a hoarse voice, still shaking from the most astonishing experience of her life. "What . . . what is it made of?"

Luke took another sip and wiped the tip of the bottle with his sleeve again before putting it back on the table. "It is not a stone, it is a crystal with a very powerful frequency which amplifies certain energies." He paused, watching for her reaction.

She'd heard something once on a magazine news show, a segment dealing with some kind of energy in crystals, how they're used to power computers and watches and lots of things, but she hadn't really paid attention.

"More simply, it was something for Maria to focus upon, other than her pain. It also amplified your strength and bravery and directed them to her. When I get it back from Maria, you may examine it, if you wish."

She slid down onto one of the chairs, listening to the

adults laughing and cooing at the newborn beyond the curtain. Feeling drained, she murmured, "I can't believe what I just witnessed."

Luke pulled a chair out from the table and turned it around. He swung his leg across it and sat with his arms crossed over the back. Smiling at her, he said, "A miracle, is it not? The wonder never lessens for me."

She glanced up from the table. "How many have you seen?"

"This is my ninth."

"Nine? What are you, a midwife?"

He chuckled and ran his fingers through his curly hair. "No. I've just been fortunate to be in the right place at the right time as life unfolded."

She didn't even want to ask where these births took place. Obviously not in a hospital, and she just couldn't handle it right now if he said it was in the time of Cleopatra or—

Before she could finish her thought, he continued, "No matter where . . . life continues to fascinate me. I cannot imagine being alive and bored, yet I have heard of people who are and I wonder how this is so."

She blinked, trying to make sense of his words. "How do you do that?" she blurted out. "Do you hear my thoughts or what?"

Again he laughed. "No, not your thoughts, but I do sense your emotions."

"That's eavesdropping!" she accused, extremely uncomfortable not being able to hide her emotions, especially after what had happened to her behind that curtain. She felt as if something, something within her, had altered, expanded. She just felt so . . . so *open*.

"I understand your discomfort, Casey, yet my intuitive ability is not something I can turn off. It just *is*." Was his smile meant to ease her embarrassment? It didn't.

She wanted to hide her eyes, shield her mind, and then suddenly figured he was just gifted or something, and couldn't help it. Yeah, most reality escapists were gifted in some way. He believed in time travel; that was his way out, and if she didn't buy in to it, she'd be okay. She found comfort in accepting her thought. "I still don't like it," she finally said. "You have an unfair advantage."

Nodding, he continued, "The reality is, you have the very same ability, Casey. You've just forgotten about it."

"Forgotten?" She wiped her forehead and sighed with weariness. "I do think, if I was ever able to *read minds*, I'd remember."

She watched him take in a deep breath and look up to the thatched ceiling. Here it comes, she thought. He was gathering how he was going to tutor her again.

"Yes . . . how shall I say this?" He paused. "Okay . . . was there ever a time when you walked into a room and, before anyone said a word or moved"—his thoughtful gaze dropped to stare directly into her eyes—"you just *knew* what was happening? Perhaps something was stirring inside you." He gestured with his hands in a circling motion around his chest. "You felt something that made you happy or uneasy . . . as though you were able to *feel* the room and sense what was to come."

Immediately her mind flashed back to something she hadn't thought of in years. She was three years old and walking into the living room of her childhood. It was as if it were yesterday . . .

She was so happy and wanted to tell her mother about the butterfly buzzing at the screen in her bedroom. The insect had seemed magical, calling her away from dressing her favorite doll. She ran over to the screen, fascinated by the colors in its slow-moving wings. Delighted, she hurried out of the room, hoping she could share it with her mother before it flew away.

Her mother was in the kitchen and didn't know she'd come downstairs. Her father was sitting in an overstuffed beige chair, drinking a cup of coffee. She was surprised to see him home in the afternoon, and then all thoughts of the magical butterfly disappeared. She immediately knew something was wrong. She *knew*, as soon as she entered the room, something was very wrong.

"How can you do this, Colin?" her mother yelled from the kitchen. She heard the anguish in her mother's voice. "Leave me with two little babies!"

She watched her father wipe a droplet from his eye. He didn't say a word as he looked down at his little girl. She could feel both their fear and pain, and it made tears come into her eyes. Why else had she rushed up to her father and pleaded, "Daddy . . . don't go!" Her eyes began to well up even now.

Of course she had felt their emotions! She didn't need the details to understand the two people she loved most in the world were suffering. She just *felt* it.

She got the details about ten years later when her parents finally split. Her father had been having an affair. He had stayed and raised his children for as long as he could and then left, ending the sham.

Casey swallowed the lump in her throat. She couldn't believe how quickly it all ran through her mind, a buried memory of almost thirty years!

"You see . . . ?" Luke's voice was gentle. "You, too, have this ability, Casey. You call it intuition, yet it is much more than that . . ." He held out the bottle to her and continued. "At some time you decided the ability to feel what others were feeling was too hard to live with . . . so, like a volume knob on a stereo or TV, you turned it down. Most people do. Then as you grew up, you believed others when they said such a thing was foolish, and you turned it down even lower."

She took the bottle from his outstretched hand, watching his eyes twinkle and his grin widen, like he was about to reveal a secret she already knew.

"But you can never really turn it off. It's a part of you."

Damn. Now he had her doing it *and* he was starting to make sense.

Must be the tequila dulling her judgment. She stared at him, not believing what she was seeing or what she was hearing, not even from within herself. It was too much. And now this fantastic man was smiling at her with such tenderness that she wanted to break down and sob like Elena. In an effort to stop such a display, she raised the bottle to her lips and gulped.

Swallowing the harsh liquid, she managed a tight grin. "So what's next?" she asked in a raspy voice. "You start calling me *grasshopper*? If I wasn't so damned tired, I'd try to snatch the pebble from your palm right now and show ya a thing or two."

He leaned his chin on his crossed arms. "I'll take Martial Arts for five hundred dollars," he answered with theatrical exaggeration. "To be a peaceful warrior . . . what is *Kung Fu*?" She watched his smile widen even further when he added, "I'd bet my life on it."

"What's this now? *Jeopardy?*" She laughed to cover any other emotion she might be emitting at the moment, for watching him smile so grandly that dimples creased his cheeks was devastating.

"You have a most wonderful laugh, Casey O'Reilly. You should use it more."

That immediately stopped her laughter. "I laugh," she said in defense. "Most people think I have a good sense of humor." It sounded like bragging, and she added, "Though mostly I laugh at myself."

"That is a fine quality. A valuable one in life. If you had

a bag of magical tools to carry with you, that one would be highly prized."

"Laughing at myself?"

"Yes, the ability to laugh at oneself."

She was grateful the curtain was suddenly pulled aside and Sergio, who still carried Elena; Esperanza; and Maria's husband joined them in the small room. Luke rose to greet them and everyone started talking at once in Spanish. Casey slowly pushed herself up from the chair, aware that every muscle in her body felt somehow fluid, as though drained of strength. She smiled at the happy people and wished she could be on her way. She simply had to reach Amy and lie down somewhere. Enough was enough. Her mind and body were weary, and the tequila intensified her need for rest.

Luke turned to her and said, "We've been invited to stay for a small celebration . . . a feast of thanksgiving for the new life."

"Oh, I can't," Casey protested. "I must be on my way." This time she was going to be firm.

Luke looked at her and, after a few moments, simply nodded. He turned to the men and said something. Everyone appeared disappointed and then Maria's husband motioned for both her and Luke to go behind the curtain. Watching the man hold the material back, she knew she didn't really have a choice without appearing rude. Besides, she wanted to see the baby one more time.

She smiled again and walked forward. Luke was behind her as they entered the bedroom area. Maria was resting, looking much better. Even her long, dark hair had been brushed. She opened her eyes as they approached, and though her smile was tired, it was still beautiful. Awed, Casey drew in her breath. Maria really did look beautiful. She was radiant, holding her new son to her breast.

Luke whispered something to her, and Casey made out the word for congratulations. Maria motioned for them to come closer. Casey felt like a kid as she took baby steps, not wanting to disturb the peace that seemed to surround the woman and child.

Maria whispered something to Luke and he smiled, while nodding as the woman extended her palm. Casey watched as Luke gently took back the crystal and then closed his hand over Maria's.

The woman said something to him and he grinned. He shook his head from side to side as if telling Maria no. Maria seemed a little disappointed and then said something more that made Luke almost beam with pleasure.

Turning his head, he told her to say good-bye to what sounded like *Ang-hell,* the baby, and to wish the child a joyful life. She felt awkward as she reached out and touched the little hand. Her finger looked so big as she stroked his tiny ones resting so close to his perfect mouth. Her arms almost ached as something raced through them, something that every *instinct* was telling her had nothing to do with the tequila. It was only when she recognized that she desperately wanted to hold the child that she pulled her hand away and smiled at Maria.

"He's so beautiful," she whispered in awe. "Thank you for allowing me to be a part of this, Maria. I know it's something I'll never forget."

Luke translated, and Maria said to Casey, "*Gracias,* Señorita Casey. *Sin duda, usted volvera a Dios.*" She then continued, and Casey was lost in a language she didn't understand. She looked to Luke, who told her that Maria said she had felt Casey's courage and she and Ang-hell would both be grateful to her for the rest of their lives, that surely she was sent by God this night.

Embarrassed, Casey shook her head and backed away a

bit. "Tell her there's no need for that. I didn't do anything."

Luke grinned. "You performed a great service. Accept it and receive graciously. You haven't forgotten how to do that too, have you?"

She felt almost reprimanded by his words. "I can receive graciously," she retorted, stunned by the realization that she almost always turned a compliment around by putting herself down. "Just tell her thank you . . . for everything, okay?" Sheesh, this guy was hitting *way* too many buttons!

"I will," Luke said, and then turned back to Maria. The two of them spoke together for a few more moments and then Luke cradled the baby's head in his palm.

Seeing this man's unabashed tenderness brought a thickness to her throat. She almost wanted to cry and thought she truly must be exhausted. She had better pull her act together and get on with finding Amy.

"*Adiós,*" Luke and Maria whispered to each other.

He straightened his body and held the curtain for Casey.

"*Adiós,*" Casey whispered, and in her mind she told the baby that she wished him a lifetime of joy. His birth had certainly affected her life. More than anything now, she wanted a child of her own. Even if it was torture to make it happen!

In the room with the others, she watched as Luke spoke to them in a friendly voice. Esperanza ran to her sister's small stove and pulled what looked like burritos from a steaming pot. She bundled them in a cloth and handed the small package to Casey, smiling and saying, "*Gracias*" over and over, along with the others. Luke picked up his coat and hat and motioned for Casey to follow him. They stepped out of the small home amid more outbursts of gratitude and waves of good-bye.

Once outside, she drew in a deep breath of the cool night air. Against the brilliant starry sky, she could now see the outline of a town just a short distance away. Casey put her hands on her hips as she turned to Luke in the street. "Okay, I didn't see a telephone in the house, but now I've got to find one. Do you know where there's a pay phone, or shall we just ask someone in town?"

Luke sighed as he put his hat on, lowered the brim, and slung his coat over his broad shoulder. "There are no telephones here, Casey. There are no cars, no electricity, no railroads, and no means for you to communicate with your sister. Look around you. In a poor section of Santa Fe, in your sister's time, there would surely be street-lights and cars. The year is 1878, and the sooner you accept it, the—"

"Stop," she interrupted before he could finish *that sentence* again. "Just point me to the center of town. My sister described a plaza, with lots of shops and restaurants. Where there's a restaurant, there's a telephone."

"You aren't going to listen to me, are you?"

"No." What did he think she was? Crazy, like him?

He grinned. "You want to see for yourself? All right, then. Come along," he said, walking forward. "I shall take you to the plaza."

"Okay," she muttered, sniffing the package she carried as she followed him. "Now we're getting somewhere."

"Oh, we're getting somewhere," he threw over his shoulder. "You're just not going to like it *when* we get there. And by the way, those are tamales you're holding. Would you hand me one, please?"

"Gladly." She opened the cloth and pulled out a warm loaf wrapped in a dried corn husk. Hurrying until she was walking at his side, she handed it to him. "Here ya go."

He whispered a *gracias* as he took it from her and then began unwrapping it. Her stomach rumbled as she got one for herself and she realized it had been hours since she'd eaten. She'd had a salad on her stopover in Denver, but hadn't had anything since. Bringing the tamale to her mouth, she couldn't suppress the moan of pleasure as she bit down into the food. Spicy beef in a sauce, wrapped in moist cornmeal, woke up her taste buds and she moaned again.

Luke glanced at her and grinned. "Hungry, I see. Perhaps when we get to our destination, we can better satisfy your appetite."

"Oh, you want to have dinner at a restaurant?" she asked between bites. "Okay, I'm sure it will take some time for my sister to pick me up, but it's my treat. You . . . ya know, saved my life and everything. My wallet's in your coat."

He merely shook his head as he continued to walk and eat his tamale. Munching on her own, she asked between bites, "What kind of name is Ang-hell? What's it mean?"

"It's a very common Mexican name. It's pronounced different than it's spelled."

"Okay, how's it spelled then?"

"A-n-g-e-l."

"Angel," she repeated, picturing the adorable infant in his mother's arms. "Yes . . . that's a good name." She would never forget that little angel and the miracle she had witnessed.

Luke simply nodded.

Casey noticed the people they passed were all dressed like peasants, and it didn't look like there was any electricity in this part of town. They really must be poor, she thought again with compassion, as she tagged along after Luke. Several people stared, some even nodding at Luke, and Casey couldn't really blame them. He was something. What, she hadn't figured out yet.

She began to hear faint strains of lively piano music filtering through the dimly lit and crooked dirt streets. "How much farther into town?" she asked as she looked around and saw it was now more crowded with people.

"Not much farther," Luke said as he grabbed her arm, pulling her away from walking directly into a large pile on the ground.

"Oh, jeez," she gasped. "Is that what I think it is?"

"Yes," he said, and continued walking. "Be careful where you step, there's more of it."

"Thanks," she muttered as she looked down and pranced over another dark blob.

Casey couldn't figure out why her sister was so in love with this place. Even in the dark it all looked kind of backward . . . as if time hadn't— She stopped that thought from continuing. Just get to the plaza and find a place to call Amy, she told herself. She was not about to entertain Luke's crazy concepts of time travel.

"The plaza is just a little more than a block ahead."

She looked around at the low, flat-roofed houses. The masses of rectangular walls and small windows made the houses appear to be much nicer than the ones from where they'd just come, but the area still didn't look too promising. She would have thought that by now they'd have come to a paved road, or something modern.

Suddenly Casey's attention was drawn toward the sound of clopping and grinding from behind them. She turned to see a large white horse and dark carriage with a driver and two passengers gracefully pass by. It reminded her of the time she'd been to New York and ridden in a carriage through Central Park. How quaint, she marveled. Why doesn't every city in America keep such time-honored traditions?

They walked on for a few more minutes, then Luke stopped and waved his hand before them. *"La plaza pública, señorita."*

Stepping forward without a word, Casey scanned the area. A white picket fence surrounded the small square, with paths laid out like a spoked wheel from the center to the edges. There were a few trees and some rough park benches. A bandstand stood off to the left of the monument in the center, which looked simply like a one-story-high spike.

Her shoulders sagged with disappointment. Where were the stores, the restaurants? Why no lights? "This can't be it," she protested.

"But I tell you, it is, Casey."

She looked around again as fear built up inside of her. "My sister said it was a busy place . . . lots of shops and galleries and . . . stuff. There must be another . . ."

"In your sister's time, she is correct. Santa Fe is one of the largest art centers in the country, but *now*, as you can see, it is less busy . . . with less *stuff*, as you so charmingly put it."

She glanced at him with annoyance. "Then is there a hotel in this place? I need to find somewhere to spend the night." She'd also find a phone at a hotel for sure.

"There is, La Fonda. But there is no need, Casey. I have friends here. Don Felipe d'Montoya will welcome us. He is a very generous host."

"You're kidding!" Her mouth dropped open with shock. "You think I'm about to go with you to a stranger's house and spend the night when my sister is someplace nearby? Show me the hotel." She stuck out her hand. "And I'd like my wallet now, please."

Again he seemed amused by her, and that only irritated her more. He handed over her wallet and she clutched it in her hand. "Okay, now, where's this hotel?"

He pointed across the plaza to the left. "You must accept what has happened to you, Casey. You are not going to be able to find your sister now. She doesn't exist here."

She felt tears of frustration well up in her eyes, and blinked rapidly to banish them. No sense in crying now. "Just show me," she muttered, determined to get away from this maddening man and find some semblance of sanity . . . somewhere.

He shrugged his shoulders and began walking across the plaza. Casey followed, blinking her tired eyes and commanding her body not to give out on her now. She had to find her sister.

"For strength, perhaps you could get something to eat in one of the many local saloons," he stated invitingly, and spun around with his hands in the air. "It might help you see things more clearly, señorita."

His glib attitude was now grating on her last nerve. "This tour is over, and I don't appreciate your sarcasm. I can see the hotel sign up ahead. I'll manage from here, thanks."

Her eyes remained fixed on the words LA FONDA as they turned left into the cross street.

"Oh!" she exclaimed as she ran smack-dab into an Indian who was leaning against the corner building. The Indian adjusted his blanket around himself and mumbled something as Casey stood frozen face-to-face with the stoic man. "Ex-excuse me, I'm so sorry. Oh jeez, I really didn't see you there, please—"

Luke immediately rushed to her side and began leading her across the street to the hotel. After he finished apologizing in the Indian's language, he turned to her with that grin again. "Yes, I'm sure you'll manage just fine."

"Well, it's dark! How do they expect anyone to see when there aren't any streetlights in this town?" she rambled as they stepped up onto the wooden sidewalk.

They walked into the small lobby of the hotel, and Casey approached the front desk. A small Hispanic man wearing wire-framed glasses and an old-fashioned suit put aside his newspaper when she caught his attention.

"Hello," Casey greeted him, and added with a tired smile, "Do you have a telephone I might use?"

"Perdóname?" The man's returning smile was mixed with confusion.

Okay, so he only speaks Spanish, she figured, but she wasn't about to give up by letting her tour guide do the translating again.

"You know, a telephone?" She mimed using one, feeling a bit foolish as she saw from the corner of her eye that Luke was grinning at her effort to communicate.

"I am sorry, madam," the man said with an accent as he pulled the small oval spectacles down his nose while taking in her clothing. "If you wish to use the telegraph, I'm sorry, the office is closed for the night . . . but I could arrange it for you in the morning."

She sighed with frustration. "You mean you run a hotel without *any* telephones? Not even in the rooms?"

The man looked at Luke as if he might help him understand her. Luke merely shrugged, allowing her to run the show.

"Okay, I would like a room then. How much?" No sense arguing with either of them. She was exhausted, and the sooner she got into a bed, the better. She would figure it all out in the morning.

"With or without a private bath, señorita?"

Sheesh, this must be like a bed-and-breakfast. "With a private bath." Yes, she could almost see herself soaking in a hot tub. The glass of wine and lengthy chat with her sister would have to wait. She opened her wallet.

"Three dollars . . . American dollars." The man swung a large book around and she could see it was a guest register.

"Three dollars?" she asked in disbelief. She glanced at Luke and saw he was still grinning, as though throughly enjoying the exchange. "Fine." Taking the bills out of her wallet, she slid them across the desk.

The hotel clerk took her money and examined it. She could see his eyes narrow with confusion. He turned them over and over, as though looking to see if they were counterfeit. She'd had that happen with larger bills, but not—

Suddenly he slapped the bills back on the counter and slipped them across to her. "I'm sorry, I cannot accept these as payment, señorita."

"And why not?" she demanded. "They are perfectly good!"

He shook his head. "I have never seen such dollars. Have you nothing else? Pesos are accepted," he added encouragingly.

"Pesos?" She looked at Luke for help. Again he shrugged his shoulders. "This *is* the United States, isn't it?"

"Since 1846, señorita," the desk clerk answered with a patriotic smile.

She was too tired to argue any further. "Okay, what about American Express?" she asked, pulling out her credit card and slapping it on the desk.

The man shook his head with confusion and started to apologize.

"Visa?" Another card hit the desk and was rejected. "MasterCard? Okay, how about a bank card? Got an ATM close by?"

The clerk said nothing, only looked even more bewildered at both of them.

Luke touched her arm. "It is useless Casey, come. We are both weary now."

She could see his amusement had subsided. Now he, too, looked tired. Turning back to the clerk, he asked if he could see his newspaper, and the man folded it before handing it to him. "Look at the date, Casey."

Fear gripped her stomach muscles and she felt faint as she read "August 21, 1878" under the heading *The Santa Fe Republican*. She grabbed up her credit cards and stuffed them into her wallet. "This can't be happening," she muttered.

Luke said something in Spanish to the man and then turned her toward the door. "Is it becoming clearer to you now, Casey?" he whispered as they went outside. "You are going to have to accept this."

She pulled her arm away and couldn't stop the tears this time. "Understand? That I'm as crazy as you are? Where am I? I feel like Alice after she's fallen down the rabbit hole! None of this makes any sense. People can't time-travel! *I* haven't time-traveled!"

"Casey, explain the newspaper."

She stared at him through the film of tears and wanted to scream out her fear. "I . . . I can't," she murmured. "Maybe this is a festival or something, and everyone is dressed in old-fashioned clothes, and to keep everything authentic, everyone even—"

"Shh . . ." he interrupted with a sympathetic smile and soft touch of his fingers to her quivering chin. "We need to rest. We've both had quite an evening. Come with me," he said, resting his strong hand on her shoulder for assurance. "My friend Don Felipe will provide us with rooms and food, and tomorrow you and I can tackle your disbeliefs again. But right now we are both weary." He slid his warm hand down her arm and into her hand. "Can you trust me on this?"

She wiped her wet cheeks with the sleeve of her sweater and nodded. "Okay, I surrender, Luke," she muttered, sniffling back her distress. "For tonight anyway. I'm too tired to fight you and a whole town that seems to have forgotten modern civilization. But tomorrow's another day, and I will find my sister."

"Come," he said, wrapping his huge coat around her again. "It isn't far from here. Everything will become more clear tomorrow after you rest."

She grabbed the sides of the coat to keep the hem off the ground and allowed him to put his arm around her shoulders. What did she care anymore? She was too weary to protest . . . No longer could she wage this inner war between the idea of time travel and the peace she felt when this man wrapped his arm around her. All she wanted to do was collapse in a bed. Any bed. In any time.

As she walked next to Luke, her mind replayed the moment she saw him emerging from that incredible bolt of lightning, walking toward her. Something had happened to her that was beyond belief . . . but time travel?

She had a nagging feeling she was going to find out soon.

She just couldn't believe she was going along with this . . .

Absentmindedly Casey ran her hand along the thick, high adobe wall, feeling the sun's warmth still radiating outward. Fragrant blossoms from vines crawling through small wooden grilled windows in the wall flashed before her dulling senses, giving her a hint of the secluded inner garden.

Suddenly Luke stopped and pulled a rope on the side of two huge wooden doors. She couldn't make out the oval plaque that was embedded over the entrance where the wall had been heightened in an ornate arch. A bell rang in the quiet courtyard beyond, and within seconds a man came and greeted them through the wooden grilles.

Luke said something in Spanish, and Casey was able to make out his name and Don Felipe's as he announced their arrival at his friend's home. The man nodded and quickly ran back toward the house. She was too tired to pay more attention. All she could think about was putting her head down and resting.

Another man rushed to the gate. The doors swung wide open and within moments Luke and the other man were smiling and hugging each other, speaking in Spanish, and laughing. Don Felipe pulled Luke toward the house, when Luke turned to her.

"Don Felipe d'Montoya, may I present my new friend, Señorita Casey O'Reilly. She is originally from the East and was separated from her family. She is now under my protection until she can be reunited."

Don Felipe appeared to be around fifty years old and was handsomely attired in a burgundy silk dressing robe with velvet lapels. His eyes remained friendly as he stepped rigidly forward and held out his hand. Casey found herself putting her own into his and was shocked as the man formally bowed over it. "I am wholly at your disposal, señorita," he said in pleasantly accented English. "Consider this your home."

"Thank you," she whispered, as the man straightened again, smiling widely. She felt Luke watching her and, wanting to make a decent impression, added, "You are very gracious, Señor d'Montoya."

"You may address me as Don Felipe," the man answered, extending his hand toward his home. "Come, Señorita Casey," he said, holding out his arm for her to take. "I see you are both in need of attention, and my household is at your command."

"That's very kind of you . . . Don Felipe." She said the man's name with hesitancy. It sounded so old-fashioned. "A bed and a bath is all I ask."

"And you shall have it," he declared, leading her and Luke into his magnificent home.

Although she was tired, she couldn't help but notice the serene ambience of the villa. Shading the incredibly bright moonlight from the inlaid stone path they walked on, a huge cottonwood tree stood in the center of the patio garden. She could make out brightly colored wooden benches, a couple of statues, and a large water fountain placed carefully around the private sanctuary. Thinking it must be even more beautiful in daylight, she then turned her attention to the portal of this grand home.

Walking under the wraparound patio roof supported by wide stucco pillars, they watched Don Felipe push open the thick wooden double doors, unveiling their gracious host's abode. *"Bienvenidos, amigos mío... Vaya a mi casa real,"* Don Felipe said in a proud tone.

"It is, most certainly, one of the finest 'royal houses' in all of Santa Fe, *caballero*," Luke replied with a big smile and slight bow.

Casey and Luke stepped over the wide stone threshold and into the warm amber glow of two huge, stamped tin lanterns adorning opposite walls of the foyer. More candles were being lit and placed into niches in the walls by the man who first greeted them at the gate.

Two small three-tiered fountains framed the broad, iron-railed, sweeping staircase at the back of the room. Glancing up the saltillo-tiled stairs to a mid-level landing, Casey spotted a large niche that displayed a painted statue of the Madonna. The landing split the stairs, which led to separate balconies under the massive cathedral ceiling. She could see dark, paneled doors lining the open-air balconies and figured they must be bedrooms.

Don Felipe latched the elaborately carved, tall wooden front doors behind them.

An older woman in a dark gown that swept the floor entered the foyer and, with her hands clasped together at her waist, bowed slightly before them. Casey thought she looked very proper with her braided hair drawn up into a coronet and a black lace mantilla attached. Don Felipe spoke to her in Spanish and the woman nodded, trying to avert her gaze from the heavy man's coat Casey was still wearing.

Luke, appearing to be quite at home in his surroundings,

smiled at her. "I shall say good night to you here, Casey. Follow this woman and you will have your bath and your bed and something to eat. Tomorrow we shall again speak, but for this night, rest as if in the arms of angels."

They were being separated? Wait . . . what was she thinking? That they would spend the night in the same room together? Mentally shaking herself, Casey began taking off his coat to hand back to him when his fingers touched and lingered on hers.

"Keep it until you are in your room. Marcella will bring it to me later."

Confused, she merely nodded. "Okay . . . well, good night then. And . . . thank you again."

Luke's smile was sincere yet brief as he turned back to their beaming host. Casey watched the two old friends walk away from her and the woman who was left to chaperone. As she heard them again begin to speak rapidly in Spanish, she thought Don Felipe was very excited to see Luke.

"*Adelante*, Señorita Casey." The woman's voice broke Casey's gaze from the two men, who were passing through another set of tall, paneled wooden doors against the right wall of the foyer.

She picked up the hem of Luke's coat and meekly smiled. The woman nodded politely and motioned with her hand to follow her.

They ascended the magnificent staircase and turned to the left. Halfway down the length of the balcony, her escort opened a door and motioned for Casey to stop.

"*Espérate una momento, por favor,*" the woman said.

Casey stared at her and smiled her confusion. "I'm sorry. I don't understand. I don't, umm, I speak . . . I speak . . . *muy poquito* Spanish." There. That about said it all.

The woman nodded and pointed to the earth-colored tiles of the balcony floor. "*Espérate*. Ah, wait. *Sí*, wait."

"Oh . . . okay," Casey answered, relieved that they could communicate now. "I'll wait."

Hearty laughter resounded around the polished plaster walls and ceiling. Casey turned and looked across the lovely foyer below. Lush greenery in large clay pots all about the house gave a feeling of vibrant life. She imagined Luke and Don Felipe smoking cigars and drinking brandy from crystal snifters in antiquated fashion beyond the closed doors.

"Venga, Señorita Casey," the woman's voice called.

Casey inhaled deeply as she turned back and entered the room. She watched as the last thick candle was placed into a lantern and hung from a wooden bracket in the wall. As the light grew, she saw it was a very warm and inviting bedroom with a heavy four-poster bed, a huge, ornately carved wardrobe, and a wine-bottle-shaped fireplace built into the corner.

"Desculpa—" The woman hesitated, as though to correct herself. "Wait, *por favor.*"

"Okay. No *problema.*" Casey weakly smiled in return.

Nodding again, the solemn woman left her alone. Casey looked around the room and sighed. She ran her hand over the soft blanket on the high bed and immediately felt gratitude well up in her chest. She might not have been able to secure a room on her own, but Luke certainly had come through with a fine one. Taking off his coat, she removed her wallet and put it on a small table before placing the heavy coat on a chair. He really had watched over her, and whenever she found her sister, they would have to reward him for all he'd done.

Looking toward the bed, she again sighed. How she wished she could just crawl up into it, yet she knew it would be terribly impolite not to wash the sand out of her hair and off her tired body first. She felt like it was in every one of her pores, and wondered where the bathroom was.

The woman she guessed was named Marcella told her to wait, so she would, but she hoped somebody showed up soon, for she found she could barely keep her eyes open.

Sitting down on top of Luke's coat, she leaned her head back and closed her eyes. Finally she could relax, and yet . . . in her mind she saw Luke walking out of that lightning and her eyes immediately snapped open. Nobody could do that.

Who was he? *What* was he?

He seemed normal, well, outside of his crazy time-travel concept that is. Maybe he was one of those New Age people, with his talk of energy and chakras and stuff that she didn't understand. And what was with that crystal? Yeah, he had to be one of them. Nice, but weird.

There was no more time to ponder as a quick knock came on the door. Even before Casey could answer, it was opened as several young teenagers, all dressed in simple white tunics with bare feet, entered with Marcella.

Two young boys placed a large, round, hammered-copper tub in the room, and Casey stood up in shock. They didn't expect her to bathe in *that*! Four pails of steaming water were being poured by two small girls as Marcella stood by and supervised. Suddenly Casey realized they must be servants, and she was saddened to think they had obviously been awoken from their sleep to attend her. Everyone appeared to be Hispanic or maybe Indian, and Casey wasn't sure she could explain her dilemma without offending anyone.

An older girl went to the fireplace and began lighting the small logs inside. The flurry of child labor around Casey made her weary body ache even more with empathy for them. This surely was one hell of a day, she thought, biting her bottom lip. Nothing was normal. Not even a simple bath!

Abruptly the reality of human necessity surged through

her entire body. "Umm, excuse me . . . Marcella?" Casey asked in a hesitant voice. "Where is the bathroom?"

"Perdóname?" The woman looked puzzled.

"Ahh . . . a toilet?" She couldn't remember the word, and she was not about to mime that one!

"Ahh . . . *sí!"* Marcella stooped down and reached under the bed. She brought out a pretty painted, glazed bowl and handed it to her.

"You don't understand. I mean, a toilet . . . where I can sit down." Casey felt tears of frustration coming into her eyes and she fought to control them.

The slightly taller woman held out the bowl to her again. *"Sí . . . lavabo."*

This was not happening. She would go without a bed before going without a real toilet! Casey turned around and looked at the polished dark wooden door they had entered from. She needed to talk to Luke, for she wasn't making any progress with this woman. They simply were not communicating.

"Señorita Casey," the woman repeated questioningly. *"Lavabo?"*

Casey spun back around to the woman still holding the heavy bowl out to her, and sighed. "Oh-kay, it's like this." Mortified, Casey mimicked sitting on a toilet and flushing, even making the sounds of running water. Everyone in the room stopped what they were doing to stare at her, the younger girl covering her mouth with her hand to hide a giggle. The stoic woman said something very sternly, sending them all rushing out of the room.

Marcella insistently placed the heavy bowl in Casey's hands and flatly stated, *"El orinal,"* then followed the others, closing the heavy door after them.

Casey stared at the closed door, the steaming tub of water, the bowl in her hands. This was unbelievable! She didn't mind roughing it, had even camped a few times . . .

but this was, well, it was a fine house! There had to be a toilet somewhere in the place . . . unless this really was . . .

No, she would not allow her mind to wander there again.

Placing the bowl back on the floor, she walked over to the tub and put her fingers into the water. It was hot and enticing and she saw there were thin linen towels draped on the crude tub handles. She resigned she could do this at least. Pulling off her sweater, she felt and heard sand scatter around her and was sorry to mess the spotless room. She slipped out of her shoes and unzipped her jeans. Folding everything neatly, even her underwear, she placed the bundle on the end of the bed. Casey bit her bottom lip again and tiptoed back to the tub. Gingerly she crawled in and slowly sat down, allowing the shallow pool to envelop her, to cleanse her pores of sand and dirt. She closed her eyes momentarily as the warmth began to ease her tired, aching body. She cupped the water in her hands and poured it over her exposed knees and shoulders, feeling the intimacy of the trickle down her spine. She took a deep breath and sat motionless for a few moments. Exhaling, she folded her arms around her legs and rested her chin on one knee. Curled in a fetal position, she opened her sleepy eyelids and gazed at the fire in the corner which was now flaming higher. Relief spread through her as the threads of fear seemed to float away with the wisps of steam surrounding her, yet the disappointment of not being able to contact her sister still lingered in her heart.

Another knock sounded at the door, interrupting her peace, and Casey instinctively covered her breasts with her hands as it slowly opened. She couldn't believe her eyes!

"Oh! I am so sorry," Luke mumbled in embarrassment as he averted his gaze back out to the hallway. "I . . . I just wanted to check with you that you . . . you had everything you needed before I retired."

"I am fine!" Casey snapped, feeling the heat rise to her

cheeks, and it wasn't the temperature of the water! Dear God, what more could this night hold?

"I . . . I sincerely apologize for disturbing your bath," he muttered, and Casey noticed his own tanned cheeks were now blushing with embarrassment as his hand grasped the doorknob.

Even though he wasn't looking at her, she tried to make her body sink farther into the water, yet it was impossible. "I told you, I'm fine. Please . . . just leave!"

"Yes . . . yes, of course," he answered, shaking his head at his own lack of manners. "I will see you in the morning. Again, I apologize for intruding." The door was quickly shut.

She stared at the heavy wood and was tempted to get up and lock the damn thing. Sheesh, was she never to get any privacy around here? What an embarrassing scene!

He did seem rattled, though. Really rattled . . .

Put the man out of your mind, far out of your mind. Relax now, Casey . . . don't think, she advised herself as she attempted to regain her last sense of peace. Sighing deeply, she pulled a dull, softened tan block from the bottom of the tub. Guessing it was the soap, she sniffed it and found the scent was not too appealing. There was no one to call now that she was finally alone, and she'd already been shown so much courtesy, she couldn't imagine requesting anything more. She began spinning the slippery bar between her hands, creating a lather.

Thank goodness her hair was short, for it took a contortionist to wash it, but she did manage and then collapsed back against the copper tub. Maybe she would just fall asleep here. As weary as she felt, she didn't know if she even had the energy to get out and make her way to the bed. All she needed was a few hours of sleep and some food when she awoke to reenergize. Then she would find

Amy and end this madness. Luke was a very nice man, but she needed to find reality . . . and a real bathroom.

Casey's mind wandered to the luxuries of modern conveniences and her sister's home, where Amy must be very worried, waiting for her to arrive. She wished there were some way to let her know she was okay. Poor Amy. Casey was sure the police had found her rental car by now and had traced it back to her. Amy would have called the airlines to make sure she'd arrived, then probably would have contacted the police . . .

The police! That was what she should do tomorrow . . . find the police.

Of course! Why hadn't she thought of it sooner? Now she had a plan that made sense. Feeling somewhat better, Casey lathered the crude bar of soap in one of the small linen towels with which she'd been provided and began vigorously scrubbing every inch of skin. As she brought her left foot out of the water, she was surprised to see that it wasn't bruised or even blistered.

What had happened to her . . . really? She'd been hit by lightning, that much she knew, and she remembered feeling like she'd been hurled into a relentless tempest of sand and wind. She recalled the intense pain that had racked her body and the fleeting thought that she might be dying. Then Luke had come and wrapped her in his coat and arms, protecting her from the storm, and she'd felt . . . safe, stronger, healed. What had he done? What kind of magic did he possess that even Maria felt while giving birth?

There would be no answers now, she thought, and sighed deeply. Deciding it was time to get out of the water, she looked around the room and realized she'd left her clothes folded on the bed, so she reached down along the side of the tub and grabbed the long length of cloth that hung from the handle.

Wrapping herself in the thin towel, she stood for a few seconds against the fire's glow and allowed the water to drip off her body before stepping out of the tub. Okay, she wasn't at the Ritz-Carlton or the Hilton, but at least she felt cleaner. She began patting her skin to absorb the remaining moisture and was startled by a quick knock and the sound of the door opening.

Marcella and another woman came into the room, carrying clothes and a tray of food.

Casey smiled shyly and thanked the older woman, who handed her a soft white cotton nightgown with layers of frills on the sleeves. *"Gracias,"* Casey said softly.

Marcella walked to the wardrobe and hung up what looked like a colorful skirt and a white blouse while the younger woman placed the tray on a small table. The two young girls who had filled the tub earlier now entered and pushed it out of the room. Marcella waited until they were finished, then picked up Luke's coat and nodded to Casey.

"Buenas noches, Señorita Casey. *Dulce sueños."*

Casey remembered enough to translate the woman's good-night wishes. *"Buenas noches,"* she replied, still clutching the towel to cover her nakedness.

The door was latched shut again and Casey let out her breath. Okay, this was it. She was here, and as far as she could tell, there was no toilet. She removed the towel and folded it over the back of the chair to dry, then picked up the soft nightgown and slipped it over her head. It fell to the floor and felt wonderful against her skin. Don Felipe certainly knew how to extend his hospitality, and she wondered whose nightgown she was wearing. It really was lovely and she felt very feminine, even though her stomach rumbled loudly with hunger, and her desire for a bathroom wasn't lessening.

She looked at the food on the tray.

She looked at the bowl on the floor.

She looked back to the food; she'd deal with the bowl later.

He stood in the hallway, willing his mind to wipe away the scene he'd just witnessed, yet he couldn't help the response in his body to the sight of such a lovely, though irritated, woman bathing. He found himself slowly grinning. She really was attractive, he thought . . . again. When he'd first come upon her in the sandstrom, he'd caught his breath at the sweet innocence in her eyes, and the sensation of her breath against his chest. Yet there was another side to her, contrasting that innocence. Casey O'Reilly would be a handful, as her feisty Irish temper had already shown him.

Luke straighted his shoulders and dug his hands into the pockets of his trousers as he walked away. It had been years since he'd let a woman have an effect on him, and now wasn't the time to allow it to surface. Better to step back and remain in the role of mentor. He was here to return her to her family. That was all.

Wasn't it?

Four

A gentle breeze played with the lace curtains in the window. She felt the sun's comforting warmth against her face as her eyelids fluttered closed again. Snuggling into the soft pillow, Casey sighed with pleasure and luxuriated in the sensuous feel of the clean sheets. Lying on her stomach, she smiled, thinking of her great dream of a handsome man who looked like a cross between Antonio Banderas and an angel . . . a man who was so sexy she moaned as she ground her belly into the mattress and swore she was in heaven. She was quite content to stay in her sensuous morning haze until—

"Good morning, Señorita Casey."

Her eyes flew open and she stared at a dark-skinned woman with long black braids and a friendly smile standing beside the bed. Casey thought she must still be dreaming, and blinked. She wanted to go back to the peaceful slumber of only moments ago, yet there was a sensation crawling over her skin now that said she was awake . . . wide-awake, and something was very wrong.

Quickly she flipped over and slid up to the pillows, clutching the sheets to her chest. "Good morning," she whispered, blowing a blonde lock of hair from her face.

The older woman smiled and stood silent for a moment, as though allowing Casey's senses to emerge and focus. From her sleepy vantage point, Casey could tell the woman was about the same height as she, but had a much healthier build. The loosely fitting natural gauze blouse gathered with strings at the low neckline and upper arms was a lovely contrast to her bronze skin. She wore a leather belt with a pouch slung to her side, and a simple brown skirt fell below calf length, revealing worn, plain leather sandals on her wide feet. The older woman's smile widened, revealing a large, toothy gleam.

"I speak English, so I was asked to attend to you," the woman finally said, sounding very pleased with herself. "Not many of the servants here can speak it as good as Juana," she added, patting her ample chest.

Casey only nodded, while still trying to make her brain work. It wasn't a dream? Luke was real? Before she could assimilate what was happening, a firm knock sounded on the door and Juana quickly walked across the room to open it.

Luke stood in the doorway, looking fresh and devastatingly handsome. His black, curly hair was slicked behind his ears, clearly still damp from a bath. He wore a long-sleeved, white cotton shirt with embroidered white stitching on the broad collar. It was loosely laced halfway down his chest and tucked tightly into his form-fitting black trousers. The sandstorm dust of the night before was now polished away from his brilliant black boots.

He smiled and Casey sat up straight, clutching the sheets tighter to her chest, acutely aware of her groggy appearance. Dear God, it was all real. He was real. This place was real. All of it . . .

"Good morning, Señorita Casey," he said, producing a deep purple blossom on a leafy stem from behind his back while stepping into the room. "Did you sleep well?"

She sat back against the pillows in an attempt to display her indifference to his gallant entrance, when her attention was drawn to Juana. She watched as the woman put the dirty jeans and sweater over her arm and then picked up the empty food tray. Juana began walking toward the door and Casey quickly sat back up. "Wait," she called out. "I need my clothes."

"They will be cleaned for you," Luke answered before Juana could speak. Casey watched the exchange between them. It was obvious that the older woman, too, saw something alluring about him as she coyly smiled at Luke in return. "Thank you, Juana."

"*De nada,* Señor Luke." Juana curtsied as he closed the door after her. Turning back to Casey and still smiling, he again inquired, "How did you sleep?"

"Like a baby," she answered, pushing the insistent, floppy lock of hair away from her eyes. "And I still need my clothes."

"I'm glad you rested well, Casey." Luke nodded, pulling a cushioned and ornately carved wooden chair near the bed. He handed her the flower as he sat down. "Again, I apologize for last night's intrusion."

She was immediately embarrassed at the thought of him seeing her naked, and tried to play it off with a shrug. Accepting his offering, she closed her eyes and sniffed the fragrant blossom. "Thanks, it's very pretty." She raised her head and looked him squarely in the eyes. "But let's not avoid the subject any longer. I need to get my day started, and you could offer me a greater gift by getting my clothes back, thank you."

An amused smile came to his lips as he brushed his forefinger over his nose. "Your clothes will be cleaned and returned to you. Last night I believe you were given something else to wear, something more appropriate for this time?"

"Oh, jeez . . ." she muttered, flopping back against the pillows and shaking her head. "We're back to time travel again? My clothes are just fine for *this time,*" she continued defiantly, "and by the way . . . where is the bathroom in this house?"

He chuckled and shook his head. "There are some adjustments, Casey. Lack of modern facilities is just one of them. You simply must accept where you find yourself now," he stated softly.

"Look, Luke . . ." she insistently began while using the flower to point at him, "I accept that I am in Santa Fe, here to visit my sister Amy, who is by now probably worried sick over me, and I need my clothes back to get to her." She waved the flower back and forth. "Now, I truly appreciate everything you've done and the kindness of these people who have welcomed me into their household—"

"And that is why I have come to speak with you so early," he interrupted her. "Before you are introduced to all the other members of this gracious home, you have to realize this is not the time you believe it to be."

She exhaled and rolled her eyes upward in exasperation at his obstinacy.

He leaned forward and continued in a low whisper. "No one here will understand if you keep insisting it is the year 2000. You must come to some acceptance of this before integrating into their lives . . . Your future, and theirs, seriously depends upon it."

She stopped twirling the stem of the flower and stared at

him. "You're nuts, you know that? Last night was one thing, but now . . . well, I simply cannot accept that I've traveled back in time, like, what . . . more than a hundred years, and that I can't find my sister. I will thank Don Felipe and everyone else for their hospitality, but I can't stay here and pretend. My sister and her family are out there waiting for me right now."

He sighed and ran his strong fingers through his damp curly hair. *"Ay. Por Dios,"* he sighed, dropping his head. "Please, Casey . . . again I request your patience. I admit, it is a strange and difficult thing . . . but you must come to accept that when you were hit by lightning, you *were* thrown back in time. You saw the newspaper last night at La Fonda. How can you explain that away?"

She merely shrugged. "I have no idea what that was about, but as soon as I get my clothes back, I'm going to find out."

"You cannot continue to wear those clothes, Casey. Not here. You see, I have created a . . . a story for you that will be acceptable to those you will meet later today."

"A story . . . ?" Her eyes narrowed with suspicion.

"Yes." He hesitated slightly while leaning back in the chair and crossing his arms. "I have said that you were a novitiate with the Sisters of Mercy in California, which would account for your cropped hair, that you changed your mind about your vocation and you left your sheltered life."

Her eyes widened in astonishment at what she was hearing.

"I explained you have been hiding from your family, dressing like a man, until their disappointment in you eases and you can be reunited with them again."

Her mouth hung open in shock. "You did *what?*"

"I know it is not a very good story"—he shrugged, sitting upright—"but I was too tired last night to come up with anything better . . . and I had to say something about your appearance."

"I can't believe this!" Impulsively she threw the flower at him and watched as he lifted his hand and easily caught it. "How dare you say those things about me! I'm not even a practicing Catholic anymore!"

"Ah, you know the religion. Good, it will be easier then."

She sat up straighter and leaned forward. "You are truly certifiable! I am *not* going along with this whole crazy story. Try and get that through your head, Mr. Time Traveler!"

That dimpled grin came to his face again as he chuckled, only increasing her irritation.

"I want my clothes. I need to get out of here."

He stood up and walked to the large, ornately carved and painted wardrobe and opened the right door. Taking out the long skirt with bands of red, white, and yellow material at the hem, along with a white frilly blouse, he held them out to her. "Here are your clothes, Casey. You will wear these."

"I'm not wearing them." She folded her arms over her chest and lifted her chin with greater defiance. "I want my own back."

"You will wear these if you wish to leave this room." He laid them at the foot of the bed and sighed, as though trying to be patient with her. "I am sorry to have to be so firm with you, but I cannot allow you to insult our hosts with your version of reality. Until the time is right for us to return to your sister and the future, we must fit in here without causing suspicion. These are my friends, trusted friends, and so—"

"So you lied to them," Casey interrupted, furious that this man seemed to think he could take over her life.

"It would appear that way to you," he answered. "Far better to make up a fictitious story than tell them they are entertaining a woman who is really from the future."

"I can't be from the future if I never went into the past!" she blurted.

"Okay, you do not believe me, Casey. However, I assure you, they would not believe you when you start asking for things like telephones and cars. You would then be the one who seems certifiable, señorita." He pointed at her playfully and grinned again.

She wasn't laughing.

"Look, we are actually in the same position. I know you came to Santa Fe to visit your sister in the year 2000. I believe you. Can you, for a moment, consider that I am in your corner, that I am trying to protect you while you find yourself in a confusing situation? Have I done anything to indicate that I wish you harm?"

She refused to answer him. She sat with her arms crossed over her chest and stared at the darkened fireplace in the corner of the room.

She heard a soft knock and, from the corner of her eye, saw Luke turn to answer the door. He thanked Juana as he took a tray and again shut the door.

"Your breakfast," he announced, placing the tray on the bed. "Take all the time you wish, señorita, to make up your mind. It would appear we are to be here for some time. I only ask that you behave like a woman and not like an unreasonable child. We can make this enjoyable or miserable . . . The choice is yours."

She watched him move out the door and was stunned when she heard a lock click. "I don't believe it!" she said aloud in shock. "He's locked me in my room until I agree to buy in to his whole mind game!" She'd have thrown the plate of eggs at the door if this were her own home . . . plus, well, she was hungry.

Jerking the tray toward her, she looked over the meal. Eggs, over easy, pinto beans, and something that looked like a red Polish sausage with a large green chile garnish invited her taste buds. She broke off a piece of the freshly baked bread on the side and jabbed at the soft egg, wishing it were her fist into Luke's so superior stomach. *Locking her in her room like she was a misbehaving kid!* What nerve! She was thirty-one years old, for chrissake!

She bit into the sweet bread covered with yolk, then waved it toward the door as though he could hear her giving him a piece of her mind. Well, he could just forget about her and Amy giving him a thank-you present when she was reunited with her sister.

She ate more of the eggs and chewed the bread thoughtfully, while trying to take her mind away from the maddening man who had just left. She had made a plan last night . . . What was it?

The police.

Right! She needed to contact the police today. Surely there was a missing-person report on her by now. When she didn't show up, Amy would eventually have called the cops. Casey blinked a few times, thinking she heard a noise coming from behind the wardrobe, and then shrugged. She'd never been in trouble with the law before, so they wouldn't even have any record of her, but her fingerprints were on the car and . . . What did happen when someone was missing?

She had no more time to think as the wardrobe door opened and a young girl's face peeked into the room.

Casey nearly choked when she yelped in fright. This was like a never-ending nightmare where people just kept popping in and out all over!

"*Buenos días,* Señorita Casey. Do not be afraid. I am Rosalinda . . . This was my sister's room before her marriage."

Stunned, Casey could only watch as a pretty teenager, dressed in a yellow gown, stepped out of the wardrobe and smoothed down her voluminous skirt.

"I am the daughter of Don Raphael Felipe d'Montoya

and Doña Isabela d'Cortez. I have heard of your courageous adventure, and even though my parents insist I wait
until we are properly introduced, I knew a woman such as
yourself would understand my impatience to make your
acquaintance."

Casey simply did not know what to say to this delightfully strange visitor, whose smile was irresistible. Swallowing the bread in her mouth, she muttered, "Hello."

Rosalinda grinned widely and swept closer to the bed.
She curtsied formally, then peeked up and began speaking
as she straightened up. "Have you really left the convent?
How brave you are! I myself would never want to shut
myself away in a convent, but I would never tell anyone
else such a thought. The good sisters of Loretto think I
may have a vocation, but I believe it is for the dowry my
father would provide the church. Fortunately, my parents
wish to see me married . . ." She took a breath. "Oh, I do
hope you will be here for my *quinceñera* feast. It will be a
grand celebration."

Rattled by the barrage of words, Casey knew she should
say something in answer. "What is a *quinceñera*?"

Rosalinda looked pleased by her question. "It is a feast
celebrating my reaching womanhood, my fifteenth year,
and announces I am available for marriage. You may wear
one of Marguerita's gowns, if you wish. She is married to
Don Carlos and he is very wealthy and so my sister has left
some of her gowns for me, and though I don't care for
them, you might."

"Marriage?" Casey sat up straighter and adjusted the
nightgown. "You're very young to be considering marriage, aren't you?" Why did this child act as though her
appearing from within a wardrobe wearing an old-
fashioned gown were perfectly natural? What kind of crazy
place was Santa Fe?

"Not at all," Rosalinda replied, daintily sitting on the edge of the bed and smiling. "My father has invited many eligible men from Mexico and even Spain . . . though I am determined to wait for my true love. I do hope he arrives soon." She seemed to dismiss that thread of conversation and veered back to her original thoughts. "Did you really run away to find your own life? How young were you when you entered the convent? Oh, this is so romantic . . . Why, you are a heroine, a woman forging your own destiny!"

Casey laughed. "I'm not a heroine, Rosalinda. In fact, I'm sort of lost right now. I need to find my family." Maybe this kid could help her. Who cared how she came to be in the room! When in Rome . . .

Rosalinda looked contrite. "Yes, so I have heard. Don't worry, I'm sure they will forgive you and you can go home to them, señorita."

Casey decided not to get into Luke's story, especially if this teenager thought it was such a good one that she wanted to be friendly. "Rosalinda, I have a favor to ask of you."

The girl appeared delighted again. "Anything."

Smiling in return, Casey said, "How did you get into this room? Is there a hidden passageway behind the wardrobe?"

Rosalinda looked at the heavy chest and giggled. "Yes. My father doesn't think Marguerita and I know about it, but we discovered it years ago. My sister and I had many adventures through its use, but I cannot go about by myself now. And there is not much one can do with a duenna accompanying—"

"I could go with you," Casey interrupted. "I'm twice your age and—"

"You are not!" Rosalinda burst with astonishment.

Pleased by the girl's reaction, Casey grinned. "Yes, I am

thirty-one and therefore quite respectable as a chaperone. I just need my clothes, and I do so want to explore Santa Fe. If it is possible, could you do me a big favor and show me how to get out of the house unnoticed?"

She held her breath as she waited for Rosalinda's reply.

"You are so old and have no husband, no children. All those years in the convent . . ."

Okay, it was an impolite statement, yet it was coming from a teenager, and the look of sadness on Rosalinda's face made Casey smile. "I would like a child someday."

"Me, too," the girl answered quickly. "I would like many children, but first my true love must find me. I know he will."

"Hmm . . ." Casey didn't have an answer. The teenager's words reminded her of her own thoughts while driving yesterday. She had surrendered looking. True love? Was there such a thing? Really? Better not to get into that discussion. There was a more pressing matter at hand. "Do you think you could help me?"

"Where are your clothes?"

"A woman named Juana took them, and Luke said they were being cleaned."

Rosalinda shook her head. "I cannot get them for you then, but here . . ." She held out the white blouse that was folded on the bed. "Dress quickly and I will change into something more . . . more suitable. I will also get you a shawl, and then if we are very quiet and very clever, we might have a secret adventure."

Grinning, Casey whispered, "Thank you so much. You have no idea how much I appreciate your help, Rosalinda."

"We shall be coconspirators then," the happy teenager said while slipping off the bed. She headed toward the wardrobe and giggled. "We shall be like sisters, united in our adventure."

Casey stopped the romantic girl with another question before she disappeared into the wardrobe. "Rosalinda, could you please tell me what year it is?"

The girl halted with one foot raised before stepping inside. Turning back, she whispered, "You don't know this?"

"I . . . I was caught in the storm last night and hit by lightning," she said stupidly. "Could you just tell me?"

"*Madre Dios!* Lightning! You poor woman, no wonder you are confused. It is 1878, señorita . . . the year of my *quinceñera.*"

Don't panic, Casey's brain seemed to be screaming at her. She numbly smiled and nodded to the teenager, and then watched as Rosalinda slipped inside the wardrobe.

Alone once more, she grabbed the edge of the sheet and threw it off. She would not think about what the girl had just said. She couldn't! If she believed her, then she really had traveled back in time and Luke was right about everything . . . and she refused to accept that. She would get dressed and leave this place to find out the truth once and for all. She picked up the frilly blouse and stared at it. Even if it meant she had to dress up like someone living a hundred years ago, she was going to find out what had happened to her!

She felt surrounded by madness as she dressed, yet she wouldn't let it stop her. She had to focus now, and within minutes she was dressed like a Spanish woman in a long colorful skirt and a thin white cotton blouse that laced down the front under an embroidered flounce. Running her fingers through her hair, she wished she had mirror, comb and a toothbrush, but small essentials weren't about to get in the way of her escape. Nothing mattered now except finding a way back . . . back to sanity.

She was ready and waiting when Rosalinda returned,

dressed in a much plainer costume. She carried a brush and a white shawl with long fringe. Walking up to Casey, the girl held out the brush.

"We must hurry before someone comes for your tray. We cannot stay long, señorita, for I shall be missed, but I will show you the way."

Casey quickly ran the brush through her short hair. "Thank you, Rosalinda. I don't want you to get into any trouble for this. If you would just show me how to get out, I would be most grateful."

She placed the brush on the bed and was stunned as Rosalinda put the shawl over her head and whispered with tears in her eyes, "I am so sorry about your hair."

Casey had to bite the inside of her cheek not to giggle. Wrapping the shawl around her and flipping one edge over her shoulder, she said in a serious voice, "It's all right, Rosalinda. It will grow back, and the shawl covers it now. Let's go!"

"Oh, one more thing I must tell you, señorita." Rosalinda stopped her before they stepped into the wardrobe.

"Yes, what is it, Rosalinda?"

"You have some yellow dust on the end of your nose . . . I think it is from the flower Señor Luke picked for you from our garden this morning." She smiled knowingly.

"Oh, jeez!" Casey blurted, and began rubbing her nose the same way she'd seen Luke gesture toward her earlier. She shook her head with embarrassment that she'd been sitting there all morning with this bright yellow pollen smudge in the middle of her face. No wonder he didn't take her seriously!

"Okay . . . we must be very quiet now, for although the household is busy, even a cough will be heard."

Casey nodded and took a deep breath. She followed the girl through the wardrobe and into the small passageway between the thick adobe walls. It was dark and Casey was really glad she didn't suffer from claustrophobia, for she could feel her own breath bouncing off the wall and hitting her in the face. Don't think, she mentally schooled herself as she followed sideways through the passageway. She wondered who had built it and for what reason.

What did it matter now, when it was serving her in escaping madness? Like walking between walls wasn't madness! Wait until she told Amy all of it. The two of them would howl with laughter. Just picturing her younger sister in her mind calmed her down. How she loved Amy, her beautiful little niece, Sara, her brother-in-law, Jim. She pictured each in her mind. She wanted to be with them, normal people who drove cars and had bathrooms and were able to recognize reality! Okay, Sara didn't drive a car, but even her three-year-old niece would be able to tell that something was definitely not right with all these people!

Rosalinda put out her hand to stop, and Casey held her breath as the girl pushed something in the wall and then leaned against what looked to be another part of the wall. Immediately Casey saw what appeared to be daylight. She let out her breath with relief. She might not be claustrophobic, but she would be grateful to breathe fresh air again.

"Come," Rosalinda whispered. "Slide behind this plant and keep close to the wall."

A plant? Casey did as she was told and saw that a large tree was planted in a huge earthen pot that hid the false wall. Her heart was thudding against her rib cage as she flattened her body to the wall and slid behind the thick branches.

"This way. Follow me," Rosalinda whispered.

"Wait!" Casey whispered back, as a terrible thought came to her. "I forgot my wallet. It's back in the room!"

The girl looked puzzled as she pushed Casey even closer to the wall. "Wallet? I do not understand this term."

"It's got my money, my identification. I need it."

Rosalinda looked relieved. "Oh, I have money if we wish to purchase something. We can't go back. Look, already Marcella is preparing for our meal."

Casey turned her head and saw the stern woman reprimanding two other women who were setting a long table in the courtyard. To heck with the wallet. She could always come back and get it later.

"Come," Rosalinda urged, and led her through a small grove of bushes to the back wall of the property. When they were outside the gate, the girl grabbed Casey's hand and giggled. "We are successful! This is as much fun as I had with Marguerita. You are a good companion, Señorita Casey."

Casey's heart was still beating furiously and she could barely smile while gasping for breath. Kids! She was too old for this stuff! Nodding her head, she finally managed to say, "Thank you very much. *Gracias*, Rosalinda. Now I need to find the police. Can you lead me to them?"

The girl held tightly to her hand and pulled her down an alley. "Hurry, we must be back before we are missed." Rosalinda turned at the corner and stopped, tightening the dark mantilla around her face. "From here I can go no further."

Casey sighed. "Why?"

"*La policía* is just down this way"—she pointed—"and to the left at the end." She shook her head firmly. "I cannot go with you, as it would be reported to my father immediately." The girl took Casey's hand and hurried her toward her destination. "Please be quick, Señorita Casey. We must get back to the house *rapidamente*."

Casey wondered if it could get any more bizarre as she made her way down the narrow dirt street alone. Here she was, feeling—and probably looking—very much like Greta Garbo in some black-and-white spy movie, with a teenager who believed she was a heroine because she'd left the convent to seek some romantic adventure.

Right. Some romantic adventure this was, she thought as she passed a grungy-looking cowboy with half the teeth missing from his leering grin.

Okay, so it could get more bizarre.

Five

Stepping onto the wooden sidewalk from the earthen road, she hesitated for a moment and turned back to contemplate where she had just been. Horses, tied to the wooden railings of the overhang on the adobe building, were fully saddled with blankets and leather bags; even a canteen was slung over one saddle's horn. Her eyes darted back out to the road, in a last attempt to witness anything that looked remotely modern. She could see many people walking around, looking into shop windows and talking in the street. There were women with shawls, much like the one she wore, some with thin blankets over their heads shading them from the intense morning sun. Across the street an elegantly clad gentleman in a very old-fashioned suit stepped out of a horse-drawn black carriage. She watched as he held out his hand and assisted a woman from the coach. A lace parasol popped open, and the woman swung it over her shoulder as she glanced toward Casey.

She refused to be drawn into this historical seduction, as she had better things to attend to at the moment. Like finding someone sane . . . not someone trying to re-create the past by wearing a Victorian-styled, high-collar costume dress of deep maroon velvet and lace. Jeez, the guy with the woman had even donned a silk top hat. It was a quiet and very peaceful scene. Everyone seemed content to be where they were. Everyone except her.

Suddenly a sense of outrage rushed through her whole body. She stamped the cold, hard wood with her foot. This just wasn't happening. Casey O'Reilly isn't buying this whole scene, she reassured herself. "I'm gonna get some answers right now!" she blurted aloud.

Just then, she noticed an elderly Hispanic man with a colorful poncho, and she watched him prod a heavily laden burro with a gnarled stick. Even with her limited Spanish, Casey could tell he was cursing at the poor creature's refusal to move.

Leaving them to their struggle, she turned away and glanced up at the words painted above the door facing her. Santa Fe Jail House. Perfect. She pulled up on the rusty latch of the iron-barred door.

The place was dark and dingy and had such an overpowering musky odor to it that Casey wanted to draw the shawl over her nose to block it. Instead, she took a deep breath through her mouth as she noticed a heavyset man sitting with his boots up on a badly scarred wooden desk, reviewing some papers. When he saw her, he immediately slipped his feet off the desk and stood up. That was when she saw he had also been eating something.

"What's yer problem señorita?" he asked in a gruff voice as his hands came to rest on his hips. He, too, was dressed in old-fashioned clothes. "One of them cowboys botherin' ya?" he demanded, carelessly tossing the papers down onto the desk, inches from a smelly burrito.

She noticed he didn't smile. In fact, he appeared highly annoyed that she had interrupted his meal. Casey decided to smile first. After all, she needed this man. He was an authority, though as she glanced around the place, her heart skipped a beat. This didn't look like a modern police station at all. In fact, it looked like it could be a western movie set, with rifles openly displayed on the wall next to a large map of the New Mexico Territory and three empty, though grimy, jail cells with actual iron bars that were rusting.

"Hey!" the man nearly yelled. "You speak English, don'tcha?"

Startled, Casey jerked her attention back to the man and smiled even more nervously. "Yes, I'm sorry, sir. I . . . I need your help. You see, I'm sort of lost and I need to find my sister."

"Lost, huh?" the man repeated, as he walked over to a broom in the corner and broke off a piece of straw.

She couldn't believe it as he actually used the thing to pick at his teeth!

"Ah, yes," she answered, trying not to watch him, yet she couldn't stop the shudder as the man seemed to dislodge some food and suck it further into his mouth. "My car had a flat yesterday and I got a ride into Santa Fe, but now I have to find my sister and I'm wondering if anyone filed a missing-person report," she hurried to explain before she backed away from the man. "Her name is Amy Maddigan and—"

"Whose name?" the man demanded as he flicked the straw onto the filthy floor.

Wincing, Casey took another deep breath to steady her nerves. "That's my sister. Like I said, I had a flat yesterday and—"

"Flat what?"

She blinked. "A flat tire . . . on my car."

It was his turn to blink at her. "Whatcha talkin' about, little lady? Car? Railcar?"

"What?"

"You tell me."

She shook her head in dismay. "Look, I *need* to contract the proper authorities and locate my sister. I mean, this place is quaint and everything, and I know this must sound crazy to you, but I want to get back to modern civilization. May I use your phone to call her? I know she'll come and get me."

"Phone?" The man scratched his oily hair. "What d'ya mean?"

Once more she looked around the place. There were wanted posters tacked to the walls, with drawings of faces and amounts of money in bold print. She couldn't find a phone or anything else that would indicate modern communication. Quickly bringing her attention back to the man in front of her, she felt her heart begin slamming into her rib cage with fear. "You wouldn't happen to have a fax or . . ."

Her words ceased as the man closed the short distance between them and stared into her eyes. He sniffed her suspiciously before saying, "You been drinking with them cowboys? What they been fillin' yer head with, huh?"

He smelled of sweat and onions and something else that she wasn't about to distinguish. She squared her shoulders and glared at the man, even though she could never remember being this scared in her life! Why, wasn't there *anything* modern, anywhere? "I have not been drinking," she insisted, insulted by the question. She was not drunk and she was not crazy! "I happen to know this is the year 2000 and I am simply trying to find my sister."

He pulled the upper part of his body away from her, as though she'd shocked him. "Maybe you need to sleep it off, little lady, until you come to your senses. This ain't no year 2000," he added with a laugh as he walked to one of the jail cells and opened a door as though in invitation.

She listened to the squeak of metal and it was like nails running over a blackboard. Shivers raced down her back and she tightened the shawl around her. "No, thank you," she muttered, trying to disguise the fear that threatened to overwhelm her as she backed up to the door. A few more feet and she would be outside. It couldn't be possible! No one was normal here! No one!

Seconds later, she was stunned as she escaped the tiny building. She tried to make her mind work, to think with some semblance of clarity, yet only one thought twirled around in her head . . .

She had traveled back in time!

There could be no other answer. Either that or every person around her was completely crazy. Maybe it was her. Maybe when she was hit by lightning something happened to her brain. In any case, there was no modern-day police station with telephones and computers . . . there were no missing-person reports, only WANTED: DEAD OR ALIVE posters like the ones hanging on the marshal's dingy office walls. She didn't want to believe she could be dreaming all of it so vividly. Maybe the electrical shock had caused her to have some sort of delusional breakdown and she was just *seeing* things . . . things that couldn't be explained . . . like every single person acting and dressing as though they lived over a hundred years ago, insisting she was in the year 1878!

How can this be? Where am I? Am I still me? Where is my sister? Does Amy exist now? Where is *now*? Her head began to pound as the thoughts flew around her mind like a raging twister and she thought it might actually explode from the pressure.

"Señorita!"

She heard the urgent cry and turned to see Rosalinda huddled against the side of the building. Blinking, she stared at the teenager. What was real?

"Señorita Casey . . . come! We must hurry back now or we shall be discovered missing!" The girl's expression showed her worry.

She couldn't move. Her feet refused to follow her command. She was frozen in fear. How had such a thing happened, and *why to her?* She needed to make sense out of it, to apply some kind of reason to her situation. Does this happen to people and no one talks about it? Luke said he time-traveled and he wasn't even upset by it.

"Señorita Casey!"

The girl darted out from the side of the building and grabbed Casey's hand. Rosalinda pulled her along and she followed meekly, not having the strength to resist any longer.

"We must hurry now. If we are discovered, I shall be punished . . . and I want nothing to ruin my *quinceñera* . . . *Por favor,* Señorita Casey. Please!"

Casey could only stare in awe at the outdated scenes taking place around her. She had just been informed her reality didn't exist. Rosalinda tugged on her hand, as though to shake her awake, but Casey only nodded in a feeble attempt to regain some focus. To believe everything around you, no matter how much you deny it, is actually happening . . . real . . . something you have been told all your life just couldn't be possible . . . Her mind felt like it might short-circuit with all she had lost. She blindly followed the teenager back through the old western town that appeared to be so *real!* What was happening to her? Was this crossing over into insanity?

But it *was* real and it *was* happening *now!*

"Come . . ." Rosalinda urged. "It's not much farther."

When they crossed several more streets and turned down the alley where they had entered the town, the girl stopped and held Casey's shoulders, as though she were the adult.

"What has happened to you, señorita? Why are you like this? You must come back to yourself or you may never wear a beautiful ball gown at my *quinceñera*, and perhaps neither will I." Rosalinda pleaded further, "*Por favor*, Casey . . . if my father finds out what has happened, *ay, Dios mío*," she whispered with a gasp, "he will have us both punished!"

That seemed to wake her a bit more. Beyond the incessant feeling of pending madness was the primal defensive instinct that no one was going to punish her or push her around . . . without good reason anyway. Not even a policeman who implied she was inebriated. She almost said it aloud, her mind recalling the sarcastic marshal. And then he'd had the audacity to threaten to lock her up until she sobered!

Now a fourteen-year-old may be leading her around by the hand, but somewhere within her was an adult who knew she didn't have to give in to this fear . . . not the fear of whatever had happened to her or the fear of someone, anyone, thinking he had the right to punish her or push her around. It was to that emancipated feeling she gave her attention.

She pulled her hand away from Rosalinda's and took a deep breath. Licking her lips, she then tried to smile with some reassurance. "It's okay, Rosalinda." she muttered. "I'm sorry. I'm . . . I'm just shocked."

"At what?" the girl asked, tightening the shawl around her face.

"At the world," Casey said, surprised at the words as they escaped her lips, yet it was the truth. Her world had tilted and she was fighting like crazy to find some equilibrium.

Rosalinda stared at her for a few seconds and then gushed, "Oh, because of being in the convent . . . yes, I understand. The world must seem very different to you."

She wanted to blurt out that she hadn't been in any convent, shut away from the world, and her world, the modern world, was so different that if she tried for a hundred years, she couldn't make this child understand where she had come from.

She was stunned for a moment as she remembered Luke's words to her last night in the wagon about not being able to explain time travel to her. Oh, she couldn't go there. Not now, not when her mind was hanging precariously by a thread. "Let's get back," she said in what she hoped passed for a normal voice.

Rosalinda nodded and again took her hand as they hurried toward her backyard. Casey looked down to their clasped hands and mentally shrugged. Right now this kid seemed more steady than she. She had to trust someone . . . until she could again trust herself.

Just to prove she might be certifiable, that damn line from the Jackson Browne song raced through her head. *The next voice you hear will be your own.*

"I need my wallet," Casey suddenly blurted. She heard the urgency in her own voice and wondered why she had to tell the girl that, but right now she felt she needed to hold on to something from her life. Inside that wallet was her identity, a Pennsylvania driver's license with her photograph and the year she was born. It was proof she was still who she was, proof of where she had come from and where she belonged. Even if she couldn't get back there, at least it was something that would help ground her through whatever madness was happening here. Rosalinda simply nodded her head in agreement, touching her fingers to her lips to indicate the need for quiet as they made their way closer to the house.

Without speaking they entered the backyard through the creaky wooden gate, sneaking past the house servants who appeared to be preparing a feast under a large tree. Casey spied Marcella and stiffened with apprehension as the woman put her hand to her hip and looked briefly in their direction. They slipped quickly behind the potted-tree branches and Marcella turned away. They were still okay.

When they entered the passageway, Casey drew in a huge breath and forced herself through the small opening. She kept telling herself to take shallow breaths, not to think of anything except getting back into the bedroom and collapsing onto the bed. There was just so much one woman could absorb!

"I will leave you now," Rosalinda whispered so quietly Casey had to strain to hear her. "This is the back of my sister's wardrobe into your room. I must change into my gown. We are both expected to be formally introduced in a short time. Remember to act surprised." The girl squeezed her hand and disappeared around a corner. Casey pushed on the wood and it slid easily to the side. She stepped into the dark, large chest and slowly opened the door to a sight that almost stopped her heart.

As if to test her endurance, it appeared that fate had decided she needed even more of a challenge to her sanity . . .

Luke was seated on the chair, his crossed legs propped up on the side board of the bed. Twirling a thin cigar between his fingers, he made no eye contact with her as he watched the wisps of smoke ride the air. In his other hand he held the brush Rosalinda had brought to her earlier, the one she had dropped onto the bed.

"I'm sure you realize your actions have endangered a child," he stated assertively.

She clung to the edge of the wardrobe, willing her foot to step down to the tile. Fear again gripped her chest and she had to fight to control it. Then she remembered that surge of strength she'd found in the alley . . . the instinct that no one was going to punish her or push her around, including this man . . . whoever he was!

Her foot slipped onto the cool, firm tile beneath it and she smiled inwardly. She'd gotten this far, she could do this. Besides, that so-called child he had just referred to was more in touch with reality at this moment than she was.

Before she could even respond to his assertion, he continued. "You went to *la policía* and they didn't believe it when you told them you were from the year 2000." He smacked the brush against his thigh. "I'll bet they even offered to let you sleep off your drunken state in one of their comfortable jail cells."

Casey smirked at him as she closed the wardrobe door behind her and drew in a breath to speak in defense of her actions. "I had every right—"

"Right?" Luke interrupted, and glared directly into her eyes. "You have no right to involve an innocent child, or anyone else for that matter, in your . . ." He began shaking his head as though frustrated and grasping for the words he wanted to use. "Your version of reality!"

"Okay, that's it, buster," she blurted. "My 'version of reality' was just fine until *you* came along. Let's focus here on who is involved and who is innocent, like me! What the hell is going on anyway? You've got a lot of explaining to do, Luke d'Séraphin," she finished, crossing her arms defiantly.

She watched as Luke's eyes became tender with compassion. "You are courageous, Casey O'Reilly. Don't cloud such bravery with foolishness." He continued calmly, "Should it be found that Rosalinda was out and about town without a proper duenna, she would be punished severely by her parents. You must respect the people with whom you find yourself now, señorita. You must also realize, in this time your actions may directly affect the future, even your future . . . everyone's future."

"Is that what you do, Luke? When this craziness happens? You just simply fit right in?" She began waving her arms around in dispute. "You pop in and out of time, like it's all part of a normal day . . . you don't mind the loneliness, the lack of anything modern . . . even a bathroom! You just follow the damned pattern?" Her voice was raised, yet she couldn't seem to stop herself. Besides, it felt better to get it out of her, all this insanity. "What the hell *are* you? Should I check under your bed to see if there's a freakin' pod? Are you some alien or something? How the hell does this happen to someone?" Casey looked up to the ceiling as though she would hear the answers she wanted from some higher source. "Where is my life? How can I have time-traveled? This isn't possible!" She felt her face flush as tears began welling up in her eyes.

"You're accepting it now," he said soothingly.

"I'm not accepting anything!" she protested. "This just doesn't happen!"

He came to his feet so quickly that Casey jumped in fright as he seemed to cross the room and stand in front of her with the grace of a cat. "But it has happened," he stated with such finality that the tears in her eyes stopped and she could only stare at him as his fingers reached up and tenderly stroked the hair back from her face. When she felt him brush a strand behind her ear, Casey thought she would lose it.

She felt her throat begin to burn with the desire to release the scream lying just below a very thin surface of control. All her stifled emotions throbbed inside her chest as they had in the sandstorm. It was as though someone had punched her even harder this time, and her body began to tremble uncontrollably as the horrible sensation of fear spread over her. She was going to have to accept this reality.

"Yes, accept it, Casey," he whispered with more compassion. "Stop fighting the fear and all your pain will ease."

"I hate it when you do that!" she said, turning away quickly. She stepped the few feet to the bed, grabbing on to the blanket and twisting it in her fists. "It isn't fair you can tell what's going on inside me! It's . . . it's invasion of privacy! Leave me alone!" Inside she wished she could twist him as she clenched the blanket harder, or punch and scream at him . . . anything to make this whole unbelievable dream disappear, and him too, since he seemed to be the biggest part of it.

She heard the click of his heels on the tile as he walked up behind her. When he placed his hand on her shoulder, it was all she could do to keep from shuddering beneath his heat penetrating her skin. Her urge to throw a tantrum momentarily subsided as she recalled when he'd first found her nearly dead in the sandstorm. Again she began to sense the protection she'd felt under his coat . . . with her head against his chest, hearing his steady heartbeat. She wanted to fall into that safety again, to know the peace she'd felt when she was wrapped in his strong arms . . . and she felt her own grip release from the blanket.

She closed her eyes and swallowed the longing in her throat. Whatever it was that this man possessed, be it carnal or divine, she realized deep down she was going to have to surrender and simply accept his help if she was ever going to get her life back. He might have the advantage, but she just didn't know if she could truly accept anything as crazy as this!

"I'm not using an unfair advantage, Casey. I'm not using any gift you don't also possess. However, I do have suggestions to make the adventure more enjoyable."

She could hear the smile in his words and she fought against his gentle pull to turn her to face him.

"Look." His voice was insistently tender. "I don't know why you were brought back to this time. Only you know your answers, and they will eventually come to you if you don't fight them with your fear. There is a pattern to all things, and you are following your pattern, Casey O'Reilly. The sooner you realize that and start paying attention, the sooner you can fulfill your purpose here and get on with your life."

She spun around, desperate for something to cling to, some explanation. "Get on with my life! Just where is my life, Luke? You said I was brought back in time. Who or what brought me back here? What is the purpose of all this? You tell me!"

"I don't know how to answer you," he whispered. "I could give you some interesting mathematical equations, some esoteric words, but I can't really describe what you are seeking. It's your adventure, Casey, and this is mine right now. At this time in history your adventure and mine have crossed. Be assured, there is a reason for it, and once we have fulfilled that reason, our paths will separate. I'm here to help you, Casey. Your fight isn't with me."

She blinked several times, trying to absorb everything he was saying. "I'm not fighting you, Luke . . . I'm not fighting anybody."

His playful smile widened.

"Who would I be fighting then?" she whispered back, secretly dreading his answer before his lips even moved.

He teasingly raised his forefinger to her lips to hush them like a child. "You are fighting, señorita . . . but you are only fighting yourself."

She saw the triumphant smile spread over his face and that twinkle came back into his eyes. She defiantly pushed his hand away from her face and glared at him.

"Okay, I'll admit it. I'm fighting, all right, but not *with* myself . . . I'm fighting *for* myself!" She felt the burning lump in her throat rising again. Memories of her life before she began this insane adventure to visit her sister flooded through her brain. Some adventure . . . full of purpose, she sarcastically lectured herself. She closed her eyes. Although she knew it was childish, she suddenly wished she could just click her heels, like Dorothy in *The Wizard of Oz*, and go back . . . only back to her time.

"Casey," she heard him say softly as she felt him lay his hands gently on her shoulders. "Stop fighting and accept where you are now, in this moment . . . stop wishing it was something else. There may be other ways of time travel, like clicking your heels together." She opened her eyes to see those dimples coming back to his cheeks as he continued. "Accepting wherever I am is being in the moment. There is no place but *now* . . . wherever it is. This is one of the first principles I learned, and I can only pass along to you what I've discovered."

He'd done it again. She shoved at his chest like an angry child to create distance between them and walked around to the other side of the bed. "Principles! Like this is some stupid course I'm taking and you're my mind-reading teacher! Ha! What a laugh."

He chuckled. "I did say a sense of humor was also a valuable tool. Go ahead and laugh. I've found it helps a great deal."

"You're mad, do you know that?" she exclaimed, moving closer to the pillow. "This whole thing is some huge, funny joke to you, a lark! Well, lemme tell ya, what I saw out there is no laughing matter! There are cowboys who wouldn't even know what toothpaste is, let alone who've seen the inside of a dentist's office in their entire lives! Or a shower! Indians selling things on corners! Women who smoke cigars and dress like they're in the road show of *Man of La Mancha*! There's horseshit and God knows what else thrown onto dirt roads, and if I really want to get into being pissed off, I could just scream at having to use a chamber pot! How's that for acceptance!" She knew her face was red, but she stared at him insolently, charging him to respond.

Luke threw back his head and laughed. "See?" he asked, still chuckling at her outburst. "You have to laugh at the way your mind is fighting this. It is funny . . . for you. Just laugh, Casey."

She wasn't laughing. As a matter of fact, she couldn't remember the last time she actually did laugh. It had to have been in Pennsylvania!

"So you're saying this was all my doing . . . coming back here, back to 1878." She rolled her eyes in disbelief at what was coming out of her mouth. "This 'adventure,' as you seem to like to call it, was all my idea? I traveled through time to obtain some greater purpose for myself?" She began hysterically shaking her head in denial. It was too much. She didn't even dream this vividly.

He nodded. "Only you could design this particular adventure, señorita. I surely couldn't."

"You . . . you're impossible!" she yelled, throwing the pillow at him.

He batted the pillow easily back onto the mattress. "I'm patient. Not impossible. Is it so difficult to accept I have nothing to do with whatever is unfolding in your life? I came upon your car and I made the choice to come back to help you. I didn't send you back here. You were already here. I came back *for* you."

Like an arrow hitting the bull's-eye, his words struck deeply inside her. She felt the tears she had been holding inside for so long burst into her eyes, demanding release. Furious, embarrassed, confused, and scared, she climbed onto the bed and clutched the other pillow to her chest. She buried her face and just sobbed . . . for Amy, her niece, her life, everything she had left behind. She just wanted her life back. There had been so much she wanted to do. She hadn't been ready to be taken away from it so quickly and—

"We will get back, Casey," he said in a gentle voice, and she felt him sitting down on the edge of the bed. "We can return to the year 2000, though only nature can provide the way. Presently it is beyond my power to change anything, except the way I view the situation. I must wait . . . like you . . . and watch as the pattern unfolds. But there will be a way for you to return. Do not doubt that."

She sniffled and swiped at her eyes with her forearm. Lifting her head, she turned around to look at him. "How?"

"I don't know . . . yet." He smiled tenderly. "But you will go *home*."

She heard the compassionate assurance in his voice and it bolstered her hope. Sniffing more, she turned herself completely around and sat up in bed. She straightened her wide skirt over her crossed knees, then scrunched the tearstained pillow under her arms. Clutching it for a sense of safety, she felt like a kid again, unsure and seeking answers as she twirled the multicolored tassels between her fingers. "So we're going to get back . . . back there?"

He nodded. "It was part of the reason I came for you, to help you return."

"And what's the other part?" She realized she owed him thanks for all his help, but she figured she could take care of that when they got back to the future. Right now she really wanted to know how he planned to get them there.

He shrugged and pulled a match out of his front pocket. Striking it on the heel of his boot, he relit the end of his cigar and puffed several times. "I'm not sure what the other part is exactly . . . I'm waiting to be shown."

Oh, she wasn't going to go down that path. First she had to get it into her head that this was temporary. She would see Amy again and have her normal, old life back. Well, her life anyway, for she certainly was a changed woman after this experience, and quite frankly, she didn't know if she would ever view anything the same way again.

He smiled and patted her knee. "You must pull yourself together now, Casey." He then stood up from the edge of the mattress and began walking to the door.

Abruptly she felt vulnerable. "But—" She was dumbfounded that she really hadn't gotten the full reassurance she had hoped would be forthcoming.

"We'll talk more about your return later. In a few moments we are expected at the noon meal and you will be introduced to the entire family. Of course, you've already met the delightfully free-spirited Rosalinda, but I would act surprised if I were you when you're formally introduced. Remember to protect the child. Her heart is in the right place, yet her impulsiveness sometimes makes it a challenge for her parents." He grinned knowingly at her.

"I don't think I can meet anyone right now," Casey mumbled, stunned that she was actually beginning to accept that she had time-traveled into the lives of these people.

"Do your best. Don Felipe and his gracious wife, Doña Isabela, are most anxious to speak with you and extend their hospitality."

"But, Luke," she protested, feeling like she could cry again. "I'm not exactly in the right frame of mind now. I can't do this!"

"Yes, you can," he insisted, his eyes narrowing as he again puffed on his cigar. "There is no other moment, save this. You must not offend our gracious hosts."

"Well, this moment brings with it a lot to assimilate," she whined. "I've never time-traveled before, ya know? And this is more than a little falling apart I've had here!"

"The next principle is to trust yourself."

"What?" That got her attention.

"Accept where you are and the customs where you find yourself and then . . . trust yourself, Casey."

Those damn, damn words from that damn, damn song raced through her head again.

"Well, get outta here then," she commanded in an irritated voice, as she waved her hand toward the door. "How am I supposed to get my act together when you're playing with my head and making me more confused?"

His smile pierced all barriers she had constructed, and as the door closed, Casey had to admit . . . she was no longer raving.

She didn't think she was going crazy any longer, or if she did, she had company now . . . and Luke said they would get back. He didn't know when or where, but she had to trust someone, and in truth, he hadn't done anything harmful to her. Except for that dumb nun story. How the hell was she supposed to pull that off?

"Trust yourself," she repeated with dismay.

Six

"*T*sk . . . such a pity! Your hair, *muy corto* . . . so chopped, señorita, but Juana will fix it. You watch."

Seated in front of the older woman, Casey could merely stare at her stomach as Juana ran the brush through Casey's feathered hair and clucked over the shorter pieces. She wanted to tell the woman that her hair happened to be very stylish, and she had paid someone a small fortune to cut it before her vacation, but somehow knew Juana would find such information impossible . . . so she shut up and allowed the woman free rein. What did she really care what she looked like now? It was enough that she was willing to go along with this charade and just pretend it wasn't the most bizarre thing she'd ever heard of happening in anyone's life.

"I will use a good pomade to your hair . . . then it will lie flat and we can pin it back."

Casey bobbed beneath the woman's strong hands gently

pressing down on top of her head. "It sounds lovely, Juana." She smiled with a wince.

"Oh, do not worry, señorita. I will create such a fashion for you that you will have everyone's *ojos*"—Juana pointed to the laugh lines around her own eyes—"looking at you," she finished with a big-toothed grin and a wink. Casey merely nodded as the woman quickly spun around and hurried from the room, telling her she would return immediately.

Worry . . . ? Nothing really mattered any longer, Casey thought with a sigh. She would just go along with this madness until there was a way for her to return to her sister. Luke had promised. Well, he hadn't exactly promised, but he did say they would return, and he had come back to this time to find her and help her. She knew she owed him a great deal already, for she couldn't even imagine what it might have been like had she been alone now. Still, a bigger part of her couldn't grasp that such a thing as time travel was possible . . . and that Luke seemed to do it regularly. Like it was a common practice. Who *was* that man?

She had no more time to ponder the question as the door flew open with a knock and Juana burst in with goodies . . . a pale pink gown over her arm, and hands full of white and pink flowers that resembled hibiscus.

"Come, change. Doña Isabela had me bring this dress for you." Juana waved it around with a grand smile. "It belonged to her daughter Marguerita, who is now married." She placed the gown on the bed and emptied her hands of flowers and tiny hairpins. "Now, come . . . we must hurry, for you must make a grand impression!" the woman said with excitement as she reached out and grabbed Casey's arms.

What a process! So many laces and slips . . . She wondered how women ever dressed themselves alone with all these buttons and layers. More than ever, she wished for her simple jeans and sweater.

"*Ay, por Dios.* What are we going to do with those shoes?" Juana worried aloud.

Casey looked down to her blue Italian leather flats. Except for a bit of a burn mark on one heel, they were nothing to be ashamed of in any time. "What's wrong with them?"

"*Bueno, está bien,*" Juana sighed. "They will have to do. Keep your feet under the gown and no one will notice, for I am going to make sure they are delighted with your face," Juanita said as she playfully patted Casey's cheeks.

"My face?"

"Now, sit," Juana commanded, pulling Casey's arm and leading her back to the chair. "I must work some *brujería* . . . some magic," the woman translated with a nod, "in a hurry."

Casey wanted to laugh. So it would take magic to make her presentable? She sat back down and patted the voluminous skirt around her. Juana was behind her, brushing her hair and slathering the oily pomade over the short locks. Using tiny, sharp pins that pricked her scalp, Juana pressed and pulled every strand tightly to the back of her head. Casey bit her bottom lip to stop from crying out in protest. The woman told her to hold the flowers and hand them to her one at a time. Casey patiently did as she was told, wondering if she was going to look like a cartoon character.

Frills, flounces, lace, and flowers were not exactly her style. She felt she was more tailored, preferring Armani to Bob Mackie any day . . . even if she didn't have the money to dress haute couture in any time. She just knew what suited her. And flowers in her hair! Juana was hiding her short hair by creating a facade of flowers at the nape of her neck. She was going to look like a blonde flamenco dancer.

She almost giggled aloud at the thought. Imagine. Well, just go with the moment.

As she handed Juana another pink blossom, she sighed with surrender. Luke was right. Instead of fighting, it made more sense to go along with the customs and try to fit in with the others. What had he said yesterday? She could make this waiting time miserable or treat it like an adventure? The choice was hers.

"There," Juana pronounced triumphantly, patting the last flower into place. "Now, stand up and let me see all of you."

Casey pushed herself off the chair and took a deep breath as she turned toward Juana.

Juana stepped back and clasped her hands together at her chest. Casey could see tears coming to her bright eyes. "Señorita Casey . . . you are beautiful, *muy bonita*."

Casey heard the awe in the woman's voice and felt the heat of a blush creep up her neck to settle on her cheeks. "If that is so, Juana, then it is your hard work that makes me appear as such." She knew she was attractive, given the right clothes and makeup, but beautiful?

"Oh, no, señorita," Juana whispered, taking Casey's hand. "You *are* beautiful. Before . . . well . . ." The woman paused and smiled, gazing at her again. "Well, now, not only God will know of your beauty, the whole world will know."

That was really overdoing it! Again she was about to put herself down and then she remembered Luke's question when Maria had complimented her. Had she forgotten how to accept graciously? She cleared her throat and smiled. "Thank you, Juana . . . for thinking I am beautiful, and for all your help. You are very kind."

Juana beamed her pleasure and, reaching out, took Casey's hand. "Now, come . . . we must hurry. Already everyone is in the courtyard and awaiting your appearance." Juana squeezed her hand with assurance. "You will make a grand entrance, *mi hija*, and their patience will be rewarded, *sí?*"

Grinning, Casey shook her head. She understood the woman's term of endearment simply by her inflection. "I'm just going along with the program, Juana. When in Rome, you know?"

"No, I do not know," the woman seriously answered as she opened the door. "But I do know," she added with a smile, "in Santa Fe you will attract many compliments and admirers. Oh, I shall like to see Señor Luke's face when he sees you now." She stifled a giggle.

"Señor Luke?" Casey asked as they hurriedly walked down the hallway. She knew where this woman was leading, but she wasn't sure how far she was going to go. Her and Luke? No . . . he wasn't interested in—

"He is a handsome one, no? It is not my place to say any of these things, but my heart senses that you are not like these others." The woman looked around suspiciously, as though making sure no one else would hear her whisper. "So, so *inflexible* . . . so I will speak my heart, as I must," she added with a nod of conviction. "Señor Luke . . . he has a fondness for you," she finished with a wink.

"Oh, no, Juana!" Casey attempted to shrug off the woman's words and perception. "You don't understand . . . Señor Luke is being very protective of me, that's all." Maybe the woman would buy it; well, she hoped Juana would, because she just couldn't imagine—

"Hmm . . . we shall see very soon." Juana didn't argue with her further. Then she reached up and pinched Casey's cheeks so quickly and so hard that Casey yelped.

"Hey! Why'd you do that?"

"To give you color, señorita. You are much too pale.

Now, go through that door into the courtyard and say *buenas tardes* to everyone in your sweetest voice. You will be fine."

Rubbing her cheeks, she felt like Cinderella being given advice from a fairy godmother right before entering the ballroom. She looked at the open gate. Okay, she could do this. Trust herself. Yeah, right. She turned her head back and smiled at Juana. "Thank you again . . . for all of this." Casey hoped the woman understood her genuine appreciation.

"*Date prisa!* Go . . ." the woman whispered with insistence, and gave a tiny shove to the small of Casey's back.

Casey started walking toward the doors and began to hear laughter and talking from the people in the garden. She took a deep breath to relax, when she heard Juana's urgent whisper from behind.

"Tiny steps!"

Turning around quickly, Casey looked back to the worried woman. "What?"

"Those shoes!" Juana pointed at Casey's feet. "Tiny steps to conceal your shoes!"

Shaking her head, Casey smiled and nodded to the woman and turned back to the doorway. Taking *tiny* steps, she proceeded through the opened double doors.

"*Buenas tardes.*" Her voice was as polite as she knew how to make it.

Everyone was seated at the great table and looked up to her. Luke immediately rose, and she saw a pleased expression grow upon his face. Don Felipe, now dressed in a formal suit and tie, also stood up, and Casey saw Rosalinda grin with excitement while clasping the hand of a lovely older woman seated next to her.

"You look beautiful, Señorita Casey," Luke whispered, then immediately began formal introductions. He led her under the tree, around the table, with his arm outstretched, as if he were offering a fine piece of art for everyone's attention.

Casey felt a little foolish, and yet it was an intoxicating experience to be treated with such respect.

Don Felipe again bowed before her. "I am honored that you grace our table, señorita. May I present my wife, Doña Isabela d'Cortez, and my daughter Rosalinda."

Casey looked at Rosalinda and read the mischief in her eyes before glancing at the very lovely, very regal Doña Isabela. This was a woman who had given a bedroom in her house, clothing, and food to a total stranger and had asked for nothing in return. For some reason, even though Luke still held her hand like a proper escort, Casey found herself dropping a few inches into a slow curtsy. "I am grateful for your kindness, Doña Isabela. It is an honor to be a guest in your beautiful home."

The woman, dressed in a gown of such dark purple that it appeared black until the sunlight hit it, and wearing a matching lace mantilla over her upswept thick black hair, smiled serenely and waved a graceful hand toward the table. "*Bienvenida*, Señorita Casey O'Reilly. *Estoy enteramente a su disposición.*"

"*En inglés, Mamá,*" Rosalinda whispered with a grin.

"Oh, yes," Doña Isabela said with a delicate smile. "Welcome, Señorita Casey. We are wholly at your disposal. Please . . . join us."

Casey felt just a tad intimidated by the complete gentility of the woman. She was someone Casey didn't want to offend, not because she intimidated by power or exuded stuffiness, but because she seemed so genuinely kind that Casey'd probably feel like crap if she ever did offend her. "*Muchas gracias*, Doña Isabela." Casey graciously nodded.

Luke held out the chair next to Rosalinda, and after she was seated, she watched as he walked around the table to his chair. He'd changed too, adding a tight black velvet vest, with black silk piping stitched in ornate swirling patterns, across his broad chest. Beneath it was the white shirt he'd worn earlier, but it was now tied at the embroidered collar with a loose, thin black silk bow. His tight, black trousers were tucked just below the knee into his shiny, black boots. She had to admit he wore time travel well, and she quickly hoped she, too, was "passing."

From underneath the table, she felt a tap on her leg and guessed it was made by Rosalinda's foot. Smoothing down her skirt, Casey nonchalantly glanced to the girl at her side. Smiling as if she had never met the impish teenager, she said in a low, polite voice, *"Buenas tardes*, Señorita Rosalinda."

"Good afternoon, Señorita Casey. Welcome to our home." Rosalinda beamed.

Nodding in thanks, Casey again looked across the table to Luke, knowing he, too, knew their secret. She watched him smile and wink at Rosalinda. He really looked so . . . dashing. Casey almost groaned when she realized her thoughts.

Dashing! Who the hell even thought stuff like that anymore! Okay, he looked handsome, fine, *whatever*. Cringing at her own thoughts, she turned her attention back to the antsy teenager.

"Luke has told me you are to have a celebration soon, Rosalinda. Congratulations."

The girl beamed with delight again at the way the conversation was proceeding. "Oh, yes, Señorita Casey. In ten days I shall celebrate my *quinceñera*. I do hope you and Señor Luke will be able to attend."

"Yes, we would very much enjoy being guests at your ball, Señorita Rosalinda," Luke interjected quickly. "But unfortunately, I must confess to you now, we do not know how long we may be here." Luke paused, picking up his glass of dark red wine and looking around at all the imploring faces. "But as the angels see fit, we would be honored to celebrate the day that you entered into this world, *querida*." He raised his glass in Rosalinda's direction, then sipped.

"Ah, señor," Rosalinda teased with a very practiced style for a teenager. "But it is more than just a celebration of my birth. It is when my true love shall find me!" she declared.

"*Sí, sí . . .*" Doña Isabela gently touched her daughter's arm, as if to ground her, and said with a smile, "I am sure our guests are hungry, *mi hija*. Let us eat before we discuss such heady matters as true love."

Don Felipe laughed, along with Luke, and Casey awkwardly smiled as she saw out of the corner of her eye Rosalinda's impatience with the stuffy adults. It was as though the girl knew something wondrous about the subject of love . . . something no one else over the age of twenty could possibly understand. Then Casey felt a surge of sympathy for both Rosalinda and her mother. The middle of the road was a weird place to be . . . understanding how the young, blossoming woman felt, yet also understanding Doña Isabela's desire to save her child from embarrassment . . . but she found she couldn't take sides right now. Maybe the middle wasn't such a bad place to be after all. One could sure see more.

Casey actually hoped they were kidding about a discussion and the subject would be forgotten even after they ate. The last thing she wanted to talk about at this point was true love. She certainly wouldn't have much to add to *that* conversation.

"You must do everything within your power, Luke, to remain for my daughter's *quinceñera*. I am certain you would enjoy it." Don Felipe leaned back in his chair. "We have an extensive guest list. There will be some very interesting people for you to meet."

The two men exchanged amused glances, reflecting their longtime friendship.

"*Absolutamente,* Don Felipe. All things permitting, I will be here to honor your beautiful daughter," he said, raising his glass again to the teenager.

Rosalinda looked very pleased by Luke's words, and Casey was happy for the young girl. At the same time, she wondered how well this family knew Luke and if they knew about his time-traveling adventures. She didn't think so, but she would have to ask him later for a full briefing on what she could discuss.

Servants appeared and soon the table was filled with bowls and platters of Mexican food. It was colorful and delicious. The strains of a Mexican guitar softly rode on a breeze to surround them. Distant birds provided accompaniment while wine flowed and, over the next two hours, she drank several glassfuls to put out the fire in her mouth from the spices in the food. The conversation ranged from politics to fashions, and the men seemed delighted to discuss anything the women wanted. It was one of the best luncheons Casey had attended in her entire life, and she was shocked to find herself enjoying it so much.

When she turned to the sound of her hostess's voice, she decided that Luke was right about one thing. She did have a choice . . . and right now she was going to choose to forget everything else, all the craziness, and just have a good time. Heaven knows, she could use it. Why, considering everything she had gone through, she even deserved it!

Turning her attention back to her companions, she focused on Doña Isabela. It appeared the woman was very devoted to an interesting cause. "The poor sisters of the Loretto Chapel had their tiny church built without a staircase to their choir loft. I find it amazing that carpenters from five states have given consultation and not one can design stairs that will not take up half the pew space. The poor sisters are desperate."

Casey wondered why a choir loft had been built without the means to get to it, but didn't think it was her place to question anything at this point. Plus, talking about nuns was too close to the ridiculous story Luke had made up about her, so she merely smiled politely while listening to the conversation.

"We could use a ladder, but Sister Bernardina refuses," Rosalinda commented in a disappointed voice.

"It is inappropriate for ladies to be climbing ladders," Don Felipe answered with a smile, before sipping his wine. His fatherly response was meant to put an end to such discussion.

Rosalinda issued a small groan and shook her head with impatience. "Oh, Papi, you speak of females as though we are fragile and will break like an old leaf in the wind. We are young, *sí* . . . and vibrant with life. We are strong enough to climb a ladder."

"Rosa, *mi hija*," Doña Isabela quickly interjected with a soft smile. "A way to the choir loft will be found. A novena to Saint Joseph is being made, and surely a carpenter such as the good saint will provide a way and our prayers will be answered." She leaned over to the teenager and added in a whisper, "And *por favor*, do not give away all our feminine secrets"—she paused to glance at her husband and smiled very lovingly—"or your papi will have us up on the roof replacing tiles."

Don Felipe threw back his head and laughed good-naturedly and then looked to his wife with such love that Casey was stunned by the man's unabashed devotion. Doña Isabela was certainly the epitome of grace under pressure, defusing a difficult situation with laughter. Even

Rosalinda was shaking her head and grinning at her mother's last statement.

I'd like to be like that, Casey thought as she chuckled along with the others and glanced at Luke. She hadn't exactly been too graceful under the pressure of the last twenty-four hours. What she saw further took her breath away . . .

Luke was staring at her with the most friendly expression. It was as though his eyes twinkled with delight just being in her presence. It seemed he was so happy to be where he was, surrounded by people he genuinely liked, great food, amusing conversation, pleasant music and laughter. When his gaze connected with hers, she felt a surge of attraction race through every cell of her body, and she sucked in her breath with awe.

It was so startling that Casey almost shook herself in response to the sensation.

"Oh, Mamá . . ." Rosalinda said in a voice that revealed she was not as upset as before, "be truthful. If you had to climb a ladder, you could do it. Even if we would have to climb wearing such an impossible costume!" She pointed, referring to her own gown.

"*Hija*," Doña Isabela said with a chuckle. "Do not even imagine such a thing!"

Glad for the distraction, Casey piped in, "Remember, Ginger Rogers not only danced backward, but wore high heels doing it!"

The silence and odd stares that followed immediately changed her enjoyment of the afternoon as a wave of confusion seemed to crash over her. Hey, she thought it was quite appropriate to the conversation, and kinda funny too!

And then she remembered . . . It might be appropriate for such a conversation, but it certainly wasn't appropriate for the time. They didn't know who Ginger Rogers was, and never would. That was history from her time. Another wave seemed to crash over her, only now confusion was replaced by a sinking feeling.

She gulped as Luke leaned closer to the table and rested his elbows on the edge.

"Señorita Casey is originally from the East, and having traveled myself, I know she speaks of the dancing partners Ginger Rogers and Fred Astaire. If I may?" He glanced at Casey with a big smile.

"Oh, please do . . ." she murmured, grateful to him for helping her save face but equally curious to know where he might be going with this.

"Truly la señora Ginger Rogers possesses an amazing gift. However, you have made another very interesting point, Casey. The female partner has a mastery, and although it is acknowledged, it is never quite as appreciated as the male's." His eyes locked into hers. "I agree, without the exquisite movement and ability of the woman, there really is no dance." He enunciated the last word and paused. "It can be applied to many situations in life." He leaned back in his chair and nodded. "Very perceptive of you, Señorita Casey."

She was stunned at how well he'd handled the situation, without once having to tell a lie.

"There, Mamá . . . even Señor Luke agrees with me!" Rosalinda stated triumphantly. "I have never heard of these dancers. Do they dance . . . the fandango?" The girl's tone was full of excited inquiry. Casey felt everyone watching and waiting for her and Luke to break gazes, when impulsively Rosalinda began laughing.

She couldn't help chuckling at how the teenager had skillfully turned the tide in her favor once more. Again she was grateful to the girl for stepping in and capturing the moment, for Casey still hadn't recovered from Luke's compliment. Well, at least that was what she thought he was insinuating. Maybe he was referring to women in a general way. She mentally shrugged.

"*Preciosa hija mía,*" Don Felipe called down the table with a humorous reproach. "You will not be dancing a fandango in ten days, so you may put the thought right out of that busy mind of yours . . . no matter how lovely your gift for dancing."

"Mamá!" Rosalinda turned to her mother for support and pleaded, "I am old enough now . . . *por favor?*" Her voice held a hint of a childish whine.

Casey smiled sympathetically and wished she had never brought up the subject of dancing. She had to remember where she was and that these people couldn't possibly know anything that she'd experienced . . . None of it had happened yet. Wow. Her mind tripped over the thought. Was it the wine or was she really beginning to accept where she was? Okay, she knew she couldn't keep making these faux pas and not expect some trouble to show up. After all, she was definitely in a different place. Now she really wanted to have that conversation with Luke about what was appropriate. If she was even considering accepting the concept of time travel, then she ought to have all the details about it. Just relax and enjoy the afternoon, she thought resignedly. At least there was good food and good company.

She again glanced at Luke and saw he was staring at her with the most devastating smile. He nodded to her as if in acknowledgment that she had said or done something that pleased him very much. Then she watched him slowly turn his attention toward the radiant Doña Isabela as she began to speak.

"Do not fret so, *mi hija.* Your *quinceñera* will be a night to remember, of that you can rest assured." Doña Isabela turned to her husband, who was tapping his pocket watch.

"Ah, *si, el tiempo*. Rosalinda." She turned back to the child, who seemed to sense what was coming. "It is time for your choir practice with the sisters at Loretto Chapel. *Corra* . . . run along now, before you are late."

"Ohhhh . . ." Rosalinda let her breath out in a rush of disappointment. "What is the point of trying to reason with adults! And why practice singing when we cannot even use our new loft?"

Luke interjected with a playful grin, "There is an expression from a tribe in a far-off land, Rosalinda . . . It is said, 'If you can walk, you can dance. If you can talk, you can sing.' "

Rosalinda appeared to be pondering his remark, then blurted with renewed humor, "Not if you heard my friend Juanita sing and saw Alvara dance. But you could teach me the fandango . . . could you not? I have seen you dance it, señor."

Luke's lips spread into a huge smile, as though he knew exactly what the teenager was doing. "I would never offend your parents, Señorita Rosalinda. Maybe you should stop all your talk about dancing and walk to your singing." He grinned mischievously.

Casey watched the young girl and Luke exchange affectionate smiles. It was obvious that even when he toyed with Rosalinda, she completely adored him . . . Everyone seemed to adore him.

"Yes," Don Felipe said in a fatherly voice. "Do practice singing, *hija*. Now you must go, or you will offend the sisters by your lateness."

"*Adelante,* Rosa *mía,*" Doña Isabela said gently to her daughter.

"*Sí*, Mami, I will not be late."

Doña Isabela called for Marcella, who appeared at the doorway as though she was waiting. Rosalinda's mother spoke to the woman in Spanish, and Casey could see Marcella's face set with determination. She had a feeling Rosalinda must really challenge this serious woman's nerves.

"Buenas tardes, señorita y señor," Rosalinda said in a proper voice to Casey and Luke as she rose from the table. "Mami, Papi . . . I shall sing my heart out."

Don Felipe looked pleased and Doña Isabela smiled to her daughter. "Stay with Marcella. She must accompany you," Don Felipe added sternly.

"Adiós, mi hija," the girl's parents said simultaneously.

The teenager gracefully left the table, and Casey got a glimpse of the woman she would one day become. She would be intelligent and yet able to play the social game to the hilt. Quite a powerful combination, she thought. Whoever Rosalinda's true love was, he would be fortunate.

Doña Isabela continued to smile after her child and said, "Forgive my daughter's impetuous nature. For all her bravado, she is still learning."

"I think she is darling," Casey said.

"She is delightful," Luke added.

Doña Isabela turned her attention to them. "Thank you both for being such charming guests. Surely it was fortune that brought you to our door. I do hope you will remain for the *quinceñera*. Why, you may even dance the fandango, Señor Luke," She grinned, then added impishly, "Just make sure Bishop Lamy doesn't catch you."

Luke laughed. "But I have no partner—"

"A lovely woman is sitting directly in front of you, my old friend," Don Felipe piped up. *"Por favor, hombre,* do not tell me your vision is clouding with age."

Casey couldn't help the blush rising to her face, yet became further embarrassed when Doña Isabela said in a chiding voice, "Felipe! Perhaps you have overstepped yourself. Señorita Casey is newly arrived in the outside world." The woman's tone was compassionate. "It is not suitable to suggest such a thing."

The man looked so chastened, Casey felt she had to come to his rescue. "Thank you for the compliment, Don Felipe. I have danced, though I have never danced this fandango you speak of with . . . with such passion."

"Ahh . . ." Luke broke in. "And that is what it is . . . a dance of passion. It *is* passion put into movement."

Casey blushed even further at his words. Why was she thinking everything he said had another meaning? Wishful thinking? That was scary and, probably, really stupid.

"*Por Dios,* such *caballeros*. You have embarrassed my guest, and I don't know that she"—Doña Isabela winked at Casey—"or I can easily forgive your inappropriate remarks."

"Perhaps I might make up for my behavior by escorting both you ladies on a stroll through this lovely garden," Luke interjected, then looked to Don Felipe. "With your permission, señor."

"*Muy bueno, caballero,*" their host said, lifting his glass toward Luke in a toast. "There is hope for mankind still," he added with a grin.

Everyone raised their glasses with laughter, and Casey once again found she was enjoying herself immensely.

"Ah, *bueno.*" Don Felipe placed his napkin on the table, then rose. "It is time I returned to my business affairs, *mi amor.*" He gently squeezed his wife's hand. "*Gracias,* Luke," he said, nodding to his friend and turning to Casey. "Your presence is a gift in our home, señorita," he finished with a slight bow.

Doña Isabela rose to her feet and smiled at her remaining guests. Looking at Luke, who was also rising, she delegated, "You may begin making up for your behavior, señor, by showing *el jardín* to Señorita Casey. I must walk with my husband back to the house and shall return momentarily."

Luke pushed his heels together in courteous acknowledgment. "It would be my pleasure, Doña Isabela," he said, then turned and smiled at Casey. "I am sure we can entertain ourselves in this beautiful sanctuary you have created, Doña Isabela."

The woman smiled and nodded, extending her hand to her husband. "I am certain you can, Luke d'Séraphin," she murmured, before placing her fingers upon Don Felipe's.

Luke bowed his respect to the woman and, as the couple left them, turned back to Casey. "Would you like to take a short walk? The garden isn't very big, but Doña Isabela has done wonders . . . and I have a feeling you would like to talk," he added with a grin.

How right he was!

Seven

*W*hen was she going to get used to it? How he could read minds, or moods, or feelings or whatever. Sheesh, and why was she now more nervous than before? "Yes. A walk in the garden would be nice. Thank you," she nearly stammered.

Luke walked around the table and offered his arm. Taking a deep breath, Casey sucked in some courage from somewhere and slipped her hand under and over his forearm as he led her away from the chairs.

"It's very formal here, isn't it?" she asked, breaking the uneasy silence with conversation as they continued to walk along the stone path.

He smiled. "Yes, it must appear so to you, but even in our age, the Hispanic people exude dignity and respect for one another," he went on to explain. "They are a very proud people, and their culture remains very polite. How one treats another holds great importance, and their hospitality is never questioned. It is a grace that lives on."

"I must remember that," Casey said, watching a small bird hop around in the branches of the cottonwood tree above their heads. "Umm, Luke," she asked, "how much do Doña Isabela and Don Felipe know about you? Do they know you . . . you time-travel?" She looked around to see if anyone else might have heard.

Luke threw back his head and laughed. "You say that as if it were a curse, instead of a gift. This afternoon did you feel cursed by such wonderful food and entertaining company?"

"No, I had a great time," she answered with a grin. "Surprised the heck out of me, too, but you're not answering my question with another question, *caballero*." Her inflection implied "buster," though she knew the Spanish word meant "gentleman."

She saw the sly smile come to his lips, as though admitting he'd been caught. "No, Señorita Casey. No one here is aware of my . . . abilities." He paused. "I have many good friends and have made acquaintances all over the world in my travels. They simply know me as a friend, and perhaps a good Samaritan, who comes and goes as the pattern unfolds."

"Sheesh," she complained aloud. "There you go again with that 'pattern unfolding.' I don't know if I'll ever understand that theory." She shook her head in confusion.

"Actually, you accepted it already, Casey."

"When?" she asked with surprise. She didn't remember saying anything to him.

"When you made your choice at the table to enjoy the afternoon."

She bit her upper lip. He'd done it again . . . Back at the table. She mentally played the scene again in her head. When he'd smiled, so sweet and knowingly, right after she'd resigned herself to relax and enjoy the afternoon. How had he known that? Had he felt it? "Actually, I think I'm still trying to digest this whole thing," she joked, and patted her hand on her full stomach. "But I don't think I've made a choice about anything yet," she added with a tone of superiority. She wasn't about to let him get away with knowing everything that was going on inside her.

He smiled and shrugged. "I sensed that you made your decision to accept where you are . . . and that when you decided to put your fears aside and just *be*, you found it enjoyable. Sounds like a choice to me," he said, and looked away teasingly.

Instinctively her fingers rose from his arm to lightly slap his chest with the backs of them. "Sheesh, Luke, I have to watch what I say all the time," she continued in awe. "Today I almost started a real mess with that Ginger Rogers remark. Thanks for the save." She glanced at him. "It was brilliant, by the way."

He smiled back at her, obviously enjoying the conversation. Shaking his head slightly, he complimented, "You were the one who had the brilliant insight."

"About women being as equally able as men?"

"Absolutely," he agreed.

A comfortable silence fell between them and she felt herself becoming more relaxed as they continued walking. "Anyway, I read that. I didn't make it up, but ya gotta admit that Ginger was some woman. She did it all without looking." Maybe it was the wine she'd had at lunch, but she felt herself leaning more heavily on his escorting arm.

He looked down to her hand on his arm and back into her eyes. "That was trust."

Why was she beginning to think this conversation could be taken another way? Why was it everything this man said seemed to be settling within her with such importance? And how in the heck did he intuitively sense what she was feeling? She thought for another moment and sobered. "Yes, it was, wasn't it? Ginger really had to trust Fred. She was the one that was always dancing backwards. For all she knew, he could have been leading her right into a wall."

"But he never did, did he? She found her equal and trusted his gift." The genuine tone of his voice drew her eyes up to his. "Look, think of me as you will, Casey," he said, holding her gaze. "I am here to help you return to your family when a way is shown. I can be your mentor," he offered, raising his finger to stop her words before adding, "if you wish help in acclimating to this time period." He gave a nod of thanks for allowing him to finish, and continued, "But do not assume that I can teach you anything. You already have all your answers. So you see," Luke said with what she swore sounded like affection as they proceeded down the path together, "you are not always the student, are you?"

She stopped and stared at him. He stood before her and looked into her eyes with an inquisitive expression. "Why are you looking at me like that?" she demanded. "As though you are waiting for me to tell you my thoughts? Why should I? You seem to read them easily enough."

"I cannot tell you how to think, señorita," he said with that charming smile.

She pulled her hand away and placed both her palms on her hips, just as Rosalinda might do. Then, surprised at realizing she hadn't done this in years, she slowly allowed her arms to slide down. "You're maddening, do you know that? If I had all the answers, I'd know what to do to get my life back and find my sister, now wouldn't I? And after what I saw in this town this morning, I *have* to trust you. And it ain't that easy for me, okay?" She paused, drawing in a deep breath before adding with a huff, "I'm not Ginger Rogers."

A serious look came over his face, as though he'd been offended and didn't know how to respond. She watched as he stepped away from her and looked up to the branches of the cottonwood tree overhead. "So . . . you think I'm leading you into a wall?" he chuckled, turning back to her.

That damn twinkle was back in his eyes. How he enjoyed playing with her head! She then thought about how he had taken her under his wing, so to speak, and she had to admit that so far she was a heck of a lot better off with him than if she were on her own. "Let's just say, I'm still looking over my shoulder, okay?"

"Fair enough," he said with more than a trace of humor in his voice. "You have made very quick progress, Casey . . . if I might compliment you without your taking offense."

"Progress?" She allowed her hands to rest at her sides. How she wished she hadn't pulled away from his arm. She really had enjoyed the contact with him.

She almost stopped walking again when the realization struck her that she was more than a little attracted to Luke d'Séraphin, and what was worse . . . *she had to do a lot better job at hiding it from him.* How confusing to have this happen with someone who could read you so well. It was . . . frustrating. She felt like Rosalinda, yet had to admit that the child seemed more practiced at bantering than she was.

"Yes, progress," Luke continued, as though having no idea of the turmoil in her head. "You have accepted where you are and now you can begin to enjoy the adventure."

"Is that what you do? Do you just pop in on friends all throughout time? Where else have you been?"

"You ask many questions, señorita."

"That's because I want many answers. This just doesn't happen in my life and I want to know everything I can about it. Like will it ever happen again? I don't know that I can go through getting hit with another bolt of lightning. I mean, what would have happened to me if you hadn't come along?"

"We will never know that, will we?" he answered. "It is unfolding differently. Do not question where you aren't, Casey. Stay focused on where you are."

"Another of your so-called principles?" She wanted to laugh at how he managed to take everything she said and put a different twist to it.

Hearing the soft strains of the guitar, she actually had to admit the afternoon had been magical. Why mess with it? "Okay, so what's this fandango?" she asked as they walked farther along the path.

"I explained it is a dance of passion. Have you ever seen flamenco dancing?"

Casey nodded. "I saw it on television and"—she got all excited—"and okay, this might be so typically female and you'll probably laugh, but I had second-row-center seats for *Lord of the Dance* and I was blown away!"

He did laugh. "Yes, there is good flamenco in it."

"You saw it?" She was pleased that a man would be interested, since all the comedians seemed to put the show down as a chick thing.

"I saw it on television," he answered, leading her as the path twisted and turned back to another part of the house. "It doesn't surprise me you enjoyed Spanish dancing, since you are of Celtic heritage."

"It doesn't? Well, it surprised the heck out of me. I can remember sitting there in awe, and then the flamenco dancing . . . God, chills ran up my spine."

"Hmm," Luke murmured in a pleased voice. "Interesting." As though to change the course of their conversation, he shifted direction again in her head when he stated, "You do know that the Spanish influence in Ireland is profound, don't you?"

"I've never been there. I wouldn't know. I was kind of surprised to see it appear in the middle of all that Irish dancing."

"In 1588 the Spanish Armada was invading England when a great storm came up and many soldiers were shipwrecked upon Ireland's shores. The people and the land enchanted the men and many stayed, thus the Spanish influence and the dark hair and eyes of some Irish. It wouldn't surprise me to find that such a man also contributed to your lineage."

"My father had dark hair and many of my cousins do."

He nodded. "So you were moved by the flamenco dancing?"

Startled by the shift again, she muttered, "Yes, it was . . ." She struggled for a good word.

Luke supplied it. "Passionate?"

She took a deep breath as they came closer to the house and she saw up ahead an older man, sitting on a bench under a tree. He was the one playing the guitar. "Okay, passionate," she whispered. "It just moved something inside of me." She wished she had never brought it up. She did not care to be speaking about passion with this man, especially if he could read her so easily.

She smiled at the guitarist, who nodded and continued to strum the strings. Luke said something in Spanish to him and the older man grinned while changing his tune. It started out slowly and then began to pick up pace, becoming very earthy, very primal, very passionate. Luke had asked the man to play flamenco music.

Her senses seemed to come alive with some kind of energy that was better left alone. This was neither the time nor the place to become attracted to someone, especially someone like Luke d'Séraphin. She had better work much harder at keeping her thoughts under control.

"Come, Casey . . . Don Felipe is correct. You would make a lovely dance partner." He swept her into his arms and held her with a formal invitation to the dance.

Immediately every nerve ending in her body seemed to vibrate with a wild surge of sexual energy. It was unwelcome. Unwarranted. Yet undeniable.

She was so startled that she pulled away, but not before he caught her wrist. "I . . . I can't do this," she whispered in embarrassment.

"Do what?" he inquired with a soft smile. "I am merely asking you to dance."

"I can't dance flamenco! That takes years of practice!"

The older man seemed to ignore them as he continued to play with such fervor that it all felt surreal to her. How could she be having this conversation? How could her body betray her like this when she so desperately needed to find some control?

"We have ten days to practice."

"You're going to teach me?" she asked, incredulous that he would even suggest it.

"This I can teach you, Casey."

"I didn't even learn the damn Macarena!" she protested.

Laughing, he pulled her back into his arms. When she grabbed his shoulder in desperation, he looked down at her and whispered, "It is not such a bad way to pass the time, is it? Remember, you have a choice. You are allowed to enjoy this, Casey."

"I can't do it. It's too . . . intricate . . . too . . . too . . ."

"Passionate?" Again he supplied the word.

She almost groaned aloud as another wave of sensuality rushed through her body, betraying and reminding her how long it had been since she was attracted to a man. Any man.

"Well, too passionate for someone who is pretending she's just left a convent, that's for sure."

"Maybe once they see you dancing, everyone will stop wondering why you left the convent."

In spite of everything, Casey couldn't help laughing. "Or they'll think I should have stayed in it!"

He held her more firmly, as though he were about to begin dancing. "Nonsense. I have watched you move, and when you wish . . . you can be quite graceful. Do not doubt yourself, Casey. I don't."

Sheesh! This guy really knew how to be charming, and she found herself surrendering. "I'm going to look like a fool," she stated between clenched teeth.

"Only you will think so. You are gifted with the ability to laugh at yourself. Use it. Now we begin . . ." He started to move, and Casey looked down at her feet. "Don't," he whispered. "Did Ginger look at her feet?"

"I told you, I'm not Ginger." Again she tried to pull away from his grasp. It only tightened, and in truth, she really wasn't trying all *that* hard.

"Can you trust me?" He stared down at her with a patient expression that said he was holding back a smile. "The walls of the house are far behind you, Casey. You won't be hurt."

She felt a thickness in her throat.

"I trust you," she whispered, and realized it was truth. If this man wanted to harm her, he'd certainly had plenty of opportunity. If anything, he was the most respectful man she had ever met.

"Then relax. We have plenty of time to practice the more intricate steps. The first lesson is to become comfortable in my arms. I am not such a poor dancer that I would lead you astray, señorita."

Relax. Right. She took a deep breath to banish and release her wild yearnings for this man. This was about trust. That was all.

She grinned. "Okay, so this is just regular dancing? Nothing fancy?"

He nodded.

"I know what this is!" she proclaimed. "You just want to find out if I'll let you lead."

He laughed and so did she. This time *she* was right on the mark!

Relaxing even more, Casey said, "Gimme your best shot, señor. Ya ain't dealin' with a complete klutz here."

He took the challenge with a pleased expression, making his face so handsome that Casey almost groaned again.

"I never doubted you," he whispered, his grin widening.

What exactly was she getting into here? A dancing challenge? She was a pretty good dancer. Damn, years of being single might finally pay off if she could meet his invitation. "You are wagering . . . señor?" she whispered back, adding the last word with a smile of her own. Better to cover her attraction with a little boldness.

"And what might this wager be?"

She thought for a moment. "If I learn, you will tell me everything I want to know about time travel."

He gaze became serious. "I can only tell you what I know."

"Okay, then that," she said, impatient to get something out of this. If she was about to appear the fool, then she wanted some reassurance it wasn't for nothing.

His smile returned and he again assumed his dancing posture, holding her firmly. "*Como tú quieres, señorita.* Agreed."

She nodded triumphantly and assumed her own posture, ready for what he had to give.

"Of course, you know . . . I would have told you what you wanted to know without all this," he muttered as he began to move.

She stumbled and slapped his shoulder. "You . . . you did that on purpose!" she accused. She tried to make her voice sound stern, yet couldn't stop the laughter. It was hopeless for her to have any pride at all around this man!

"Just dance," she said, resuming her former position. She was ready for him now.

"Don't look at your feet," he whispered, trying to match her serious mood. The creeping smile betrayed him.

"I'm not," she retorted, staring straight into his eyes. Little did he know that in college one of her best male friends taught her about following at too many frat parties for her ever to forget. With any luck, Luke d'Séraphin would be the one stumbling soon.

He took a big step forward and she followed easily as she caught the rhythm of his body and matched it. Two shorter steps and she knew she could follow him. He was a very good dancer, she thought, staring into his eyes and trying not to think of anything else, trying to just allow the music and this man to lead her. They danced in a circle, her dress sweeping out like a pink cloud, and she thought surely, for this moment, she had landed in heaven.

"I'm going to swing you out now," he whispered and, grabbing her waist with one hand, flung her toward the house. She twirled twice quite gracefully and then stumbled when her vision caught something dark standing not far away.

"Oh . . ." Casey stopped and tried to get her head back to normal. *Normal?* Ever since that lightning struck, nothing was normal. Especially this! And now her head was spinning! "Doña Isabela," she said, catching her breath. "I didn't see you."

"I am sorry I interrupted," the woman answered, and came closer. Smiling, she looked at Luke briefly. "I see I owe my husband an apology. Señorita, you dance beautifully."

"Oh . . ." Casey was so embarrassed that she had to stop herself from wringing her hands together. "I danced a great deal when I was younger."

"No wonder Rosalinda has bonded with you in such a short time. You have an admirer in my daughter. I'm afraid she will monopolize your time, and you must continue your dancing lessons before the *quinceñera*. I believe I have some shoes that would be more appropriate."

Luke came forward and placed his hand on her back very gently. "I'm afraid I have worn out this gracious lady."

Casey shot him a look. "You didn't wear me out."

He chuckled as he turned his attention back to Doña Isabela. "Perhaps you might escort the señorita back to her room. There is something I must attend to while there is daylight."

"Of course, Luke," the woman answered, and held out her hand to Casey. "We don't want to tax your strength, señorita, since you just arrived last night and need to be gentle with yourself. A siesta would be most helpful now."

"I will return before the evening meal, *damas*."

He bowed to both ladies, and Casey was stunned as he walked away. Luke was just leaving her? Like this? Pulling herself together, she turned to her hostess.

"Come, señorita," Doña Isabela urged. "Rest. It has been a very busy day for you."

Yeah, you could say that!

As she walked with Doña Isabela into the house, Casey remembered that, according to Luke, the d'Montoyas knew nothing about this time-travel adventure. She was simply a welcomed guest, traveling with a friend of theirs. How she would love to grab the woman's shoulders and ask her what the hell was happening. Someone wiser than she must have some answers, cause Casey was certainly shaken by this whole encounter, especially this last one with Luke. She remembered Juana telling her that she thought Luke might be interested in her. She wanted to burst into nervous laughter at the crazy thought.

Nah . . . someone like him must have plenty of women around him whenever he wanted. He wouldn't be interested in her as anything more than a diversion to pass the time until he could return her to her sister.

"I will send the shoes to you," the woman murmured, as they began to climb the stairs.

Casey smiled and nodded. "Thank you."

Maybe that was why he had to leave so suddenly. Maybe he had a woman in this time. Now, who could she ask about that? And why did she even care?

She did.

That thought created an uncomfortable feeling in her belly. Well, she would just have to cleverly ask Luke when she talked to him again at the next dance lesson. Or maybe Rosalinda knew.

She wondered how long choir practice lasted . . .

Eight

Rosalinda patted her braided coronet as she stared into the long standing mirror that days ago had been brought into Casey's room. "All right, señorita . . . now, watch me. Grasp your skirt and hold it to your hip. Lift your chin, knowing you are equal to any man, especially a man who challenges you with passion. And then . . . stomp your foot, like *so!*"

Casey watched as this child/woman did a remarkably simple yet sexy move of her body, as though not only answering a male's challenge but raising the bar a notch or two with staccato footwork. "Hmm," she murmured, catching her bottom lip between her teeth. "I don't know, Rosa. That looks good on you, but I think I'm a bit too old to be the femme fatale. Didn't exactly work for me . . . before."

Rosalinda turned around and grinned. "Well, *of course* it didn't work for you before! You thought . . . thought you were someone else then. A nun." The girl seemed to be try-ing not to hurt her feelings. "Now you have put that behind you and you will see what kind of woman you truly are."

Slumping back to sit on the edge of the bed, Casey stared at her. "How did you get this smart? It was your mother, wasn't it? She taught you?"

Rosalinda sighed. "Yes, my mami is very wise, but it just makes sense to me, Casey. I, too, thought once I might have a vocation, that I might want to devote myself to God. I was very serious and talked to my friend Alvara, and Sis-ter Bernardina. That was when I knew whatever I wanted to do, I could do it as a vocation. If I wanted to be a wife and a mother, I could. If I wanted to dance the flamenco on stage, I could." She resumed her dancing position and stomped her foot. Grinning, she added, "I could serve any way I choose."

"I think your parents might disagree with your last example." Casey laughed and shook her head at the teenager. "You are something else, Rosalinda d'Montoya, you know that?"

"I don't understand. Of course I am something else. I can't be you." Chuckling, Rosalinda reached down and gently pulled Casey back to her feet. "Only you can be you, Casey O'Reilly. I think it's now time to begin finding out who you are, don't you?"

How she wanted to tell Rosa that she hadn't been in any convent. That the whole thing was made up. She paused, and suddenly she felt like she really had been away for a very long time. In truth, she might just as well have been in a convent for all the good being available had gotten her. Four serious relationships had ended for the same reason. The men didn't want to commit. Now, what the hell had made her think of that? As soon as she asked the question, her mind played out that scene of her father wanting to leave and her mother pleading, accusing. And she experienced the fear she had felt as a child at the overwhelming situation.

What the hell had made all those relationships fail? Had she pushed too hard? Was she really that clingy? Was it some childhood fear of betrayal or abandonment? She wanted to take that tiny, frightened girl into her arms and hug her until she wasn't scared anymore. What a thing for a child of three years old to walk into without any warning!

"Casey . . ." Rosalinda shook her arm. "What's wrong? You look just like you did the other day in the street."

Casey blinked and smiled at the girl. "Don't worry. I'm okay. Maybe better than okay." She did feel better, now that the shock of that buried memory and its power had lessened. What had this teenager said to her? It was time to find out just who she really was?

Was she someone different? If she was, then who had she been? she wondered. Could she be someone different in a relationship now, without that buried fear? It was mind-boggling and yet she almost wanted to laugh at the lightness she felt.

"*Bueno*. I'm glad you are feeling better." Rosalinda smiled, then added, "But you have only a short time before you meet with Señor Luke for your next dance lesson. You have done fairly well with the steps. Now we must work with . . . how do you say it . . . ?" Rosalinda once more grabbed her gown, exposing the ruffled underslip, and held the material in a fist that rested upon an outthrust right hip. "We must work . . . with *attitude*!"

Both females burst out laughing.

Even though many things had changed over the last hundred years and it was hard to communicate at times, the language they were speaking now was one that was understood by women throughout *all* time. What a riot to have this happen with this particular person, someone she'd had to travel back in time to meet!

Stifling her laugh, Casey said, "All right, girlfriend. Show me. This is my fourth lesson with Señor Luke, and I want to knock his socks off." Holy shit, was *this* who she really was? Again she had to bite her bottom lip not to giggle like a teenager. Well, she certainly was enjoying herself now!

She was passing the time with interesting, gracious people, learning to dance the flamenco, and falling for a man who—

She froze with her last thought. She couldn't be! She wouldn't allow this to happen. Not now! Not with *him*! Attraction was one thing, but falling in love?

"Casey, whatever is going through your head is not the attitude I was speaking about. Look, you must do it like this," Rosalinda said with an extremely poised look on her face.

"You're right," she answered, making up her mind that she was in charge of herself now. There wasn't anyone here to give her advice, not about being attracted to a time traveler. She knew now these people didn't really know what Luke did. She had no choice but to listen to herself in this situation. She could get through this.

All she needed was the right attitude.

"All right then, Rosa," she said, holding her soft cotton skirt in her hand and resting it on her hip. "Show me again."

The two practiced dance steps, with *attitude,* for the next half hour until it was time for Casey to meet Luke and Manuel, their faithful guitarist, in the courtyard. Wearing a full green skirt with a white ruffled petticoat, Casey adjusted her white, gauzy blouse and, daringly, opened the top button. She glanced down at the tips of the black leather shoes Doña Isabela had given her. The heels were chunky; when she stomped, she had to admit, it sounded pretty . . . well, attitudinal. She was ready.

He was studying the smoke from his thin cigar when she entered the courtyard. She stopped for just a moment to take in the scene. Wearing dark brown slacks and a thin white cotton shirt with ruffles at the cuffs, Luke appeared like a hero out of a romance novel. Casey almost groaned. She didn't read those books . . . Well, okay, maybe she'd read a few on vacations, ones recommended by a co-worker, but she never thought that type of man could really exist. And now here he was, standing right in front of her. He was so handsome the very thought he might be interested in her as anything more than a traveling companion seemed ludicrous. She didn't care what Juana had told her, a man like Luke could have any woman he wanted. They seemed to gravitate toward him and melt in his presence.

She was not about to become a groupie to a time traveler!

He glanced at her and immediately smiled, as though very pleased by her arrival. She was not about to read anything more into it than that. Or possibly give anything more for him to pick up on with his crazy spidey senses. They had spent the last four days meeting and dancing for an hour or so, being dinner partners, and enjoying the company of this delightful family. They were friends now. Strange friends, but friends nonetheless. And that was all, regardless of what her body was telling her.

"Ah, señorita . . ." Luke said as he walked in her direction. "I do think the Southwest agrees with you. Even this time period, it appears. You look *muy bonita*."

She knew that meant very pretty. He was always complimenting her, but then he complimented everyone, even Manuel when he played with passion. Why should she think anything else? She shouldn't. She couldn't. What she needed was some of Rosalinda's attitude right about now.

"*Gracias, señor*," she managed to say smoothly, as she walked into the courtyard and met him halfway across the rough tile they used as a dance floor. She really did like the way her heels clicked over it, announcing each step.

"You seem . . . different this afternoon, Casey." His smile widened with appreciation.

She actually grinned. "Ahh, so I wasn't lovely before and now I am?"

"You actually think I'm about to walk into that one?" He chuckled and puffed on his cigar. "Please give me credit for more intelligence than that."

"Oh, I give you credit for intelligence, Luke," she answered, wishing she had a cigar of her own to make her point, or something with a little more attitude, for Luke's close presence was devastating. "I was merely teasing."

He raised his head slightly as he exhaled. "Lightheartedness becomes you, señorita," he said with a smile. Tossing his cigar butt to the grass, he turned and added, "let us see if your steps are as light . . . Shall we dance?" There was that smile again.

She nearly groaned. How in the world was she supposed to pull this off?

"Casey?"

Blinking, she stared into his soft brown eyes, which held flecks of amber and gold and— *Stop it!* She simply had to get control of herself. "Yes. Let's dance."

He held out his arm and she placed her hand on his palm, watching the way his fingers closed over her own and pulled her into his arms. This was dancing, right? She *had* to get anything more out of her mind. Attitude. That was it. She needed some attitude.

They assumed their usual dancing position and Casey took a deep breath as she was held in Luke's arms. Dancing really can be so intimate . . . No wonder some men are intimidated by it, she thought. But not this one . . . He seemed to like intimacy, especially with her mind, and now her own body was falling under his spell.

He nodded to Manuel and the passionate flamenco music began.

She followed easily, now somewhat accustomed to the steps and to Luke's sure guidance. It was like a tango, not that she'd ever danced the tango, except at Amy's wedding when she'd had too much to drink and had dragged her sister onto the dance floor. What she was doing with Luke was nothing quite so silly. This really was romantic, or one could choose to take it romantically. She didn't know what she wanted at this point, except not to stumble or stomp on his foot, as some of the steps were pretty intricate.

"*Muy bien*, Casey. See? How easily you have learned to trust."

"Trust? I'm just hopin' my feet don't fail me now," she remarked, as she held on to his shoulder. "I'd rather *not* trip the light fantastic, thanks," she joked with a grin.

He laughed, twirling her around, and Casey found herself forgetting her insecurities, her fears, and just going with the graceful movement. She knew he could see her smiling big time, but she just couldn't help it. What did any of it matter? Why not just have fun?

As she spun around, his handsome face flashed before her in blips and she was grateful for the anchor, as it helped to keep her equilibrium. There he was, and there he was again. So what if he had a woman he saw every night, for she'd found out from Juana that Luke had left right after dinner the night before and hadn't returned until sometime in the early morning. He was here now and he was her friend, that was all. Concentrate, she told herself. And don't fall!

He spun her out, holding on to her hand, and then pulled her back so that her shoulders were now in front of his chest. His arm, along with hers, was crossed over her stomach, and his other hand was resting on her waist to push her out again. Instead, he paused and whispered in her ear, "That's why I'm here. You won't fall."

His breath created a ripple of pleasure in her ear that raced down her body and settled, quite alarmingly, between her legs. Damn . . . she had to watch herself here. She really could fall for this guy who seemed to innocently flirt with her mind, her body, and her soul. Jeez, concentrate on the dance. He wasn't for her, she mentally rebuked herself. Besides, it was obvious from all his late night absences that particular space in his life was already occupied. Yet somehow, the thought of him in another woman's arms did make her back stiffen a little.

He twirled her out, and for some unknown reason, she found herself letting go of his hand and standing there, staring at him. He stood, inhaling deeply, and stared right back, as though wondering what she was going to do.

Casey felt the surge of determination rising in her veins. Slowly, deliberately, her fingers grasped her green skirt and, clutching it to her hip, she actually stomped her foot in challenge!

Luke seemed startled for just a moment. She saw it in the slight widening of his eyes, and then watched as he slowly pulled back his shoulders while bringing both of his hands to his hips. He not only stomped, but threw in a few extra intricate steps. Casey saw the challenge was accepted and sighed deeply, drawing in energy from someplace and willing her feet to perform as she had practiced with Rosa.

Attitude. Now was the time to bring it on full force.

From some untapped reservoir deep within, she found more attitude than she had originally thought she possessed. Lifting her chin, she stared right back and answered his footwork with a staccato of her own and a flip of her petticoats to show him she wasn't about to be intimidated.

"Brava!" Luke broke the tension by clapping and

laughing. "I see you have been practicing . . . Rosalinda has been helping you?"

Casey raised one eyebrow and grinned slyly. She was pleased by his praise; even Manuel had stopped playing and was tapping the side of his guitar. "Yes, the girl has been wonderful," she exhaled, allowing her shoulders to relax. "Rosalinda said all I needed was more *attitude*." She pronounced the last word with her best Spanish accent. Suddenly she felt a little let down that he had stopped the momentum they'd been building in their dance. Especially the thrust of her newly found *attitude*, for if she wasn't mistaken, she had just seen something in his eyes . . . something with primal intensity aimed directly at her.

He now appeared delighted and moved across the tiles to her. "A very good subject . . . attitude. Perhaps, after this dance, you would allow me to escort you through the garden once again?" He finished by tilting his head invitingly . . . with that smile again.

It was the first time he had asked her to stay after the lessons, and she found it pleased her greatly. If he wanted to talk about attitude, fine. She'd talk about anything, just to be in his presence, for there was no denying that there was something unique about the man. He was like no one else she had even dreamed could exist, and she just wanted to be around him, to be in his company. Everything didn't seem so scary then; as crazy as it might seem, it was starting to make sense. He had the uncanny ability to calm her down, to soothe her fears, to—

"If you are otherwise entertained, we could always speak at some other—"

"No," she interrupted, and then realized he might be confused. "I meant . . . yes," she blurted out. "I would love to walk with you again."

Jeez . . . did that sound desperate or what?

A quick smile of agreement and then he held out his hands again. "Let us begin once more then." He nodded to Manuel to resume playing, and Casey came back into his arms. "We shall surprise more than a few guests next week. You are quite good, Casey."

Hating the betrayal of her own blush, Casey said, "Oh, I don't know, Luke. Here with you is one thing, but dancing in front of others . . . ?" She turned slightly away from him and added, "I . . . I just don't know."

"It's about trust, Casey. With me, yes," he softly said, touching her arm to turn her back to face him. "But more so with you. Trust yourself."

"Myself?" she said, gazing up into his penetrating eyes. "I've never even attempted to dance like this before in my life, and now with a little less than a week's practice, you're saying I can be trusted not to make a fool out of myself in front of hundreds of strangers?"

He laughed. Laughed!

"I'm glad you find me so amusing," she muttered, wanting to slap his shoulder.

"There will not be hundreds of people. Okay, maybe a hundred," he chuckled.

"Oh, okay then. That makes a big difference. Now I feel so much better." She surrendered and joined his laughter.

"Listen," he said lowly, grabbing her attention with a more serious face. "Trusting yourself is merely believing in your own self-worth. I'm telling you, Casey, you are a good dancer and you can trust that gift."

Well, she'd always thought she was a decent dancer, but she'd never had a partner like this, and now it was getting just too serious with the thought of an impending performance.

"Hey, just have fun," he added with a lighter tone. "This is a dance of passion, señorita, the male and female energies coming together as equals. It's quite a show."

Male and female energies coming together as equals . . . what exactly did that mean? Sounded more like making love to her. "I don't want to perform any show," she muttered.

"What do you want?"

And what could she answer to that? That she wanted it to be private, like this . . . ? Wasn't that the reason everyone thought she was learning this dance? A performance? No one suggested it was for personal reasons. "What I want . . ." She paused, refusing to allow the thought of what she really wanted to enter her brain again. "Is not to look foolish," she finally answered.

"If you haven't learned yet to trust yourself, at least momentarily"—he winked—"trust me. Ginger Rogers has got nothing on you, señorita. I assure you, you will not look foolish. You will look equal to anyone who may be watching. And they will know it."

She sighed, thinking about how he always seemed to turn all her fears around. How did he know just what to say, to respond so perfectly to how she was feeling? It was eerie, and yet comforting at the same time. How could she not want to stay around him? What woman wouldn't?

"Okay," she said resignedly. "Let's continue practicing then."

Nodding, Luke pulled her closer. As she placed her hand in his, Casey knew that though she was fighting it like crazy, she was losing her inner battle. She really, actually, insanely, was starting to fall in love with the most weird person she had ever encountered in her entire life!

She couldn't help it. She laughed at herself.

And it felt good.

A half hour later, she was sweating from her efforts and her legs were aching and tense. They had danced the fandango and flamenco until she felt like a weary woman with a rapidly waning attitude. She wanted to call a halt to the lesson and walk in the garden, anything but have to pull together more energy to match Luke's.

"You are tired, señorita," he said, releasing her. He turned quickly toward Manuel and thanked the man in Spanish. The older gentleman got up and bowed slightly, tipping his floppy straw hat and leaving them.

"Gracias, señor," Casey called out with a smile to the kindly man who had played so well, and for so long.

"I apologize for becoming so carried away," Luke exhaled as he walked toward a table where a pitcher of water and goblets were waiting.

Watching his fluid movement, she realized during the last half hour Luke's hold on her had been less rigid, more relaxed, as though he was now trusting she could carry more of her own weight in this dance. "Yes, I think I've had enough for now," she admitted with a smile, pleased at her realization. It was very complimentary, even if it was raising the bar another rung and she had to focus more now. Still, it was nice to know that he respected her.

The sun was still high and Luke poured fresh water into both goblets and handed one to her. "You have much stamina, señorita." He smiled, raising his glass to her in toast.

She accepted the goblet with a nod. Hmm. That was an interesting comment, she thought. *Don't contemplate it now, Casey, you haven't the strength,* she mentally advised herself. "That was a good lesson. You had me concentrating to keep up."

She watched as he drained the goblet and couldn't help staring at the movement of his Adam's apple while he swallowed. She had to remind herself it was *water* she was thirsty for and not anything else. Bringing her own glass to her lips, she took a huge gulp and then turned toward the garden path. "I need more shade," she announced, and starting walking. She didn't even care now if he wanted to walk with her. Maybe it would be better if he didn't. She was so rattled by the realization that she was falling in love that she was going to need some privacy to figure this out.

"Your rhythm is excellent, Casey," he said, coming to walk beside her. "It's been quite some time since I have danced."

"Really?" She glanced at him and smiled. "I would think you would do it a lot . . . considering you're such a good dancer."

What was this? Were they verbally dancing now? There was just too much irony with the innuendos flying between them, Casey mentally suspected.

"Well, thank you, but it's been quite a while. I believe it was my last visit here," he said, looking up to the branches of the trees and nodding. "It was about four years ago."

"Wow . . . I mean, why were you here? Did someone else get thrown back and you—"

"No," he interrupted, as he held his hands behind his back and settled into the stroll. "I was alone." He glanced at her and grinned. "Not that time can make you forget, you understand, but you gave me a good lesson in remembering that I can dance . . . as I tried to keep up with you."

Her heart expanded even more with his genuine smile. "I think you have that backward. I was trying to keep up with you."

"Oh, you think so?"

"Yes." Sheesh, wasn't it obvious to him?

He stopped abruptly, and after a few steps, she turned back to him.

"You really have no idea about your self-worth, do you?" he asked.

It came right out of left field, no preparation, no gentle setup for such a personal question. Flustered, she tried to get her mind to function. "What are you talking about?

I . . . I like myself," she stammered. It was a way to buy time until some neuron found a receptive connection in her brain . . . somewhere. Jeez, this man could rattle her.

"Yes, but I'm talking about your self-worth, Casey."

Deep down she knew what he was talking about and wished she could change the subject quickly, as it sounded like it might begin a dissection of her ego. She really didn't want to go there right now . . . It was enough that this man could read her feelings so well; she didn't want to reveal anything more.

"I wish you could see yourself through my eyes."

His words interrupted the barriers she was mentally building to shield her emotions, and a pull took hold of her to look up into his eyes. She wished she could too! It sure was a different picture than she was seeing.

After what seemed like a very long pause, he asked, "Would you like to know what I see, Casey?"

She could imagine herself, like Alice, falling further down that rabbit's hole if she even acknowledged she would love to hear his answer. "Okay, what?" God, she was so easy!

Walking again, he passed her and continued down the path with an invitational wave to join him as he said, "I see a woman with great potential who, for whatever reason, has hidden from it . . . yet she is seeing glimpses of it, but believes it is better to be humble and not admit it to herself, or anyone else for that matter." She swore she could hear the smile on his face as he continued. "Actually, it is very funny to watch someone pretending to be less than who they are." He paused, turning back to her, as though waiting for her to resume their walk. "Haven't you ever secretly thought that a greater destiny awaited you?"

She almost stumbled into his arms with that last statement. The first part felt like a nudge and the last like a shove, as if to awaken her from sleepwalking. She sure as hell felt like something was happening as this man seemed to lead her down a path not only in a garden but also in her mind. How much did she dare reveal to him? How vulnerable would it make her? Unsure in this exposed territory, she merely shrugged.

"I think you have," he added, when it was obvious she wasn't about to speak. "I think all humans do at some point in their life. They may have been young, and have forgotten, but I'm sure they did. It's part of the human condition, that realization you are more than what you are being told you are. That you are here for a purpose. Your life is no accident."

"Okay," she admitted, deciding it didn't make much difference now if everyone thought it at least once in their lives. "There was always this nagging thought," she murmured. "I mean, I . . ." How could she explain this?

"I know," he answered in a soft voice, and then began to walk again.

She quietly walked beside him. For once she didn't feel the need to fill the silence with words. He knew the feeling she was talking about, as though something was waiting for her . . . , pulling her forward through time to find her purpose. And somehow, as crazy as it might seem, she was also beginning to feel she might have traveled back in time to find it.

After a few minutes, Luke said in a quiet voice, "You brought up a good subject earlier. Attitude. It ties in well to self-worth, don't you think? Ironically, our mischievous Rosalinda hit upon a powerful topic."

Casey grinned. "She certainly has attitude aplenty. I like her a lot."

"As do I. She has not yet lost her belief in the magic of love."

Surprised, she asked, "You think love is magical?"

"Don't you?"

She shrugged. "I don't really know."

"I've seen love transform situations that seemed hopeless. Nothing physical was necessary, just love and its many derivatives."

Derivatives? Casey was wondering what he meant when he began to answer her mental question. She was getting used to that now.

"Like forgiveness or humor."

"Hmm, yes, you're right. I've seen that too. So love is an attitude?"

He glanced at her and grinned. "Love is magic."

She stopped again and waited for him to halt and turn around. He did.

"Okay, what are you? A time traveler? A magician?"

"Both," he answered as she watched that twinkle come back into his eyes.

"Are you one of those New Age people with all their belief in love and light and crystals and . . . bizarre stuff?" It was time to find out.

He chuckled. "First of all, there is nothing new in New Age. Truths are timeless, and they can be found everywhere, in all cultures and movements. I do not belong to any organization or church, if that's what you mean."

"Well, that's good, 'cause I don't understand them. How can everything be all light and love? It's not. In the real world ugly things happen. It's just not realistic."

He was nodding. "There is darkness. And that comes from the other side of love, the denial of it. That's fear. You know how fear makes you feel, don't you?"

She couldn't help it, she laughed. "Ah, *yeah!* I think I've had a few good opportunities in the last week to experience that one."

"Yes, you have," he answered with a widening smile. "How did it make you feel?"

"Scared!"

"And did it make you feel heavy? Tired? Like you just wanted to lie down and not get up?"

She paused, recalling the sensations. "Yes, it did."

He nodded and then waved his hand toward the path to continue their walk. "Fear carries a very heavy frequency to it. It's a difficult thing to handle when you have so much gravity pulling you down to begin with. Adding that band of energy can make life grueling." When she caught up with him, he asked, "And how did you feel when you surrendered to the situation, accepted where you were, made a choice to stop fighting it and stop putting up resistance?"

She didn't want to admit that she was actually *enjoying* herself more now than at any other time of her life. There was just so much of his being right she could acknowledge!

"Are you a preacher or something?" Now, wouldn't *that* just be her luck!

He threw back his head and laughed again, this time from his belly. "I am not a preacher. I apologize if I sound as though I have been preaching, Casey. It was not my intention."

She couldn't help joining in his good humor. Chuckling, she said, "No, not preaching, but everything you say does sound . . . I don't know, like everything is about life and how . . . how . . ."

"How magical it is?" he volunteered.

She stopped chuckling. "Yes, like that. How do you do that? How do you take everything I say and make it so . . . so meaningful? I don't get it. Who *are* you?"

The twinkle in his eyes was even brighter when he said, "I am no different than you . . . just a fellow traveler."

Yeah, right! She began shaking her head with her own abstract amusement. "No, see . . . I was born on the East Coast of this country . . . *on this planet!*" She mentally mimicked his inflection: *A fellow traveler*, indeed! "C'mon, tell me . . . where do you come from? What planet are you from? I mean, people can't just up and time-travel, like it's a freakin' vacation or something!" Okay, that should put his asteroid in park for a while.

"Really?" he broke in without hesitation. "Explain you and me walking this garden path then. In this moment you could very well imagine it is the year 2000, and although you are dressed in a costume, right now just imagine, outside that wall are automobiles and telephones and TVs and computers. For this moment you could imagine that, and yet something within you . . . something you can't define, reaffirms you have done something few others have. You have time-traveled into the year 1878. Quick," he ordered, as he suddenly grabbed her shoulders and stared into her eyes. "Tell me what is in your heart. You can't see the house. Where are you? Are you in the past, a place you have already visited? Are you in the future, a place you are only wishing to visit? Or are you here, on this path, right here, right now . . . where all the presents are?"

"Well, yes . . . I'm here," she whispered, feeling like something inside of her was breaking away as she gave her answer and Luke patted her shoulders before withdrawing his hands. She had spent her life time-traveling . . . right *out* of her life! She was always worrying about the past or the future. It wasn't until she was forced in the last four days to live in the present that she actually began to enjoy each day as an adventure. It was great! She had time-traveled, lost her past, had no idea what the next hour was going to bring, let alone the next day . . . but she was truly experiencing the present, and she was loving it!

"I need to sit down."

Luke held her arm and led her to the wooden bench in the shade. Sinking down upon it, Casey kept holding her chest. This was unbelievable!

"Breathe," Luke counseled.

"Okay," she breathed. That advice was acceptable.

"Breathe deeply."

She nodded and found herself calming down. Luke sat beside her and placed his hand on her back. He made soothing circles, and Casey experienced even more peace enter her body. Soon she was breathing normally and she turned her face slightly to see him. "Do you do this often?" she asked, and paused. "I mean, time-travel?"

He shrugged. "I can't say that I plan it. It unfolds before me and I follow the path. I do have a choice, Casey. I simply choose to be of service when I am called."

"Who calls you?"

"Life does."

"That's a pretty broad statement," she replied, wondering if he heard the hint of frustration in her voice.

"Okay, Life . . . it's that lighter-wave energy we were talking about earlier. I guess you could say that I made a choice to be in service to that frequency."

"Wait. You said love was that frequency. You're in service to love?" If he said yes, she might just slide off this bench to the ground.

"What are the real choices any of us have?" he asked softly. "Let's not complicate it with too many words. Bring it all down to basics," he said, holding his hands out in example. "I choose love"—he turned his right palm upward—"or I choose fear." She watched him make a weighing motion between his hands, then close his right hand gently and turn his left palm to the ground, as though releasing something. Okay, she got it. He released the hand with fear as a choice. He paused for a moment, then looked directly into her eyes. "Just like you, I, too, have chosen love, a much lighter frequency . . . so in answer to your question, yes, I am in service to it."

Okay, she was not about to make a total fool out of herself over this man, so she fought to keep her balance and stay on the bench. But she needed to turn this conversation away from love and toward something less personal. "So tell me, have you met other time travelers then?"

He grinned. "I am looking at one right now."

"You know what I mean. There are more than the two of us, aren't there? I mean, we can't be the only ones."

"There are others. Actually, many of them are here, all over the world, in all time periods. It's a question of balance, Casey."

"Balance? To time-travel?"

"No. In the world. Okay, picture a child's playground seesaw. Sitting on one side is fear, with all its recalled sensations, heavily keeping the opposite side, love, in the air and away from the ground. To balance that out, obviously, the opposite side needs more weight. I'm just throwing my weight on that side of the seesaw. But it's all balance, Casey. One needs the other to stay in balance. You were right when you said it can't be all light. The darkness serves a purpose."

"Serves a purpose?" She couldn't believe this was coming out of his mouth. "I don't get it. How do pain and horror in the world possibly help anything?"

"Maybe it shows you your prejudice, what you are holding yourself back from in your own life. I can't answer that. It's personal for each life experience. I don't know your pains and your horrors, though I'm sure, like everyone else in the world, you have gone through them, and somehow . . . when you eventually get far enough away from the memories, or recalled sensations, you can see more clearly how they served you."

She remembered several times when she'd thought her heart was broken, from her own life and choices she'd made, or hearing the tragedies of others, yet everything always seemed to work out . . . somehow. She was still having a problem with what this all meant. She thought a moment longer. "Prejudice, huh? That's part of the darkness on the seesaw?"

"One of them anyway," he said, sitting up straight. "Okay, for instance, you asked what planet I'm from. What if I told you I'm from the planet Venus? What would you say?" he asked seriously, though she thought she might laugh at his exaggeratedly dignified posture.

"Are you?" Her heart was beating faster. He could be an alien! What did she know? Crap, she hadn't even watched *The X-Files*!

"Answer me, if you would. I would like to make a point . . . I think it will help."

"Look, you're always making points . . . umm, good examples. But quite frankly, some of them are kind of scary and I'm a little afraid of what your next one might be."

"Don't put your weight there, Casey. It's way too dense to carry, especially when you're time-traveling. Does your choice to fear mean you would be afraid of me if you believed I was from . . . from somewhere you couldn't believe?"

"Gimme a break here. I am allowed to be rattled at the thought of extraterrestrials, I mean, little green men running about!"

His full lips spread into a grin and Casey found herself letting go of some of her fear.

"So you have a prejudice of little green men?"

That stopped her. "I don't know if I'm prejudiced against them, but—"

"But you wouldn't want to meet one."

"Right." She stared at him. "I haven't, have I?"

He seemed to enjoy her confusion. "Have you ever seen a picture of our universe?"

"I guess," she muttered. "Wait a minute, answer my ques—"

"In a moment. Patience is very important for a time traveler."

She shook her head and crossed her arms over her chest. Patience was not one of her strong suits. "Okay, I've seen a picture of the Milky Way. It's enormous, huge . . . Oh, and once I saw a poster of it with an arrow pointing to this tiny speck, indistinguishable from a billion other tiny stars, and it said, '*You are here*.' Kinda blew me away not to see Earth or be able to make it out from that distance."

"What you saw was a powerful message. Do you honestly think there is absolutely no intelligent life outside of Earth, inside that Milky Way, or beyond that universe you saw in the poster?"

"Well, no," she answered truthfully. "I mean, in view of the fact that no evidence has proven otherwise, I guess it stands to reason there could be another form of intelligent life out there . . . somewhere . . . I guess." She'd never seen a ghost either, but that didn't mean they didn't exist. Plenty of reputable people had claimed to see one. She'd never time-traveled either, but nobody she knew ever claimed to be able—

"Casey, can you see the air?"

His question interrupted her mental rambling. She thought about it. "Well, I can see the wind."

"Yes, you see the effect of the air upon something. Air is invisible and yet the most vital ingredient of life, and you believe it is there because you feel it. Just as you feel there must be intelligence beyond this Earth."

"So . . . are you admitting you're from . . . from Venus?" Her heart was thudding against her rib cage as she waited for his answer.

"No, señorita, I am not."

She squinted her eyes suspiciously at him. "You're sure?"

He laughed. "Well, if I was, what kind of greeting do you think I would receive, being little and green?" he said, making a peace sign.

She had to laugh. Just watching this incredibly handsome man making a silly pantomime melted her fears. "Well, you wouldn't get a very warm one, that's for sure. Damn, we can't even stop being prejudiced within our own species. What a shame. We can't seem to get along with the neighbors we've got, let alone a new one."

"So why wouldn't 'little green men' be hesitant to introduce Earth into a universal community"—he paused—"if one should exist?"

She looked into his eyes and saw something that at the same time thrilled her and frightened her. "What are you?"

"I am someone just like you, Casey. There is little difference between us. I just see that the darkness serves. I'm not aligned with it, yet I can recognize even its ugliness is showing us the prejudice within most hearts, even for little green men."

"So you're saying that until we can get along with each other, make peace and play nicely, we can't go outside to play?"

He burst out laughing. "Not quite, but I do like your metaphor. It's appropriate." He settled himself and paused as another comfortable silence settled between them.

The sound of people talking in the house carried into the garden. It sounded as though preparations were being made for the evening meal.

"Now, your mentor believes you've had enough for the moment and I have a few errands I must do before dinner," he said, sitting up.

"Okay, nice talk about attitude," she said with a smile,

even though her mind was wondering where he wanted to run off to in the middle of the afternoon. The same place he went every night? Wherever it was, he wanted to leave her now.

He stood up and she rose with him.

"I believe we began speaking about self-worth. This long conversation was merely my way of suggesting that you strengthen your feelings of inner confidence so that others are not so easily able to break down or deflate your sense of well-being. You can be trusted now, Casey, to trust yourself." He nodded formally. "Señorita, as always . . . it has been a pleasure being in your presence."

She could only nod as he smiled and walked away.

Sheesh . . . Now, how was she supposed to integrate *that* conversation with the way her body was betraying her? It was too much for any woman. What was going on here? Was she falling in love with a man, a time traveler, who claimed she, too, was a time traveler, and maybe all they needed to do was enjoy themselves and throw their weight into it?

She needed a drink, and water just wouldn't do.

Luke left the Montoya household and walked toward the plaza, all the while going over the conversation with Casey in his head. He sighed deeply as a realization hit him. He was not only attracted to her physically, but her mind intrigued him as well. It had been many years since he'd had such a philosophical discussion with a woman, and a beautiful woman at that. It would be very easy to take their friendship to a deeper level, and that thought made him stop walking and stare at the ground in a moment of deep reflection. He'd better be very careful in his dealings with her, for something told him that Casey O'Reilly was going to challenge all his beliefs and all his resolve.

Still, he couldn't deny that he really enjoyed being in her presence, watching her move, hearing her laugh, seeing her eyes sparkle with mischief. She was quite a woman, and she captivated him.

Nine

*F*our days she had spent in his company, watching him, listening to him, falling in love with him. *Only four days.* What kind of person fell in love in four days? She'd heard of love at first sight, but didn't think she believed in it. And then her mind ran an image of her in the desert watching him leave that incredible spiraling light, walking up to her and folding his arms around her. Didn't a person have to get to know someone really well, before *knowing* he was the one?

Sipping her wine, Casey snuggled into bed and pondered this great matter in her life. She had left the courtyard, returned to her room, stripped off her clothes, and asked Juana for wine. When the woman had came back with a tray holding a decanter of ruby red wine, she'd thanked her and asked her to leave it. Changing into her nightgown, she had assured Juana she wasn't sick, but wanted to remain alone.

She had some heavy thinking to do.

First, she accepted that somehow, by some crazy method, she had time-traveled. She couldn't deny it any longer. It had happened. What she couldn't seem to accept and what she would love to deny was that she was falling in love. Could she stop it? Could she somehow turn off this valve once it was opened? And did she want to?

What was the point of falling in love with a man who could time-travel *out* of her life at any moment? Talk about lack of commitment! Could her heart stand it? Could her head stand it that this same man seemed to find someone or something so interesting he stayed away for half the night? What was the point?

The point was . . . her heart was pounding out a primal rhythm to her, telling her Luke might just be *the one*. Somehow, she had never felt like this in any relationship. How could she? For one thing, none of the other men was a time traveler, and none was so honest, so wise, so charming, so handsome, that she seemed to melt as soon as she saw him. It was pathetic. *She* was pathetic!

Luke said to trust herself.

Right. When her heart and her head were telling her to go for it, her fears were whispering that she was a fool even to try. What had he said this afternoon about fear? Not to add weight to it? That it was a very heavy frequency? Way too heavy to be carrying around when time-traveling. That *was* what he'd said!

Here she was, before the sun even set, in bed, exhausted, and she couldn't blame it on dancing. Her mind was whirling with confusion. What did she want? What had she always known she wanted out of life?

To be a mother . . .

She almost laughed out loud, but caught her bottom lip between her teeth to prevent it. She could just see herself walking up to Luke before their next dance lesson . . .

Excuse me, but I'm like falling hard for you, and I know it's insane, but I've always wanted to be a mother and I'm not getting any younger and I've tried this dating game and you're the first male I've met who seems like the perfect match. Would you mind donating some sperm and fathering my child?

This time she couldn't hold back a guffaw. It was madness!

It also made perfect sense.

She poured more wine and then settled back against the pillows to really think this through. Okay, he would be perfect, not just because he really did seem perfect but because he would be time-traveling, or something, and he . . . Why, it would be like going to a sperm bank without all the red tape and the cold clinical atmosphere!

He had more integrity than any human being she had ever met. He was intelligent, virile, in great physical health; he had dedicated his life to love, for crying out loud! There was also a hint of something around him, something that said if challenged, he would be a formidable opponent, and yet he was the gentlest man she had ever met. She really was falling in love with the man, so there had to be a bond established. He was perfect for her . . . and she wanted him.

Did it really matter whether he wanted her for a lifetime? What had he said today about worrying right out of the present? She had spent her entire life worrying whether she'd done the right thing, worrying over the consequences of every action as though some dark force was going to confront her in the future and slam her behind the knees, making her fall on her face. She couldn't do it anymore. She was right here, right now, there was no past, and she hadn't a clue about the future, so she might as well collect some of those presents Luke had talked about today in the garden.

Now, how exactly did one approach a man and ask him to donate genes?

She fell asleep picturing Luke in the back of that wagon, playing with Elena. He loved children and they seemed to love him. He would say yes; he had to. It might take some effort on her part, to go beyond herself, her *old* self, and do what Rosa said . . . discover who she really was now, but she could do this if it meant finally fulfilling her only true desire. To be the mother she wanted to be, she was first going to have to become the woman she was always meant to become.

To hell with worry, was her last thought.

It was exciting!

She had no idea how exciting her life was about to become. In retrospect, she was quite unprepared for the very next evening . . . She sat across the dinner table from a dark-haired, single man who seemed to be flirting with her, and he wasn't Luke. Earlier in the day, nursing a sick headache, she'd heard a commotion in the hallway and was later informed that Don Miguel Cortez had arrived all the way from Spain for Rosalinda's *quinceñera*. Juana had hinted Don Miguel might even be a suitor for the hand of young Rosalinda.

Casey had expected Don Miguel to be young, in his twenties, yet the man with the slicked-back hair was at least as old as she, and Casey could see that Rosa wasn't too thrilled with this first prospect. The girl was polite, even coquettish at times, yet underneath her actions it was clear there was no deeper interest. Casey was secretly glad since Rosa deserved her one true love, as she liked to remind anyone who would listen. Maybe the man sensed he wasn't making headway with the teenager and had turned his attention to her now. He was looking directly at her and saying something and . . . Shit, now she was expected to respond. Everyone, even Luke, was looking at her with expectation.

She smiled down the length of the table and whispered, "I must apologize. I was daydreaming." Might as well be truthful, rather than get herself into more trouble.

Everyone grinned at her honesty, and Doña Isabela announced, "Señorita O'Reilly has been indisposed today." She turned to Casey and smiled. "We are happy merely by your presence tonight. Thank you for gracing our table when you are not fully recovered."

Wow . . . what a nice save, Casey thought, and smiled with gratitude. "*Gracias*, Doña Isabela. I am much better now."

"*Que bueno. Con tu permiso,*" the woman said, nodding and turning her attention back to Don Miguel. "Then, with Señorita O'Reilly's permission, I will answer your question. She comes to us from her family. She has been away on a sabbatical for many years and is spending this time with us now until she can be reunited with them. We are honored to have her with us, especially as it appears she will be here for Rosalinda's *quinceñera*."

"Ah," the man said, nodding his head as if the entire thing made any kind of sense.

Casey glanced down the table to Luke. He was calmly cutting his meat, without a shred of concern.

Don Miguel cleared his throat and spoke again. His voice was heavy with a Spanish accent, and Casey could tell he wanted to be sure of his words. "I understand, Señorita O'Reilly. I find that travel within this country is most taxing. But tell me, this sabbatical that Doña Isabela speaks of . . . That would be spiritual in nature, yes?"

He sipped his wine and smiled into her eyes. Casey wasn't sure what to say.

"Couldn't everything be spiritual in nature, Don Miguel . . . from a certain viewpoint?" Luke interjected, as he intensely examined a roasted red pepper with the tip of his fork. "Even purchasing horses from the Indians for your farm in Mexico. Wouldn't you agree, señor?"

"I would say that is business, Señor d'Séraphin. There is nothing of a spiritual nature involved with such matters."

Luke shrugged and smiled. "I suppose you could be right. Pardon my interruption, *mi amigo*. In what part of Mexico is your farm located? Don Felipe tells me it is most beautiful."

"The western part, señor. It has been in my family for generations, even surviving the French occupation, and yet this is the first opportunity I have had to visit. I am most anxious to bring it back to a proper state."

The man kept talking about his farm, and Casey could only stare at her plate of food. Luke had smoothly turned the conversation around and had saved her from telling a lie. Again she felt her heart expand toward the man. She was like a moth being drawn to the light. Could she trust herself to survive this if she went through with her plan? Didn't most moths die? She'd already been hit by lightning and had survived. Why not go for the whole shooting match? What the hell did she have to lose at this point?

And she had everything to gain.

She focused her attention and was so proud of Luke as he held his own with this slightly pompous guest, while still remaining charming. He was quite a man and she was more than ever determined to ask him. If he said no . . . he said no. That was it. She could accept it. She might be embarrassed, but she wouldn't die of it since, once they returned, she'd never have to see him again. That thought made her stomach muscles clench with regret. She had to stop thinking about this stuff and pay attention.

Rosalinda was going to sing for them after dinner, and Casey was really looking forward to hearing the talented girl. She realized as she glanced down to Rosa that she was going to miss her when she left. In such a short time she felt like she had made a friend.

Her attention didn't seem to be required as the talk of Mexico seemed to hold the conversation. She was glad she had an excuse not to converse as Don Felipe spoke of his extensive importing business. Even though the discussion was pleasant, she wanted to be alone with her thoughts now more than ever. With each day, she was becoming more and more sure that she had been sent back in time for a reason. What was it Luke had said? She was on this adventure for a purpose? Stuff like this just didn't happen all the time, and since it had, then maybe she should begin to wonder how it might all fit together in her life.

Here she meets this fantastic man, back in time, and has the perfect opportunity to get pregnant without anyone ever finding out who the father is or where she met him. What could be more perfect?

In the back of her mind was the nagging thought that perfect would be him loving her, but she pushed it back even further. He didn't have to love her exclusively forever and ever, and with a time traveler, that could be a *mighty* long time! He already respected her. She'd gotten that far. Suddenly Casey realized this was the first time she had truly been the pursuer and not the pursued. It was an odd feeling. She had dangled out her line a few times with some of the best bait she knew how to conjure and had had a few serious bites, but this . . . this was going after *the* catch of all time.

What if she lost? Fear crept up her back, making her shiver.

"Are you chilled, señorita?" Doña Isabela asked, calling over a servant with her raised fingers.

"I'm fine," Casey answered, even though she wasn't. What if she lost out on this opportunity? It might never come again in her lifetime.

Doña Isabela whispered something to a servant and turned back to her guests. "Perhaps, *damas y caballeros,* with everyone's permission, we will have a dessert after our concert?"

Everyone agreed and the men pulled back the chairs for the ladies. Couples seemed to pair up, Don Felipe and his wife, Rosalinda and Don Miguel, and Luke held out his arm to her. Her smile was hard to keep under control as she accepted the invitation to walk with him into *la sala,* the large living room with the piano. There was more than enough room for all to sit down, and Casey was about to sit the farthest away when a servant handed her a beautifully embroidered shawl that looked lovely with her borrowed pink gown.

"Gracias," she whispered to the man, who nodded and walked away.

"May I help?" Luke asked, taking the shawl from her and holding it out.

She turned her back and he gently draped the material across her shoulders. Pulling the edges closer, she smiled her thanks. "That's the fourth time you've saved me in as many days. Thank you, Luke."

"The shawl was Doña Isabela's idea, not—"

"You know what I mean," she whispered, as she watched the others move about the room. She noticed Manuel discreetly slip in through a side doorway then sit on a stool by the end of the piano. "I mean, Don Miguel almost had me with that spiritual question."

"Ah, that . . . You're welcome, but I'm not keeping score." He paused and looked at her with a grin, adding, "Are you?"

"What? Of course not." She shrugged, answering in a voice she hoped wouldn't give her away. "I was just thanking you and making polite conversation until the concert began."

"Are you warm enough?" Don Felipe asked in passing.

Gliding into the room on her husband's arm, Doña Isabela added, "I can have a fire lit."

She held up her hand to them. "Please, everyone . . . I'm fine. Enjoy yourselves now. You are wonderful hosts and I thank you for your hospitality." She couldn't seem to say it enough. She really was so grateful to be in their home and accepted as a family friend, and all on the good word of this man at her side.

Don Felipe looked pleased and Doña Isabela affectionately patted her arm as she and her husband passed.

"They're a happy couple, aren't they?" she whispered to Luke.

"Yes, they are. I enjoy their company."

"So do I. They're great examples of a good union." She threw the line out there to see if there was any interest.

"I agree, and their children reflect it."

Oh, that was *big interest*, maybe even a bite!

"I think I would like to talk to you about that the next time we are . . . How did you put it? Mentoring?"

"The subject of children?" He sounded surprised.

"The topic of a happy union producing happy children."

"Hmm . . ." He grinned. "That's sounds like it would be a most interesting topic, señorita. I warn you, it might get pretty philosophical."

She cleared her throat and grinned. "*Get*? Excuse me, but every discussion I have with you turns into a philosophical discussion."

"And that bothers you?" he asked as Rosalinda walked toward them.

"No—"

She had no time to answer further as the teenager grabbed her hand and whispered, "*Ay,* Casey, Don Miguel . . . he is much too old and I know he isn't my true love, but tonight my mother insists that I sing this song.

Don Miguel will think I am singing to him and I will never be rid of the man. You must help me!"

Casey, who had thought the whole thing funny until the last sentence, pulled her shawl more snugly around her and said, "What do you mean? How can I help you?"

"If you could sing in Spanish, I would ask you to perform a duet and—"

"Yeah, well . . . I can't," Casey interrupted to stop that crazy thought.

"I know," Rosa declared with a hiss, and lowered her voice. Leaning in, she whispered, "You must catch Don Miguel's eyes and . . . and distract him."

"*What?* I can't distract him!" Casey declared, and was acutely aware of Luke's body beginning to move with suppressed laughter. She glared up at him. This was not funny. This kid meant it!

"But you must, señorita!" Rosa pleaded. "My true love is coming to my *quinceñera*, I know this . . . and I also know it is not Don Miguel Cortez! *Por favor*, Casey. You must help me."

"Rosa *mía*."

They heard Rosa's mother call her, and Casey quickly whispered, "Oh, I'll try, but I'm not promising anything!"

"*Gracias!*" Rosa whispered, and turned to her mother, standing at the piano.

Watching as Doña Isabela sat down in front of the large instrument and began adjusting her gown, Casey whispered to Luke, "Can you believe that little imp?"

His voice still sounded amused. "Yes, I can believe her. She is determined. You have to admire that."

"Yes, determined to get me in trouble with her!" Even though her voice was low, she couldn't stifle the frustration. "What the hell am I supposed to do now?"

"Distract the very proper gentleman from Castile, Spain. He has shown some interest, in case you hadn't noticed."

She glanced up at his expression. There was none, save amusement.

"You're enjoying this, aren't you?"

"It has the potential to be quite a performance, I think. Perhaps I should take my seat now to throughly enjoy it."

"Oh no . . . you're not leaving my side now," she declared. "I'm going to need you here so Don Miguel doesn't think *I'm* interested in him. Think you can pull off an interested party there, Mr. Time Traveler?" It was an ambiguous question, and she awaited his answer.

He looked into her eyes and she swore there was interest. He didn't say anything for so long that she finally asked, "You just said you were going to sit down. You did intend to stay, didn't you? I mean, I know you have someplace to go, since you always leave after dinner and—"

"I'm staying," Luke murmured. "Now, sit down and I shall stand here, behind your chair, and lean against the wall."

"You won't leave?"

"Trust me." He smiled, looking directly into her eyes, then added, "I won't leave you."

"Okay," she said, walking around the chair. She smiled at the others and realized they were waiting for her to take her seat. *I trust you*, she mouthed to Luke, right before she turned and sat down.

Trust . . . It was becoming a pretty big issue in her life lately.

Ten

The soft romantic strains of Manuel's guitar accompanied Doña Isabela's beautiful melody on the piano as Rosa began singing in a sweet, innocent voice. It was lovely, and Casey would have enjoyed it even more had she understood Spanish.

"The sun announces your arrival. The flowers open for your enjoyment. The trees cradle my joy as I reach out for your love."

Casey almost leaped in fright when Luke began whispering the words behind her. She saw Don Miguel glance at her and smile, and she couldn't help smiling back, especially since she was very pleased to hear those words coming from Luke's lips . . . even if they were a mere translation. Don Miguel wouldn't take that as an opening with Luke so close, would he? How could she have agreed to distract the man, especially with the man she really wanted standing so close to her that she could almost *feel* him?

What a situation!

Breathe, she reminded herself. *Now, breathe again!*

It was difficult to concentrate as Luke's soft whisper seemed to vibrate the nerve endings of her ear . . .

"Birds sing your praises. The sky receives them and sends them back with . . . with passion on their wings," he translated, stumbling just a bit on the word *passion.*

Good sign, Casey thought and, since he couldn't see her, smiled with a secret satisfaction. Shocked, she watched as Don Miguel's eyes widened as he seemed to catch her meaning and secretly smile at her!

No, wait, no . . . her mind seemed to scream. Wrong man!

"The wind caresses your heart with a gentle breeze and the moment is now, for all eternity stands waiting for our love."

Oh yeah . . . Now, what were the chances of Rosalinda singing this song and having Luke translate it for her? Pretty slim, she thought, and took it as another sign she was on track, that she was moving in the right direction with asking Luke to father her child. And if this took a serious turn toward the romantic . . . well, all the better.

Why, she would make the best use of this time-traveling gig. She hadn't asked for it, but now that she was here, she could see how it all fit together perfectly. And Luke d'Séraphin was the perfect candidate for fathering her child!

Now, how to convince him of it? Hell, how to get up the nerve even to approach the subject? But then, he'd said he would talk to her about unions and children, and somehow, someway, she had to steer the conversation around to fit her purpose.

She tried to listen to the words Luke was translating, but her mind was too excited now to really concentrate, other than registering that it was a song about love and the seasons of nature corresponding to the seasons of the heart. Well, at thirty-one, it was her season now. This was an opportunity she wasn't going to miss.

A feeling of being watched came over her and she glanced up to find Don Miguel staring at her. He held a white handkerchief in his hand and dabbed at his lips, as though to hide his smile from the others in the room.

Oh jeez . . . now what? The very last thing she wanted was Don Miguel's attention. She could almost cringe at the pompous man's flirtations. Not that he wasn't handsome. He was. Though compared to Luke, any man paled, at least in her estimation. She turned her attention to Rosa as the teenager finished her lovely song and immediately clapped her hands in appreciation. The rest of the group quickly followed suit, and Rosalinda blushed prettily as she gracefully curtsied. Casey glanced at Don Miguel and saw something in his eyes as he turned his attention to Rosa, something that seemed predatory, and it immediately scared her. She didn't want to see Rosa hurt.

Casey turned quickly as Luke extended his hand to her. Rising from the chair, she said, "Thank you for the translation. It is a very pretty song."

"Yes, it is," he agreed with a sexy grin. "Love is very important to this culture."

She nodded and brought the shawl more closely around her. "Perhaps that's why you enjoy it so much."

Luke tilted his head, as though trying to grasp her meaning. "Enjoy this time period, this culture?"

"That, and the whole subject of love," she answered. Casey smiled at the small group and added, "I've never been around a man, any male, who was so comfortable with the concept."

"You think love is a concept?" he asked with a chuckle.

Sheesh, he was so damn handsome, and when he laughed, the lines around his eyes made them almost sparkle. It was quite a picture, and Casey tried to halt the rush of warmth that was quickly spreading through her veins. She wanted to run her fingers through his dark curly hair, to feel the texture of his lips upon her own. She simply *had* to get a grip, and she clenched her fist around the shawl to stop the crazy urges. "Okay, it's more than a concept," she conceded. "It's just that most men tend to shy away from speaking about it, and you don't seem intimidated at all."

He leaned in closer to her, and Casey inhaled the clean, citrusy scent of him.

"I will tell you a secret," he whispered with a provocative grin.

She couldn't help grinning back. "Oh, goody, a secret. Do tell."

"Most men crave love just as much as women do. It's a natural instinct to seek love, isn't it, from the time we are children? Why should it change as we age? A man's hopes and desires don't lessen as he grows older. We celebrate the warrior, the athlete. Why not the lover?"

Why not indeed? She remembered driving in the rental car and thinking almost the same thing. More than ever, she thought he would make the perfect father for her child. "I like that," she murmured, staring into his deep brown eyes. "Celebrating the lover in the male."

An extraordinary thing happened then, some shock of realization, as the two of them stared into each other's eyes and Casey thought she was being drawn into a place she had never been, a place that seemed to pull her with a wildly hot, yet free, abandon. Her heart began beating faster and a deeply penetrating sexual surge rushed through her body, inviting her to go even deeper and close the distance between them, as Luke lowered his gaze to her lips and inhaled sharply, causing his chest to expand toward her aching breasts.

He would kiss her. At any moment, he would kiss her. A woman knew these things . . .

"Perdóname, señorita," he muttered in a hoarse whisper. "I must take my leave."

She merely blinked in shocked dismay as she watched him brush past her and walk up to Doña Isabela, who was rising from her seat in front of the piano.

How could Luke just walk away and leave her . . . like that!

He bowed over the woman's hand and said, *"Muchas gracias, mil gracias,* my most gracious hostess, for another delightful evening." He then turned to Felipe. *"Con tu permiso,* I beg your leave, *amigo,* as I must immediately attend to some personal business in town."

Don Felipe rose, smiling, and nodded. "Of course, Señor Luke. Thank you for joining us tonight."

Luke turned to Rosa and took her hand. "A most beautiful song, señorita. *Gracias.*"

Rosa looked pleased by his compliment and whispered, *"Buenas noches,* Señor Luke."

"Buenas noches," Luke said to the room, and quietly slipped through the door.

Casey was stunned. How could he just up and leave? What was it that was drawing him every night? It must be very powerful . . . *she* must be a very powerful attraction, for now Casey was convinced it was a woman. It had to be a woman. A sinking feeling lodged itself in her belly and she tried to hold a pleasant smile. She wasn't successful.

Rosa came up to her. "What is wrong, señorita?" the girl asked. "You did not enjoy my song?"

Casey looked at the teenager. She had to banish all thoughts of Luke and what had just happened from her mind. "Oh, yes, Rosa. It was lovely and I didn't know your voice was so beautiful. You certainly are a talented young woman."

"*Gracias*." Rosa leaned forward as though to kiss her cheek. "And you did well with Don Miguel. I am indebted to you."

"Now, listen, kiddo . . . about Don Miguel—"

"Sing us another song, *mi hija*," Don Felipe called out, interrupting anything more Casey might have said.

Rosa smiled at her father. "Oh no, Papi, *por favor* . . . I am weary. Today at choir practice, Sister Bernardina had us singing so long my voice is tired. You sing. Remember *los cantos* you used to sing to Marguerita and me when we were children?"

Don Felipe grinned at his daughter. "You have most certainly mastered the art of distracting one from his purpose. You know it has been years since I have sung."

"All the more reason to resume, Papi."

Don Felipe looked around the room at his guests as though they, too, should be amazed at what they were hearing. "*Tú eres una niña imposible,* Rosalinda," her father said with jovial affection. Casey watched everyone smile, even as a sly smile crept up onto Rosa's cheeks.

"I am not an impossible child, *Papi*. I am a woman now, and the possibilities for me are endless," the young girl retorted, still grinning.

Suddenly Casey found herself clearing her throat. She needed some space for clarity of thinking. "I am terribly sorry, but I must ask if I may be excused." She looked to her hosts with a smile of apology. "I find I am tired, after all . . ."

Doña Isabela rushed to her and clasped her hand. "*Ciertamente*, most certainly, Señorita Casey. Do you need assistance to your room?"

"Oh no, thank you, Doña Isabela. I can see myself upstairs."

Both dons rose quickly. *"Buenas noches,* Senorita O'Reilly," Felipe said, bowing to her formally.

"Mucho gusto, Señorita O'Reilly," Miguel added, clicking his heels in an extremely proper manner before Casey could even respond. "I am very happy to have made your acquaintance and I look forward to the pleasure of seeing you again." He smiled, taking her hand and adding, "When you are feeling better, señorita."

"Yes . . . well, thank you, Don Miguel. *Gracias,*" Casey nearly stammered as she curtsied slightly to them all.

Rosalinda came up to her quickly. *"Gracias, hermana,"* she said, taking Casey's hand and leading her out of the room while adding, "I think it worked. Don Miguel hardly noticed me at all tonight," she confided with glee.

"Believe me, little sister," Casey whispered the returned endearment. "I want to talk to you about that later, okay?"

"Okay," the young girl mimicked with a smile.

"Buenas noches," Casey called back to everyone as Rosalinda left her in the foyer.

Casey brushed thoughts of Don Miguel's ambiguous advances to get to know her better from her mind. There was something more gnawing at her, and with each step she ascended, it became more persistent. She was really interested in where Luke disappeared to every night. "Personal business" . . . What was that all about? she wondered. Was he meeting with some woman he couldn't bear to be away from? Was he gambling at one of those saloons by the plaza? Where *did* that man go?

Juana was sitting in the chair dozing when Casey walked into her bedroom. The light had been lit and the older woman had her arms crossed over her ample chest. Casey tried to be quiet as she closed the door and nearly jumped out of her skin when she heard the low voice behind . . .

"You are retiring early, señorita? Does your head still ache?"

"Yes," she answered, spinning around. "A little."

"Ahh," the woman answered, pushing herself up from the chair. "It must have been a long time since you drank so much *vino*, eh?"

It took Casey a moment to piece together what Juana meant and then she nodded. It was the convent thing again. Sheesh . . . she was getting tired of trying to live up to an ex-nun's reputation. "It's been quite a while," she said, and realized it was the truth. She had never been much of a drinker, even when she was younger.

"I will fix you a . . . how do you call it . . . a potion? Yes, that is it, a potion for your aches." The woman came up to her and turned her around, beginning to unlace the bodice of the gown. "Tomorrow I will wash this dress and speak with Doña Isabela about what you are to wear to the *quinceñera*."

Casey spun around. "Oh, no . . . Doña Isabela has already been more than generous to me. Please don't ask her for anything else."

Juana turned her back to the door and continued unlacing her undergarments. "*Ay*, la doña is very blessed indeed, and she won't mind sharing. Besides, she would want you to look your best as her houseguest. Juana will take care of you."

Casey sighed, realizing that it was useless to argue with the woman. Staring at the ornate carvings on the door, she asked in a thoughtful voice, "Where do you think Señor Luke goes every night?"

"That I do not know, señorita. Now step out of the skirt."

She did as she was asked and began undoing the tiny hooks at her belly. It would be good to breathe without the tight, corsetlike bodice. "He must be going to see someone, some friends. He goes every night."

"It would appear so," Juana answered, throwing the skirt onto the bed and then opening up the wardrobe.

The woman brought out a fresh cotton nightgown, and Casey added the bodice to the skirt on the bed and walked to the table under the window. She poured some fresh water into the large bowl and then splashed her face over and over, wanting to wash away the sick feeling in the pit of her stomach. She also wished she could wipe away the annoying thought of Luke being so drawn to someone else that he couldn't wait to leave.

"You don't look so good, señorita," Juana said, interrupting Casey's mental list of physical ills. "I should bring the potion now," the woman added with a worried tone.

Casey stopped splashing and, keeping her head over the bowl, said, "I don't need a potion, Juana. I'll be fine now."

"You are certain, señorita?" The concern in the woman's voice was obvious.

Grabbing a cloth, Casey held it to her face and nodded. She patted her skin and said, "All I need is a good night's sleep."

Juana smiled sadly. "Your heart is heavy."

"No, I'm fine . . . It . . . it's the headache. That's all."

Shaking her head, Juana said, "*Mi hija*, you cannot fool me. I know of these things. I can feel the heaviness of your heart."

She could only stare at the older woman, who was clutching her chest in empathy.

"Really, I'm fine."

The woman's eyes squinted in obvious disbelief. "You ask about Señor Luke . . . and your heart is heavy. I tell you, he is interested in you . . . as you are interested in him, but you cannot trust this old woman." She paused, gesturing with her hands in the air, as if to accept Casey's interruption. It didn't come. "*Bueno*." The woman's voice told of her resignation as she turned toward the bed. "I will allow you to sleep. Maybe your dreams will tell you more." She looked back to Casey with a sincere smile and added, "I pray you feel better in the morning, Señorita Casey."

Casey murmured a slow thank-you as she watched the woman pick up the gown and carry it to the door.

"Buenas noches."

"Buenas noches, Juana . . . and thank you."

The woman nodded and closed the door after her.

Casey stared at the door for a few moments, realizing she wanted to run after Juana and ask her to come back, to tell her all she knew about her heart and about Luke's interest. Sadly, she couldn't. She was frozen with indecision. Until she found out where Luke went every night, she didn't know what to do about her heart.

Changing into the nightgown, Casey figured she hadn't any right to feel jealousy. She had no rights concerning Luke. As she pulled the soft cotton material over her naked body, she wondered why she cared anyway. She wasn't the jealous type, and she'd always believed that if someone didn't want to be with her, why in the world would she fight to keep a relationship together? Just the idea of someone being around her who would rather be somewhere else was not in the least bit appealing . . . so why now?

She pulled the pins out of her hair and picked up the antique brush. Turning back to the mirror, she looked at her reflection and tried to be impartial. She wasn't ugly. Her body wasn't too bad. In fact, now that she was back in a time when women were allowed to look like women instead of adolescent boys . . . she looked pretty darn good. She'd never even known she had an hourglass figure until she began wearing that pink gown with its tight corseted bodice.

She was passable.

Suddenly Luke's words seemed to replay in her mind.

You really don't know your self-worth, do you?

She took a deep breath and looked again at herself.

She was better than passable. She was an attractive woman. It was okay to admit that, even if only to herself. Years of being brought up to deny one's self in the cloak of humility came crashing in on her and she actually felt guilty for the admittance.

"Wow . . ."

The word hung in the room as she stared into her own eyes, wide now with an intense realization. She really had been denying herself. Not that she was model-pretty. She wasn't. She was more real, more natural, more *her*. She didn't have to measure up to anyone else's standards to admit she had a nice smile, pretty blue eyes, a decently rounded figure. Why was it that fashion designers wanted women to look underdeveloped, like young boys? And she had bought in to it! She had been embarrassed because she'd thought she was twenty pounds overweight and had starved herself to lose ten pounds before she gave up feeling like crap and just accepted that she would never measure up to society's standards. What freedom now to just *be* herself, however she looked. There were no magazines telling her what needed to be improved, no commercials showing her how inadequate she was compared to models. There was just freedom.

Juana's words came back to her, telling her that Luke was interested. She immediately reached for the oil lamp. Turning down the wick until there was only a slight yellowish glow cast in the room, Casey replaced it on the table and then crawled into bed. She pulled the coverlet up to her shoulders and stared at the wardrobe.

She would simply have to find out where Luke went every night before she could proceed further down this path!

Until she knew if his heart was turned in another direction, she couldn't dwell any more on the thought of him fathering her child. It was a pretty wild shot anyway, but if he was seeing a woman, she certainly couldn't ask him.

Tomorrow night she would slip out of the house through the wardrobe's secret passageway and follow Luke d'Séraphin. It was the only thing she could do. She could take it . . . if she just knew.

It was the not knowing that would drive her crazy.

The next day she began slowly to develop a plausible reason for another early retirement. Although her body was simply vibrating with anticipation and worry, she tried to appear listless and tired. She even told Luke she didn't feel like practicing. There was no way she was going to be in his arms again until she knew whether another woman was also occupying them during the night. Casey told herself he had every right to see whomever he wished. She had no claim on his affections, for it was her own desire to be in his presence that had brought on this yearning and thus her plan for obtaining his genes.

Some might think it was madness, yet she couldn't seem to help falling in love with a man who had made no overtly romantic moves on her, at least none that couldn't be explained away by a dance of passion . . . and yet that dance was going way beyond the courtyard for her. It was taking her *way* out there . . . into the future. Before she continued on *that* trip, she had a few things to clear up. Primary was her need to know what drew him away in the night.

She had to remind herself that it was vampires who couldn't be seen during the day, and then almost giggled at the crazy notion. Her laughter ceased as a thought crossed her mind. He was away a lot during the night, though. She had to shake herself as fear raced through her body.

Luke as anything evil?

No. That thought was merely her fears again, projecting her away from her objective. She wasn't afraid of Luke. She was afraid of her heart, and whether it could stand the disappointment should she follow him tonight and see him in another woman's arms. No matter what the outcome, she had to know . . .

That evening, she excused herself from the table early and everyone seemed to understand as she apologized and left the room. Everyone except Luke. He appeared concerned, yet puzzled. Casey didn't even look at him. She didn't want to give him an opportunity to *read* her again. Not tonight.

Once back in her room, she quickly changed into the black skirt and grabbed the black shawl she had borrowed from Rosa. She stood in front of the mirror and wrapped the material around her head, throwing the end over her shoulder as she had seen the other women do. She quickly pulled the edges of the top down to cover her blonde hair and rearranged the sides to hide most of her face. It was the best she could do. She had to hurry and get out of this house to be waiting by the front gate when Luke left, something he could be doing right now.

She had already informed Juana that she wanted to be alone tonight, and although the woman had looked at her suspiciously, she had nodded her acceptance. As an added precaution, Casey hurried to the bed and turned the long pillows sideways and covered them with the blanket. Sheesh, she hadn't done this since she was a teenager, sneaking out of the house with Amy to go into Philadelphia to a dance club by the river.

Casey refused to think about it anymore. If she did, she would lose her nerve. Right now being young seemed more reasonable than being a so-called adult. She blew out the flame in the lamp and walked over to the wardrobe.

Opening the heavy door, she cringed at the slight sound,

sure that Juana or someone else was standing in the hallway and could hear her. Letting out her breath, she pushed
aside her borrowed clothes and entered the huge wardrobe.
In the dark, her fingers felt the back and sides of it until she
touched a small notch in the wood. As she pressed it, it
released and slipped a tiny bit to the right. Using both
hands, she pushed harder and the back of the wardrobe
seemed to disappear into the side wall. Taking a gulp of
fresh air, Casey closed the front wardrobe door after her,
rearranged her clothes, and then stepped into the concealed
passageway. She then pushed on the wall to her right again
and the panel slipped back. Not wanting to search for it
when she returned, she didn't press on it to latch it. Better
to risk being caught then to be stuck in a damn wall until
morning.

She might be acting like a teenager, but she wasn't without some common sense!

Right . . .

Walking through a wall in the pitch black, feeling the
rough adobe as she made her way blindly down a secret
passageway, was *sensible*? She simply had to somehow get
back to Amy and tell her all this. It was such a wild ride,
somebody had to hear it!

That's it, she told herself. Think of Amy. Do not think
about this closed space that seemed even smaller without
Rosa's guidance. Just keep moving. There was no turning
back now. If she got through this, the worst was over.
Everything else would be a piece of cake.

Well, she might have a tough time if she saw Luke in a
woman's arms, but she'd prepared herself and she had to
know the truth. She would accept it and wish him happiness.

Of course, she wasn't about to admit that she wanted his
happiness to coincide with her own, but it was enough to
know she was ready to face whatever awaited her. She
might be disappointed, but she wouldn't be destroyed.

It wasn't like she was *in* love with him.

She was just falling in love with him. It hadn't happened yet.

Had it?

She suddenly felt so claustrophobic that she hurried down the passageway like a sand crab, sideways and frantic. When her hand felt the outside door, she almost cried out her relief. Biting her tongue, Casey searched the frame around it for a depression, anything to release the door and set her free.

Something inside of her said to calm down, that in her frantic searching she would never find it. She needed to take a deep breath and yet it felt like all her breaths were on the other side of that door, fresh and clear and—

There it was again. Fear. She recognized it and remembered Luke said it was a heavy frequency. Okay, she needed some peace now, some calm, or she might lose it, and she was so close now and—

Stopping her desperate thoughts, Casey inhaled the stale air and slowly began moving her hand over the frame again . . . this time methodically feeling each inch of the wood. There! There was the depression. Relief swept through her as she pushed on it with all her might and the door clicked open. She almost stumbled out into the night air and gulped in huge breaths as she tore the shawl away from her face.

Her heart pounding, she bent over slightly to fill her lungs more fully. After several deep breaths, she leaned against the wall and tried to get her bearings. The heavy limbs of the tree hid her and she thought it was fortunate the courtyard had not been used for supper tonight. Ever since Don Miguel had arrived, they'd been eating the evening meal more formally. Briefly grateful for the man's influence this night and how it served her, Casey turned around and closed the door to the passageway. She readjusted the shawl over her head and pulled it closer as she left the safety of the house and approached the garden. If she could keep to the shrubs, she would be at the back gate in less than a minute. No one was outside, and Casey hoped all were still busy serving the meal. She had very little time before Luke excused himself, if he hadn't already. Her last thought made her risk it all as she ran for the wall. The last time she had done this, she'd been with Rosalinda, and even the girl had hesitated to walk around this town without a chaperone. Well, she wasn't about to let anyone else mess with her, especially not until she found out the information that could change her life. She was a woman on a mission now. Somehow, she knew, nothing in her life would ever again be the same.

Lifting the heavy wooden latch, she opened the back gate very slowly and slipped out of the walled property. Casey closed it and was grateful it stayed closed without locking.

She ran around the property and hid at the corner, slipping into the shadows with a good view of the front gate. From her vantage point, she wouldn't be able to miss Luke when he left the house. If she could keep to the shadows, she should be able to follow him without being detected. For once, she was glad there were no streetlights. Suddenly her attention was drawn to two men, one of them Luke, walking down the road. She pressed her body against a large old tree trunk, wanting to blend into the bark, to disappear and just watch.

Yes, nothing in her life would ever be the same after this night.

She would *know* . . .

As she made her way through the narrow and dusty streets, ducking in and around people, the pungent aroma of liquor and cigar smoke that filled her senses almost made her choke. Saloons and cantinas flowed with men and women laughing and cajoling each other in drunken happiness. It certainly was a scene, with gay piano music tinkling a different tune from each bar she passed—and there seemed to be plenty in this small town, with the roaring cheers of gamblers inside each one. Sauntering cowboys in full regalia—shiny, clinking boot spurs, holsters with guns, and fringed chaps—tipped their hats with a "Howdy, ma'am" when she used them momentarily for cover along her way.

In her mind she began rationalizing the surrounding chaos by realizing television and movies hadn't yet been invented, so this was the way of leisure. Suddenly she was acutely reminded of the severity of it all when she heard a loud pop and instinctively hunkered against a wall. She watched as a crowd gathered along the sidewalk. An inebriated cowboy had shot off his pistol and was laughing, probably to express his merriment with the moment, but he was immediately subdued by the local law enforcement officers. The Santa Fe night life, circa 1878, she mentally mused. Yes, it was reality for her now, and the guns were really loaded.

Yet she would not be deterred from this quest. Her mysterious prey was not far ahead as she slipped from shadow to shadow, keeping a safe distance from him, his awareness, and his uncanny ability to sense her. Luke d'Séraphin was some guy to warrant her obsession, and she knew she was stalking him, but she just had to know what drew him out into the night. She needed to know everything she could about the man before she could ask him to father a child with her.

Slamming her back against an alley wall, she stood panting, and wondered if he'd seen her when he turned and looked behind him just before entering the bar. Okay, that was where she must be . . . the woman who had enchanted him, this incredible man who was . . . well, he wasn't of this earthly stuff, she had to admit to herself. He was heavenly, and that was one of the reasons she believed his genes would be the best other half in creating the child she wanted to mother. And this other woman who obviously had captured his attention, to the point of him leaving even his good friend Don Felipe and family, well, she must really be something. Casey resigned herself to the inevitable . . . It was now or never, and all her answers were just beyond the swinging sash doors of a bawdy saloon. Talk about your irony. She had to laugh.

Pulling the shawl tightly around her face again, she drew in her greatest breath of courage, quickly turned the corner of her hideaway, and stepped right into the chest of a young man. "Omph!" she exhaled, with the wind nearly knocked out of her. "I'm sorry . . . I mean, excuse me," she stammered.

Bursts of laughter resounded as she looked up to see the face of the young fellow.

"Pardon me, ma'am." He nodded and smiled a big-toothed grin.

"Billy, yer such a galoot," his friend chuckled as he picked up and brushed off the hat that was knocked off the young man's head when they collided.

"Yeah, Kid. Why don't you watch where yer goin'?" another voice snickered as the group moved on, still chortling about the incident.

"Sheesh," she said aloud, pulling herself back together. Wait a minute. She mentally and physically froze. *Billy . . . the Kid*? Naw. She shook the insane thought from her rattled brain. *Okay, gather your wits again, girl,* she silently commanded herself, and forced her feet to continue their walk toward the saloon doors and her destiny . . .

"Gracias, amigos!" Luke's voice suddenly called out as

he made his way through the throngs of characters lining the sidewalk . . . and right toward her.

"Ohmahgawd," she blurted, and threw her gaze to the ground as she spun around. Deadlocked where she was, the moments felt like an eternity as he passed right behind her. Had he noticed her? Should she look up? Was he gone yet? Turning ever so slightly, she peeked one eye out from behind the shawl that shielded her, to see him stepping around the corner of the very alley where she'd been hiding minutes earlier. Jeez, she was beginning to think this whole scenario was a sitcom for the gods, and she was the starring clown. *Gimme a break,* she almost said aloud, looking up to the starry night sky. It really didn't matter if anybody was listening . . . Just the absolute absurdity of her situation seemed to blend quite well in the moment.

Okay, so what was going on now? He needed a quick drink first before going to . . . to *her*? Casey had talked herself into believing that it was a woman. He had passed by the rest of the bars, the gambling houses. What else was drawing him every night? It had to be a woman.

Nothing, not anything she could possibly imagine, could have prepared her for the answer she so desperately sought and thought she could handle.

The sitcom of her life continued . . .

Eleven

$\mathcal{S}$he watched from the shadows as Luke went into a run-down building and closed the door behind him. Puzzled, Casey kept taking deep breaths to calm down. What kind of woman was he meeting there, through an alley behind the big church? As bizarre as that sounded, it couldn't be much more bizarre than a time-traveling woman, in a barely settled western town, masquerading as a nun/Garboesque spy, running after a mysterious, time-traveling angel/man of the night, with whom she was considering having a child!

This was just not a normal life!

Was it that she had begun adapting to the times, or were there more serious issues at work here? Like insanity? She couldn't deal with answers right now, unless it was to find out what drove Luke into the darkness every night.

More curious than ever, Casey waited until she saw through a window the dim glow of lamplight before she stepped out of the shadow for a closer look. Creeping stealthily across the alley to the small window, she found it was higher than she'd anticipated and she could barely get a peek on her tiptoes. What was going on in there? She needed something to stand on for a clearer view to satisfy her ardent curiosity. Walking as quietly as she could back toward the street from the alley, she passed a horse. Thinking twice, she literally shook her head no, better not try it . . . that could unleash too much comedy. She didn't need any more of that tonight, and truly, she was becoming tenaciously serious about this whole affair. As a matter of fact, she was beyond frustration, she was beginning to panic.

She did her best to blend in to the ancient town while moving around the front of the building to find another window or door. With each step that she took, she felt her heart pounding even harder against her breast, while the sound of her own pulse raced in her ears. She caught the material of the shawl and clutched it to her chest, as if the action would slow it down. *Stay calm and breathe,* she commanded herself once more. In just a few moments she would know all that she needed. She simply had to know, and as the inevitable approached, Casey felt dizzy.

Making her way around to the other side of the building, she kept her feet moving, commanding them to cross the distance and end her torture. She flattened her back to the wall of the building and listened. There was no sound. No voices. Was he waiting . . . ?

Taking a deep, steadying breath for courage, she pushed herself away from the wall and stood on her toes to peek inside another small window. She could only cling to the rough adobe for support as she blinked in disbelief.

Luke was unbuttoning his shirt. Even though she knew this was highly personal, she couldn't turn away from looking. What woman could? A nun? Well, this temptation proved she could never have been one!

He was disrobing in what looked like some kind of workshop. Whom would he be meeting here? She couldn't see anyone else. His back was to her, and just as he was about to pull his arms out of his shirt, Casey dropped to the balls of her feet and pressed her forehead against the adobe building wall.

What was she doing, spying on this man?

Had she gone over the edge? Did she so desperately want a child that she would humiliate herself like this? Damn, she owed Luke an apology.

And then her mind began playing with her, reminding her that beyond the wall this man was undressing for a reason. He was about to do something . . . and she would be able to find out something about him. He was so evasive about himself. What if, when he undressed, he wasn't normal? What if he really *was* from another planet? At any other time in her life, that question would be cause for admittance into a locked ward, but this wasn't like any other time in her life or anyone else's life either. He said he wasn't from Venus, but there were seven other planets. He could be from Jupiter, or Mars, or Uranus . . . or she could just be certifiable!

Too curious now, she pushed back up on her toes and was astonished to see him changing into a loose white shirt and baggy pants. What in the world . . . ?

While buttoning his shirt, he walked to a huge mound covered with a large rough cloth. Pulling the drape back, he revealed two big tubs with one long, curled wooden beam resting in them. He slowly, gently, almost reverently ran his palm over an exposed smooth curve and then stood with his hands on his hips to stare at it.

Casey's toes were aching from holding up her weight and she sank to her heels again. He'd left the house every night to work with wood? She felt as if she'd just been popped in the back of the head with a fly ball.

He may be the strangest man she'd ever known in her entire life, but she could now safely say she was falling in love with this incredibly strange man. He wasn't meeting a woman . . . he just needed some masculine *Tool Time*!

She rested her forehead against the adobe wall again. Her breath was ragged as she tried to process what was happening inside of her. Okay, Luke was working, making a wood something. He wasn't meeting anyone else. Her plans were still on . . . but did she really, in the deepest core of her being, intend to go through with this? Could she live with the definitive consequences? Could she take possible disappointment and yet be graceful about it? Could she stand that much happiness if he somehow agreed?

She felt as though her entire being were literally on a huge scale in that moment. It was truly a life-altering choice she was about to make, shifting the balance completely one way or the other. She mentally weighed it all. Okay, playing it safe had brought her to being thirty-one years old and working in the accounting department of a soap manufacturer. She didn't have a partner. She didn't even have a cat. Playing it safe also had every single serious relationship ending because the man couldn't make a commitment. How could she now ask for any kind of commitment from a man she'd just met and . . . when she didn't even know what century she would wake up in from one morning to the next? It was mind-boggling.

If she did what Luke said, stayed right here, where she found herself, she'd realize there wasn't all that much safety outside of the present moment. And after everything she'd already been through, she owed it to herself to know one way or the other. Just then the truth of the entire matter slammed into her consciousness with the force of a freight train. It felt like the most important decision she had ever made in her life. She had to stop time-traveling into fear, wondering if she could find the courage to risk it all. She had to stop and trust herself to follow her heart, instead of her head, and walk through that door. Regardless of what he said about sharing his gene pool, she still wanted Luke.

In a flash, memories of their time together raced through her mind . . . the desert meeting, the birth of Angel, dancing lessons . . . Oh yes, she admitted, she wanted him.

And now she had to be willing to risk everything to find out if he also wanted her.

Fear assaulted her, but she quickly recognized it and shook her head. This time she wouldn't allow it. For once in her life, she wasn't going to play it safe. If she backed away from this because of fear, she knew she would always wonder *what if* . . .

She'd had enough *what ifs* to last two lifetimes, she thought, and pushed herself away from the wall. Hearing a man's distant yell from the direction of the plaza, she rearranged her shawl and pulled it more tightly around her. She couldn't just remain here. She had to follow through on her decision.

Taking a deep breath, Casey willed her feet to move toward the door.

She could do this. She didn't have to blurt out the question. It could be days before she worked up the nerve to actually ask him about considering fatherhood, but she did need to let Luke know she had followed him tonight. It was the only honorable thing to do. Somehow she felt very strongly about being honest now. If anything beyond friendship developed and he found out later, he might think she had deceived him. Instinct was telling her this was way too important to screw up.

She stood in front of the door and brought her hand up. Her knuckles remained motionless inches from the rough wood. Courage. She just needed courage from someplace. Her mind replayed scenes of how she had handled the adventure so far, and then she realized she was a pretty courageous woman. She'd had a brief moment of distress, but she hadn't completely fallen apart. She was functioning fairly well for a woman who had time-traveled 122 years and who found herself, as far as she was concerned, with the most incredible man on the face of the planet, perhaps in the entire universe.

She had courage.

Knocking on the door, she inhaled deeply and waited.

The old wood creaked and, through the small opening and the light beyond, Casey was able to see Luke's silhouette. She was stunned as the light behind him seemed to spread out from the back of his body.

"Casey . . ." He said her name without too much surprise. What seemed like an eternal silence fell between them as her voice went mute.

"Well, are you just going to stand there, or are you going to tell me why you're here?"

She blinked a few times while swallowing in an attempt to bring moisture into her dry mouth. "Yes," she muttered. "I mean, I'm going to tell you."

More rowdy shouts were heard in the distance and Luke opened the door wider. "Perhaps it would be best if you came inside."

She nodded, grateful for the admittance. Now that she was here, in this makeshift workshop, how was she to begin? Looking down at the dirt floor, Casey whispered, "I followed you."

"I can see that."

She heard the door close. "I want to apologize to you. I . . . I don't know why . . ." Her words trailed off when she realized she had just vowed to be honest with the man and she was already straying from the truth. "Yes, I do know why I followed you," she said to fill the silence. "I wanted to know where you went every night."

She heard him pause and exhale. "And you never thought to just ask me?"

She quickly looked up at him and answered, "I thought if you wanted me to know, you would have told me. So I guess I'm apologizing for not respecting that."

He nodded and slowly walked away from the door. "Thank you." Heading for one of those long troughs of water, he added, "Since you're here, you might as well see what all the mystery is about. You may be disappointed. It isn't very exciting."

She didn't say anything as she crossed the room, careful to step over any pieces of wood on the ground. She was in his space now and she had already trespassed upon his privacy. Standing before the strange wood soaking in some liquid, she whispered, "What is it?"

He turned briefly and smiled. "I'm hoping it's going to be a staircase."

She glanced at him. "A staircase? Who are you building it for?"

"The sisters at the Loretto Chapel. They need one for access to their choir loft."

She remembered Rosa telling them about it during her first meal with the d'Montoyas. "How . . . ? I mean, do they know you're doing this?" Casey allowed the shawl to drop to her shoulders and she let go of the material. Leaning forward for a closer look, she saw the wood had taken a graceful, swirling form. A staircase?

He again turned to her and grinned as he lifted his finger to his lips. "Shh . . . it's a surprise. That's why I'm doing it at night. Sister Bernardina has been sworn to secrecy." He paused for a moment, staring into her eyes as though he was reading her confused thoughts. "Since space is so limited in the tiny chapel, I'm making a spiral staircase."

"Wow . . ." She truly meant it. This man had all sorts of hidden talents. "How did you come up with this idea?"

He brushed past her to a makeshift table on two saw-horses. When she saw him pick up a long piece of paper, Casey crossed the short distance.

"Here is what I'm hoping it will look like."

She saw a rough sketch of a beautiful, flowing spiral staircase. "How lovely," she murmured, before gazing up into his eyes again. "You can do this?"

He grinned. "Yes. Does that surprise you?"

She couldn't help it, she started to laugh with nervousness. "Well, yeah . . . everything *about* you, Luke d' Séraphin, surprises me! I keep wondering who you really are."

"I told you—"

"I know," she interrupted with a grin of her own. "You're a time traveler, just like me."

"So what did you think I was doing, Casey? Afraid I would beam up without you and leave you here to face a *quinceñera* alone?"

She relaxed and smiled even more. "Beam up, huh?"

"It's an expression I thought you would appreciate."

"Hey, remember, I'm learning a little bit more each day to trust you, but as I already told you, I'm still looking over my shoulder."

"So you did," he said with a chuckle, and turned back to his soaking wood. "Now, answer *my* question. What did you really think I was doing at night?" he inquired again, as he began rolling up his sleeve.

Oh jeez . . . This was the part she was dreading. Wasn't there any way not to answer that question with the whole truth? "I just wondered what drew you every night away from the house. I thought it must be something very important to you."

"It is."

"I can see that. It's quite impressive," she said, hoping her tone would help to change the subject.

"I'm not doing this to impress anyone, Casey," he stated with a laugh as he rolled up his other sleeve. He looked back at her and added, "It's my wish that no one ever finds out who built it. Much more fun that way."

"You not only *are* a mystery. You *love* it, don't you?"

"You really think so?"

Grabbing the ends of her shawl, she twisted the fringe between her fingers. "What I think is that I know nothing about you, and you seem to know everything about me. You even know my thoughts. Kind of seems a bit unfair, don't you think?"

"And even though I said I wasn't keeping score on anything, you calculated it would be fair to follow me tonight, is that it?"

"Well, no . . ." She thought about it for a few seconds. "I told you I wanted to know who—I mean *what* drew you away from the house every night." That was a close one.

Again he chuckled. "You are very funny, Señorita Casey O'Reilly."

"Well, I'm so glad I amuse you," she answered, not quite sure what he was finding so humorous.

"You wanted to know if I was seeing a woman."

Jeez . . . to have him say it, like it was some kind of joke, didn't make the shame of the reality seem any better. "All right . . . so I was curious."

"Would you be disappointed if I told you it was a female that draws me away every night?"

Her mind was racing. What did that mean? "A female?"

"The good sisters are devoted to the Madonna. It is her praises they will sing in their choir loft. So I do this for them."

She watched as he bent over the trough of liquid and began applying pressure to the wood. "You do this for . . . for nuns?"

"Have you ever heard women singing?"

Confused, she tried to make her mind function. "I don't get it. You are building this to hear women sing? That's why you come here every night?"

"I do it for a few reasons. That's one of them. As I have already mentioned . . . it *is* female energy that causes me to leave Don Felipe's every night."

"Could you just stop being so cryptic?" she asked, trying to keep the desperation from her voice. Her heart was telling her there was something else besides the good sisters that was the source of all this.

His voice, when he spoke, was barely audible and she had to strain to hear him.

"I also do it to provide an outlet."

"For what?" she whispered, coming closer to his back. She could see him shaking his head.

"Must I say this even more plainly?"

"Obviously you must, since I'm still confused."

He looked over his shoulder at her. "Okay, I'll tell you." He paused, taking a deep breath. "I do it to get away from you," he exhaled with resignation.

"From me?" She hoped her shock wasn't apparent in her voice.

"You." Abruptly he turned around to her and wiped his hands on his baggy pant legs. "All right, let's have this discussion. It's been coming and I suppose we've both been avoiding it."

"This doesn't sound promising," she muttered, and was shocked that her words were audible. Shrugging, she said, "You probably already know what I'm thinking, don't you?"

Shaking his head again, Luke said, "Casey, I will admit there is something, some attraction taking place, yet I don't think it would be a very good idea to pursue it. Not for me, and especially not for you."

Yes! There was an attraction!

Feeling so much better now that he had admitted it, Casey boldly came forward. Placing her hands on her hips, she asked, "Oh, so now you're making decisions for me? What about all these choices you love to talk about? Don't you think who I am attracted to and when that happens is my decision?"

"I was afraid of this." He grabbed a cloth and wiped his hands more thoroughly. "Now I see how you take my words and give them back to me, yet you must believe me, it is you I am more concerned about." He stared into her eyes. "I am not like most men, Casey."

There was an almost pleading look, as though he was asking her to back away. A part of her wanted to; another, stronger part wanted to close the space between them and cradle his cheek in her palm. She decided to compromise.

She took a few steps forward and leaned her hand on a barrel for support. "And you think I don't know that, Luke? You've been blowing my mind ever since you walked out of that lightning. How could I not be attracted to you?"

"Casey, you don't understand . . ."

"Then tell me," she said in a firm voice. "I'm risking everything by being here. I've never done this before and it's like standing completely naked in front of someone. I'm not used to exposing myself to this degree of vulnerability. So tell me, Luke. Help me to understand why you are not like most men."

His expression appeared to be strained, as though he knew his own moment of truth was fast approaching. No longer could he put her off with evasive answers, and Casey realized he was struggling inside.

"It is a strange life I live," he began, throwing the cloth onto the worktable. He suddenly looked at her and said in a direct voice, "And I wouldn't have it any other way."

"Are you saying that this . . . this attraction between us would threaten your way of life?"

"I am saying that it would change my life and alter yours in ways you can't even begin to imagine right now. I'm not afraid, Casey. I just know what I want and what I don't want."

"And you don't want me?" There, she had said it. You couldn't get much more naked than this!

He groaned and turned back to the vat filled with wood. "When I said I wasn't like most men, I didn't mean I didn't want you. It is best that I don't have you."

He began working the wood, and she lifted herself on top of the barrel to sit. This conversation was getting better all the time. He wanted her! "How are you different from most men then? You *are* human, aren't you?"

He nodded. "I'm human," he whispered. "And . . . something more."

She sat frozen, staring at the back of his head, not quite believing what she was hearing. "Something more?" She held her breath.

"It's the part that's hard to explain," he muttered, and she watched as the muscles in his back strained with the pressure he was applying to the wood. "It's been labeled many things, and when the time is right I hope I'll be able to explain it to you and you'll understand. Right now you'll just have to take my word for it."

"Are you some kind of holy man, sworn to celibacy?" *Please, please say no!*

" 'Holy' is another label, Casey. I don't consider myself to be holy, at least if you spell that word with an *h*. Now, if you meant it as 'whole,' with a *w*, well, that's a bit closer to the truth."

"I don't understand! What is it about you . . . ?" The words, laced with frustration, popped out of her mouth. Again she found herself twirling the fringe of the shawl more tightly between her fingers.

He stopped working, his head bent over his creation.

"I don't know *what* to think anymore," she blurted as a few threads came loose from the fabric she was pulling on. "You certainly aren't like most men I've ever known or even heard about."

"I'm like you, Casey, just—"

"I know. We've covered that already," she interrupted. "We're both time travelers. What else can you add to the story?"

He laughed, as though caught. "What do you know about time?"

Casey dropped the threads she'd inadvertently yanked from the shawl and watched them fall slowly to the floor. "Time? It's . . . it's just there. It measures everything, I guess."

"You're right, it does seem just to be there, doesn't it? Yet your perception of it can change if you're having a tooth pulled or working a job you can't stand. It can seem to drag on endlessly. How many people do you know who have wanted to escape time?"

It was her turn to laugh, breaking the tension. "Millions, myself included."

Nodding, he resumed working on the wood. "But what happens when you're enjoying yourself? Time passes more quickly. So what's the trick then?"

She thought about it. "To enjoy life more? That's the way to escape time?"

He looked over his shoulder. "Very good, Casey."

She slipped off the barrel and walked up to him. "And since we're time travelers, our mission, *should we choose to accept it,* is to have a good time?" She burst out laughing.

"That's about it," he said with a grin. "By a 'good time,' I would mean not resisting where you are and what you're doing. You're doing it all for a reason, so accept the reason and—"

"Wait, wait," she interrupted again, watching his strong hands tightening the vise that was twisting the dark wood beam. "So if we're time travelers who are supposed to enjoy the time we find ourselves in, why are you fighting the attraction you have in this moment?" Wow, she was impressed with herself for coming back with that one!

He laughed and looked to her with affection. "You're a very good student, Casey O'Reilly. Somehow I knew you would be an even better teacher."

Oh, so now she was the teacher, eh? Well, she had a few lessons up her sleeve she would love to use. "You didn't answer me, Luke."

"I didn't because I am making a choice."

"Hmm, a choice, huh? Is that why you are working here, to make time, the night, pass more quickly? Perhaps you might rethink your choice, Luke." Wow, she had never been the pursuer, but this role wasn't bad at all.

"You think I haven't been rehashing it every night and nearly every moment I am here?" His words were low and hoarse, filled with what sounded like torment.

"Why not end it then? Why not just turn to me and let time take care of itself?"

He stood up straight and stared at her. His hands were dripping and he wiped them on his pants before grasping her. "You are a temptation, Casey," he muttered, tightening his strong hands around her waist and pulling her closer.

Pressed against his body, Casey didn't say a word as she stared into the depths of his dark eyes. There was an intensity there that she hadn't seen before. It was as though he were penetrating her very soul, searching within her and finding a key that ignited her senses. His hot breath flamed her resolve and she leaned even closer. Her breasts began aching in rhythm to the pounding of his heart as she *felt* his frustration and his yearning battling with each other. And she felt something else . . . his desire between them, betraying him and thrilling her.

"Well, Luke?" she whispered, knowing at any moment he was going to kiss her.

A near growl escaped his lips as he tightened his grasp on her waist even more and, without warning, abruptly picked her up and plopped her back onto the barrel.

"Argg . . . There. It's much better when you are over here."

She couldn't help it. She sighed loudly with her own unfulfilled desires. "You're a prisoner of time here in this workshop, aren't you, Luke? If you keep busy enough, you won't have to think about this attraction. Why is it you still dance with me, then?"

"I dance with you because I enjoy it so much." He quickly turned back to the wood.

Casey was glad, because now she simply couldn't hide her grin.

"Okay, so do I," she conceded with a giggle of triumph. She'd applied enough pressure for one night, and to have his admittance was a great first venture in being the pursuer. "Since you don't want to talk about yourself right now, tell me about this staircase. Sister Bernardina knows you're building it, but no one else?"

Nodding, he said, "She gave me use of this space and has promised to keep my secret. Now I must ask the same from you."

"Sure. I won't tell anyone." That was easy enough. "So have you ever done this before? Built a staircase?"

He paused, as though thinking of something private. "I guess I have been building them for a very long time. This one will be in the shape of a double helix. When you saw my sketch, did it remind you of anything?"

Casey glanced at the curling paper on the worktable. It was too far away now for her to see clearly, but it did seem vaguely familiar. "I don't know what it is, but it does remind me of something I've seen before."

"DNA?"

Immediately she saw it in her mind and said, "Yes, that's it. Pictures I've seen of DNA. That spiral. You said time was like that . . ."

"Yes. I thought it would be an appropriate way for a time traveler to leave his mark on a chapel."

"I appreciate the irony, Luke."

He looked over his shoulder at her and smiled with genuine warmth. "Thank you. Somehow I knew you would."

DNA. Uniting of the life force. Multiplication of cells . . .

Her purpose for being here came to the forefront. What if he already knew about it? He seemed to know everything she was thinking anyway. What if he knew she wanted him to share his genes and help create a child?

Yikes . . .

Twelve

"*W*hat is troubling you now?"

She was startled from her thoughts and, after taking a deep breath, said, "Maybe we could have that talk now about great unions producing happy children."

"You want to talk about it now?"

She nodded. "Why not? That is, if you don't mind talking while you're working. If you'd rather I leave, I will."

"No, you can stay. Actually I find I'm enjoying working with you here."

"Okay, I will," she pronounced. She ran her fingers across the edge of the old wooden barrel. "So what's your take on this unions-and-happy-children thing?" This was going better than she could have ever hoped. He was attracted to her and now they were going to talk about children.

She watched him shrug and then continue with his work,

saying, "I am not a parent, but as an observer I can see that children sometimes pay the price for their parents' haste."

"Haste?"

"The rushing into parenthood, without first cleaning up or growing up, or whatever one wants to label becoming responsible. I wish women, especially young women, could clearly understand what they are taking on when they make love to a man."

This was coming from a man?

Stunned, Casey whispered, "Go on . . ."

"Women are receivers, wondrous receivers . . . and what they receive from a male is more than they realize. In union, along with the physical comes everything else the man hasn't resolved yet in his life. All the frustration, anger, stagnation, fear of intimacy beyond the physical joining, come along with him. Most young women are resolving those same issues, and when a young girl becomes pregnant by someone who is looking for nothing more than the physical, she's hit with a double zap of low-frequency energy. Hers and his . . . and those two have just created a third. Sounds to me like a perfect setup for a challenging life."

"Doesn't it work the same way with men if they are intimate with a woman who hasn't resolved those issues?" She was thinking of herself and why Luke might not want to take this attraction any further. It was starting to make sense and it scared her.

"Of course it does. But men don't become pregnant, which makes it easier for a man to walk away. Most of the time he doesn't realize what he's walking away with. The energy exchange has already taken place."

"What energy exchange? You mean love?"

"Hopefully that's a big part of it, but it goes beyond the seen. What do you know about electricity?"

She glanced at the oil lantern. "It hasn't been invented yet?"

"Electricity has always been a part of this planet, Casey. Think of lightning. The air is like an insulator between the clouds and the earth. The difference in the electrical state between earth and clouds builds up until it becomes so great that it isn't enough to keep both apart, and in one explosive burst, the electricity discharges across the barrier. Perhaps in this time where we find ourselves, the potential for conventional uses of electricity hasn't been discovered yet, but no human invented electricity. What do you know about the properties of it?"

"Electricity?" Her shoulders sagged. What did she know? She'd just taken it for granted that if she threw a switch, light appeared. "Not much. I'm . . . ah, not very scientific." In truth, the subject of science had never appealed to her.

"Would you like to know?"

Honestly she would rather get back to him being attracted to her and wanting her and the possibilities and properties of *that,* but since she had changed the subject for his sake, she'd go along. Besides, she had a feeling somehow all this was interrelated, that this science was a part of him. Because she wanted to know everything about him that she could, Casey said, "Okay, but you're going to have to bring it down to a *Sesame Street* level for me."

He laughed. "You understand more than you give yourself credit for, Casey. You know that your brain sends out electrical impulses and makes connections. You know that your heartbeat is an electrical pulse. Electricity is a part of being human."

"It is?" She thought about it for a moment. "Okay, I guess it is. I was thinking this was going to be more scientific, but so far I'm with you."

"Good," he muttered, applying more pressure to the

beam. She couldn't see too much from behind him, yet she could make out the muscles of his back straining. "Think of yourself as a battery, charged particles with electrodes and conductors. Electricity flows with discharges from one place to another place. The same principles that apply to the scientific study of electricity can be applied to you as a human being, for that's what you are . . . a marvelous electrical source. You are discharging electricity all the time and you're not even aware of it."

"I am?" Well, she sure had some impulses of electricity discharging from her right now that she hoped he could pick up.

"You are. You give off negative charges to the ethers and—"

"Negative?" she interrupted. What she was feeling couldn't be termed negative.

"Negative and positive are just labels, arbitrary words to identify electrons and protons. The protons that make up the nucleus of every atom have a positive electric charge. The electrons that surround the nucleus have a negative charge. Scientists could have easily called them anything. Don't get stuck on labels."

"Okay," she answered, hoping she would be able to understand this. "I'm a marvelous electrical source that gives off negative charges. Got it."

"After a while all your negative charges will be discharged and you won't have any energy left. You'll be diluted, so to speak. That is the point when you need to be recharged again."

Oh, she liked where this was leading. Recharging sounded just fine to her. "How does one recharge?"

"First you need to understand discharging. When you discharge energy, it goes through some sort of conduit. When you recharge, all you're doing is forcing electrons back into yourself through the same conduit. Then you're charged again. It's important to remember when you discharge, you do it through something. It's not . . . random. It actually has focus. It can be through a fingertip, an eye, a thought, an action, but it manifests itself through some conduit. To get that charge back, you have to bring it through the same conduit, otherwise it doesn't work."

"Okay, now you've lost me," she said with more than a hint of frustration. "Are we talking about electricity or people?"

"Both." He stood up straight and stretched the muscles in his back for a few moments before resuming his work over the trough. "If you discharge love, for example, and you give off that electrical energy for the sake of love, the only way to get it back is through love."

All right . . . now this conversation was heading back in the right direction! "Okay . . ."

"If you discharge through anger, the only way to get it back is through anger. See? You discharge through sadness, the only way to get it back is through sadness. But most importantly, we have to realize that whatever we give out, or discharge, we can get back."

"That's kind of scary," she muttered, thinking of all the times she'd been angry in her life and sad . . . Well, she'd certainly had it returned to her, so the circuit was complete. "What about love? You get back what you give out and complete the circuit there too?" She envisioned the love and trust she had given in relationships and suddenly realized it really had been returned in proportion to what she'd discharged. She had always held back, waiting for the other person to show his cards or make a commitment. There was always fear too.

"Glad you brought up circuits. A circuit needs three things . . . a source of electrical energy, an output device, and a connection between the source and the device."

"You're losing me again," she said with a laugh. "*Sesame Street*, remember?"

He chuckled as he continued to work. "Okay, how about this? When you discharge, you're not just discharging out into space. There's usually an object for your discharge. When electricity is discharged, it causes something to happen somewhere."

"What about the emotional part, about humans?" She was far more interested in that than in abstract electricity.

"There are literally billions and trillions of electrical circuits out there between human beings. Discharge is not random; it's going to follow a circuit. The source and output device must be connected so that electrical current can flow from the source to the device and back again. The return part is necessary so that an electrical charge does not collect at any point in the circuit. A collected charge would oppose the flow and keep the circuit from functioning."

"What happens if there is opposition to the flow?"

"If you try to discharge more, everything will come to a standstill. Just stop. Nothing will happen. There has to be a place for it to go into and a place for it to come out of, or nothing will happen. Does that make sense?"

"Is this like when you're walking and suddenly you make eye contact with a person, a stranger, and you either smile or look away?"

"Exactly. If you smile and the connection through the eyes is made and the other person accepts your discharge and smiles back, how do you feel?"

She grinned. "I feel good."

"Energized?"

"Yes."

"We are all electrically connected as people, so the electricity will continue to flow from one person to another person to another person and so on. As soon as one person lets go of the connection, nothing happens, the electricity between them stops. Then sometimes we need something to break the current when it is too high."

"We do?"

"Certainly. We have them all the time. Why do we want to break it if it's too high? Well, if you're a lightbulb, you'd blow up if you got the main surge of electricity from the source, the power plant. If you're a human, you might have chaos . . . anger, sickness . . . you can go on overload. You can become too energized and things can happen to you. You can break down. It's intelligent to have a circuit breaker."

"You mean something to break the tension?"

"Yes. If you're a parent and you and your spouse are having a high-level energy discharge, the juices get going, charges are flowing, and both parties are amping up with negative energy. Then a child walks into the room and breaks the circuit."

She thought of that time when she was a child and had broken the circuit between her parents. It made sense.

"Humor is a great circuit breaker too."

"That's why you said it was an important tool for a human to have."

"You remember. Anything that lightens a situation works as a circuit breaker. All of a sudden all of the energy that was flowing, causing that problem, whatever it might have been, just stops. Circuit breakers are very important."

Sitting on the barrel, Casey thought back to when she was a teenager and had been making out with a boy in his car. They had been at a lake, a place where high school kids parked after a dance or a date, and things had started to get hot and heavy. Suddenly they'd heard a sharp rap on the window and it had scared them both. A policeman had been clearing all the kids out and it certainly had put a stop to any other thoughts. That had been a circuit breaker, for sure. "Okay, I think I've got circuit breakers and how important they can be."

"Good," he said, and turned around to face her. He grabbed his rag and wiped his hands. "Now we'll talk about potential energy, for it's the key to directing energy from one place to another."

Oh, she had some potential energy she wanted to direct, all right. From her to him . . . but she knew he was serious and so she merely nodded.

"It's nothing more than the difference between your positive energy and your negative energy. In a person it's like when someone exudes so much positive energy that it just goes out and goes through everybody else. Everyone has met someone like that, and everyone has a degree of this positive energy. Some people have a potential difference in the opposite direction and are in such need of positive energy, someone else's electricity, that they seem to suck all the energy out of that person and into them."

"I've met people like that. Both kinds."

"Most everyone has, Casey. It's nice to understand it, though, and how it can be directed. If you are an electrical source of energy yourself, isn't it time you understood how you and every other human being works?"

"I never knew all this. I mean it makes sense, just no one has ever talked to me like this." She paused for a moment. "Maybe you're right. Maybe I didn't give myself enough credit to understand and so I turned my attention elsewhere."

"But you understand now?"

"I'm beginning to."

"Good, because we're getting to the most important part. Types of current and magnetism."

She sighed and, looking into his eyes, smiled.

He seemed to catch her current and smiled back.

Casey felt a sizzle of electricity race through her body and settle in her solar plexus.

"See?" he asked. "You do it all the time. Now you know what is happening."

"Hmm . . ." Why was it she wished they would stop talking and amp up the voltage? "So what are you, Luke? A copper-top Duracell?"

He laughed. "More like an Energizer, I think."

"I must be an Eveready," she said with a laugh. "Loyal, constant . . . that's me."

He smiled and this time he was the one sending an electrical discharge, and it was warm and exciting. She didn't want it to end. He obviously thought it was enough, for his next words seemed to dissipate all her warm thoughts.

"There is, scientifically, direct or alternating current. DC, direct, always flows in the same direction. AC, alternating, flows back and forth. What do you think a person who is always angry, always depressed, is? AC or DC?"

"Ahh . . . I didn't know there was going to be a pop quiz," she said, and laughed. Here come the questions. "DC? Going in one direction?"

"Well done, Casey," Luke said with a grin. "The majority of people are AC, alternating current, always giving and receiving. What happens when one person is AC and he or she hooks up with someone operating in DC mode, only focused on one direction?"

"They blow a fuse?"

He laughed and she just loved the way his eyes seemed to sparkle with affection. "You can't have AC with DC without a rectifier. At some point in time both have to become AC or DC."

Rectifiers? What the heck were they? She was getting confused with all these electrical terms, yet she was still attempting to get the gist of his conversation because she still felt like it was leading up to something. She'd go along for a while and watch it play out. "Well, I like AC, giving and receiving," Casey declared with a grin.

"Most women are AC, great givers and, sometimes, unaware receivers."

"Ahh, now I see we are back to unions and children and how women receive from men more than just the physical. It makes sense now why a lot of relationships just don't work out. People are operating on different currents."

"Yes, but the discharge of energy has taken place, the connection has been made, and remember I said the only way for it to return is through the same conduit. If a young girl opens herself to a male who is operating on DC, merely physical, and then he breaks the connection . . . she is going to have to get it back through something, or someone. She feels the loss and needs to get it back somehow."

He smiled a little sadly. "She can be self-destructive, enter into another relationship, or remain stagnant, in a state of loss. She has an open current. All she knows is that she discharged love and is waiting for it to be returned to her. If she stays like that, nothing happens."

"This doesn't sound very hopeful," Casey muttered.

"But it is," he assured her, turning back to his work, "when it's seen without the false images that are fed to men and women about sexuality. It's the mingling of the energy of the physical, and of something else that is beyond the physical, that for a glorious, timeless interlude takes us beyond our human existence into something . . . more. Some have merely forgotten the real power, the electrical charge, behind sexuality and treat it like a toy instead."

"Children having children . . ." She murmured her thought aloud.

"Yes."

"I want a child."

She said it because it was the truth and because the opportunity presented itself.

"I know you do."

She stared at his back, willing him to turn around and face her once more. "How do you know that? You reading my thoughts again, Luke?"

"No. I saw your face when you touched Angel after he was born. You will make a wonderful mother, Casey. Responsible and still playful."

"Well, I'm not having much luck in that area, Mr. d'Séraphin," she said with a laugh. "Care to assist me?" It was one of those moments when the setup was just too perfect not to go forward. She could always laugh it off later.

He turned around. "Marriage is not something I intend to enter. It wouldn't be fair to any woman."

She stared right back at him. "I wasn't asking you to marry me, Luke. I was asking for a little assistance in having a child. I'm thirty-one years old. I'm working through most of my issues and I feel I'm responsible for my actions and I was thinking about being a single mother right before I was zapped back here."

He looked like she'd picked up a piece of his wood and batted him on the head.

"You . . . you were thinking about what?"

"About wanting to have a child and yet not wanting to dive into the gene pool at a sperm bank. I know I could do it . . . raise a child, a happy child."

"And you were thinking this right before you were hit with lightning?"

"Well, right before my front tire blew and then I was hit with lightning. Why?"

He quickly turned back to the soaking wood and rested his hands on the edge of the trough. His shoulders slumped and he exhaled heavily. A long silence followed and Casey patiently waited, for she knew that somehow she had just shaken his world a bit. What could he be thinking?

"I think I should walk you back," he said in a shaken voice, as though answering her mental question. "Suddenly I'm tired and this diversion of wood isn't helping."

She slipped off the barrel. "What did I say?"

He walked over to the table and picked up the rag. Wiping his hands, he muttered, "It's getting late and you should return before someone discovers you're missing. You did sneak out from the wardrobe in your room, didn't you?"

Casey nodded. "But what did I say to upset you?" She didn't want to let it drop.

"You didn't upset me. You surprised me." He returned to his staircase and pulled the long cloth over it. Picking up his clean shirt and the dark trousers, he added, "The pattern is becoming clearer, but I can't explain it right now. Let's get back before Doña Isabela finds out you're gone."

He blew out the lantern and took her hand. "Be careful. Follow me."

Grateful for his hand, Casey clutched it as she walked slightly behind him. Why was he in such a hurry now, after their discussion about electricity? Whatever she'd said, she'd rattled him for sure. All her progress and now . . . what? One remark about time traveling and children ruins it all?

She was going to have to think about this one when she was alone.

Still, it had turned out far better than she could have hoped. He was interested. He wanted her. And now she was holding his hand . . . Yeah, far better.

He led her through the noisy streets, determined to see her back in her room and *far* away from him. It was bad enough that he'd almost kissed her last night after Rosa's recital, so strong was the attraction, but now she had confirmed his worse fear. Casey O'Reilly, this wild, wonderful, incredible woman who was capturing his mind and his heart, had been thinking about finding a father for her child right before she had time-traveled, and he had made the choice to come and assist her! This pattern was unfolding in such a way that his normally peaceful state was altered into one of confusion. Choices . . . He knew it was all about choices and responsibility for them, and now he was being challenged by one of the biggest he had ever faced in his life.

It was obvious she had chosen him.

Thirteen

The preparations for the *quinceñera* took up the next few days, and Casey pitched in as much as she could; however, the staff seemed to have everything under control and she found herself with time on her hands to think. Lots of time. Still, the house was bustling with activity. Deliveries were made all day long. Relatives, aunts, uncles, numerous cousins, and family friends began arriving to pay their respects. Marguerita, Rosa's older sister, showed up *encinta,* three months pregnant, and the d'Montoya household was brimming with joy.

Casey liked the shy Marguerita and could see the young woman's eyes almost shine with an inner light. There were too many other relatives to remember all the names. Most were staying at the hotel in town, yet every night the house was filled with people and music and laughter. Casey excused herself early each night so everyone could be more comfortable and speak in Spanish, plus she wanted to return to her room. Luke stayed away more than before. She had only seen him twice since the night they were alone at the workshop, and now there were so many people around they hadn't had a chance to talk privately. She knew she could always sneak out again and visit him, but something held her back. It was obvious he was avoiding her.

What had she said?

She must have gone over their conversation ten times, and the only thing she could come up with was that he'd seemed startled when she'd told him she had been thinking about being a single parent and the possibility of going to a sperm bank right before she was taken back in time. Now, he could be shocked at her thoughts or . . . he could be following the pattern, as he so loved to say, and watching as it unfolded before him. He just never expected it to unfold like *this*.

He also mentioned there was a purpose to everything, it all happens for a reason . . . What if the purpose of this whole time travel for them both was so Luke *could* father her child? It was a plausible theory for what was unfolding . . .

That was the way he thought, that one thing leads to another and one should just be aware of what is unfolding. Wasn't that what he kept saying to her? Why was it so shocking to him now, unless he was struggling with his own desires?

Snuggled in bed, she listened to the guitar music the others were enjoying in the courtyard and stared at the beautiful gown Doña Isabela had given her to wear tomorrow night. It was a gorgeous creation of pale yellow silk, off the shoulders, with white silk flowers attached to the scooped neckline. When she'd first tried it on, she had felt like a fairy princess. A silly thought coming from a thirty-one-year-old woman, and yet that was how she had felt . . .

beautiful and unearthly, and she couldn't wait to see Luke's reaction when he saw her in it.

The night in the workshop had taught her many things. He was not only attracted to her, he wanted her and he stayed away from the house at night to stop himself from having her. He had said he was more concerned for her, and yet even that drew her to him. It was like they were on this course, and for once, she could see more of it than he. He was trying to stop the electrical connection, just like he'd stopped the lesson on electricity before they got to magnetism. Well, now that she knew this was definitely AC current, going both ways, she was not about to allow anything foolish to break it. She no longer needed to pursue him. She had stated her case. Now it was up to him.

So she could wait, allowing him his space. It wouldn't be long. The party was tomorrow and he couldn't avoid her there without appearing rude. And Luke d'Séraphin was anything but rude. A smile played at her lips and she blew out the lantern. Lying in bed, listening to the flamenco music, Casey hugged the light coverlet to her breast and looked into the moonlit bedroom. Yes, tomorrow she wasn't going to plan anything. She was just going to allow the day to unfold and be aware of everything around her. She would create memories, but more than that . . . she would create some magic. Her wish was out there now, waiting to be fulfilled. And the great part was, she realized she didn't have to do a thing . . . only be herself.

Sometimes she just loved being a woman.

Suddenly she heard a noise in her wardrobe, and tensed as she waited to see if it was a rodent or—

"Rosa!"

The girl's head peeked past the door of the huge chest. "Shh," she admonished, as though her walking through walls were an ordinary thing! "I wanted to make sure you were feeling better for tomorrow."

"And you couldn't have knocked on the door?" Casey asked with a laugh as she sat up in bed and watched the teenager emerge completely and walk toward her. She was dressed in a light cotton nightgown and robe. Truthfully, Casey was delighted with the company.

"Everyone thinks I am resting for my big day tomorrow, but I am far too excited to sleep." She stood at the edge of Casey's bed.

Scooting over, Casey threw open the cover and said, "Come on, then. Get up here."

Smiling, Rosa climbed into the bed, and when Casey pulled the cover over them both and settled back against her pillow, Rosa threaded her arm through Casey's and rested her head on Casey's shoulder.

For just a moment, Casey tensed at the innocent gesture, and then she found herself enjoying it. Many times she had done the same thing to Amy while growing up when she wanted to talk. Smiling with fondness, she said, "Okay so how are all the plans going for your *quinceñera*? Everyone all set?"

"Oh, yes," Rosa whispered. "All the *chambeláns* and *damas* are fully rehearsed. We shall make a good presentation. This afternoon was the last practice."

Casey was learning about the Hispanic custom of presenting a fifteen-year-old girl to society. Fourteen couples, representing each year of the girl's life, prepared a special dance. It was going to be some celebration, full of tradition. "And your sponsors have arrived?"

"Yes, my *padrinos y madrinas* are all in Santa Fe now. *Tía* Concepcion and *Tío* Arturo arrived today, so all is ready. I am more anxious about the mass tomorrow than the reception after it. It is very serious, Casey."

She nodded. "Because you will then be considered a woman?"

"I will renew my baptismal vows and make a public statement about my commitment to my family, my faith, my chastity, and how I will contribute to society. I am anxious, for I don't like speaking in front of many people."

"*You* don't like speaking?" Casey asked with a laugh.

Rosa squeezed her arm with affection. "Not in front of so many! The church will be filled with friends, relatives, and . . . and my one true love. This may be the first time he hears me speak. I must speak words that will ring true within his heart."

"Yes," Casey said thoughtfully. "I can see why you'd be nervous, but your parents love you very much, Rosa. Don't rush into anything or expect too much. Just relax and enjoy each moment tomorrow. It's certainly a grand party they are giving you."

"*Sí*, Casey. I know this. Papi is sparing no expense for my *quinceñera*. I think it might even be more grand than Marguerita's was, and people still speak of that. I am blessed for certain, and tomorrow I will meet my one true love." The girl sighed deeply in thought.

Casey put her hand over Rosa's smaller one resting on her arm. It was odd how quickly she had become fond of this impetuous teenager. She felt like an older sister. "Now, wait a minute. Do you think it's wise to put that much pressure on yourself tomorrow night, of all nights? What if it doesn't happen?"

"But it will. I know this. In *here*," she whispered, touching her heart. "Tomorrow I go to church a child in the eyes of everyone and leave a woman. I am entering womanhood, and women know of these things."

Casey didn't want to argue with her about that, but still felt she should say something more. "Okay, but promise me if . . . if you need me tomorrow you will seek me out. I hope your one true love does appear, Rosa, for your sake."

"He will come. He, too, has been waiting. I know this."

"How do you know?" she asked, truly curious how this girl could be so sure. Was it more than romantic fantasies placed in her mind by others?

Rosa leaned her head closer to Casey and whispered, "I have been talking to him."

"You have?" Casey was surprised. "Is he here in Santa Fe? Do your parents know?"

Rosa giggled. "I have been talking to him in here," she whispered, touching her forehead. "And in here." Again she placed her fingers to her heart. "I know he hears me, and tomorrow he will make himself known. I have been talking to him since I was a very little girl. He is my true love and tomorrow our souls will meet in person."

Casey could only stare at Rosa and blink. "I know what you mean," she finally whispered back. "I've done that myself, that yearning for *the one* to appear in my life. Telling him everything, opening my heart to him, whoever and wherever he is. I guess I gave up a long time ago and didn't believe it anymore, but I will tell you a secret now . . ."

Rosa raised her head to look up, and her beautiful brown eyes widened with anticipation. "Yes . . ."

"I think I have found mine."

"No! *De veras?* Really?"

Casey giggled like a teenager and nodded. "Yes."

"It is Señor Luke, is it not? It must be!"

"How did you know?"

Rosa smiled. "Oh, Casey. It could only be him . . . or Don Miguel."

Both females stared at each other for a few seconds in the dimly lit room and then burst out laughing. "Definitely *not* Don Miguel!" Casey managed to get out as Rosa nodded.

At the same time both of them were aware their laugher might attract attention, so they restrained their giggles.

Rosa sighed deeply and murmured, "Oh, Señor Luke . . . he is so handsome and . . . and I watched you two dance and I knew something was happening. Has he declared his love to you? You must tell me everything!"

"Calm down, Rosa," Casey said with a smile. "He's admitted he's attracted to me, though I don't think he's thrilled with that, so no, he hasn't declared his love. But I just know he's the one," Casey said, glad to have told someone what was in her heart. She felt she would burst if she kept it in any longer.

"He is attracted to you but does not love you? Don Miguel might say such a thing, but Señor Luke would never admit his attraction if love was not behind it. He is too honorable."

Casey realized the girl was thinking with the mentality of someone living in a very formal household of 1878, when people didn't declare a sexual attraction at all unless a marriage proposal was first given. "Well, marriage isn't even the question in my mind," she said firmly. "But love . . ." She sighed. "That, I would like to hear from his lips."

Rosa leaned in closer. "I have seen him dance with you, Casey, and I will tell you this . . . He is part Spanish and his passion for you is real. This I know." She nodded her head with confirmation.

"If you are being pronounced a woman tomorrow, then there is something you should know right off the bat. Passion isn't always love, Rosa. There is a difference."

"I know the difference. Do you think I do not see Don Miguel's advances? They are done without the respect of love first. Do you believe Señor Luke respects you?"

"Yes." Her answer was immediate. Luke hadn't even tried to kiss her.

"Then if he has admitted his attraction to you, it is because of love and respect, Casey. I know Hispanic men and I have seen his eyes when he dances with you. There is great pleasure and affection in them."

Pleased, Casey smiled. "I hope we dance tomorrow. He's been avoiding me."

"Oh, you shall dance. I shall request it!"

Casey burst out laughing again. "You are too much, Rosalinda d'Montoya!"

They heard voices in the hallway and both stopped speaking until they'd passed. Whispering, Rosa said to Casey, "I have to prepare myself. Wait until you see my gown. It has been made by my relatives. All my accessories come to me from my relatives and are cherished. Even Marguerita has given me her fine comb and mantilla for the mass. Later, it will be replaced with a jeweled crown. All of my female relatives will attend me and I will thank them before I am dressed. It is a long process, but I shall see you tomorrow when my flat shoes are traded for heels and I am finally adorned as a woman and no longer a child. Rest now, Señorita Casey, for tomorrow we shall both be certain of our loves. It is fated."

Casey stared as Rosa leaned over and kissed her cheek. *"Hasta luego, hermana."*

She touched her cheek as she watched the teenager scamper out of the bed and rush to the wardrobe. *"Dulce sueños!* Sweet dreams," she translated right before she pulled the door closed behind her.

Casey was suddenly so filled with emotion, she felt like crying. Rosa had called her "sister." How she missed Amy. She missed her mother who had passed away four years ago. She missed that female connection to her past. She wanted to get back, but what good would it do to go mentally time-traveling there? she thought, and stiffened against the onslaught of emotions that seemed to be poised right above her, waiting to crash down.

She turned her thoughts back to Rosalinda d'Montoya. What a gift to the world the young woman was. Rosa's faith in herself was remarkable for someone of such tender years. Immediately her mind started racing when she realized she wanted to give something to Rosa for her birthday. What could she give this child who seemed to have everything? She had nothing with her except her clothes, and hopefully one day soon she was going to need them. Just clothes, shoes . . . and her wallet!

Scrambling out of bed, Casey opened the wardrobe and searched the side shelf for her wallet, stuck inside one of her blue flats. She grabbed it and raced back to bed. Money was out of the question, but there might be something . . . and then before she even opened it, she knew the only thing she had to give to the girl.

She crawled back onto the bed and pulled the cover over her. Slowly she opened the wallet and with her fingers searched the compartment in back of the bills. Amid a few coins, she felt it and pulled it out. Placing the wallet on the bed, Casey sat back and opened her palm.

In the light of the moon she stared at a tiny glass pendant, sealed with a gold bezel. Preserved inside was a perfect four-leaf clover.

It had been a gift to her from her mother so many years ago when she'd graduated college. She could almost hear her mother's voice saying, *One leaf is for hope. The second is for faith. The third is for love. The fourth is for luck.* Casey had carried it with her since that day, transferring it from wallet to wallet as a sentimental keepsake, a token of love she just felt better having around her. Most of the time she forgot about it in the day-to-day routine of her life, but now it seemed like a wonderful gift to give another.

She thought about what the clover, part of her own Celtic heritage, represented . . . all the things Rosa was professing tomorrow. Hope, faith, love, and luck . . . *Luck* didn't seem like the right thing now. Since traveling back in time and learning more about herself, she wondered just how much luck had to do with anything. Could everything that had happened to her be attributed to luck? If it wasn't luck, what was it? Fate? Destiny?

It dawned on her that she'd never pondered such thoughts, realizing she had preferred to think of everything happening as a matter of good and bad luck. Did she believe in destiny? Of course she did, though she secretly denied it most of the time. Since she was a small child, she had felt *something* awaited her, something wondrous that would point to her purpose. She had never told anyone about it, not even Amy, thinking it might sound vain to someone else. But now, in the silence of this night, she could be honest with herself. She had been taught that it was humble to belittle herself, to make herself out to be less than she was. Now she believed she and her mother and so many other women had been taught incorrectly. Sure, she had lots of room for improvement, but if *she* didn't recognize her gifts, how could she ever hope to fulfill her purpose? Secretly it was what kept her going, knowing that she was meant to be something, to do something with her life that had meaning. And everything in her life has been leading up to it, whatever it was.

Maybe it was what Luke had said . . . to just be happy with where she was and stop questioning everything. Just allow it all to unfold around her. Turning the tiny pendant in her palm, Casey realized that trust took faith and hope and love . . . So then, who needed luck?

Yes, she finally decided. Tomorrow morning she would give Rosalinda the clover and tell her it represented hope, faith, love, and destiny.

She had made a choice, and it felt right inside of her. Suddenly she was pleasantly tired and couldn't suppress a yawn. She wished she had remembered the clover while Rosa was with her and they could have talked more. Sometimes the teenager seemed so wise and Casey felt like a kid herself when she was with her. And tomorrow Rosa would be thought of as a woman, welcomed into society. It was a nice tradition, and she wished there had been something in her own life to celebrate the passing of her childhood and youth into womanhood. It might have made the journey a little easier, instead of leaving her to spend years trying to figure out if and when she finally *was* a woman and responsible for her life.

She leaned over and placed her wallet and the pendant on the small table by the bed. Lying back into the pillows, Casey sighed with contentment. She had a fine gift for her little sister.

Wondering if Luke would ask her to dance, Casey punched her pillow down and turned to her side. She stared at the beam of moonlight, thinking Rosa was going to have a full moon tomorrow night for her reception. How perfect. Closing her eyes, she allowed her mind to let go finally and rest. No plans . . . that was her new resolve. All she had to do was be herself, enjoy where she found herself, and be aware as life unfolded before her.

Sounded like a pretty cool gig, this time-traveling . . .

Casey walked into Rosa's bedroom hesitantly, for it was a hive of feminine activity. Women were rushing around, making last-minute alterations to Rosa's beautiful white gown, laying out lovely lace undergarments, crinolines, and an exquisite veil, and speaking in an excited voice to each other. One would think it was a wedding about to take place.

"Casey!" Rosa called out from in front of a vanity, where an older woman was curling the girl's hair with a hot iron. "*Venga aquí,* come," she added with a sigh of what sounded like relief.

Smiling to the other women in the room, Casey hurried to her friend's side and clasped Rosa's outstretched hand. "I'm sorry for barging in on you now, but—"

"Do not apologize," Rosa interrupted, glancing around at the excited older women. "It is a most welcome visit. Have you ever seen such activity for one person? I keep telling everyone all will be fine, yet no one believes me. They insist on fussing endlessly, though I am not complaining, for I know it is done out of love too."

Casey reached into the pocket of her borrowed robe. "I have something for your birthday," she murmured, hoping not to take up too much time. "I wanted to give it to you before all the excitement started, but I see I am already too late." She brought out the pendant and offered it to her friend.

Rosa inhaled with pleasure and stared at the four-leafed clover. "It is beautiful. I have never seen such a thing." She said something to the woman who was fixing her hair and the older woman backed away, giving them a few moments of privacy.

Casey placed it in Rosa's hand and said, "It was given to me by my mother when I was a little older than you, as I was going off into the world on my own. It's an Irish four-leafed clover. Each leaf represents something. One is for hope. The second is for faith. The third is for love. And the fourth is for your destiny."

She watched as tears came into Rosa's eyes. "But I cannot accept such a priceless gift from you, one that your own mother gave you."

"I would be honored if you would accept it, Rosa," Casey whispered, reaching out to tenderly wipe a tear from her friend's cheek. "You are my sister now, so it will stay within the family, no?"

"I am honored, *mi hermana*. I will treasure it always. *Gracias* . . . from my heart to yours." She reached up, and Casey leaned down to embrace her.

Rosa turned her head and kissed Casey's cheek so hard that Casey started laughing before she, too, started crying. "Now you'll have to wipe your eyes or all these women will scold me for ruining such a beautiful face on this special day."

Rosa sniffled and wiped her fingers under her eyes. "I cannot wait to get to the church and begin the festivities. I feel like I will be here preparing all night if they have their way," she said with a chuckle.

Casey saw the older woman returning with her hot curling iron. She looked a little impatient. "I should leave now so you can finish up here. Happy birthday, Rosalinda. May you always be as happy as you are today."

"*Muchas gracias*, my sister of the soul. Never will I forget this moment and your generous gift. I will see you in the church. I am saying all my vows in English, for Papi has invited many of his business and political acquaintances. Say a prayer for me that I do not stumble over the words."

Casey quickly placed a kiss on Rosa's cheek. "You will do fine. Don't worry. What could go wrong on such a day?"

Rosa smiled broadly. "You are right. The saints are with me, and already I have a charm to ensure it is the best day of my life." She held the pendant up and placed a tiny kiss upon it.

"I will see you in church," Casey called out, and headed for the door, very pleased with her decision to give Rosa the pendant. Even though it was precious to her as a sentimental reminder of her mother, she knew she had done the right thing . . . for it just felt so good!

*   *   *

It had been years since Casey had been inside a Catholic church, and she found herself falling into the routine of kneeling and standing and sitting. The scent of incense wasn't any more appealing to her than it had been in her past. The priest, a bishop, said Rosa's mass in Latin, and the young woman, dressed in a gorgeous white gown, gave a beautiful presentation when she renewed her baptismal vows and placed a bouquet of red roses at the feet of the Madonna. Rosa then told the bishop and all in attendance that she wanted to contribute love to the world, that she was blessed by her family and wanted to share those blessings with others. It was a very pretty speech, and Casey was happy it was in English, so Luke wouldn't have to translate. Even though he sat next to her in the church, he didn't say anything more than politeness demanded. So she was still being shut out, huh?

Back in her room, dressing with Juana's assistance in the lovely yellow gown, Casey felt a surge of anticipation as she heard a pianist and a violinist playing a romantic bolero while people arrived for the reception. She knew from Juana that an excellent mariachi band had also been hired for the party. Even Juana and all the servants were invited guests as Marcella supervised the hired men and women who specialized in these grand affairs. Helping Casey to dress was Juana's last official duty of the day. This was a day to honor all those who had contributed to Rosalinda's life. She remembered how Rosa had cried when she'd presented her with the pendant earlier, and thought with a small twinge of pleasure that she, too, had contributed in a tiny way to this young woman's life.

"Francisco Tomás Sandoval and his parents have arrived, señorita, all the way from Spain," Juana gushed as she tightened the laces behind Casey's back. "Señor Sandoval is Señor d'Montoya's business partner, and there are great hopes for a union beyond business. I have peeked. Tomás Sandoval is a most handsome young man."

"Really?" Casey asked, her own interest piqued by Juana's gossip. "His father is also an importer?"

"*Sí,* and training young Señor Tomás to take over his business."

"Has Rosalinda met him yet?"

"No," the woman answered, tying off the laces. "They arrived after the mass started. I saw them quietly come in as Señorita Rosa was speaking her vow to the Virgin and I watched as they found seats in the back. She will be introduced to him later tonight."

Could he be the one? Casey wondered, almost believing Rosa's prediction that her one true love would make his appearance tonight. How romantic . . . "When we get out there, point him out to me, Juana, all right?"

"*Sí,* but he is not for you, señorita."

Casey laughed and turned to the smaller woman, who was dressed in a festive costume of red and white with flowers in her hair. She looked wholesome and pretty, and Casey wondered if Juana was married. She had never asked.

"Of course he's not for me, Juana. There are just so many people here tonight, I want to make sure I know who this Tomás is when Rosa meets him. I would like to see that."

"*Sí,* I would like to see that also. Something tells me this is going to be an . . . how do you say it . . . an exciting night for many people."

"Juana, are you married?"

The woman blushed prettily. "Yes. Manuel and I were married by his priest many years ago. I allowed it, for it is necessary for the man to feel most married. A woman can feel it in her heart, but a man needs the . . . the ritual of it to bind him, I think."

"Manuel plays a beautiful guitar. You are a luck—" She stopped herself from using that word. "You are a blessed woman, to be surrounded by music from the man you love."

Again Juana blushed. "*Sí,* some nights he plays just for me and I know the gods are smiling down on me." The woman adjusted the scooped neckline of Casey's gown and patted a silk flower into place. "You, too, I believe, señorita, are a blessed woman. Señor Luke is a very fine man also."

"Señor Luke?" It was Casey's turn to blush and look away.

Juana chuckled. "Do not think I have not seen you two together. I was right when I told you he is interested. Even more so now that he shies away from you. I have brought you something for this night."

Casey watched as Juana reached into that small pouch she always had attached to her waist. She brought out a tiny plugged vial and held it out.

"Here. Use it."

"What is it?" Casey asked with more than a tad of suspicion.

Juana again chuckled. "It is a woman's secret, collected from far away . . . jasmine flowers and spices. It brought my Manuel to me and sealed the union."

Casey continued to look at the thin brown vial. "I don't know. Is this magic?"

"Of course!" Juana exclaimed. "Women have used magic forever to draw in their love. Use this perfume and you will be irresistible to him. Do not try to make me think he is not already irresistible to you. I have seen you, Señorita Casey. He *is* your love, and tonight is your opportunity to draw him closer. Take it or not . . . but know, it is nature's magic that is at work, not mine."

Curious, Casey unplugged the vial and sniffed. The most wondrous scent wafted to her nostrils and she smiled at the woman. "Wow . . . it's . . . it's beautiful."

"Like you," Juana whispered with an answering smile. She took the vial from Casey's hands and tipped her finger over the opening. She then touched the skin behind Casey's ears, whispering, "May tonight you hear words of love." Her wrists were then scented. "May you feel the caress of your lover's skin." Then Juana tipped the vial again and placed her finger above Casey's cleavage. "May tonight you feel his love in your heart and know you are blessed to be born a woman."

Casey felt Rosa wasn't the only one indulging in ritual tonight, and suddenly she caught her breath as she turned around to the long length of mirror and saw her reflection.

Incredibly, tonight she *was* beautiful!

The soft yellow silk of the gown complemented her hair, again pulled back and decorated by Juana with a full wreath of tiny white flowers hiding the short strands. In her billowy gossamer gown, she looked like she had walked right off the pages of a fairy tale. Her skin was bronzed by her days in the sun, making her blue eyes stand out even more, and her cheeks were flushed with excitement.

"Thank you, Juana," Casey breathed in disbelief. "You've done it again. I . . . I look beautiful."

Juana laughed. "You always were beautiful, señorita . . . only now *you* see it."

Casey spun around and impulsively hugged the older woman. "How can I ever thank you?" she whispered.

Juana patted her bare shoulders. "You have thanked me, but I will tell you what you can do that will make Juana very happy."

"Anything," Casey answered, pulling back and looking into the woman's suddenly mischievous eyes.

"Do not let that one get away. He is a treasure and will make you very happy."

Casey suddenly wanted to cry. "I don't know . . . I don't want to force anything. I'm . . . I'm falling in love with Luke, and he isn't too happy about it, Juana."

The woman held up her hand and dismissed the notion, before dropping her vial back in her pouch. "Pah . . . *hombres!* If they only knew what is best for them, they wouldn't be fighting their wars with themselves. They would be making love and keeping their women happy."

Instead of crying, Casey laughed. "Sounds like a good idea to me. How do I convince him of it?"

"You do not have to do a thing, señorita. Tonight you have the magic about you."

Casey blew out her breath in a rush. "Well, I can use all the help I can get, 'cause I have a feeling this is the most important thing I have ever wanted."

"Trust," Juana whispered. "The moon is full and magic is already in the air." The woman opened the door and smiled. "Come, Señorita Casey . . . come dance in the magic."

Fourteen

A myriad of *ramilletes,* or candleholders with ornately designed punched-tin shields, illuminated the entire length of the patio walls. Casey found the ambiance quite romantic and had to know what they were called. She was still accompanied by Juana, and all her questions were gladly answered or translated by the kind woman. Hanging from the huge cottonwood tree were larger lanterns filled with oil, and towering torches surrounding the area provided additional light. A five-piece mariachi band played stirring traditional music and, between songs, strolled about the crowds of guests to different locations. Aromatic scents of spicy food drifted through the evening air, making Casey's mouth water. They walked beside a long table that was piled high with colorful displays of Spanish cuisine. Juana pointed out and explained what each dish was made of as wine and tequila flowed amid everyone's laughter and celebration. Casey thought the scene was incredibly lovely as she shyly smiled and made her way through the courtyard, looking around for another familiar face.

She didn't see him.

She didn't even see Rosa. Casey smiled at Marguerite and her husband as she walked further into the crowd. She spied Manuel talking to another man and turned to Juana. "There's your husband. Go to him and enjoy yourselves tonight."

"I don't want to leave you," the woman answered. "Let us find Señor Luke."

"No, that isn't necessary, Juana," Casey said. "There's no need to find him. He's here. He'll find me. Now, go . . . celebrate with your husband."

"*Bueno,* I will go to my man as you ask," she said, moving slightly as a woman's full skirt brushed past her. "You will remember the magic of this night?"

Chuckling, Casey nodded as she looked up to the full moon. "Kind of hard to forget it, Juana, but I promise I shall remember that tonight is magic. Now . . . go! And tell Manuel I said the musicians are very good, but they aren't as gifted as he is."

"*Muchas gracias,* Señorita Casey. He will be touched by your compliment," Juana said with a smile. Patting the pouch at her side, she whispered with a sly grin, "Tonight there is magic. I can feel it."

"Hmm . . ." Casey murmured with a smile. "I think you are right. Tonight life does seem magical."

Juana nodded, squeezed Casey's hand, and then slipped into the crowd. After a few moments of feeling lost, Casey smiled into the faces of more strangers as she walked toward the garden and found a place to observe the activities without getting in the way. How odd to be here in this place, in this *time*, and finding herself falling in love with it all. There was a charm here that she had never felt anywhere else when she had traveled in the States, no matter what the year was. But here it felt . . . *different.*

"It is a beautiful night, is it not, Señorita O'Reilly?"

She turned, slightly, startled by the voice, and smiled back at a grinning Don Miguel. "*Sí, señor.* It is very beautiful. Rosalinda is very blessed to be highly respected and loved by her family and friends."

The man, formally dressed in a Spanish costume of a dark suit with a short jacket, adjusted a ruffled cuff and again smiled back at her. "The d'Montoya family is respected around the world for its integrity in business. This is the first time I have enjoyed their hospitality, and considering this backward country, I must say they have presented themselves well."

"Backward? I'm afraid I see nothing backward tonight, señor," Casey answered, smiling out to the crowd. "I see people who are enjoying themselves. They could be in any country, in any time."

"You must come and visit my country, Señorita O'Reilly, to see there is a difference."

"Thank you, Don Miguel, but I haven't yet finished exploring my own yet. This really is such a beautiful country." Casey didn't care to be around the arrogant man, yet didn't know what she could do without appearing rude. She also didn't want to say anything that might ruin Rosa's party and her own evening.

The music suddenly ended and a man announced something in a loud voice. It was in Spanish and Don Miguel was kind enough to translate what was happening. "The honor court is being introduced."

She clapped along with everyone as each couple made their entrance. All the girls had lovely dresses in the varying shades of the rainbow. Their escorts, the young men, looked very serious in their formal suits. Standing on tiptoes, she could see that as the announcer introduced each couple, the *dama* dropped her handkerchief and then her escort lowered to one knee, picked it up, and remaining in the humbled pose, offered it back to her. When she took it, he kissed her hand, rose, and led her into the courtyard. Casey thought it was very much like a wedding reception, that same kind of romantic and joyous atmosphere with all its traditions.

Suddenly, across the sea of people, she spied Luke speaking to a woman as the last of the honor court was being introduced. He was dressed in a black suit, with silver studding on the short jacket. Even across the space of at least a hundred people, Casey felt the surge of love well up in her breast as she looked at him. It wasn't that he was so handsome. He was so wonderful, so—

As she was thinking he was just about everything she'd ever wanted in a man, he turned his head and looked straight into her eyes. Stunned, Casey could only stare back as he smiled at her and nodded his head slightly. He said something to the woman at his side and then bowed before moving away. She watched as he made his way through the crowd to her. Her heart was beating so hard that she barely heard Don Miguel's conversation.

"And now the *quinceñera* presentation will begin . . ."

"I'm sorry," Casey muttered. "I . . . I wish to be closer to see Rosalinda. Excuse me, Señor Miguel. Enjoy your evening." Quickly Casey left the man's side and began walking toward Luke. The very last thing she wanted was for Don Miguel to be with her when she finally got to speak with the man who now occupied her mind and her heart.

"*Hola,* hello," Casey kept murmuring politely to those she passed. She saw Luke's dark hair and knew they were closing the distance. Within a few moments he stood in front of her and, after staring into her eyes, smiled softly.

"*Soy muy seguro, tú eres la angelita mas bonita que todos aquí esta noche,* Señorita O'Reilly."

Casey let out her breath and smiled back. "What?"

"I was complimenting you, telling you how beautiful you are."

She found herself blushing like a teenager and tried to accept the compliment gracefully. "Thank you, Luke. And may I say that you look very handsome tonight. It's a beautiful suit."

He smoothed down the jacket that ended at his waist and, still smiling, accepted her words. "Thank you, señorita. Don Felipe was very generous to share his wardrobe."

"We're both wearing borrowed clothes," Casey said with a grin. "The d'Montoyas have been very gracious to us. Thank you, Luke, for bringing me here and allowing me to meet your friends. I like them very much."

"Yes, so do I."

"How . . ." She leaned closer to him to continue, "How is your project coming along?"

Looking down to her, he winked. "Very nicely. It should be ready in a day or two, maybe a bit longer if I am able to put up a railing."

She didn't have time to answer as a great buzz started in the courtyard and the announcer introduced Señorita Rosalinda Maria Theresa Concepcion d'Montoya.

Luke tilted his head to be heard over the intense applause. "Rosa is soon to be officially presented as a woman."

Casey thought surely she was applauding the loudest. She wanted to whistle and throw out a few shouts of congratulations, but restrained herself as this wasn't a crowd to get too rowdy. This was a ritual that all honored. Rosa wore a gorgeous creation of white tulle and satin, with layer upon layer of ruffles that reached the floor and thousands of seed pearls sewn onto the fabric in a design of tiny flowers. She still wore Marguerita's mantilla, studded with pearls, attached by an elaborate comb nestled atop her dark curls and—

Casey sucked her breath in surprise.

Around Rosa's neck was a long thin chain of gold, and the clover pendant dangled to her waist as she moved to her place of honor. Casey felt tears coming to her eyes. "She's wearing my gift," she whispered.

"Your gift?" Luke asked with a perplexed look on his face.

"Yes, the pendant around her neck. It's a four-leaf clover, permanently sealed in glass. My mother had given it to me years ago, but I wanted Rosa to have it." Casey didn't want to explain anything further about why she had given it to the young woman. There were just some things women held privately, especially when it concerned destiny.

Luke smiled and said, "Then you should be honored. For her to wear it tonight means Rosa thinks of you as family."

"I think of her as my little sister," she said, watching Don Felipe escort his daughter to a decorated chair, behind which he stood as the honor court gathered in front of Rosa. Doña Isabela moved to stand beside her husband. Everyone pushed back to make room for the honor court, and soon the courtyard became a dance floor. The girls formed a semicircle in front of Rosa, and Casey watched as her young friend rose up from her chair and joined her *damas,* all fourteen of them, one for each year of her life. The music began and soon all the young girls were dancing together in a playful mood. It seemed to signify that her time of childhood was at an end. Casey watched with a twinge of sadness that the impish Rosa was now supposed to be a grown-up. Somehow she hoped Rosalinda wouldn't lose her curiosity and become too serious.

At the sudden end of the dance, all the *damas* scurried back to their escorts waiting for them behind the chair of honor, leaving Rosa alone on the dance floor. Immediately the musicians began another waltz as Don Felipe slowly extended his hand to his daughter and then swept her up in his arms. Together father and daughter glided across the tiled courtyard floor. He was presenting his daughter to his guests as a woman.

Tears came into Casey's eyes at the touching scene as she witnessed the love of this man for his child, the father for his daughter.

"The music is a very important transitional part of the *quinceñera*," Luke whispered to her as he offered a handkerchief. "First Rosa playfully danced with her friends as a young girl, and now she dances with her father as a young woman."

Dabbing at her eyes, Casey sniffled with emotion. "It's just beautiful." She had never danced with her own father. He had died of a stroke when she was a teenager. She didn't know if she was crying for Rosa, for herself, or what was happening inside of her. She wanted Luke to put his arm around her, to hold her close and let her get this emotion out as she continued to watch father and daughter gracefully waltz.

When the dance ended amid great applause, Don Felipe escorted his daughter back to her chair. Soon a woman, one of Rosa's godmothers, came to stand before the teenager. The woman knelt down and removed Rosa's flat childish shoes and replaced them with chunky high heels. Then Marguerita came forward and stood behind her sister as she removed the mantilla and placed a jeweled tiara upon Rosa's dark curls.

The transition had been made.

Looking like a regal princess, Rosalinda Maria Theresa Concepcion d'Montoya was now officially a woman.

The young girls came hurrying back onto the dance floor and stood in another half circle while their escorts returned and stood in front of their partners.

"This is *la bailar un vals,* a waltz. They have been practicing for weeks."

Nodding, Casey said, "Rosa has told me about it." She was so glad she'd moved away from the garden area and now had such a great view, especially since Luke was next to her. Putting aside her own emotions, Casey clutched the handkerchief in her fist and watched as the girls curtsied to their escorts and were swept up gracefully in the arms of the young men. It was another lovely waltz and the young people dipped and swayed in time to the soothing refrain. Casey thought it was beautiful as all that fabric in all those shades, billowing out like clouds of pink, violet, green, and yellow, passed in front of her. The girls' faces were radiant, as though all the practicing had finally paid off. Casey felt shivers run up her arms, signaling that she was viewing something she would always want to remember.

"Are you cold?" Luke asked as be bent his head to whisper in her ear.

Great! Now she *really* had shivers! Something, some instinct, made her turn her head slightly and whisper right back in his ear, "And if I was? What would you do?"

She saw him stare straight ahead as though startled by her words, and then a slow grin spread over his lips. Without looking at her, he straightened and said, "Why, I would be a gentleman, señorita, and offer you my jacket."

Casey smiled and turned her attention back to the dancers. "Refuse no sincere offers, I say," she answered with a chuckle. "Especially if you're a time traveler. Ya never know when or where you'll get another."

He had to hide his chuckle, but she saw his shoulders shake and she knew she had scored a connection. Yeah . . . she thought, watching the couples wind down the dance . . .

he's the one who had taught her about electricity. Maybe she didn't remember everything perfectly, but she did remember that for a circuit to exist, it must have three things. A source. *Her.* An output device. *Him.* And a connection between the source and the device. *The laughter.* It had worked! His entire mood had changed because hers had too. No longer was she nervous and afraid, worrying that he might not want her. Suddenly she remembered, she had promised herself to *be* herself without any plans!

How could she have forgotten already? She wanted to throw back her head and laugh at her silliness. In fact, the urge was so strong that she had to put Luke's handkerchief to her mouth to cover her giggles. It was worse than being in church because then you could hide behind someone else. Here she just *had* to get a good view and put herself right in front of everyone! Thankful that the *vals* was over, Casey clapped so hard she was glad the hankie was still in her hand. She couldn't even look at Luke or she'd start laughing again. He was so right about laughter being a circuit breaker too.

She really had a new appreciation for the gift of laughter, and vowed to use it more often just as he had said. Obviously it made a good connection between them.

The applause lessened while the floor cleared, as glasses of wine were served to the guests and Casey wondered what the next tradition would be. She noticed Rosalinda saying something to her father and then she looked around her at all the nice people having such a good time. Feeling very happy, she turned her attention back to the dance floor as Don Felipe walked to the center, carrying his own long-stemmed wineglass. What a great party, she thought, glancing at the moon and really liking this magic!

"*Un brindis,* a toast," Luke informed her.

She nodded happily as she held her glass of wine in anticipation.

Don Felipe cleared his throat and looked back once to his beautiful daughter with an endearing smile before turning to the crowd. "*Damas y caballeros*, Bishop Lamy, honored guests. Tonight I toast my daughter Rosalinda, a young woman possessed of a great heart. Before I fulfill this honor, Rosalinda has made a request, an *addition* to her court of honor to complete her presentation. She has requested that two of our fine guests honor her by dancing . . . *un fandango*."

Don Felipe was actually looking straight at Casey!

Casey immediately felt her soaring, bright mood begin a nosedive, and no matter how hard she pulled back on it, her good spirits threatened to crash.

He couldn't mean her! And Luke?

She felt Luke touch her arm and she immediately pulled back. "I can't do this," she muttered between a tightly clenched smile. "No!"

"Do you not realize what an honor this is?" he whispered, leaning down to her as applause began. There were murmurings amid the applause. "This is a very rare occasion, Casey."

"No!"

Don Felipe raised his glass in their direction and smiled with warmth, as though he were including her and Luke in his family. Casey felt her heart drop. She simply could not dance in front of all these people!

The man turned back to his daughter, and Casey looked at Rosa. The girl was holding the clover pendant up for Casey to see. Rosa smiled with such love that Casey felt tears come into her eyes as her new young sister touched the pendant to her chest for just a moment before turning her attention to her father.

Hope. Faith. Love. Destiny. The words she had whispered to Rosa earlier in the day came back to haunt her.

Casey found herself swallowing down the lump in her throat as she listened to Don Felipe begin his toast.

"Congratulations, Rosalinda *mía*. I raise my glass to the future of this beautiful young person, who is an example to many families and graces mine. You are the pride of my life. I pray to God, to your guardian angel, and your grandfather Francisco, that they guide you with steady hands all through your life and assist in making all your dreams come true. I congratulate your mother, your friends and teachers, everyone who wishes blessings upon you, for you have blessed us all by being on this earth. We are all so very proud of you, no one more than your mother and I. May you always be blessed with life's sweetness, the way you have brought sweetness to our lives. *Salud!*"

Casey kept swallowing and blinking to hold back the tears. Everyone shouted, *"Salud!"* She threw back her head and swallowed the entire glass of wine in one huge gulp, as though it might drown the encroaching tears.

"Casey, now is the time. You cannot refuse the honor Rosa has requested of us!" Luke rasped in her ear as he applauded with the rest of the guests.

Watching Rosalinda sip her wine, Casey knew she couldn't either. "This is crazy," she muttered. "How can I do this?"

She watched as Manuel joined the band and she saw Juana standing on the sidelines. The older woman nodded to her and touched her pouch. Sheesh . . . ! Casey needed some big kind of magic right now to pull this off, and she wasn't sure Juana's little ditty bag contained it!

A servant took their wineglasses.

"Shall we dance?" Luke held out his hand to her, and she couldn't move as he lowered his lips closer to her ear and said in a sexy voice, "I got some good advice earlier. Refuse no sincere offers."

He was throwing her words back at her!

"Is this a challenge, señor?"

If possible, his smile became sexier. "This is an opportunity for a man and a woman to dance . . . with passion. Do you accept?"

Oh, he was good.

Suddenly she laughed. She couldn't help it, and the tension left her body as she placed her hand in his. Glancing at Rosalinda, she shook her head, as if to tell the imp that she, too, was good. Rosa had promised they would dance and she wasn't kidding! Walking to the center of the cleared dance floor, Casey kept taking deep breaths, telling herself that all she had to do was forget there were more than a hundred people about to watch as she took on Luke d'Séraphin publicly.

The band began playing slowly as they reached the center of the floor.

"Shall I take my handkerchief?" Luke offered.

"You'll need it later," she whispered with a grin of her own as confidence started to build in her body. She had danced fairly well with him before. There was nothing to fear except what she would think of herself when it was over. She began shutting out the crowd, concentrating on the man, and dropped the white cloth as the *damas* had done earlier. Just like the young men, Luke knelt down on one knee and picked it up. He gently kissed her hand and slowly rose while stuffing the handkerchief into his breast pocket. The edges stood out in sharp contrast to his dark jacket. He then held out his hand to her. She took it and was pulled into his arms.

There had to be some Spanish in her blood, she thought again while remembering Luke telling of all the Spaniards who had been shipwrecked on Ireland . . . 'cause this just felt so natural to her, to be held like this, with a man staring into her eyes, demanding her attention. Maybe it was just this man who brought it out . . .

"Trust me?" Luke whispered.

"Yes." She took a deep breath. "With a passion."

His eyes lit with something that Casey would have sworn was passion itself. His smile reappeared and he whispered, "Good," right before holding her firmly in his arms and taking the stance to alert her he was ready.

Never shifting her gaze from his, she straightened her spine and lifted her chin.

He turned her as the music slowly built in tempo, beginning with Manuel's guitar. It was comfortable and familiar and the other musicians stomped their heels to the rhythmic beat. Casey followed easily, focusing all her attention on Luke's eyes. She allowed her feet to automatically move with his. He twisted her at the waist as the other musicians joined in and the tempo increased. Castanets were suddenly added to the already sensual music.

She swore there must be some gypsy in her and for a moment she wondered what everyone was thinking . . . a blonde woman dancing like this. Almost missing a move and a step, she was glad for the full skirt to cover it.

Stop thinking about them, she admonished herself. *Focus on Luke. This is between the two of you, and everyone else is merely a witness now.* Somehow it was the only way she was going to get through this, she thought as he twirled her out and then back again to wrap his arm across the front of her waist. With her back to his chest, she could feel his heartbeat against her bare skin. His breath in her ear. It sent chills racing across her skin.

"Ginger would be proud of you," he whispered into her hair.

She grinned widely as all tension left her body. She felt fluid, moving along with him, her steps sure as he abruptly twirled her and then turned her until she was back in his arms, staring into his eyes again.

The crowd cheered and Casey suddenly realized she didn't really care what anyone thought. She was having a great time!

She allowed herself to go limp in his strong arms as he dipped and swirled her out and right back in to him. Recalling the theatrical, pointed gestures, she moved with rhythmic confidence as she felt them becoming one with the music. She stomped her foot at the appropriate beat of the moment. He put his chin to his chest, looked her square in the eyes, and stomped back, displaying his acceptance to her challenge. She felt the dew of her own sensuality rise through her pores as he grasped her waist once more and pulled her firmly to his erect body. Oh, this was passion, all right . . . passion with a fever boiling between them.

She trusted him completely, accepting his lead without fear or hesitation, and it was magnificent. Never before in her life had she been this reliant on another human being without trying to take some control. Now it was Luke who guided her across the floor with an expertise that was remarkable. If possible, he was pulling out all stops and she was matching him step by step, move by move. The next time she was twirled out, she dropped his hand and stared at him, daring him to take it higher. She slowly lowered her hand to her skirt and lifted the edge of it up to rest her fist on her hip. In one swift move, she stamped out another staccato of deeper invitation.

The side of Luke's mouth lifted in a sexy grin, as the men and women around her shouted out their approval.

He slowly brought his hands up to his hips and answered her movement with a stunning one of his own. Knowing she wasn't practiced enough to match it, Casey lifted her chin, raised her skirt a bit higher, and repeated her staccato . . . with *attitude* this time.

The women's cheers were even louder than the men's, and Casey almost laughed at Luke's expression. He looked as though he not only wanted her . . . he wanted to have her. Bless Rosa's impetuous heart!

He held his hand out to her and she slowly closed the distance between them.

As he pulled her back into his arms, they again resumed the beginning dance steps. She seemed to be floating above the ground as she effortlessly followed him, all the while staring into his incredible soft brown eyes. Yes, there was magic.

It was called love.

When the dance ended abruptly, Casey was so stunned that she could only continue to stare at Luke, gulping for breath and feeling dizzy at the sudden stop.

"Well done, Casey O'Reilly," he breathed into her mouth.

"You weren't bad yourself, Señor Luke d'Séraphin," she said, adding with a grin, "at least we were far enough away from the walls . . ." She figured he would understand her joke.

He chuckled and spun her out of his arms. When she saw he was presenting her to Rosa, Casey grinned at the teenager and slowly curtsied as Rosalinda stood up and cheered along with the crowd.

Luke turned her around and they slowly bowed to the crowd. Rising, he led her off the floor and back toward the house. Everyone kept applauding, and Doña Isabela seemed to have tears in her eyes. Casey felt a blush cover her skin . . . from the heat of her body now that she'd stopped dancing, and from all the attention. She wasn't used to it, and it was a pretty heady thing for an accountant to experience. Her job felt like a lifetime away.

Don Felipe patted Luke's back as they passed, and the man's smile was full of approval. Casey couldn't remember a time in her life when she'd felt so alive, and as a servant offered her a glass of water, she gratefully accepted and decided staying in the moment was the only way to go, time-traveling or not.

"You were wonderful, Casey," Luke said, accepting his own glass of water. He sipped a few times and Casey could see beads of sweat popping out on his forehead.

Grinning, she pulled the white cloth from his pocket and said, "Why, thank you. Your handkerchief, señor?"

He laughed and grabbed it from her hand amid the chuckles of those surrounding them. "Touché," he said, blotting his forehead, then added, "I believe I have met my match in you, Casey O'Reilly."

It was her turn to laugh.

Eureka! The connection was made and the circuit complete. They had power.

In that moment she glanced up at the moon and felt the magic of being a woman. She was now fully prepared for the next lesson.

Magnetism . . .

Fifteen

"*Y*our dance was magic."

Casey spun around and grinned when she saw Juana beaming up at her. "Oh, thank you so much for everything, Juana. It was your magic that worked."

"It was *your* magic, señorita. Oh, look . . ." Juana pointed to a young man about twenty-five years old who was walking toward the house. "There is Tomás Sandoval."

Still breathing heavily, Casey looked at the handsome man who seemed to have his gaze fixed on Rosalinda. "That's him?"

"*Sí,*" Juana answered. "Señorita Rosa has not met him yet. I see his parents following him. It must be time."

"Time for what?" Luke asked, replacing his glass of water with one of wine.

Casey grinned. "Tomás Sandoval. He is the son of Don Felipe's business partner in Spain. Rosa is about to meet him."

They all watched as the man and his parents approached Don Felipe. Their host greeted his friends warmly and then introduced them to Doña Isabela. Casey held her breath as Don Felipe brought them around the chair to meet Rosalinda.

She watched Rosa's eyes light up and sparkle with interest. The young woman clutched the clover pendant briefly before extending her hand to Tomás. The young man bowed very slowly over Rosa's fingers and, before releasing her hand, he said something that made Rosa's smile widen with pleasure.

Well, how about this? Casey thought in awe. What if Rosalinda was right about meeting her one true love tonight? And what if it really was Tomás?

The musicians began to play again and the atmosphere was expectant as Rosalinda stood up and once more extended her hand to Tomás. The man seemed very pleased as he gracefully led her to the center of the dance floor.

"Now Rosa dances with a man who is not her relative, signifying she is a woman of marriageable age and fully presented to society." Luke grinned as he watched the couple begin a waltz. "Looks like she has picked your Tomás fellow to be the first."

"And maybe the last," Casey murmured, seeing Rosa blush prettily and shyly in Tomás's arms. Casey turned to Juana. "What do you think?"

"I think," the older woman said with a satisfied sigh, "that this night is full of magic and anything is possible."

Nodding, Casey turned her attention back to Rosa. Halfway through the dance, Don Felipe and Doña Isabela joined their daughter. Soon other relatives began dancing and the dance floor became crowded as all were invited to join.

"I must find my man and make sure he doesn't play his

guitar all night with these *hombres* and then desert me,"
Juana proclaimed. "I, too, wish to dance."

Casey smiled at the kind woman as she walked away.
Standing next to Luke, she had turned her attention to the
dancers, trying to find Rosa, when she heard a male voice
behind her.

"Would you honor me by joining me in this dance,
Señorita O'Reilly?"

She turned around and saw Don Miguel, smiling into her
eyes with what he clearly intended to be an invitation.
Feeling awkward with Luke at her side, she was about to
turn the man down when Luke suddenly spoke up.

"*Gracias, señor.*" He looked at Casey and added,
"*Perdóname señorita.* I must step away briefly. Thank you
for the honor of our dance. Perhaps, before this night is
over, we might share another, but now I must beg your
leave."

Stunned, she could only stare at Luke. What the hell was
he doing? Leaving her to Don Miguel? And what did he
have to do that was so important he had to be excused?

"Señorita?" Don Miguel held out his hand.

Casey nearly glared at Luke before placing her palm in
Don Miguel's. "Thank you, señor," she said as politely as
possible. "It would be my pleasure."

The man led her into the circle of dancers, and she was
grateful the waltz had already begun as she didn't know
how long she could hold up. She still wasn't cooled off,
especially now that Luke seemed so eager to dump her.
What was that about? She smiled again at her dance partner and then tried to look into the crowd with every turn.
Where was he?

"You dance very well, Señorita O'Reilly," Don Miguel
complimented her with another inviting smile.

She stared at the tall man before her for just a moment,

this odd visitor to the Montoya home who, as a business acquaintance of Don Felipe, seemed welcome to stay as long as he wanted. The Hispanic culture was certainly different from her own, and far more hospitable. Most of the time he remained in the background, as though not really wanting to socialize with people he considered to be less cultured; at least that was her perception of him. He also appeared to have given up on Rosa as a prospective wife and now seemed free to pursue whom he pleased. She was just glad it was no longer her young friend, who truly did deserve to have her dreams fulfilled.

"Thank you, señor." Casey knew this man had a vague interest in her ever since that night Rosa had begged her to take Don Miguel's attention away from the teenager. Not that she wasn't flattered, as the man wasn't hard to look at and he seemed to be highly respected by these people, but . . . he wasn't Luke. No man she had ever known was anything like Luke, and she didn't think she would ever meet anyone who could surpass him in her eyes. That was why she knew what she was feeling was true.

He was the one.

He was her one true love. Somehow she knew he always would be. No matter what happened between them, Luke would remain the love of her life, even if he never professed his love for her. It just *was,* and she knew she could never deny it.

"Are you certain you have never been to my country, señorita? There seems to be a . . . a passion in your blood, in your dancing, that speaks of Spain."

"Luke taught me to dance," she blurted out, and then regretted her words when she saw the narrowing of Don Miguel's eyes. "And no, I have never been to Spain . . . though I have heard recently that the Spanish Armada was shipwrecked off the coast of Ireland and many of your ancestors left traces of their visit with mine. So perhaps, señor, there is a bit of Spanish blood in my veins after all," she finished with a courteous smile.

"Interesting." Don Miguel didn't seem too impressed with the history lesson.

"Isn't it? I thought so too. Now, here I had been brought up convinced that I was Irish by descent. We Irish are very proud of our heritage, you know. Like the Spaniards, I would think." She saw in the man's eyes his displeasure with her words. "And now," she continued, as though oblivious to the situation, " I have strong suspicions that my so-called pure bloodline just isn't so. It makes me wonder if anyone's actually is. Now, *that*, I find very interesting, señor," she finished with a chuckle. There. That ought to make him think. Plus, his superior attitude was starting to annoy her. Where was Luke? Again she tried to find him, but couldn't as Don Miguel spun her around. She did manage to catch a glimpse of Rosa, and when their gazes connected, both of them smiled with delight to have found each other. In such a short time she had opened her heart, not only to Luke, but also to this giving family . . . especially Rosalinda.

Don Miguel didn't continue the conversation, and on the next sweep around the floor, Casey spied Luke in conversation with a tall, stocky man. The more she looked, the more she was convinced that Luke was not pleased. In an instant of seeing him, she sensed that his body posture was different, and even from a distance, she could see that his expression wasn't its usual serene self. Something was wrong.

The music ended with applause, and Casey allowed Don Miguel to lead her back to the house. She thanked him and hurried off in Luke's direction. As she wove through the crowd, she found that more and more people were smiling at her and nodding in acknowledgment. She nodded back and smiled in response, yet her heart was beating faster as she closed the distance between herself and Luke. His back was to her, though she kept his head as her focus now as she passed the last couple. Even though she couldn't see to whom he was speaking, she did make out the heavily accented English words . . .

". . . and I am scandalized that you, señor, would dance with a woman in such a fashion, a woman who has abandoned the Lord and the church for . . . for carnal knowledge of the world!"

Casey couldn't move when she realized that the man was the same man who had said mass for Rosa. It was the bishop, and he was slamming her for dancing!

"Again I will ask how you, of all people, Bishop Lamy, can sit in judgement."

"I am the representative of the Lord in Santa Fe, placed here by Pope Pius the ninth . . . that is how, señor." The man spoke English with a heavy French accent, yet his voice was clearly firm.

"Ah, yes. Your church," Luke said in appeasement. "The very one that is based upon the teachings of one who spoke of love and nonjudgment. Señorita O'Reilly has nothing to be ashamed of this night, and neither do I."

"You are not a Catholic?" the bishop stated with surprise.

"I am not. I belong to no earthly organization. I am free."

Casey felt like she was eavesdropping as she stayed behind Luke's back, yet she didn't want to interrupt.

"A Hispanic who is not Catholic," the bishop pondered aloud. "I find that . . . very interesting, to say the least. Yet you are not free, señor. You are lost if you do not belong to anything. I will pray for your redemption. It is no surprise to me now that you have willfully corrupted the soul of this woman!"

That did it. Casey came around Luke and slipped her arm into his. "*Buenas noches*, gentlemen." She smiled up at him and then extended her smile to the outraged cleric. "Please excuse me, sir, I don't mean to interrupt, but this fine, *honorable* gentleman has promised the next dance to me, and I believe it's about to begin."

The staunch bishop appeared shocked by her arrival and her words. Casey increased her smile. "Do you like dancing, sir?" she teased, and continued not to give the bishop an opportunity to respond. "Oh, I do so love dancing. It's so . . . so passionate, almost divine. Surely God must be passionate, don't you think? Wouldn't Creation have to be passionate?" The startled man didn't answer and looked as though he couldn't believe what he was hearing. She looked up to Luke's barely contained grin. "My dance, señor?"

The music began just in time, as if perfectly cued, and Luke placed his hand over hers resting on his arm, while he bowed slightly to the man. "Enjoy the rest of your evening, sir. These festivities shouldn't be marred by such a serious conversation. We might continue this at another place and another time, but for this night I will ask to be excused as I join with others who celebrate the life of a young friend. Bishop . . ."

He left the man staring after him and led Casey back onto the already crowded dance floor. As he took her into his arms, she whispered with a loving smile, "Now it's my turn to say 'well done,' Luke. And thank you for defending my honor."

"*De nada,*" he whispered back, smiling into her eyes.

She saw that twinkle return and her heart soared again. She realized the love she had for him had just expanded even more.

"Your honor, señorita, should not require defending. I was simply reminding the man that there is always another perspective." He chuckled as he dipped her slightly and then added, "I am glad you came along before I got into the passion of King David's dancing as he entered Jerusalem!"

"Oh, that was a good one," Casey said with a giggle. "We can go back and tell him, if you like." She clung to his shoulder as the tempo seemed to increase, segueing into another dance.

"I think not," he said with a laugh. "I was holding my breath, waiting to see what else was going to come out of your mouth. 'Wouldn't Creation have to be passionate?' " he added, repeating her words. "That was brilliant, Casey. A little direct for a bishop in 1878 to comprehend, but still brilliant."

"Well, wouldn't it?" she insisted.

As they passed the table of food, Luke suddenly inhaled and said, "Are you hungry?"

"I am," she admitted with a laugh. "I've been too excited to eat all day."

"Let's eat then," he declared, pulling her off the dance floor.

Giggling, Casey realized she liked this more relaxed version of Luke, who stood up for her and himself without making excuses and now seemed determined to satisfy his hunger. She felt like she was on a date.

They piled their plates with an array of cultural delicacies: beef, pork, and chicken enchiladas, frijoles, *arroz con carne asada,* red sauce, green sauce, guacamole, and rich, hot salsa, all topped with flour tortillas and blue cornmeal muffins. There was still more to choose from, awaiting them if they had any room left after the huge meal.

"Let's find seats at a table . . . We can come back for more later if you're still hungry," Luke said as he looked around the courtyard at the crowd. Most chairs were taken.

Casey sighed, not really wanting to share him with anyone. "Why don't we find our bench in the corner of the garden, where we practiced?"

"Good idea," he said, standing back to allow her to lead the way.

Within minutes they found the bench and it was miraculously deserted. "Perfect," she said with a sigh as she sank down onto it. "After all that dancing, it will feel wonderful to get off my feet, and this plate was getting too heavy to hold any longer," she added with a grin.

Luke smiled, sitting next to her, and she pulled aside her gown to give him more room. When she let go, the material fell back, covering his leg, and she felt pleased by the intimacy of it. The party taking place behind them provided a pleasant backdrop with laughter and music.

"It all smells so delicious," Luke murmured, flipping his napkin over his exposed thigh and inhaling the wonderful, spicy aroma of the food.

Casey did the same. "It does," she agreed. "You know, it's funny. I never really ate Mexican food before and now I love it."

"That's part of the adventure, Casey, expanding your base of knowledge, and that includes your palate." He smiled, looking down at his plate as if wondering where to begin.

"Hmm, well, if I eat everything I piled onto this plate, it won't just be my knowledge that expands," she said with a laugh.

Luke bit into a tortilla with gusto. Grinning, he chewed while shaking his head. When he'd swallowed he said, "Stop worrying and enjoy yourself. You have nothing to worry about in this moment, Casey. You are a beautiful woman. Hasn't tonight shown you that?"

She was biting into an enchilada. "Mmm," she murmured in appreciation as she swallowed. "Thank you for saying that. Tonight seems . . . I don't know, magical."

"It does, doesn't it?" he answered, and paused, glancing up at the tree limbs filtering moonbeams down to their private picnic. "Don Miguel seems enchanted by you."

It came out of nowhere, and Casey almost choked. "Enchanted?" Was that a tinge of something in his voice, something that said Don Miguel's attentions were unsettling to him? That was interesting. "Why did you just dump him on me?"

He almost choked and had to swallow hard in order to laugh. "I didn't dump him on you. It was merely the polite thing to do. I couldn't monopolize you all night, especially after everyone saw how wonderfully you dance. I'm sure you enchanted him even further."

"Why, thank you again, kind sir." She smiled. He was brimming with compliments for her, and she was secretly wishing he would monopolize her. "But I don't know about the enchanted part." She stifled a giggle. "I brought up a history lesson and he didn't seem too pleased with the version."

"You didn't reveal anything about the future to him, did you?" Luke suddenly became serious. "A time traveler only talks about these things with another time traveler. You'll know them when you meet them."

She playfully nudged her elbow into his arm. "Oh, give me some credit, Luke." Laughing, she added, "You said I was a good student and I remembered that we shouldn't meddle in the affairs of the time. I didn't think telling Mr. Superiority that probably none of us could call ourselves purebred was meddling with anything."

"Except his mind," Luke offered with an answering laugh.

"Yeah, well, he deserved to have his mind meddled with a bit. Have you listened to him when he goes on and on about being a *gente fina,* as though he's better than . . . than Maria's precious little Angel who was just born? It really annoys me."

Luke grinned. "You are seeing all kinds of prejudice now. It doesn't have to be just about race, you know. It could even be so simple as thinking not having a bathroom ruins an entire adventure."

Casey burst out laughing and almost slapped his arm. "Oh, you! It was an adjustment, a *big* adjustment, okay?"

Shared chuckles became a shared companionable silence as they satisfied their hunger. A few couples strolled along the torch-lit path and nodded greetings as they passed. Casey's mood lightened even more as she felt like she was also part of a couple. Luke seemed to want to be with her, and appeared to be enjoying their time together too. This was just about the best adventure any woman could ask for . . . in any time!

She thought of his statements to the bishop, and her heart expanded again. Luke was certainly a man to have in her corner. She had never seen him really lose his temper, though she'd come close a few times in trying his patience, but she had felt his tightly held control when he'd spoken with the stuffy cleric.

"Imagine that man attacking you when you're building that beautiful staircase for his church!" Her internal thought came through her lips without check.

Luke chuckled. "I'm not building it for him. I told you, I'm building it for the chapel, for the good sisters of Loretto, although I have heard that his niece is mother superior."

"No comment," she said, bringing a fork filled with spiced rice to her mouth.

"Well, I still have compassion for the man, as he has certainly had his share of earthly problems here in Santa Fe. He is carrying a very heavy burden in his heart since his nephew shot the architect of the chapel."

"Oh my," Casey managed to interject between bites.

"Yes, it is quite tragic."

"What happened? I mean, why would someone do that?"

"Since it is a known fact and history will bear witness to the truth, I'll share the story with you." He paused and turned to look in her eyes before continuing, "However, I don't like to involve myself in rumors, Casey."

"I understand and respect that, Luke," she responded sincerely.

"The bishop's nephew discovered the architect was in love with his wife. It ruined his marriage and he shot the man dead." He sighed. "You see, a man's passions can boil over into irrationality when his honor is challenged or insulted, especially in a culture where honor is so revered."

"I guess that's the other part in the definition of passion, that it can also mean fits of anger and rage," she interjected.

"Exactly," he continued, "and Bishop Lamy hasn't had an easy time of it here, since he also alienated many New Mexicans when he disapproved of *santos,* which are primitive carvings of saints. He has demanded they be removed from the people's church, Saint Francis's. I suppose it's because, being French, he may not understand the Hispanic culture."

"That's actually quite sad," Casey thought aloud, feeling a bit of compassion for all involved. "Maybe that's why he's so strict about dancing and . . . how did he put it . . . carnal knowledge of the world?"

Nodding, Luke wiped his lips and said, "Although, to his credit, he has established the academies for both boys and girls, and he is known for being an honest man. Bishop Lamy is a complex mosaic."

"Sounds like it," Casey agreed.

"Enough of the bishop," Luke declared. "What else shall we discuss this fine night?"

"How about . . . us?" She wasn't about to miss another great opportunity when it was presented.

"Us?" Luke appeared startled by her direct approach.

"Yes . . . us. When do you think we'll be able to go back? And when we do, will I ever see you again?"

"Well, at this moment in time, I don't know the answer to either of your questions," he said, taking her plate and putting it on top of his. He placed them on the ground and looked at her. "As you know, Casey, I am only following the unfolding pattern."

She thought about that for a moment. "Yes, and along those very lines, you know what I've been wondering?"

"I'm almost afraid to hear."

She grinned and looked him straight in the eye. "I've been wondering if I was brought back in time so I *could* find you, Luke d'Séraphin."

"Is that what you're wondering?" he asked, staring back at her as though he couldn't tear his gaze away.

"Yes," she whispered, leaning her head closer ever so slightly. "Could it be that we were meant to meet and explore this time together?"

"That could be . . ." He was now staring at her mouth, just inches from his own.

"Remember, you are the one who said you thought I was your equal, Luke. Now I think so too."

"Admittedly, you are like no other woman I have ever met, and I have met many women from many places and times, Casey O'Reilly. You are kind and intelligent, humorous and courageous. You challenge everything in me." He sighed deeply. "And you are beautiful."

"Thank you, señor. Now do I have to tell you all the reasons why I'm falling in love with you, or will you just shut up and kiss me?"

His smile was almost tortured. "Don't fall in love with me, Casey."

"Too late, *amigo*."

He slowly shook his head and stood up, breaking the connection. "This just won't do," he muttered, looking out to the night.

She stood up and pulled on his arm. "Tell me you don't want to kiss me, Luke. Right now, in this moment, which is unfolding, try and tell me that."

He glanced at her and blew his breath out with frustration. "Look, all I can tell you is that this is very dangerous territory you are venturing into, Casey, and—"

"Enough of your double talk, d'Séraphin," she interrupted with more boldness than she ever had before. If she was going to take this risk, then she was going to give it her all. "Luke, I have listened to you for over a week now, successfully changing this subject and avoiding me altogether. I'm not going to let you do it again. Just tell me you don't want to kiss me." In the brief pause that followed her last words, Casey felt she could now read his feelings as the air around them filled with sexual tension. He wanted to and she was certain of it.

Within an instant, she heard his low growl of surrender as he pulled her firmly into his arms and kissed her so perfectly, so passionately, that Casey's head was spinning and she had to grab on to his shoulders just to stay upright. His lips were warm and insistent, sending shivers of delight racing through her blood, melting away any doubts, taking her higher than she thought possible.

When they broke apart, he stared into her eyes and whispered, "I don't want you to be hurt, Casey. I cannot promise you anything."

"I'm not asking for promises," she whispered back, shaking in the aftermath of that kiss. She felt like she might be sinking into the soft brown of his eyes. "I'm just doing what you told me to do. I'm living in the moment."

He continued to hold her tightly against him, and she almost moaned with the pleasure his body aroused in hers.

His smile was soft, and maybe a little sad. "And now the student becomes the teacher."

She was about to raise her hand to brush back a curl from his forehead when another couple made an appearance on the path. Pulling apart quickly, they tried to look nonchalant while smiling and nodding to the other couple. After they passed, Casey smoothed down the front of her gown and adjusted the neckline.

"So what am I teaching you, Luke?" she asked, still wishing to be in his arms.

He sighed deeply again, running his fingers through his hair. "Can you not see how foolish this is? I never know where I shall be or how long I will remain. It would be unfair to you, and to me."

"I'm not asking anything of you," she responded in a trembling voice as she felt him withdraw his energy.

"You are asking everything of me, Casey. You are asking me to alter my life. Sexuality isn't something casual to me."

"And you think it is to me?" Shocked, she added, "Do not mistake my . . . my attraction to you as casual, Luke. I've never been casual. I would rather remain alone than casual. I happen to believe I came back in time to find you. I'm sorry if my love complicates your life, but I won't play coy at this point and pretend, for this hasn't been one-sided, and that kiss just proved it. I'm not innocent like Rosalinda. I'm thirty-one years old and I know what I want now. I've waited a lifetime for you to show up. If I'm not honest now . . . when? What else do we have but right now? Isn't that what you've taught me?"

He closed his eyes briefly and then sighed. "You are making this very hard."

"Good."

Another couple came strolling by and they again nodded and smiled, as though the interlude they were having were mere party conversation. "This is not the place to discuss this matter," Luke muttered, picking up their plates from the ground. "We should get back to the celebration before you are missed."

"Where is the place then to discuss this, and who's going to miss me?" Casey asked, disappointed that again he was managing to backpedal. "What is it that scares you so, Luke? You keep telling me not to fear, that it's such a low-density frequency. What was all that? Do you really believe it?"

He looked tortured. "I don't believe it. I know it."

"And . . . ?"

"And you really don't know that much about me. You have no idea what my life is like and—"

"Wait," she interrupted. "You told me in the garden that you were in service to love, Luke. I'm offering it to you." She hoped he didn't perceive her boldness as whining, but she had to be truthful.

There was a long pause. "There's more to it, Casey."

"Then you're in service to something else? To whom, or what?"

"I don't know how to explain it."

"Try."

He looked up at the moon. "Do you remember when we were talking the other night about electricity?"

"Yes."

"Do you remember I said there must be a source?"

"Yes."

"I am in service to the source."

She blinked. "Wait a minute. This is starting to sound like a *Star Wars* kind of thing and—"

"No," Luke interrupted her with a chuckle, breaking the

tension between them. "The Source . . . The Force . . . they are just labels."

"God?" She said the word, and it took more courage than she thought she had.

"That's just another label to describe the indescribable, which is why it is so difficult to explain this to you. I am in service to something beyond human labels."

She stared into his eyes and knew he meant it, that it was truth to him. "But you said you weren't some celibate holy man."

"I'm not. I'm human and I'm connected to that source. What does that make me? Right now, a time traveler who has come back to the year 1878 because he followed a path and came upon your car and knew he had to come and help you. It was my time of being in service."

"I know you're serious, Luke, and I respect that. It's just that you seem to be stopping the connection that's happening between us, and it feels like fear to me. I'm not afraid. For one of the rare times in my life, I'm not afraid. This just feels so right, I know I'd be regretting it for the rest of my life if I didn't at least give it my all to find out why we were brought together."

"You would tempt the angels, Casey," he whispered, gently brushing a stray strand of hair behind her ear. "You have no idea how much I want you, how much of my thoughts you occupy every single day since I've met you. Just like you do with everyone who gets to know you, you have enchanted me."

"Thank you, for admitting that," she whispered, before adding, "Seems to me, Luke, you have a choice to make. Is it going to be fear, or will you choose love? May not be very romantic to put it like that, but there you are . . . It's unfolded and now it's up to you. I've made myself clear." She looked at him, holding the plates in one hand, staring at her as though she'd just punched him in the stomach.

Reaching out, she pulled his handkerchief from his breast pocket again and dabbed at the corner of his mouth. "There. A little sauce." When she finished, she held the cloth between her fingers and offered it to him with a feminine smile. "I told you you'd need it later. Now I do believe my task here is finished for the night."

Still appearing shaken, Luke slowly pulled the handkerchief from her hand.

"Buenas noches, señor. Enjoy the rest of your evening."

Turning, she walked away from him, away from his fear, back to the house and to her bedroom.

Luke watched the way she held her head, the way her shoulders were pulled back, the sway of her skirt as she walked away from him and was lost in the crowd. He felt as though the breath had been knocked from his body and his mind was spinning. Sitting back on the bench, he set the dishes down and stared into the night sky. What had happened to him? How had everything in his life changed with the appearance of this incredible woman, who more than lived up to her name? She triggered old emotions inside of him, ones he'd thought he had mastered. He felt like there was a short circuit inside of him, reminding him that those emotions were always there, perhaps just dormant. Now they flared up with even more intensity.

He wanted her . . . probably more than she could ever imagine.

Sixteen

*C*asey slowly undressed herself, carefully hanging up Doña Isabela's beautiful gown. She was glad she hadn't soiled the material with her dancing and was again reminded of how generous this family had been to her. That graciousness was kind of lost in her own time, the feeling of giving to another without expecting something in return. She was very grateful to the d'Montoya family for showing her many things.

Walking away the wardrobe, she suddenly stopped and remembered how frightened she had been a little over a week ago, and now . . . now she was grateful to have time-traveled! She had learned so much about herself and had found a new way to view life.

Casey could still hear the party going full swing as she pulled the flowers from her hair and laid them on the small table. Somehow she knew she'd had enough excitement for one night and now she wanted to be alone. She didn't even want to talk to Luke. He needed some time to think, and so did she, she thought as she puttered around the room in her bare feet. The soft cotton nightgown caressed her skin as she washed her face and brushed her hair while preparing for bed.

How strange that she wasn't fearful of what Luke might do. She had made her case and there wasn't anything left to be said about it. It was his choice now.

Blowing out the flame in her lantern, Casey climbed up onto the bed and snuggled back against the pillows. She had never been the pursuer, and she suddenly had a feeling of what men must experience while trying to help their woman see their love. It was a night for odd feelings . . .

But he had kissed her!

And what a kiss! Wow, she had never felt such passion in her entire life. Oh, he wanted her, all right. Now he just had to slay his mental dragons and realize they were being given this great gift, this love, for a reason. There had to be a purpose to it all, even if it was just to be given the opportunity, for once, to follow their own hearts and not worry about the future and what it may or may not bring.

She could admit to herself, if no one else, that she had done well tonight. It wasn't often that she could remember feeling this kind of self-respect. She didn't cry or cling. She just spoke from her heart and prayed Luke could hear it.

The glow from the full moon interrupted the darkness of her room, as she heard the mariachi band begin another spirited song. Casey grinned and thought back to the way she and Luke had danced. Wait until she got hold of Rosalinda and thanked her! And what an honor to be part of her new little sister's *quinceñera* presentation. Rosa had shown by wearing the clover that they were sisters of the heart. As she pictured the way Rosa had arranged everything, Casey's eyes filled with tears of gratitude to the young woman.

Smiling, she punched her pillow down and snuggled deeper into the bed, listening to the music and the laughter, thinking about sweet Rosa and her family, Don Miguel and the bishop . . . and Luke. She knew this night would be burned into her memory. Surprisingly, she was calm, and she closed her eyes and breathed deeply, welcoming the peace of slumber. She had already done enough today. She needed rest, for she had a feeling that whatever was about to happen was going to come on fast now. It was just a feeling, an instinct that told her once Luke made his choice, whichever way it went, something big was definitely going to happen.

Maybe she wasn't the only one who had time-traveled to find out more about herself. Perhaps Luke wasn't just her guide, but was also learning. What had he said about the student becoming the teacher, and the teacher becoming the student again?

She shook the question out of her head. Enough for one night.

The music became softer, less passionate, and Casey felt the last residuals of tension slowly leaving her body as she surrendered. She cleared her mind of everything but the sound of the music and her own rhythmic breathing. She lost all sense of time as she seemed to relax more and more and welcomed the comforting arms of sleep around her.

She had no idea how much later it was when she was awakened by silence and realized the party was over. Then she heard a soft noise from her wardrobe and gasped when she saw Rosa walking toward her.

"*Rosa!* What . . . ? Why . . . ?"

"Shh," the girl called out, and tiptoed up to the bed. "I couldn't sleep without talking to you, my sister. This has been a night of all nights, and it has happened! I have found my true love!"

Wide-awake now, Casey automatically moved over and opened the coverlet for her. Rosa snuggled in, and Casey turned on her side to face her. "Tomás?"

Rosa's gleaming smile showed through the darkness. "You knew!"

Shaking her head and chuckling, Casey said, "I guessed and Juana pointed him out to me. I saw him lead you in the dance."

"Is he not most handsome? And the very best dancer, and his heart is kind and compassionate and *ay, Madre de Dios*, he is most charming!"

"You think he is the one, Rosa?"

The girl nodded her head vigorously. "He is the one. I am certain of it. Already he speaks of feeling as though he has always known me. That is the way I feel too. When I say something, he can finish my words! I think he would have told me he loved me but for it being our first meeting. Such a thing is possible, is it not? My parents tell me they both knew as soon as they met. Is that not remarkable? I am so filled with love, my sister."

"Should you, I don't know, go a little slowly?" Her words sounded a bit hypocritical. Who was she to tell another to love slowly?

"For the sake of our family, Tomás and I have agreed to proceed with proper respect for tradition. He will be here for three more weeks as both our fathers conduct business. Do you know that Tomás's father is Papi's partner in the importing company? We have time to prepare our families."

"You've decided all this in one night? To get married?" Talk about taking a risk!

"I have three weeks to decide, though I must admit my

decision is already made. You simply have to meet Tomás, Casey, and you will understand."

"Yes," she breathed, stunned by Rosa's sudden news. "I would like to meet him."

"He thinks you are a most remarkable woman. We have talked about you and Señor Luke, and Tomás's words were, 'The *caballero* is very much in love with the beautiful *senorita*.' It was plain for all to see when you danced."

She liked this Tomás more and more. Grinning, she reached over and hugged Rosa. "Thank you for including me in your presentation and for wearing the pendant. I am honored, little sister."

"I feel that, Casey. Though you are not of my blood, you are a sister of my heart. You are not stuffy, like Marguerita is now. You still remember that life does not have to be so serious. That we are here to experience the happiness too!"

She looked at Rosa and smiled widely. "The optimism of youth. I guess I've gotten it back while I've been here. Thank you for that too."

They heard voices in the hall and both of them remained silent until they passed. "I must go now," Rosa whispered, flipping the cover back. "I am sure when the house is quiet, Mami will pay me a visit. Promise me you will meet Tomás tomorrow."

"I will, I promise."

"And then promise you will meet me in the evening, after the house is again quiet."

Casey was confused. "Why?"

"There is more to tell you. Meet me at the fountain at nine o'clock. Promise me?"

"Okay," she whispered. "I don't know what this is all about and why you can't tell me now, but—"

"I must get back," Rosa whispered from across the room as she entered the wardrobe.

"Happy birthday, Rosa!"

"*Gracias*, it has been the happiest day of my life."

The door to the chest closed and Casey fell back upon her pillows, certain she would never get back to sleep now!

She sat on the edge of the fountain, waiting for Rosa to show up. At exactly five minutes to nine, she had left the house and come to the courtyard. What was so important that Rosa had kept putting her off during the day, making sure that every conversation was either about Tomás or with him? Casey had to admit she really liked the young man, who seemed very serious about his commitment to his family, his career, and now to his new love. In observing Rosa and Tomás together, Casey realized the young woman might just be right and have found her one true love. Amazing . . .

Twisting the fringe of her shawl with her fingers, Casey sighed at the moon, still bright and magical. Her attention was drawn toward the sound of footsteps across the tiles. "Rosa?"

"Casey?"

It was a male voice. Luke's.

Standing up, she watched as the man who had successfully avoided her all day now walked in her direction. "I'm waiting for Rosa."

"She told me to meet her at the fountain," Luke said, looking around the darkened courtyard. "She said it was important."

"She said the same thing to me."

They looked at each other and Casey started to laugh. "You don't think she arranged this, do you?"

Luke grinned. "I wouldn't put anything past that young lady."

Casey listened to the pleasant sound of the water and

said, "You might as well know, she knows how I feel about all this."

"Don Felipe has been bending my ear over you. Do you suppose this is a family conspiracy?"

Laughing, she shook her head. "I'm learning since I've been here that anything is possible. Don Felipe, huh?" She was thrilled to have Luke's friend in her corner.

He looked back at the house, as though willing the girl to show up. "Yes. He said after seeing us dance, it was obvious to all but a blind man that something deeper was happening. You will be happy to know he called me a fool."

"Good for Don Felipe."

They heard a noise from the patio door and soon a tall figure was walking toward them. It certainly wasn't Rosalinda.

"Señor Cortez," Luke greeted the man, who was looking around the courtyard.

When Don Miguel recognized Casey, he seemed surprised and bowed formally. "I didn't expect to see you, Señorita O'Reilly. I was told to meet someone at the fountain."

She held up her hand. "Let me guess. Rosalinda?"

"*Sí.*" The man look surprised.

"She told the same thing to Luke and to myself. Why do you think she wants us to be here . . . together?"

"That I do not know. She was very . . . what is the word? . . . mysterious about it. I had hoped, ah . . . thought she might make an announcement about her affections."

"Oh," Casey murmured, and glanced at Luke. He didn't seem pleased.

"May I walk you back to the house, señorita?" Don Miguel asked, pointedly looking at Luke before adding, "You should not be out here alone."

"She isn't alone, señor. I am with her."

Casey heard the formality in Luke's voice and decided

to say nothing. This was getting interesting. She would just watch as it all unfolded before her.

"Señorita Casey is without a proper chaperone."

"Are you implying she isn't safe with me?"

The air seemed to bristle with tension as both men looked at each other, and Casey swore she had seen this scene before. Two men, trying to claim territory . . . It was like some sort of primitive male contest.

Don Miguel backed down and said, "I shall see what is keeping our young Rosalinda."

As she watched the man walk away, Casey whispered to Luke, "Feel better now?"

Even though there wasn't much light, Casey could see his frown. "See what you have me doing now?"

She laughed. "That's okay, Luke. Good to know you still have some buttons that can be pushed. You aren't perfect."

"I never claimed perfection. How boring that would be."

"And you certainly aren't boring," Casey added. "So that proves you are imperfect, just like the rest of us."

"You are baiting me, aren't you? Like last night when you walked away after making that statement about choices." He was staring into her eyes.

She merely smiled. "Hmm . . . choices. If I were really baiting you, señor, I would tell you that I have fallen in love with this place and I might just remain and have lots and lots of *bebés* with Don Miguel. As we've learned . . . when an opportunity presents itself—" She was unsuccessful at keeping the laughter from her voice.

He chuckled. "You are impossible, do you know that? Let me walk you back now. I am installing the staircase tonight and must leave."

"I don't want to go back," she stated with a bit of defiance. "Maybe I'll just stand here by the fountain and wait for Don Miguel. He never runs out of conversation." She now realized why clever Rosalinda had asked Don Miguel to meet them. It was to put a bit of pressure on Luke. Pretty smart young lady, Casey mentally mused.

"I can't stand here and argue with you. I must leave."

"So go . . . See if I care. Make a choice, one way or the other. I can—"

Her words were cut short as Luke pulled her into his arms. Staring at her mouth, he murmured, "I have work to do, woman. Go back into the house."

And then his lips slowly, gently, grazed hers, a mere whisper of touch. "Please don't torture me anymore," he murmured into her mouth. "How can I work if I cannot sleep for thinking of you day and night? Will you release me from this spell?"

"This is no spell," she whispered back, running her hands over his shoulders and then threading her fingers, ever so softly, into his hair. "This is love, and the sooner you accept it, the better off everything will be. Take it from someone who's done it."

"Ay, mujer," he muttered before capturing her mouth under his lips and kissing her so thoroughly that when he released her she was swaying.

"Go back inside," he rasped, and then walked away.

She was left there, astonished by the intensity of emotion that had passed from him into her as their tongues had dueled in a passionate mating dance that rivaled anything they had done on a dance floor. She held out her hand as she lowered herself to the ledge of the fountain, for she needed to sit down until her equilibrium returned. Suddenly her hand slipped, and before she knew what happened, she found herself falling into the water.

"Shit!" She sputtered and attempted to pull herself out. She couldn't believe it! Enough was enough. She must have needed the water to make her see it plainly. If this was a dance they were doing, then it was time for the finale. She was going to get some answers, away from this house. Standing up and wrapping her damp shawl around her with as much dignity as she could muster, Casey began to walk out of the courtyard.

She wasn't going back to the house.

She was going to have a showdown.

Seventeen

She knew she must look ridiculous, wet and furious, so she kept to the shadows as she walked through the streets of Santa Fe, building her mental rant as she passed by drunken cowboys and several women standing against buildings, smoking cigars. No one dared to approach her as she kept mumbling to herself . . .

How dare he just kiss her and walk away? She had listened to him for over ten days, watched him flirt with her, deny her, want her, and deny her again. Enough! It was time for Luke d'Séraphin to get off the fence and make a choice. Who knew how long they would be here, and she wasn't about to spend this time trying to make him see what was obvious to everyone else, even his friend Don Felipe! She wasn't asking for a commitment, just a decision.

What caused his fear? she wondered as she turned down the street toward the building in which he worked. He couldn't promise anything. Okay, she wasn't asking for a promise. He never knew where he would be, or how long he would remain. Fine, he was here *now*. Hadn't he taught her to accept the present and not worry about the future? He was in service to some mysterious, unnameable force or source of everything. Terrific, she'd throw in her weight, too, if it meant living in the moment and seeing that life was meant to be enjoyed. Sounded like a pretty adventurous path, and she was finding that being in Luke's presence was a catalyst for her being more true to herself. He just wanted to keep this attraction as a flirtation, and she wasn't going to have it. They could be friends or they could be more than friends, but this torturous in-between state was going to end.

It was like he was talking himself out of happiness.

That made her wonder why in her time people so willingly agreed that shit happened, but were suspicious when joy happened? She guessed she, too, had talked herself out of happiness plenty of times because of fear, and that was why she could recognize it so easily in Luke now.

She blinked in surprise as she looked across the street to the building Luke had been using. It was dark. He wasn't there. It made no sense and she turned around in a circle, not knowing what else to do. Where could he be? Maybe he had stopped in one of the bars again and hadn't arrived yet. Standing against the rough adobe wall of a building, she decided she wasn't about to check out the bars, so she'd just wait. He would show up.

And then they *were* going to have it out!

She was ready. It was no longer just about having a child. She wanted Luke, if not for forever, then for right now, and she wanted him to want her without fear. She wanted him to make a decision. She realized she could live with it, no matter the outcome. She went over in her mind everything she wanted to say to him, giving him back his own words, his own mentor advice to her. The longer she waited, the more she built her case. A faint flicker of light down the road caught her attention and she looked to see what it might be.

The chapel.

She had never been inside, and it was far enough away from the bigger church that if one did not go down the side street, it couldn't be seen. Luke must be there. She suddenly remembered he'd said he was installing the staircase tonight. Pulling her still damp shawl tighter, she ventured out from the shadows and walked toward the light.

Within minutes, she pushed on the side door and peeked inside.

"Casey!"

She didn't say anything in response to him as she entered the tiny chapel and walked around the pews. Her voice was silenced by the magnificent sight of the double helix spiral staircase reaching up to the choir loft. It had two 360-degree turns in it and seemed to stand by itself. "How does it stay up?" she breathed in awe, her rant completely forgotten for the moment.

"The inner radius is so small that it acts as a support pole." Luke seemed to accept her presence and even smiled as she admired his work. "You like it?"

"Like it?" She turned to him. "It's magnificent, Luke! I can't think of any other word to describe it." Instinctively she rushed up to him and hugged his arm. "Congratulations," she whispered. "Well done."

The muscle of his upper arm tightened in response to her hug and he chuckled. "Thank you. It does serve the purpose well. Now the sisters can ascend to their choir without worrying who might be looking up their skirts."

Laughing, Casey pulled back and turned once more to the staircase. The small chapel was dimly lit by the few lanterns he had placed around his work space. The lighting added to the ethereal atmosphere. "Oh, Luke, it really is magnificent," she whispered, coming closer and reaching out to run her fingers over the smooth wood. "What a wonderful thing you have created. Its takes you almost magically up from ground level."

Again he laughed. "Well, it will get them where they want to be."

She spun around and saw that in the front of the chapel, behind the altar, was a big portrait of the Madonna and Child. "And you shall hear women singing praises, as you wished."

He shrugged. "That was only part of the reason."

She turned her gaze to him and whispered, "Yes, I know. I'm the other part. Now that it's finished, what are you going to do, Luke d' Séraphin? We're still here together and you explained you don't know exactly when we're getting back . . . How will you occupy your nights now?"

He shook his head and walked past her to the staircase. "You are too much for me, Casey," he muttered, picking up a tool and sanding out a rough spot on the wooden curve. "You won't allow this to rest, will you?"

She brought her hand up to her hip. "Hey, I'm not the one who kissed you back there in the courtyard. You grabbed me, remember?"

He glanced at her. "Why are you wet?"

Brushing her damp hair away from her face, she stood up straighter. "Never mind trying to change the subject. You're very good at that, Luke, but tonight I'm not going to allow it. I came over here to let you have it."

"It?"

"Yeah, *it!*" she almost yelled, and then lowered her voice when she remembered she was in a chapel. "You think you're the only one who's filled with doubts about love? Is that your fear? Because if it is, your fear is going to drive me away. We can be friends or we can be more, but we can't stay like this. It's driving both of us crazy."

"You don't understand what you're asking."

"I understand that I'm asking you to make a decision. Maybe one you've managed to sidestep for God only knows how many years. Since you're in service, time-traveling God only knows where, it might have been thousands!" She felt better now that she had gotten it out. Calmer, she continued, "But you have to make a choice now, Luke. I don't deserve less, and truthfully, neither do you. I have a right to know if I am loved."

His arms dropped to his sides, and he stared at the wood in front of him, as though not having the strength to finish. "Casey . . ." His voice was a mere whisper of torment.

"Luke, if it's about not making promises because you don't know where you'll be, I accept that. No promises. I don't want to take away your freedom. I know how important it is to you. If it's because you've got some contract with this unnameable source, I accept that too. I'm starting to realize why it will always come first in your life and I can respect it. Heck, I'll even come on board myself if *this* is part of it, because I had never known I was capable of this much love for another. Whatever your fear is, Luke, you've got to listen to your own advice. You're the one who taught me not to hold on to fear, but to accept where I was now and not fight the way life was unfolding. Well, it unfolded with me loving you, and I deserve to know what your fear is, because it's blocking both of us now. I deserve the truth."

She surprised herself by her words, yet as she heard them, she recognized they were as true and sincere as she knew how to communicate. Swallowing several times to bring moisture back into her mouth, Casey tried to be patient as she waited for him to speak.

He laid the tool back on the ground and walked up to

her. Standing a few inches away, he reached out and pulled her damp shawl from her shoulders and draped it over a pew. Her heart started thumping in her chest and she knew he had made a decision.

"You are the most wonderful and the most maddening woman I have ever encountered, Señorita Casey O'Reilly," he whispered with a tender smile as his fingers brushed back her hair. He looked more deeply into her eyes. "You have sharpened my mind with your never-ending lists of questions, and—"

"There weren't that many and I had every right to ask questions when I'd been thrown back in time and—"

"Shh," he said with a smile as he held his finger to her lips. "Allow me, for once, to finish without interruptions."

"Okay," she murmured against his finger, for he left it resting ever so gently on her chin.

"You have reminded me with laughter and intelligence not to take myself so seriously. And finally, you have probed every last recess of my resistance with your words of truth and your incredible, amazing love, making it impossible for me to deny it any longer. How could I not love your warmth, your humor, your intelligence, your compassion, your faith, your agility, your complex and fascinating beauty?"

"You love me?" Tears were coming into her eyes.

"Here, *mi querida,* my beloved one, in this chapel that honors truth, I confess mine now. You must already know the truth of my soul . . . I adore you. You had my love long ago. Perhaps from the moment I looked into your incredibly honest eyes." His finger was slowly tracing the outline of her lips. "I do love you, my precious angel."

He lowered his head, and when his lips touched hers, she whimpered in relief and threw her arms around his neck as he drew her into the most beautiful kiss. Holding him close, she met his kiss with tenderness, with respect, and with a love that she thought might burst through her heart.

"You love me," she whispered through her tears as she broke the kiss and laid her head on his chest.

He stroked her hair and kissed the top of her head as he cradled her in his arms. "I apologize for not telling you earlier. I was worried for you, *querida*. This will not be a normal relationship by any means," he whispered, tilting her head up to look at him.

"Believe me, I know that. I'm willing to do whatever it takes. I've waited forever for you to show up, Luke. I'm not about to blow this because of fear."

"You are courageous, my love. Your parents named you well."

"I never thought of myself as being brave. This doesn't feel brave, Luke. This feels *right*."

"It does," he agreed. "Again, I am so sorry I made you wait to hear a truth we both felt in our hearts. I was worried for you, my time traveler. Already you have surpassed me in faith. Truly you are the teacher now."

"We'll teach each other and learn together."

"You must know something first," he said, looking deep into her eyes. "I have never said what I am about to say to anyone else, and I want you to know it is a love such as I never knew existed that prompts these words . . . I am committed to this love now, in every way, physical and beyond. I will always honor and respect it, for it is beyond you and me, it has a life of its own, our union." He took her hand. "Will you, Casey O'Reilly, share with me whatever time we have together?"

She felt like a bride, and the tears she had been trying to hold back started to fall onto her cheeks. "I will."

His eyes were filled with intense love. "As will I," he whispered into the silence of the chapel, while brushing away her tears with his fingers. "You are wise when you say you deserve the truth. Above all, such vulnerability deserves it. My fear, beloved one, was loss of freedom, and now that I have told you of my love, I feel more free than I ever have before. We are blessed, you and I, for however long we travel together. May it be eternity . . ."

Slowly, no longer needing words, they came together, joining lips, minds, hearts, souls, and silently sealed their union.

"Surely no wedding service performed by a priest was more accepted in the eyes of God."

They broke apart and turned toward the voice.

A nun stood at the doorway.

"Sister Bernardina!" Luke identified the woman as he continued to hold Casey to his chest.

"It is beautiful," the nun whispered in awe as she came into the chapel and looked at the staircase. "You have performed a miracle, señor."

"Gracias." Luke released Casey and held her hand as the nun came closer. "It still needs a railing, but any good carpenter can do that for you."

"And it works?" the robust woman asked in disbelief.

"Try it."

"Oh, there is no time!" Sister Bernardina exclaimed, as though remembering why she was in the chapel so late at night. "The light has been sighted by the sisters and they are sending Father Taladrid to investigate. I came to warn you. If you do not wish to be discovered, señor, you must leave immediately."

"Thank you, Sister," Luke said, grabbing his jacket and Casey's shawl, and pulling Casey toward the door.

"Wait . . . señor!"

They looked back to the nun.

"Who are you really?" she pleaded, awe still in her

voice. "How . . . how did you perform this miracle in such a short time? What shall I say when asked?"

"Say nothing, sister," Luke insisted, leading Casey to the door. "You cannot tell what you don't know. *Vaya con Dios, Hermana.*"

"Tell everyone an angel built it," Casey yelled with a joyous laugh as Luke pulled her out the door.

He stared at her, his eyes wide with disbelief as he led her away from the chapel.

"Well, you are, aren't you?" she asked with a giggle. "Angels are messengers, and you're delivering messages everywhere you go, to everyone you meet. You must be an angel!"

"*Angel* is another label, Casey," he muttered, pulling her into the shadows of the alley. He suddenly pressed her against the side of the building, concealing her with his body and looking like he was about to kiss her. "Does it matter what I am?" he asked, and Casey heard hurried footsteps. It must be the priest.

"No," she answered with a whisper, looking into his eyes and knowing it was the truth.

The footsteps passed them.

"If I told you I was an alien, or an angel, or just a simple man who happened to have time-traveled once, just like you, and found himself while doing it . . . would any of it make any difference to what you know in your heart?"

She shook her head. "Nothing will change my mind. I love you, whoever you are."

"And I love you, Casey O'Reilly." He smiled and squeezed her hand. "Now let's get out of here while Father Taladrid thinks we are a scandalous couple who can't control their emotions on a public street."

They both laughed and Casey felt like her feet didn't even touch the ground as they hurried through Santa Fe.

Casey . . . the married lady. A nun, no less, had pronounced it!

They stood at the foot of her bed, staring at each other. Luke had entered the house with her, using the passageway, and now it appeared the moment of real truth was upon them.

"Why am I so nervous?" Casey whispered, staring into his eyes. She had wanted this, dreamed of it, desired it. Why did she look like a drowned rat *now* of all times?

"There is no need, *querida*." He brushed the tips of his fingers over her brow. "What if you knew that for the rest of your life you never again had to worry what someone thought of you, because you knew you were totally loved? Every thought. Every gesture. Every laugh. Every curve of your body. What if every inch of you is so precious that no thought save love could ever be applied to it?"

"I . . . I would be in heaven."

"Welcome to heaven, Casey," he said with the most tender smile.

"This is gonna be intense, isn't it?"

"Yep." His slight chuckle was even more endearing, that he could go along with her playfulness. "This is gonna be intense. But you're an excellent teacher and you've taught me there's nothing to fear. Allow me to lead you. I will never hurt you, my precious angel."

"Right," she breathed, as his fingers slid down the side of her face to her neck, and the laces that bound her blouse. She kept her gaze locked with his, taking her strength now from him.

"I have imagined, dreamed, of this moment," he whispered, pulling on the laces until the top of the blouse dropped down her arms. He gently removed the blouse and placed it on the bed beside them. The chemise had more laces and he slowly began untying them, whispering, "Beautiful, beautiful . . ." as more of her was revealed.

She drew in her breath as his hands gently touched her breasts, as though paying them honor with his reverent touch.

Gazing into her eyes, he said, "Thank you for trusting me."

Sensing the tears returning, she pulled him to her, feeling his shirt against her breasts. "Thank you for loving me," she answered, burying her face against his neck and inhaling him. "I . . . I've never felt like this before."

He brought his head down and lightly ran his cheek against hers, creating an intimacy that inflamed every nerve ending in her body. "Nothing exists, *querida*, but this moment . . . Stay here with me."

"Always, Luke . . . I'll always stay with you, anywhere, anytime."

Their mouths came together, as though starved for each other, and Casey nearly ripped his shirt from his chest. Luke helped, and when his bare skin touched her breasts, she moaned with the searing contact and her head fell back as he placed kisses along her neck and shoulder. He took his time, savoring each inch of skin, extracting for them both such pleasure, all that was heard was their ragged breathing. Kissing, licking, nipping, his mouth devoured her. Her breasts ached for his touch again, and as though knowing everything about her, he bent his head and paid them homage. Everywhere he touched, her blood rushed to that spot, leaving her feverish for more. His hands caressed her back and waist, tugging at her skirt until it pooled at her feet.

Without words, they quickly removed all remaining barriers of clothing. Shoes were kicked off, slip and underwear dropped on the floor along with his trousers. As she stood naked in the moonlight, Casey realized, incredibly, she wasn't scared. She could feel she was loved beyond anything she'd ever imagined, and fear had no part in this . . . This was timeless.

"You are so incredibly beautiful." His voice was low and husky with desire.

She smiled and brought her hand up, as though to sprinkle something before his eyes. "Juana's magic," she murmured. "To keep you thinking that."

"I need no magic beyond this moment, *querida*." He captured her hand and kissed her palm, running the tip of his tongue up to her wrist and planting a kiss at her pulse. "I wish you could see yourself through my eyes. You would know you never need anything else. You *are* beautiful."

She sighed as she stroked his chest, feeling the beat of his heart under her hand. "I love you, Luke," she whispered as emotion crept up her throat.

"C'mere." He shocked her by sweeping her up into his arms and carrying her to the bed. Placing her gently against the soft pillows, he reached down and kissed her tenderly. "I'll be right back."

"Where are you going?" she demanded, feeling his loss as he walked across the room.

He picked up the chair and carried it to the wardrobe. "I just want to make sure we aren't disturbed."

Casey grinned. He was the beautiful one. His strong lean body was perfection. "Good thinking." She turned on her side and ran her hand over the coverlet. "Now *you* c'mere . . ."

"As you wish, *mi querida*," he answered, sliding onto the bed and pulling her into his arms again.

They came together with a passion kept in denial for far too long. Hands were instruments of discovery and pleasure. Their mouths tasted and memorized the landscape of each other's body. Casey felt herself melting into him, giving of herself so freely, and when he moved to lie on top of her, she gasped with the scorching connection. She could feel his heartbeat at their intimate meeting as he held her close and breathed her name . . .

"Casey . . ."

She opened her legs to welcome him and he slid between them. This time he gasped and stared at her in wonder. Stroking her hair back off her face, he said, "I have never felt this close to another. Always I held something back, for fear of the uncertainty in my life. This time . . ." He shook his head slightly. "This time there is no holding back. If there is nothing more than this moment, then I shall not waste it with anything but love. I, too, have waited a lifetime to adore you."

He lowered his head and kissed her lips, her eyes, her nose, her chin. He began a course down her body, lingering at her breasts, and when he left them to go lower, Casey moaned and reached up to cling to the iron bars of the bed.

He adored her, using his tongue to caress her tender flesh. Over and over he graced her with his attention, creating such exquisite pleasure that she moaned his name as his hand came up and captured her breast. Waves of intense sensations permeated her body, and when she thought she couldn't take any more, he slowly, deliberately, slid up her electrified torso and stared into her eyes.

"You were made for me."

"Yes," she breathed back heavily, trying to make her brain work again. The throbbing between her legs didn't ease and she wrapped them around him to again make contact.

"Not yet, my beloved," he whispered, and then glided down to kiss each breast, the tender skin beneath, her belly, and again he adored her. "I want this night to be burned in our memories." His hot breath against her inflamed body sent a current of heat laced with pleasure rushing through every inch of her. Every tiny nerve ending was alive, awakened, and demanding release from this magnificent torture.

"Oh God . . ." Casey gasped, not knowing how much more she could stand. Over and over he repeated the same thing, bringing her to the brink of orgasm and then stopping. She had never been loved with such total abandon, and a part of her knew she was being altered, for she felt herself expanding to him, opening her mind, her heart, her soul, even more.

"Please, Luke," she pleaded, wanting to unite with him. "Please come to me . . ."

For the last time he kissed her throbbing flesh. "My pleasure, *mi amor,*" he whispered, coming to lie above her. "You are mine."

"I am," she murmured thickly. "Forever . . ."

She wound her arms around his back and pulled him to her, gasping and pressing her head into the pillow at the exquisite, breathtaking sensation of him slowly, gently, sliding into her. The warmth, the fullness, the rightness, overwhelmed her as he kissed her chin and whispered in a raspy voice, "Thank you, my precious one, for loving me. I . . . I didn't think you existed, except in my mind."

"I'm here," she cried. "And I do love you . . ."

He thrust into her and she moved in response, wrapping her legs around him to pull him closer. Again he began a rhythmic motion, this time with his body, and Casey followed easily, for they had danced before and she trusted him with her life. He brought her back to the edge again, urging her onward with words of love, encouraging her to leap, to fly, and it built and built until she burst beyond and she *was* flying, as wave after wave of divine energy seemed to race to every atom of her being and seep out through her pores, sending her into the universe to dance amid the stars.

It was magnificent.

"Casey . . . Casey . . . *mi amor* . . ." He called her name as his body stiffened with release and he joined her in the heavens, granting her the honor of leading him home. They clung together through the aftershocks, gasping as the dance crested on and on in an unnameable timelessness. Everything they each desired was fulfilled in one exquisite, glorious, eternal moment.

"Oh . . ." Casey gasped, settling back into her body with such sweetness that she wanted to cry.

He lifted his head from her shoulder and gazed with love into her eyes. "We are united now, you and I," he whispered with a smile as he brushed her hair off her face. "We are forever altered, *querida*. There is a poet who said it well, something to the effect that you and I are not going to be who we were going to be because we changed all that for each other, and we are now going to be who we never would have been without each other. I pray you will always be happy with the change."

"I am so happy, Luke," she whispered, sniffling and cradling his face with her palms. "Happier than I have ever been in my life. I feel so peaceful, as though I have finally come home and my seeking is done. Whatever happens after this, I promise you . . . I will always be grateful that you changed my life."

"As will I, Casey. I am more of me now."

"Yes," she said in an excited voice. "That's it. I'm more of me now, too."

He slid off her and pulled her into his arms. She lay on her side and casually, as if they had been married for years, drew her leg over his body and her arms around his chest. "That was exquisite, Luke," she murmured, running her hands over his skin and reveling in the sensation.

He stroked her back and sighed contentedly. "Thank you for receiving so beautifully and for giving so completely. You honor me with your love."

"I could stay within your love forever like this," she

sighed, feeling as though she never wanted to leave his arms. It was as if she had been on this long, arduous journey to reach him her entire life. And now she felt safe, secure, loved.

"I must speak with you about a few things now, my precious time traveler."

She lifted her head and looked into his eyes. "You sound so serious. What's wrong?"

"Nothing is wrong, *querida*, but the time has come to explain some things. It's about time-traveling. Do you remember making a bet with me? That if you learned how to dance with me, I would tell you everything I knew about it?"

She thought back and did remember that conversation in the garden before their first dance lesson. "Yes. I did win, didn't I?"

He chuckled and continued to stroke her back. "Yes, you won . . . and you danced magnificently."

"So now the time has come for you to pay up. I think I like this part," she giggled.

"I hope you feel that way when I've finished."

"Why?" Again she raised her head to stare at him.

"Because I believe the time is approaching when we shall return."

Now she sat up and stared at him. "*Really?* How do you know?"

He closed his eyes briefly, as though collecting his thoughts. "I can't explain it. It's something I feel . . . A *knowing* starts to build inside of me that a change is about to take place. You will feel it, too, when it's evident, and you must trust yourself . . . for now you are a time traveler, Casey. It may happen to you again."

"What do you mean?" she demanded. "I could time-travel again?"

He nodded and opened his eyes. "You are not the same

woman you were when you were driving that car in the storm. You *are* altered, Casey, and you will never be that same woman again."

"I'm okay with that," she whispered. "Actually, I like myself much better now."

He smiled. "Good. But just as the opportunity to serve you was presented to me when I drove along that interstate, you, too, will be presented with opportunities to be of service now."

"*What?* You mean I could be zapped back in time to anyplace . . . *alone?*"

Once more he gathered her in his arms and she clung to him. "Do not fear. You will always have a choice, *querida*. To be of service or not. I have found in my experience that things unfold exactly as they will, and if I fight the circumstances, it only leads to difficulty. You will not be forced, for if you do not do something with an open heart, is it really of service to another?"

She thought about it, all the times she had done something because she thought she should, not because she wanted to. "I guess not."

"When your cup is filled to overflowing with love, then you have something to give without expecting anything in return . . . for you are full, whole, complete . . . no fear."

"Will you be with me?" She asked the question with a trembling voice.

"I honestly can't say right now. But you will feel me. In that sense I will always be with you. Our connection cannot be changed after tonight. Still, we will have to see how the pattern unfolds before us."

"Oh, Luke . . . this sounds scary." She felt the burning in her eyes and shut them tightly to stop the tears.

"Do not allow fear to enter into it, Casey." His voice was firm as he held her tighter. "I am only telling you this because you have a right to know. You are an intelligent woman and you understand the pattern now. You will see the signposts. You will read the directions. You will make the choices. Trust yourself now . . . your own inner voice."

The words to the song she had been listening to in the car, a lifetime ago, played through her mind.

The next voice you hear will be your own . . .

He hugged her tighter to his chest. "Let's stay in this moment, for I'm afraid I will have to leave you before it gets light."

Casey sighed. "Yes, this is not the house to be discovered in bed together. I think Marcella would faint away in shocked outrage."

He chuckled.

"And I don't want to disrespect Doña Isabela. She has been so kind to me."

"Everyone has grown to love you, Casey. Should you ever come back to this time, you now have a place that will welcome you with open arms."

"I don't even know if I want to leave anymore . . ."

"Don't think, *querida*. I am sorry I took you away from the moment. Stay with me now, here," he whispered, lifting her chin and kissing her lips with such tenderness that Casey moaned with renewed pleasure. "Let us dance once more . . ."

Her sigh seemed to fill the room as she slid over his body and stared down into his beautiful brown eyes.

"Oh, *sí*, señor. I accept your invitation . . . with great pleasure."

Eighteen

"Señorita! Señorita! Wake up. I have food to break your fast and *news* such as you will never believe!"

Hugging her pillow, Casey blinked several times and saw that the space next to her was empty. Luke was gone. "Oh, Juana," she murmured sleepily, "let me sleep for a few more minutes. Please . . . ?" She felt like she had just closed her eyes.

"Why are you not wearing your nightclothes?"

Immediately awake, Casey pushed the hair back from her face and pulled the cover over her. She turned around and saw a nightgown was placed at the foot of the bed and her clothes from the night before were neatly folded on the chair. Bless Luke's heart. He thought of everything.

"Ah . . ." she stammered, fumbling for an excuse for her nakedness. "I was so hot last night, so I removed my nightgown. Weren't you warm, Juana?"

"No," she answered, coming closer and putting her hand to Casey's cheek. "Are you with fever?"

What a leading question!

"No, I don't think so," Casey answered, wishing Juana would not look into her eyes so directly. How could she possibly hide such a night of lovemaking? Surely it was written all over her face.

The older woman looked around the room and inhaled. "I will ask no more questions, for I have news of a miracle."

"A miracle?" Casey sat up in bed and pulled the cover under her arms as Juana placed the tray of food in front of her. She had to clear her mind of last night and concentrate on the conversation. Talk about challenges, since her body was still tingling with the memory of Luke's touch. A shiver ran through her body as she instantly recalled the sensations of making love with him.

"Now you are cold?" the woman asked with concern.

"Yes . . . I mean no. What about a miracle?"

"Oh *sí* . . . the entire town is speaking of it," Juana said with renewed excitement. "A staircase, such as has never been seen before, has appeared in the Loretto Chapel! *Gracias a Dios*, the sisters' prayers to the carpenter Saint Joseph have been answered! They say it was the saint himself who built it and left when the priest discovered him last night. I have seen it myself, Señorita Casey. It was my Manuel who told me and took me this morning to the chapel . . . and it is round and round and . . . Oh, you must see it yourself. Everyone is going. You must eat and get dressed quickly for Doña Isabela is going to a special mass the bishop is going to say there. She has invited you to go with the family."

Casey could only hide her smile as she stared at the woman's animated gestures. Luke's mystery had created a miracle for these people of Santa Fe. Her love for him grew and she couldn't wait to see his face and talk to him about this. Plus, her arms ached to hold him again and hear him say he loved her. He loved her! Now, *that* was her miracle.

Thunder sounded in the distance and Juana's face brightened even more. "And perhaps also rain! What good signs. We are doubly blessed today."

Casey inhaled the spicy eggs and tortillas, figuring people living in the desert would always welcome rain, and it would be nice to lie in bed and listen to rain on the tiled roof. Her stomach growled to confirm her hunger. "Juana, I don't feel up to mass this morning. Will you ask Doña Isabela to excuse me from the mass? Perhaps I will see the miracle staircase this afternoon."

"But there is a great feast planned on the plaza to celebrate and you must go, though if it rains, I do not know where it will be."

"I will go to the plaza later. I promise. It's just that I didn't sleep well last night and I'm so tired." She smiled pleadingly to the older woman.

"*Sí* . . . I will make your excuses, señorita. Rest for the celebration. Imagine, another fiesta so soon. *Ay, Dios mío!* We all will be tired this night!"

"Yes, it's been quite a few days, hasn't it?"

"Eat. Rest. I will return later for the tray."

"Oh, Juana, enjoy yourself. Don't worry about me. I'll take the tray back down to the kitchen. I can take care of myself."

The woman looked once more around the bedroom and smiled knowingly. "*Sí*, I can see that."

Casey could feel a betraying blush creep up onto her cheeks and she quickly looked down at her tray.

As Juana moved to the door, Casey called out in a quiet voice, "Thank you for everything, Juana . . . You have been a good friend to me."

"*Gracias,* señorita Casey. It is a pleasure to serve you."

The door closed and Casey dug in to her food with relish. Miracles . . . miracles . . . The one taking place in her life right now was mind-boggling. Last night seemed more than a dream. The memory of it still made her body vibrate with love.

Love . . .

Casey finished her eggs and sat back against the pillows. She thought she knew about love, but she had only scratched the surface of it. What an all-encompassing emotion. It was vast and she didn't see a limit at all. Last night when she'd had an orgasm, Casey had felt like *she* was love. It had saturated every atom of her, and when she couldn't contain it any longer, love had seeped out from her pores and just expanded into the room, beyond the room . . . into the night and whatever was beyond that. *She* was the love that went out there, wanting to share, needing to share. Receiving intense pleasure *because* she shared.

She thought about the past when she had been in love. Then she had held that love close to her, protecting it, keeping it safe. Safe? Hell, she had smothered it! No wonder those men hadn't wanted to make a commitment. Now, through Luke, she realized that love was about freedom. There was safety in freedom.

No wonder Luke had held back. He'd finally admitted his fear was loss of freedom.

How could she share it with him when she hadn't even given it to herself?

Now she could, and *that* was her miracle. The freedom to love without conditions. She knew Luke finally felt that from her, she knew she had healed the part of her that was so frightened of abandonment, of loss . . . so fearful of love. She hadn't understood. She had taken all her role models and mixed them up and had come up with the crazy thought that love hurts. It was really only her holding on too tightly that made it hurt.

Love, real love, doesn't hurt. It's freeing.

She looked down to her left hand and focused on her ring finger. She'd always thought when she united with someone it would be in a formal marriage . . . the dress, the witnesses, the ring . . . all the official marks of a legit union. She couldn't help laughing at herself.

Last night, looking like a drowned rat, she'd joined forces with a man. So much for the white dress. There was no ring, nothing official, save a nun who, against everything her religion taught, could not deny the sincerity of their love and had pronounced them man and woman, united. She didn't need a ring. She didn't need anything now. She had what was most important. She actually *was* love.

That woman in the car, listening to a man singing about trusting yourself . . . that woman was forever changed. She couldn't go back. It was as though she had emerged into a space that was much bigger and she couldn't make herself small enough anymore to fit back into something much tighter and confining. It just didn't fit any longer. She felt reborn in love.

It sounded so corny and yet she couldn't deny the truth of it. If she was going to trust herself and this newfound freedom, then she had to be honest with herself now. She was altered. When the words to that song ran through her head again, she burst out laughing.

"Okay, okay . . ." she said aloud, followed by the thought, *I'm altered and I'm listening!*

She found she actually liked this new and improved model. Somehow she had a feeling it was only going to get better and better. Grinning, she picked up her fork to finish the now cooled breakfast. In her present frame of mind, it was delicious. Life was delicious. Everything was!

Whatever this source Luke had tapped into, it was the best thing to come down the pike since . . . she thought about what to compare it with and couldn't find a single thing . . . since anything. No wonder it was unnameable.

Luke had so lovingly helped her to make her own connection. And now she was a full-fledged time traveler. Jeez, this was certainly not the life experience of a rational, logical, linear-thinking accountant!

She thought about the conversation she and Luke had had last night before they'd made love again. She'd collapsed into his arms and had fallen asleep with the sound of his heart beating against her temple. She hadn't even thought about what he had said earlier about her being in service now. Her worrying mind had been quieted and she'd only wanted to remain in Luke's arms while she slept. And oh, how she'd slumbered.

Now the idea of being in service to something nameless, something that could present opportunities for her to do this again, was too much to handle. She didn't want to think about it, for something inside her said she wasn't ready . . . just yet. She was the rookie and needed some time to learn this stuff!

A soft knock on the door stopped her mental wanderings. It didn't sound like Juana. She had a feeling it was a man on the other side of that door, and pushed aside her tray. Grinning, she ran her fingers through her hair and rubbed them over her face while calling out, "Come in."

He walked into the room, wearing his blue chambray shirt and his dark trousers. His hair was damp, as though just washed, and he was carrying a yellow cactus flower.

"Good morning, *querida*."

She couldn't help the sigh that escaped her lips. Just

looking at him caused her heart to expand. "Good morning, my love," she answered with a tender smile.

Closing the door, he came over to the bed. He offered her the flower, and when she accepted, he bent down and kissed her forehead. "You look . . . delicious this morning."

She giggled and held the flower to her heart as she reached up and hugged him. "Oh, Luke . . . Thank you, thank you, thank you . . ."

"I must remember you love flowers so much," he said with a laugh.

She let him go and grinned up at him. "I do love flowers, but I wanted to thank you for everything. For being here with me, for loving me, for showing me what real love is, for folding my clothes, and for watching my back like you always do. I love you. I love life. I love it here!"

He sat on the mattress and faced her. "You are so beautiful," he breathed.

Casey realized the cover had slipped down and she grabbed it up to anchor it under her armpits. Embarrassed, she blushed and wiped under her eyes. "I do clean up so much better. I must look a mess!"

He gently pulled down her hands and looked into her eyes. Smiling, he said, "You look like a woman in love . . . exquisite."

"Aww," she murmured. "Is it any wonder I love you?"

"It is a wonder," he answered with a grin.

"Oh! Speaking of wonders, my love . . . it seems everyone in Santa Fe is talking about your miracle."

Shaking his head, he laughed slightly. "I've heard. It appears everyone loves a mystery."

"Hmm, you think Sister Bernardina will keep your secret?"

"I think she will. She is devoted to Saint Joseph and was the one who asked for the novena. To have it answered and credit given to her saint will only please her. And what does it really matter?"

"It doesn't," Casey agreed. "Still, it will be hard to go to this celebration later and pretend I don't know anything, when I'm going to be standing next to the miracle worker."

He smiled and Casey could sense something else was occupying his thoughts.

"I don't think we'll be going to the celebration, my love."

"We won't?" she asked.

Again he shook his head and smiled at her as he placed his hands on her shoulders. She felt something inside of her and blurted out her thought.

"This is it, isn't it? That's why you're dressed like that."

He nodded solemnly, and she instinctively grabbed his wrists as she stared into his eyes. "I don't know, Luke . . . I love it here. I . . . I'm . . ." Her words were broken off by a distant rumble of thunder. "We're leaving, aren't we?"

"Shh . . . Don't fear. Remember, we are only following the pattern and presenting ourselves for the opportunity. We must hurry if we are to catch its unfolding."

"Oh, Luke . . . I can't help it. I am scared. After last night . . ." She felt tears welling up in her eyes.

"Last night will always be with us, anytime we choose to remember, *querida*. We're together right now, in this moment, and remember to trust what you know in your heart to be true. Everything is happening at exactly the right moment. Just relax, Casey . . . so you can enjoy the adventure."

"I know you're right, but I've never had adventures like these and . . . I'm a rookie!"

He chuckled and caressed her face. "Oh, my sweet one . . . you are never without guidance. Don't you know that yet?"

Again she grabbed his hand. "I know, I know, but I'm so

new at this! What if I screw something up and something happens and you and I aren't—"

"Stop worrying, Casey," he said in a firm voice, as though to stop her chaotic thoughts. "We must hurry. Dress in your jeans and your sweater. Don't take anything from this time with you, not even this flower." He picked up the blossom and handed it to her.

Clutching it in her hand, she watched him stand up.

"Now, make sure you are wearing everything you came in with and—"

"Luke!" she interrupted. "I'm afraid of the lightning."

He cradled her cheek within his palm. "There is a controlled way to interact with such power, Casey. I would never let anything happen to you. Trust me. I told you you would be returned to your family when we were shown the way."

Reaching up, she clung to his hand as she listened.

"*Mi amor,* I believe we are being shown the time has come to leave. We must make our preparations. I have to take care of some things and I will come back here in an hour. We'll have to ride out to the desert, so I'll have a horse in the alley behind the house. We'll leave by the passageway and no one will see us depart."

"Can I say good-bye?" Casey asked, swallowing down her tears.

Luke smiled sadly. "I know how difficult this is for you, *querida*. You have become close with the others during this time, but they would not understand and it would be very emotional for you. We don't have time for explanations now. Perhaps it is best if we leave their lives quickly. Don Felipe knows this is my style and does not take it as an insult."

"But Rosa . . ."

"Rosa is in love, and love forgives any action, especially one that is done without malice. Besides, she knows of your love for her. Her father will help her understand it is not personal."

"Yes," Casey reluctantly agreed. "I guess you're right."

"Now I must leave you for a short while as I arrange for the horse. Use the time wisely and be ready in an hour." He again kissed her forehead. "You are safe, *querida*."

"Yes," she affirmed, stunned by his announcement. "I was just thinking that before you came in the door."

"Hold on to that thought, Casey," he whispered, kissing her lips. "And remember . . . it's an adventure."

"Right," she muttered, and swallowed deeply. "An adventure . . ."

He carried his heavy raincoat and his black cowboy hat, and held her hand as they stood before the wardrobe door. "You're not bringing anything with you? You're not leaving anything? You must be wearing the same underwear. *Everything*."

"I am," Casey insisted nervously. It felt so weird to be wearing her jeans and cotton sweater again. Even her soft Italian flats felt strange on her feet. "The only thing I came back with was my wallet, and you gave that to me."

"Where is it?"

She lifted up her sweater and showed him it was tucked into her waistband.

"Then we're ready."

His words, spoken to reassure her, sent a shiver of fear through her body. "I don't know if I'm exactly ready, but I'm following you."

Using his free arm, he hugged her and whispered, "No fear."

"Right. No fear," she whispered back as thunder rumbled closer. She wrapped her arms around his waist and hugged him tightly. "I love you, Luke. I trust you."

He kissed the top of her head and said, "Thank you for your love and your trust. Now we must leave quickly, *querida*. The storm is fast approaching."

She nodded and released him. Looking up, she watched as love filled his eyes and he lowered his head to kiss her. She felt renewed in his incredible love, and when they ended the kiss she breathed, "I'm ready."

"*Adelante,* then," he whispered, squeezing her once more before opening the door. "I will lead you."

She made sure all her lovely borrowed clothes were in order before slipping into the passageway and closing the hidden door behind her. Luke took her hand and together they walked sideways through the narrow opening. It seemed this time they made it through much more quickly, and Casey had no time to ponder as they hurried from the garden and out the back gate.

She saw a brown horse, saddled and tied to an overhanging tree limb.

"We're riding that? Together?"

Luke chuckled as he pulled her closer. "Yes. Stop worrying."

She almost laughed out loud. "Ah, we're not *stealing* this horse, are we?"

Joining her laughter, Luke slipped his arms into his raincoat and stuck his hat upon his head. "I am not stealing this horse. It will be returned, as it's branded with the d'Montoya mark and Don Felipe is a man well respected. My friend will reward the person who returns it and know I have moved on. Now, come, my worrying time traveler. Let us ride."

Her mind kept repeating, *It's an adventure, it's an adventure* . . .

Fortunately, everyone in town was gathering for the celebration of the miraculous staircase. They rode out of town swiftly and unnoticed. Casey was reminded of everything she had experienced in Santa Fe, witnessing the birth of an Angel, the unexpected friendships, the bonding of like souls and love . . . all of it laced with love. It helped to take her mind off the jostling ride. She could see the lightning in the distance and winced as she clung to Luke's torso. Burying her face in the raincoat, she kept muttering, "It's all an adventure, an adventure."

He patted her arm as they left the town behind, and the horse broke into a gallop as they headed out to the desert. Casey cast one last, loving look backward and clinging more tightly to Luke, reminded herself it was all worth it. No matter what happened now, she was a blessed woman. They rode hard for what seemed almost half an hour, and she felt sorry for the horse carrying their combined weight. She saw the mountains were closer and cringed as lightning crashed in the distance. She remembered the last time she had been there, and fear again raced through her body. She closed her eyes and tried to think of Amy, of her niece, of everything that awaited her in the year 2000, but her mind was playing pictures of a beautiful young woman with a stunning smile who crept into her bed and called her *hermana*. She couldn't just have left without saying goodbye. Surely the note she had left in the pocket of her skirt was harmless.

Casey's eyes burst open as louder thunder seemed to rock the ground beneath them and she could see a flash of lightning crash into the desert. Oh dear God, they were riding into the storm.

"Luke! Luke!" she called out to him as the wind picked up.

"It's all right," he shouted back to her.

"No . . . Luke, I . . . I left a note for Rosa."

She could feel the muscles in his body tighten as he slowed down the horse. "You did what?" he asked over his shoulder as thunder crashed again, frightening not only herself but the poor horse.

"I left a note saying good-bye to Rosa. I couldn't just leave and—"

She couldn't explain more as a flash of brilliant white light seemed to surround them, and the horse reared up in fright. She grabbed Luke, yet found that her fingers slipped on the oily material of his coat and, unbelievably, she was sliding back off the horse.

"Luke! *Luke* . . . !" she screamed as her world tilted and she felt herself falling backward toward the ground.

"Casey!"

As though in slow motion, she watched Luke spin around in the saddle to reach out for her, but her hands seemed too heavy to move and she couldn't reach him as she continued to fall. Terrified, she felt herself suspended in this slow-time as she sank back toward the desert floor, away from Luke, and into a hard, painful thud on her back.

The last thing she remembered was her head hitting the sand and flopping just once before darkness descended and wrapped her in oblivion. Moments later, as her head swam with pain and confusion, she thought she heard him calling her name.

"Open your eyes. Wake up!"

She wanted to wake up, to make the pain stop, to be held in his arms again . . .

"Can you open your eyes?"

She blinked and then abruptly closed them again to shut out the bright light shining in them. "Luke . . . ?" Her mouth felt dry and her lips parched. Even swallowing was painful. And her head was throbbing . . .

"Ma'am, you're going to be all right," a man's voice said to her. "Don't try to move now. We're cutting away your jeans."

She forced her eyes open against the pain of the light and stared at the stranger with a helmet on his head. Confused, she could only mutter, "What . . . ?"

"Looks like you're lucky," he said with a reassuring smile, and Casey noticed that there were others, all helmeted and looking like firefighters, or policemen or rescue workers or . . . "Where . . . am I? What happened? Where's . . . where's Luke?" Even speaking was painful.

"Luke? Someone else was with you?" He turned to a man who was looking at her wallet. "Look for another one," he shouted.

More confused than ever, she heard sirens screaming, saw lights flashing and people kneeling around her, using scissors to cut the leg of her jeans and wrapping a big white collar around her neck.

"Here's the ambulance," the kind man's voice announced. "We'll have you to the hospital in no time. You're a lucky lady."

She tried to smile at him, but her gaze was searching the small crowd of people above her. Attempting to lift her head, she heard the man admonish her.

"Don't move. We saw the burn mark on your heel and we're checking for any more burns, but we don't know yet and you could do real damage to yourself if you move now."

"Luke, where's Luke?" she pleaded, too shocked to cry. Desperate, she reached out and clung to the man's arm. "You *must* find him!"

"I don't know, lady," another man answered. "A driver called in the 911 on a cell phone, but we haven't found anyone else yet."

"No, he's got to be here," she insisted, terrified that she was alone in this madness. "Please, please, look around for him." She had to close her eyes against the painful glare of the lights. "I'm not leaving until . . . until . . ."

She couldn't finish her words as the pain in her head seemed to wrap around her mind and block out all thoughts, save one. *Where was he?*

No longer able to think, she clung to his image and surrendered to the darkness.

This couldn't be real. It couldn't. It couldn't . . .

Nineteen

The hospital room was cold and frightening, yet not as frightening as what was racing through Casey's mind as she stared at her sister and wondered how in the world to answer her question.

"Honey, please . . . tell me, what happened?" her sister pleaded, while clutching Casey's right hand. Casey's other hand had an IV in it.

"I . . . I'm not sure," Casey muttered through the tightness in her throat. What could she say? Her brain was still trying to make sense out of her surroundings. She wondered if she was having a dream of being with her sister, and she would wake up in Luke's arms . . . or was he the dream?

What the hell *was* time? Was it ours to play with, to make drag on or speed up? Was that what Luke had learned, what made him so . . . so real that everyone who met him recognized there was something about the man that made them want to be around him? Was Luke really a time traveler, or was she crazy?

Amy stared into her eyes with a worried expression. "Casey, the doctors have told me you're all right. Don't be frightened. You were hit by lightning. Do you remember anything?"

She could only nod. "Yes . . . something happened," she again muttered, for she found using her lips to make sounds was hard and annoying, taking too much effort.

Amy reached out and stroked strands of hair off Casey's forehead and placed a kiss upon her skin. It felt warm and loving, and Casey found herself smiling at the familiarity. Her sister . . . She had been traveling to meet her sister. "Amy . . ."

Amy came back into her line of vision. "Yes?"

"I'm glad to see you, lady."

Her sister finally really smiled, and something within Casey burst open as she squeezed Amy's hand. "Did . . . did they find anyone else? Was I the only one?"

"Just you. Why? Did you see someone else? Maybe they were the ones who called 911."

Casey sighed with the effort it took to make her brain work. She couldn't think about this right now. None of it made sense, and yet a deeper part of her, which she couldn't access right now, knew it did. Sensing she should answer her sister, she said, "I thought I saw someone else."

"Oh, sweetie, you're going to be confused for some time. The doctors advised me about it. Just take your time, they said." Amy pushed her dark hair back and added, "But the good news is that you've been thoroughly examined and they can't find anything wrong with you." Her face brightened considerably. "They're calling it a miracle you came through that with no injuries, considering what happened to the car."

"What happened?"

"Well, I haven't seen it, but the police say the door was almost blown off the hinges. You're lucky to be here." Her sister became more serious.

Casey found herself smiling and shaking her head. "Wasn't luck," she whispered. "I don't know that I believe in luck anymore."

"What?" Amy chuckled, holding her hand tighter in a familiar bond. "I think I would legally change my name to Lady Luck if I'd just gone through what you did."

In spite of the confusion and aches, Casey couldn't help chuckling, too. "It's good to see you, Amy. I've missed you."

Again Amy kissed her forehead. "I've missed you too. And as soon as the doctors say it's okay, I'm taking you home and pampering you."

"Sounds like a good deal to me," Casey murmured, suddenly very tired. "When I woke up I . . . I thought I had been dreaming."

"Let me get a doctor and I'll come right back."

"Amy . . ." she called to her sister.

"Yes, I'm coming right back."

"What day is it?"

Amy looked confused for a moment, before saying, "August twenty-first, sweetie. The day you flew into Albuquerque. Though it's nighttime now."

Casey could only stare blankly at her sister, who again grinned and quickly turned away. She watched Amy leave the room and then closed her eyes. Same day? How could that be possible? She had spent over ten days with Luke! She remembered him . . . Rosalinda . . . Juana . . . all of them. They were *real*. She didn't understand this, but she knew what Luke had said to her about being a time traveler must be true, for she couldn't deny where she had been. It had been every bit as real as this hospital room and her sister's kiss. Somehow, in the space of moments, timeless moments, she had been taught to live there, and escape *time*!

Panic seemed to be bubbling right at the edges of her consciousness and she breathed deeply as Luke had taught her. She somehow knew she could go two routes . . . One was fear, as Luke had said, a heavy and dense energy. She knew that would only make it harder. Or she could stay in the middle of the child's seesaw Luke had talked about, which was teetering at the moment, and try to make a decision. Fear or love? To give power to fear would only make the situation much worse. To deny the love she had experienced would be insane, for she knew she was altered. The woman in that car before the lightning struck might have been able to deny it, but she just wasn't that woman any longer. There was more to her now. Love had changed her into something more.

A time traveler . . .

She would have laughed again, except her muscles ached. There was nothing wrong that rest wouldn't cure, plus Amy had promised to pamper her. She was going to hold her sister to it! She needed some space and time to integrate all of it.

Luke was real.

All of it was real.

Casey O'Reilly. Accountant by necessity; time traveler by choice!

To heck with the pain, she thought, letting out a guffaw. It was funny! And didn't she already know the best medicine was laughter? Thank heavens she could laugh at herself. It was quite a story she had to tell, if she ever did . . . and then she remembered Luke's firm advice to only speak of time traveling with other time travelers. What in the world was she going to tell Amy? Anyone? She would have to keep this to herself until she found Luke.

She didn't doubt for a moment that she would be reunited with him. She might be the rookie, but he was a seasoned vet. He would find her. She *felt* it.

If she told others, they would have her committed, and she couldn't blame them for their beliefs. Before she was hit with lightning, she, too, wouldn't have believed such an incredible story. But now she knew, because she had experienced it, and she couldn't go back to the old way of thinking any longer. She had been given an extremely rare gift: to travel through time, not once, but twice. She felt that was just too sacred to share with anyone who couldn't understand. What she had discovered about herself and love was far too precious to be judged by anyone. Now, somehow, she had to dance between two worlds, two times, the memory and the reality.

Just accept where you find yourself and stop fighting it with fear.

She remembered Luke's words to her when she'd fallen apart after her visit to the jail and had finally accepted that she was in 1878. And he'd been right. She'd had the time of her life after she'd allowed the fear to abate.

Well, she might be a rookie, but she wasn't about to forget anything she had learned.

He'd find her.

It's an adventure. An adventure . . . she told herself. Sheesh, how had Luke ever gotten used to this?

Closing her eyes, she was about to call out to him to hurry up when Amy rushed back into the room, followed by two doctors.

"Here we are, Casey," her sister announced, as though she were now in charge. "The doctors want to examine you again."

Casey watched as two men, one in his forties and the other looking like he was still in college, came forward. The older one pulled out a penlight and smiled into her eyes while the younger one held a clipboard with her file.

"I'm Dr. Woolery. How are you feeling, Casey?" the older man asked.

"Tired," she replied, staring at a spot on the wall above the doctor's hair.

"You're a lucky lady," he murmured, concentrating on her eyes as he shined the light into them.

"So I've heard," she whispered back. "Thank you for all your help. And the paramedics too."

"Well, we're all amazed. You seem to have walked away from this with no damage," he said, turning to her other eye and focusing his attention there.

Casey smiled and repeated his last words. "No damage." She might have been a rookie, but she must have gotten something right. Luke was a good teacher.

"Well, it appears you're just fine," he said, flicking off his penlight and holding her wrist to take her pulse. "You just need some rest, young lady."

"Wonderful," Amy pronounced. "So I can take her home?"

The doctor looked once more into Casey's eyes. "It's up to you. You can stay the night for observation if you want. Your insurance would pay for it. Your EKG and blood pressure are normal. We've checked every inch of you with exams and ultrasounds, and can't find a thing wrong even though your shoe was burned. Not even a blister, which is amazing in itself. No bruises, nothing . . . and you were thrown from the car. I've never seen anything like this."

Casey could only stare into his eyes and smile.

"Well, you can stay the night, or you can go home with your sister and see me in ten days for a follow-up. The choice is yours."

Everyone was looking at her, waiting for her answer.

"I'll go with Amy," she whispered, smiling at her sister.

"Fine," Dr. Woolery pronounced, "but I want you up and walking to the bathroom before I'll release you. I'll call the nurse and have her help you. Remember, I want to see you in ten days for a follow-up. You'll have all the information on your release form. Your sister says you will be here for two weeks?"

"Yes," Casey said, feeling stronger at the thought of getting to Amy's house.

The doctor nodded and held his hand out for the clipboard. He started scribbling. "Headache?"

She nodded. "Not bad, but yes."

"Body aches?"

"A little."

"Blurred vision or speech? Anything?"

She shook her head.

"All right," he said, reaching out to shake her hand. "I'll have them remove this IV and then you can use the bathroom. And I'll see you in ten days."

Casey smiled. "Thanks. I'll be there."

"Rest and be gentle with yourself. Things may seem a bit confusing. That's normal after the jolt you received. Take your time and recover at your own pace."

"Thank you, Doctor," Casey said, slowly placing her hand in his.

The man shook it and grinned. "You're one lucky lady."

She could only smile and nod her head. She didn't think he would understand that it wasn't luck, but love, that had pulled her through.

"Ten days."

"Ten days," she repeated.

He gave the clipboard back to the younger man and walked toward the door. "Get some rest."

She closed her eyes and took a deep breath. "I intend to."

She had a lot to do now. And the first was to acclimate to being back in this time.

"We're going home," Amy pronounced with happiness, after she, too, thanked the doctors.

Opening her eyes, Casey grinned at her younger sister. "Looks like it."

"That is, if you can stand up and walk over to that bathroom and pee."

Laughing, Casey reached out her hand. "Help me sit up. I'll show ya!"

Amy rushed to her aide. "Now, stay right there until the nurses come!"

"Amy," she said with a strong voice, "you have no idea how long I have waited to sit on a damn toilet! Now help me up!"

Giggling as if they were kids again, Amy pushed a button on the side of the bed. "Going up," she announced.

"Slower!" Casey called out as her head swam with the quick ascent.

Amy laughed nervously. "Oh, sorry. How's this?"

"Fine," Casey answered with a giggle as she sat upright. "Now take this side down."

"Shouldn't we wait for a nurse?"

Casey almost glared at her sister. "Amy, I am about to burst. I am not waiting for anyone. If you only knew, you would just take down the damn side and not argue with me."

"Okay, okay . . ." her sister conceded, fumbling with the metal bars. When she finally got the side down, she stood with her hands on her hips and added, "You're still hooked up to the IV. You'll have to wait."

Casey looked up to the bag hanging on a hook. "It's got wheels. You hold it and walk with me."

"Me?" Amy demanded. "You need a nurse."

"I need help," Casey said. "You can do it."

"Oh, jeez . . ." Amy muttered. "You are going to get me in trouble, just like when we were kids."

"I never got you in trouble," Casey retorted, throwing back the sheet and slowly bringing her legs to the side of the bed. "I wasn't the one who had to go to summer school for too many detentions."

"I was framed," Amy answered with a laugh as she gently held Casey's heels and placed them on the floor. "And don't you ever tell Sara that when she gets older. I'll lose all parental control."

"Yeah, right . . . framed. Now, that's funny," Casey said, slowly sitting and finding her balance. "Okay, if you can help me stand, I'll be able to do something I've waited a long time to do."

"Walk?" Amy asked with a chuckle, holding out her arm as Casey rose slowly.

"No, sit on a toilet, you fool," Casey answered with a giggle. "And if you make me laugh again, you're taking care of any accidents. Now, move with me, girl. I'm a woman on a mission."

The two of them struggled to find a successful arrangement and soon they were crossing the room, Casey holding on to her sister as Amy dragged the IV with them.

"I forgot to ask. How's that handsome husband of yours and your gorgeous daughter?"

Amy was breathing heavily. "Fine, everyone's fine. Let's just get you into the bathroom and then we can have a reunion. Right now I don't want to get caught."

"Where'd we get that?" Casey asked, seeing her luggage on a built-in table against the wall.

"Oh, the police brought it with you. They got it out of the trunk of the rental. No sense in going back there."

"Right . . ." Casey muttered. At least she had some clothes.

"Okay, now wait until I turn on the light," Amy said, letting go of the IV and flipping a switch. She pushed the door open and then, together, they entered the bright room.

"Jeez . . ." Casey closed her eyes briefly. "It sure is bright."

"Wait until you sit down and I'll turn them off."

It was a comedy of errors as Amy held up Casey's hospital gown and she sunk onto the toilet seat. Sheltering her eyes with one hand, she used her other hand to cling to the metal support bar next to the toilet. "Turn off the lights and wait for me," she whispered.

Amy did as she was asked just as a nurse came into the room and demanded to know what was going on.

Sitting on the toilet seat, Casey lifted her hand from her eyes and squinted up to the older woman in white. "I'm in . . . heaven," she muttered, finally releasing the pressure and laughing at the sheer ridiculous joy of the moment.

"And there, there! That's the Governor's Palace, right?"

"How do you know all this? You've been reading maps or something?" Amy demanded as they crossed the plaza.

Filled with energy from ten days of unabated pampering by her sister, Casey pushed the stroller carrying her precious niece and sighed. "I'm telling you, Amy, it's like I've been here before. I know all this."

Shaking her head, Amy said, "Talk like that fits right in

around here. Kinda weird, but I'm starting to get used to it."

Wearing a pair of jeans and a white T-shirt, Casey breathed in the fresh air. "I know the La Fonda Hotel is right down that road, and I know the chapel . . . Oh, Amy, is there a chapel on the other side of that big church?"

Amy looked at Saint Francis Cathedral and nodded. "The Loretto Chapel."

"Come on," Casey said with much excitement. "We have to go. There's something I have to see."

Amy kept pace with her, asking, "Casey, what the heck is going on? Did you do research on this before you came? How can you know this?"

"I can't answer that, Amy," she said, rushing past the plaza, past art galleries, souvenir shops, jewelry stores. "It's to the right, isn't it?"

"Casey, what's wrong?" Amy demanded as they turned down the side street and she stared at her sister.

Casey looked at the small building and stood perfectly still. It was real!

"C'mon," she murmured, pushing the sleeping Sara toward the chapel. "We have to go in. Is the staircase still there?"

"You know about that? Yes, it's there," Amy said, keeping up with her. "Will you please tell me what's going on? You've been acting strange ever since . . . well, ever since you were released from the hospital. All those days of sitting and staring out the window, and now *this*!"

"I can't explain it now, Amy. I haven't figured it all out yet."

Casey was astounded to find out that the chapel was now privately owned and you had to pay money to go in and see "the miraculous staircase." Walking into the chapel, she heard the story of the itinerant carpenter who came to Santa Fe, built an amazing staircase out of a single piece of wood that grows many miles away, and left without accepting payment or even recognition.

Giving over the stroller to Amy, Casey sank down on a pew and stared at the still beautiful work of art. Someone had finished it by added a railing. It was magnificent. How Luke would love this. Again, for the hundredth time, she called out to him in her mind and in her heart.

Oh, Luke . . . come see this. Come find me. Please . . .

"Casey, are you okay? You have your appointment soon. Should we leave?"

Sara had awakened and Casey reached out to touch her niece as more tourists filled the tiny chapel where she had united with the most extraordinary being and now felt more married than she could have ever thought possible. It was as though he were away, a traveling salesman or something.

She almost laughed at her last thought and had to cover her mouth to stifle it in the hushed atmosphere of the chapel. That was Luke . . . a traveling salesman for a source without a name . . . And then she stopped and stared at his handiwork.

The source had a name.

It was love.

"Casey, hon, we can come back, but we've got to get going if we're not going to be late for Dr. Woolery."

"Right." She blinked a few times, telling herself she would definitely be back. "Isn't it beautiful, Amy? Do you believe the legend?"

Her sister shrugged. "I don't know. This city challenges all my beliefs. Ya know Santa Fe means Holy Faith in Spanish?"

Smiling, she rose from the pew. "Yes. I was told that once before."

* * *

"Okay, Casey, you seem to be in perfect health," Dr. Woolery pronounced. "Can't find a thing wrong with you, but just to make sure, I would like you to wait until the results of your blood test come back. It should only be a few more minutes." He gave her a friendly wink. "One of the advantages of having your office in a hospital. Less waiting."

"Well, Doc," Casey said with a grin as she buttoned her blouse, "I don't care what your tests show, I feel great."

"Good. Stay that way."

"I intend to do just that."

A nurse knocked and then came into the examining room. "Excuse me, Doctor. Here are the results."

Casey continued dressing as Dr. Woolery perused the sheet of paper while leaning against a counter. Casey was so excited as her mind filled with possibilities. Now that she had a clean bill of health, her entire future was before her. She could do whatever she wanted, even—

All thoughts ceased as the doctor cleared his throat and asked, "Is there any possibility of you being pregnant?"

She stood frozen in shock as she turned her face to him. "Why?"

"Your hormone levels are way up. Maybe we should take another test to make sure there wasn't a mistake at the lab."

Casey felt a surge of pleasure rush through her body and she gripped the edge of the examining table to steady herself. "There's no mistake," she whispered as it all slammed into her with such clarity that she almost hugged the doctor.

It was real! It was all real! And now she had proof!

"You knew you were pregnant? You should have told me."

"I didn't know until right now. It can only be weeks. I was expecting my period any day."

"When you get back home, I want your doctor to call me and I'll send him a copy of your records. He should know all the tests that have been performed." Dr. Woolery looked at her and smiled kindly. "I take it you're all right with this?"

Casey could barely contain her grin. "Better than all right, Doc. I'm thrilled!"

Hours later, Casey closed the door to Sara's bedroom after putting her niece to sleep with a story. Sighing deeply, she walked through the rambling ranch-style house to find her sister. She knew she couldn't put it off any longer. She had played with it in her mind for hours and she knew what she wanted to do. It was the only thing that made sense.

Amy was snuggled in the corner of the sofa, holding the phone to her chest.

"How's Jim?"

Her sister smiled. "He said he's sorry he's missed all the excitement and hopes he gets a chance to visit before you leave. This new job as VP of sales and marketing keeps him away on business trips, and this trade show in Seattle has been grueling for him." Placing the phone on an end table, she asked, "How's Sara? Did she give you any trouble?"

"I must have bored the kid with my storytelling. She fell fast asleep." Casey sat down in an overstuffed chair and curled her legs up under her. "I need to talk to you, Amy."

"What's wrong? The doctor released you and—"

"I'm fine, Amy," she interrupted. "Better than fine. I'm pregnant."

Her younger sister just stared at her. "What did you say?"

"You heard me," Casey answered. "I'm pregnant."

"My God! Did you know this? Is this why you were coming out here? I know you've wanted to have a baby, but . . . who's the father? Where is he? Does he know? I didn't even know you were seeing anyone. When did—"

"Hold on," Casey interrupted with a smile. "I know it's a shock. Was for me too. I just found out today at the doctor's and—"

"And you waited until now to tell me? That was hours ago!"

"I know, I know," Casey answered, trying to placate her sister. "Believe me, I've thought of little else. I've had some decisions to make."

"So answer some of my questions. Who's the father?"

Taking a deep, steadying breath, Casey said, "His name is Luke d'Séraphin." It felt good to say his name, to speak the truth.

"What kind of name is that? Where's he from?"

"I don't really know," she answered truthfully. "We met and spent some time together and . . . and I fell in love, Amy, like I never knew love could be, and now I'm having his child."

Amy got up and sat on the edge of Casey's chair. She wrapped her arms around her and whispered into her hair, "You've really had a tough time of it, haven't you? Okay, I'm shocked, but I'll get over it. Now, what do you want to do?"

Casey looked up into her sister's eyes and smiled. "I knew I could count on you. I've been thinking . . . if it's all right with you and Jim, I'd like to move to Santa Fe and have the baby here. There's something about this place that calls to me."

Amy looked doubly shocked, yet pleased. "All right with us? Are you kidding? You know how much I've missed you. Oh, to have you here with me and . . . and a new baby too! When are we going to meet this Luke d'Séraphin character?"

"That, I can't tell you," she said, holding her sister's gaze. "I don't know when I'll see him again, but I know I will. He loves me, Amy, like I've never been loved in my whole life."

"Well, let's look him up. The man will want to know he's going to be a father!"

Casey laughed. "I have a feeling he'll show up when the time is right." She became serious. "Thanks, Amy, for accepting this, as bizarre as it sounds. It'll be great to live near you again. I even saw an apartment yesterday in the paper that sounds perfect. It's a large old home that's been turned into a complex, and there's a rental if I seize the moment and take it."

"Oh, take it, Casey," Amy declared. "We'll figure everything out later. So you'll go back east and quit your job and pack up to move here?"

Nodding, Casey whispered, "I'm just following the pattern and watching as it all unfolds, but that's my plan so far. I figure I can do freelance accounting until after the baby is born and then figure it out from there."

"I'll help you, and Jim has all sorts of business contacts in the city. Being in the hotel industry, he knows just about everybody in the city. When are you thinking of doing all this?"

Taking another deep breath, Casey said, "As soon as I return. Day after tomorrow I'll fly back and give my notice. It feels right, Amy."

"Follow your heart on this one, sweetie," Amy whispered, gathering her once more into her arms. "Follow your heart."

It was the only thing she knew how to do now, for she

was committed to Luke and to their child. How could she not follow love all the way, wherever it led her?

She had to have faith it would lead to happiness, and she was willing to risk it all to find out.

Twenty

$\mathcal{C}$asey grabbed her coat off a hook by the front door and grinned. Slipping her arms into it, she looked around at her cute apartment and felt a sense of satisfaction that would be hard to define to anyone else. Somehow everything had fallen into place. The apartment she had read about in the newspaper turned out to be perfect, a completely renovated wing in an old, yet very familiar house. Warm colorful rugs over Saltillo tile enhanced her green leather furniture and gave it a genuine southwestern look. She even had an office behind the kitchen, and she was preparing the nursery in the small second bedroom.

Casey felt like a truly blessed woman.

She almost forgot the swatches of material for the curtains in the nursery and she rushed back into the bright kitchen to grab them off the counter. She was meeting Amy for lunch later, and the two of them could decide together.

How wonderful to be close to her sister again, she thought as she dropped the material into her purse, picked up a ledger, and hurried toward the door.

Walking down the street, she couldn't help but grin at everyone who passed as she murmured "Good morning." How she loved this city with its many cultures and creative energy. As always on her daily walk to the plaza, she paused in front of a gallery and stared at the bigger-than-life sculpture of an older Indian woman assisting a younger woman into a shawl. It always made her think of Juana. Right there, right on the street, a masterpiece for all to admire. It was part of why she so appreciated this city. Santa Fe *was* a city different, as it was now known.

Sighing with a love of life in any time, she walked toward the plaza and her first stop—the coffee shop and her new friends who greeted her every morning.

"Casey . . . great to see you again."

"You, too, José. I'll have those papers ready for you to sign tomorrow," she called out.

"Casey, you look so happy. Want to share some of whatever you've got?"

"I sure can, Andy," Casey answered with a laugh as she moved past the people sitting at the counter. "It's called happiness."

Andy, standing behind the counter at the old-fashioned coffee shop, wiped his hands on his apron and said, "You want the usual? Herbal tea and a bagel?"

"After four months of me coming in here, Andy, do you think I'm going to change now?"

Still grinning, the man leaned over the counter and muttered, "Hey, it's a heck of a lot easier than shrimp and sherbert. My wife used to send me on hunting trips in the middle of the night!"

Casey giggled as she laid the ledger she was carrying on

the end of the counter. "I guess herbal tea and bagels ain't so bad then, huh?"

"Oh, and speaking of wives," Andy said, "mine informed me that we're going to Hawaii with the money you saved us on the state taxes. Thanks again, Casey."

Smiling with happiness, she nodded. "Thank you for referring me to José. I really think I'm going to make it here, Andy."

The man brought her a take-out cup of steaming water and placed a wooden box of neatly lined tea bags on the counter. "Pick your poison."

Laughing again, she refused to egg on this man who seemed to love to tease her. Andy, who looked like an ex-hippie, had quickly become a good friend. "Let's see . . ." she pondered while looking through the selection. "Yesterday I had chamomile. I think I'll try"—she paused as she picked up a tea bag—"Strawberry kiwi!"

Andy lifted his lips in an expression of distaste. "If you say so."

"I do," she pronounced, tearing open the wrapping. "Now, what about my bagel? Lightly toasted with cream cheese."

"I got it, I got it," Andy said, while walking over to the commercial toaster. "One bagel, coming up!"

Leaning her elbow on the counter, she looked past the friendly faces of the people sitting there to the booths that lined the front window. Casey opened the first three buttons on her coat and watched the steady stream of people on the plaza. She never tired of it, and spent almost every morning sitting on a bench, eating her breakfast, talking to Luke about everything that was going on in her life . . . the pregnancy, the move, the apartment she had miraculously found in the d'Montoya compound, her work, things she was learning. She told him everything, knowing that somehow their connection could never be broken. She had finally come to peace about it all . . . realizing that she didn't have to have all the answers, for what was happening was a much bigger picture than she had been used to viewing.

She was content to be a rookie and learn now at her own pace.

"Here ya go," Andy said, interrupting her thoughts and sliding a brown paper bag across the counter.

"Great," she said, grinning as she picked up her ledger, the bag, and the bill. "I'd leave ya a tip, but then you'd just have to declare it, and we're trying to keep your gross down, remember?"

Laughing, Andy said, "That's what I get when a customer does my books!"

"See you tomorrow, Andy," she called out as she walked toward the cash register in the front of the shop.

"See you, Casey. Keep on keepin' on . . ."

Without turning back, she raised her fingers in a peace sign. "*Adiós.*"

Standing at the cashier's counter, she watched a man walk down the street with his baby strapped to his chest. She smiled at the sight as she handed over her check.

"How are you this morning, Maria?"

"*Ay,* if it gets any more busy, I'm going to pull out my braids. It's the skiing season and I hear Taos is so crowded this year you can't drive down the streets without stopping for the tourists." The Indian woman took Casey's money and gave her the change. "How are you doing, hon? You look good. No more morning sickness?"

Casey shook her head proudly. "Haven't been sick for over a week. I think I'm finally over it."

Maria pushed up from her stool and leaned closer to her. "Now the best part comes. This is when you start radiating it to everyone else. That must be some baby you're carrying, 'cause you're beamin'!"

Both women giggled together, as though they shared some wondrous secret. Casey realized she did that a lot . . . giggle. She couldn't help it. She was too happy to contain it and simply *had* to let it out.

As she walked out of the coffee shop into the brisk morning air, she again wondered about something that always crossed her mind when she was people-watching.

Why weren't there bumper stickers proclaiming the joy of life? It was real. She was living it! Was there such a thing as being too happy? She didn't think so.

Walking to the corner, she sighed deeply with contentment. Despite not having seen or heard from Luke in four months, she was still happier than she had ever been in her life, at least since she was a little girl. She was living in a great community, in a great apartment, exactly where she wanted to wake up every morning. She was gainfully self-employed, had her sister within walking distance, and had more genuine friends than ever, friends who invited her to gallery openings, concerts, plays, festivals, workshops . . . Her life was full of joy.

She rubbed her palm over her stomach as she waited to cross the street. And a miracle growing within her to boot! Being a time traveler was the best thing that had ever happened to her, and she wouldn't have changed a moment. Luke was right, everything was evolving at exactly the right time. Why not enjoy the adventure?

She crossed the street and entered the plaza, happy to see that her familiar bench was unoccupied. Only once had it been taken, and then she'd gone back to the coffee shop. That was when she and Andy had really started to talk. She figured that was meant to be too, and so not much tended to bother her anymore.

As she sat down and arranged her things around her, Casey had to admit that only one thing could bring up any clouds on her horizon. And it was her own lingering desire for Luke to find her. She wondered where he was, what had happened to him when she'd slipped off that horse. She worried that he might need her and then reminded herself he was a seasoned traveler. She didn't have to worry about him, as it certainly didn't help either of them, but she did miss him so much.

At night, in bed, she recalled the sensation of being with him . . . talking to him, watching him move, listening to him, dancing with him, laughing with him, making love with him. The yearning and desire had only increased.

Although Amy was totally behind her lifestyle change and the pregnancy, she was not too thrilled that the father hadn't shown up. Casey had told her sister about Luke—well, what she could tell her about Luke—and Amy was very protective. Casey couldn't blame her. If the situation were reversed, she probably would feel the same way, yet she knew something her sister didn't. Luke was not an ordinary man.

Luke d'Séraphin was an angel in disguise and he had delivered quite a message into her life!

She opened her teacup and blew away the steam before gently sipping. She had wanted someone special to be the father of her child, and she'd certainly gotten her wish. It was actually okay with her to be alone now. The love she shared with Luke could never be diminished by time.

She watched an older couple, dressed in winter clothes, walk hand in hand across the street. The woman stopped at a window to admire the spectacular sculptures being offered for sale. The man put his arm around the woman as the two of them admired the artistry.

That would be nice, she thought, to grow old with Luke . . . to share adventures and dreams. She should make that her next wish, since all of them seemed to be coming to pass.

Closing her eyes for a moment, she smiled as she centered herself and took a deep breath.

I wish to grow old with Luke . . . no matter where we are or what we're doing. I just want to share my life with his, my love with his, always.

She opened her eyes and sent it out there into the universe and didn't worry about how much time it would take to fulfill it. Satisfied, she opened her bag and took out her bagel. Chewing happily, she saw the Indians across the street selling their beautiful silver jewelry in front of the Governor's Palace and thought she might reward herself for getting José's huge Mexican restaurant as her latest account.

Why not pamper herself?

Making up her mind to do just that, she wrapped the remaining bagel in its wrapper and dropped it into the bag. Taking another sip of tea, she replaced the lid and stood up. She gathered her things and started across the plaza. Something silver . . . a bracelet maybe, or a ring with a stone to mark this time when everything in her life seemed to be unfolding so beautifully. Some might call it luck, but not her. She could see how one thing led to another now, how at each crossroads she had made a decision, and each time she had called on something within her that had been labeled faith, trust, or love to make the appropriate choice. Somehow it all worked out.

She was filled with happiness, her attention captured by a certain blanket. The sun was glittering on a wide silver cuff which seemed to capture the shining brilliance. She began to cross the street when suddenly everything started to slam into her consciousness . . .

A car approaching too fast.

Her feet frozen in fear.

In an instant she thought her mind had separated from her body. Everything began to move in slow motion, as though she were watching herself in a movie. All she heard was the pounding of her heart and the rush of blood in her veins. Somehow she sensed she couldn't stop what was unfolding in front of her. Just as she began to accept the inevitable, she felt a force that nearly took her breath away . . . a force so hard, her teacup flew out of her hand and she was spun around and stumbled into a dark figure as the car whizzed past.

"*Buenos días, señorita.* I believe we have met before."

The voice! She squinted hard to make out the face.

"When I told you to enjoy the moment, *querida,* I didn't mean to become oblivious to everything around you." He leaned closer and whispered, "Part of being a time traveler is being aware of where you are."

Luke!

Yes, it was he! Luke d'Séraphin, philosopher, builder, time traveler extraordinaire, and let's not forget, father-to-be!

Stunned, she watched him take her bag and the ledger. "I don't think I want you going anywhere without me again," he said with a breathtaking smile.

She could only stare at him, wearing his cowboy hat and that big riding coat. Her hands free, she suddenly pushed him on the shoulders. *"Where have you been?!"*

He laughed at her actions and said, "Oh, my love . . . how I have missed you. Come here and give me a kiss, for I've been busy and have dreamed of this moment."

All questions vanished as her body relaxed with gratitude. She slipped her arms around his waist and hugged him closer. His lips gently brushed hers for just a moment in greeting before becoming more insistent, demanding a response that Casey gladly gave.

I knew he would find me, her heart sang.

She had followed her heart and here she was . . . in a moment of sheer bliss.

"Come, let's get off the street," he whispered into her mouth.

Realizing they actually were in the street, she giggled and allowed him to lead her back into the plaza. It was like waking from a dream, one that she'd had so often. It was why she kept coming back to the plaza, day after day . . . wanting, dreaming, wishing . . . and here it was. She was protected beneath Luke's strong arm.

"I still want to know where you've been," she announced in a falsely stern voice while leaning her head against his upper arm and squeezing his waist.

He chuckled. "I've been busy arranging some things and—"

Her head snapped up. "You think *you've* been busy?" she interrupted in disbelief. "Well, let me tell you a thing or two, Mister Time Traveler . . . I've quit my job, moved out here, hustled myself a fine little business, and—"

"*Estoy aquí, mi amor* . . . I am here, my love," he whispered, bending his head and looking at her beneath the wide brim of his cowboy hat. "You are brave, Casey . . . and irresistible." It was his smile that was irresistible. "Not many would seduce an angel and then draw him back again and again. Have you no shame for the quandary you have created? Have you no regrets?"

The child within her seemed to quicken with soft butterfly movements. "None," she answered truthfully. "If I had any, it would be that I didn't meet you years ago. We've lost so much time."

His brown eyes seemed to sparkle with mischief. "What's time, my love?"

She giggled again. "I would say an illusion, 'cause I know that answer would please you, but I've got to say in five months we're going to be on a whole new adventure."

"You know this?" he asked with a smile, placing her things on an empty bench.

"Uh-huh," she replied. "I know this."

He looked at her again, closely . . . smiling into her eyes, connecting with her deeply. "You have changed," he whispered in an impressed voice. "You must have been learning on your own, for you're literally beaming now."

"There's a reason," Casey threw out to see if he would catch her drift. Maybe being pregnant, she wasn't so easy to read. There could be lots of bennies to her condition she had yet to discover.

"I'm sure there is a reason. Would you care to share it?"

"I'm pregnant. Four months pregnant, to be exact. In May of next year, you and I will be entering the adventure of parenthood, Luke."

She watched as his eyes became huge with shock. She was right. He didn't know. He seemed stunned and slowly lowered himself to the bench. Stifling a laugh, Casey sat next to him and started rubbing his back.

"Breathe," she ordered, and watched as he took a huge gulp of air.

"Now, breathe again," she advised just as he had done in a different time, under different circumstances. It was obvious that on this new adventure she wasn't the rookie. Luke was. "Now calm down and tell me how you feel."

He stared out at the street for a moment before turning to her. He still looked surprised, yet there was something in his eyes and she swore it was tears. "Do you remember when you first told me that you had been thinking about having a baby right before you were brought back in time?"

She smiled. "Yes. You looked like I had dropped a brick on your head."

"That's because I knew your thoughts had been so powerful that you were making your future unfold, and it was obvious I was to be a part of it. It really shook me. Me, a father . . ."

"And now?" She held her breath as she waited for his answer.

"I came back to you, Casey, *for* you, but this . . . this miracle makes the adventure all the more beautiful, *querida. Gracias,* from my heart."

He gathered her in his arms. "We must get married at once!"

Casey sank into his embrace with such love that she couldn't contain it. She started giggling.

"What?" He pulled back and searched her face. "Why are you laughing?"

"Oh, Luke," Casey said, wiping at the moisture under her eyes. "I'm giggling like a bloody fool all the time now. I just love the way this pattern is unfolding. Of course I'll marry you . . . *again!*"

He was staring at her and she felt herself lost in the past, in their shared memories, in his dark fathomless eyes, his tender yet sensual smile.

"Fools rush in where angels fear to tread, my love. I could not stay away. You've enchanted me with your love, and a love such as yours, anywhere, in any time, is irresistible to my kind. We have all the time we need to live as one."

"I know," Casey breathed as it all fell into place. "Two fools."

"You will understand when I must disappear for short periods? That I still have services to perform?"

"I understand." She could think of a few services he could perform as soon as they were back at the apartment.

He nodded. "That is what I was doing. I had to retrieve that note you left for Rosalinda, and I have something for you." He reached into the inside pocket of his coat and held out his hand.

Casey opened her palm and watched as her four-leaf-clover pendant fell into it.

Staring at him, her hand, and then back at him, she whispered, "Rosa gave it to you?"

"*Sí*, she said it worked for her." He closed his eyes briefly. "I must get her words right. She said to tell you that hope, faith, love, and destiny all came together when Tomás asked her to be his wife. Now it's your turn and she hopes we will attend her wedding feast."

"Rosa's getting married to Tomás?" Why that surprised her, considering how everything else was unfolding, she didn't know . . . Just the shock of holding her pendant again was startling.

"*Sí*, a summer wedding is planned. Do you think we could find a baby-sitter, my love?"

Still stunned, Casey held up her hand and began her rant. "Oh, I am not planning that far ahead. And you still have to meet my sister. She isn't too pleased with you at the moment, but when she gets to know you, she'll understand. Whether she'll baby-sit or not is another story."

Luke pulled her into his arms. "Oh, my precious angel . . . I am so sorry I wasn't here for you. When you said you had left something behind, I had to go back for it."

"I caused this?" Casey murmured against his neck.

He shook his head. "There is no blame, my love . . . there is only now. We're together. I am honored you are carrying our child beneath your heart. I will be here for you. I promise. We are a united force now."

She sighed as she looked down the street to the chapel where his staircase drew hundreds of visitors each week. How many women could claim to be loved by someone whose very name means angel of light? There were no detours on the road to grace, only side trips, all leading back to this moment of joy. Again she counted her blessings.

Why, she'd almost given up until Luke had come along, enchanting her, reminding her of what every unmarried person secretly feels and often denies . . .

She just knew she had a greater destiny.

Acknowledgments

Lyssa Keusch—my editor, for her excellent skills and her encouragement.

Marcy Posner—my agent, for her optimism and her belief in this genre.

Kristen and Ryan Flannery—my children, for their patience, their humor, and especially their love.

Ann O'Day, Colleen Quinn, Pat Trowbridge, Leslie Esdaile—my mother, my friends, and all sisters of my soul, who have never failed to be there.

Cristopher Cornell Sterling, for the selfless hours of research and organization so I can write faster, and for the unending support and love that has brought joy not only into my life but also into my work.

Welcome to the world
of the Avon Romance Superleader
Where anything is possible . . .
and dreams really do come true

We all know there are unspoken rules that govern the acts of courtship. There are the rules of today (if he doesn't call by Wednesday he won't, even if he says he will!) and the rules of days gone by (a lady should never dance more than three times with a gentleman).

But often, what is expected is at odds with what is longed for . . . and how you're allowed to act is different from the way you feel. Heaven help you if you take a wrong step . . . but sometimes it's better to toss the rules away, take matters into your own hands—just as the heroines of these upcoming Avon Romance Superleaders are about to do.

HERE COMES THE BRIDE
Pamela Morsi

JULY AVON ROMANCE SUPERLEADER

Gussie Mudd, the proprietor of a small ice business in
Cottonwood, Texas, has determined that at some point in a
woman's life she must get herself a man, or give up on the
idea entirely. To get her man she decides to play by the
rules . . . the rules of business. And she makes a business
proposition to her employee, Mr. Rome Akers.

"PEOPLE, MR. AKERS, ARE JUST LIKE BUSINESSES. THEY
act and think and evolve in the same way as commercial enterprise. People want and need things. But
when they are vastly available, they prize them differently."

"Well, yes, I guess so," Rome agreed.

"So when we consider Mr. Dewey's hesitancy to
marry me," she continued, "we must avoid emotional-
ism and try to consider the situation logically."

"Logically?"

Rome was not sure that logic was a big considera-
tion when it came to love.

"Mr. Dewey has been on his own for some time

now," she said. "He has a nice home, a hired woman to cook and clean, a satisfying business venture, good friends and myself, a pleasant companion to escort to community events. Basically all his needs as a man are met. He has a virtual monopoly on the things that he requires."

Rome was not certain that *all* of a man's *needs* had been stated, but after his embarrassing foray in that direction, he chose not to comment.

"He is quite comfortable with his life as it is," Miss Gussie continued. "Whyever should he change?"

"Why indeed?" Rome agreed.

She smiled then. That smile that he'd seen often before. That smile that meant a new idea, a clever innovation, an expansion of the company. He had long admired Miss Gussie's good business sense and the very best of her money-making notions came with this smile.

"I can do nothing about Mr. Dewey's nice home, the woman hired to cook and clean, his business, or his friends," Miss Gussie said. "But I can see that he no longer has a monopoly upon my pleasant companionship."

"I'm not sure I understand you," Rome said.

"In our business if Purdy Ice began delivering smaller blocks twice a week, we would be forced to do the same."

Rome nodded. "Yes, I suppose you are right about that."

"We would be forced to change, compelled to provide more service for the same money," she said.

"Yes, I suppose that's right."

"That's exactly what we're going to do to Amos Dewey," she declared.

Rome was listening, but still skeptical.

"You are going to pretend to be in love with me," she said as if that were going to be the simplest thing in the world. "You will escort me about town. Sit evenings on this porch with me. Accompany me to civic events."

That seemed not too difficult, Rome thought. He did not normally attend a lot of public functions, but, of course, he could.

"I don't see how that will change Dewey's mind," he told her honestly.

"You will also let it be known that you are madly in love with me," she said, "and that you are determined to get me to the altar as soon as possible."

Rome got a queasy feeling in his stomach.

"Amos Dewey will no longer have a monopoly. *You* will be the competition that will force him to provide the service he is not so willing to provide—marrying me."

Gussie raised her hands in a gesture that said that the outcome was virtually assured.

Rome had his doubts.

"I'm not sure this will work, Miss Gussie," he told her. "Men . . . men don't always behave like businesses. They are not all that susceptible to the law of supply and demand."

"Don't be silly," she said. "Of course they are."

"I'm not sure I'm the right man to be doing this. Perhaps you should think of someone who would seem more . . . well more suited to the task."

Her response was crisp and cool.

"I was hoping for a late-spring wedding," she told him. "When the flowers are at their peak. But I suppose, in this instance midsummer would be fine. Let's say the Fourth of July; that sounds like an auspicious day for a wedding. It is going to be absolutely perfect. The most perfect wedding this town has ever seen. I do hope you will be there, Mr. Akers."

~ ❧ ~

HEAVEN ON EARTH
Constance O'Day-Flannery

AUGUST AVON ROMANCE SUPERLEADER

For Casey O'Reilly the world was supposed to be an orderly place where you met, married, and had children with the man you love. But nothing had gone according to plan. Mr. Right never made an appearance, and now, at "thirtysomething," Casey figured she had a better chance at being struck by lightning than struck by love . . . but then the unthinkable happened . . .

SHE WAS MAKING THIS UP. WHATEVER WAS HAPPENING was all in her mind. *It had to be!*

Desperately, Casey rubbed at her eyes and then cupped her hands around them to shelter her face as more lightning, familiar narrow streaks, flashed around her and thunder rumbled.

There was no time for questions as a man slowly, deliberately, walked closer, as though he had no fear of the lightning or the sandstorm. Casey's voice was stuck in her throat. She wanted to ask him who he was, but only garbled noises emerged from her mouth as she watched him unbutton his dark coat above her. His face was hidden by a wide turned-up collar and the cowboy hat pulled low over his brow, but somehow the closer he came, the less she feared him.

He knelt before her and, without a word, wrapped the edges of the raincoat around her, pulling her to his chest and sheltering her from the sandstorm. She could feel the strength of his arms around her back, and immediately sensed peace as she was gathered into the sanctuary of his body. She felt the strong beat of his heart reverberating against her face. She smelled something citrusy, very earthy, about him, and lifted her hand to cling to his soft shirt.

"You are all right, Casey O'Reilly."

She almost jumped at the close proximity of his voice resonating from his chest and into her ear. The low soothing tone sent shivers throughout her body and she found herself clinging even more tightly to his shirt.

"Who . . . Who are you?" she managed to mutter.

"I've come to help," he answered, holding her tighter as another crash of thunder made the ground shake violently beneath them.

"Thank heavens," she sobbed.

Somehow she felt incredibly safe, more so than she had ever felt in her life. Her body was tingling with some strange and powerful energy that was unfamiliar and yet . . . so perfectly wonderful. She felt a renewed strength welling up in her muscles, spreading through her body down to her burning foot. Her chest stopped aching and her headache eased as she held this man who had just walked out of a bolt of lightning and into her life . . .

&

HIS WICKED PROMISE
Samantha James
September Avon Romance Superleader

Glenda knew what was expected of a Highland lass—she must wed a man bold and strong enough to protect her. Love could come later . . . if it came at all. But although she was now without a husband, she had once known the joy of the marriage bed . . . and the pleasure that Laird Egan was willing to reacquaint her with . . .

"WELL, YOU ARE EVER AT THE READY, ARE YOU NOT?"

He cocked a brow. "What do you mean?"

"I think you know quite well what I mean!"

He was completely unfazed by the fire of her glare. A slow smile rimmed his lips. "Glenda, do you speak of my manly appetites?"

"Your words, sir, not mine," she snapped. Her resentment blazed higher with his amusement. "Though I must say, your appetite seems quite hearty!"

"And what of yours, Glenda?"

"Whatever do you mean?"

"You are a woman without a husband. A woman

without a man. I am not a fool. Women . . . well, women have appetites, too. Especially those who know the pleasure that can be found in another's body."

And well she knew. She had lost her maidenhead on the marriage bed, but she had never found lovemaking a chore or a duty, as she'd heard some women were wont to do. Instead, she had found it a vastly pleasurable experience . . . All at once she was appalled. She couldn't believe what they were discussing! To speak of her lying with a man . . . of his lying with a woman . . . and to each other yet!

He persisted. "Come, Glenda, what of you? I asked you once and you would not answer. Do you not find yourself lonely? Do you not miss the closeness of a man's body, the heat of lips warm upon yours?"

Suddenly she was the one who was on the defensive. "Nay," she gasped.

"Nay?" he feigned astonishment. "What, Glenda! Did you not love Niall then?"

Glenda's breath grew short; it seemed there was not enough air to breathe, for he was so close. *Too* close. So close that she could see the tiny droplets of water which glistened in the dense forest of hair on his chest. Niall's chest had been smooth and nearly void of hair, and it was all she could do not to stare in mingled shock and fascination.

She was certain her face flamed scarlet. "Of course I did! You know I did! But I"—she made a valiant stab at reasoning—"I have put aside such longings."

He did not take his eyes from her mouth. "Have you?" he said softly. "Have you indeed?"

A strong hand settled on her waist. In but a half breath, it was joined by the other. His touch seemed to burn through the layers of clothing to the flesh beneath.

"Egan," she floundered. "Egan, please!"

"What, Glenda? What is it?"

She shook her head. Her eyes were wide and dark. Her head had lifted. Her lips hovered but a breath beneath his. The temptation to give in, to kiss her, to trap her lips beneath his and taste the fruit of her mouth was all-consuming. Almost more than he could stand.

She wanted it, too. He sensed it with every fiber of his being, but she was fighting it, damn her! Yet still he wanted to hear her say it. He *needed* it.

"Tell me, Glenda. What is it you want?"

She shook her head. Her hands came up between them. Her fingers opened and closed on his chest . . . his *naked* chest. Dark, bristly hairs tickled her palm; to her the sensation was shockingly intimate. Yet she did not snatch back her hands—she did not push him away—as she should have.

As she could have.

"Egan? Are you here, lad?"

It was Bernard. They jerked apart. Egan moved first, stepping back from her. Did he curse beneath his breath? Glenda did not wait to find out.

She fled. Her heart was pounding and her lungs labored as if the devil himself nipped at her heels. Her feet did not stop until she was safe in her own chamber and the door was shut.

'Twas then that her strength deserted her. She pressed her back against it and slumped, landing in a heap on the floor.

Thrice now, Egan had almost kissed her. *Thrice.*

What madness possessed him? Sweet heaven, what madness possessed *her*?

For Glenda could not deny the yearning that still burned deep in her heart. Just once she longed to feel the touch of his mouth on hers. Just once . . .

RULES OF ENGAGEMENT
Christina Dodd

OCTOBER AVON ROMANCE SUPERLEADER

Miss Pamela Lockhart knew that proper behavior could guide a governess through any trying situation. The rules were straight-forward: never become too familiar with your employer, always take your meals upstairs on a tray, and remember your station at all times. But what happens when your employer is devastatingly handsome . . . and his behavior is anything but proper?

"YOU CONSIDER MARRIAGE THE SURE ROUTE TO MISERY."

"Not really." He stroked his chin, a gesture he had adopted from his grandfather. "The trick to marriage is not letting expectations get in the way. A man needs to understand why women get married, that's all."

Her mouth drew down in typical Miss Lockhart censure. "Why, pray tell, do women get married?"

"For money, usually." He could tell she was offended again, but with Miss Lockhart he didn't have to worry overly much about offense. After all, she didn't. Besides, he thought his assessment quite fair. "I don't blame them. The world is not fair to a spinster.

She has no recourse but to work or starve. So if she's asked, she marries."

Obviously, *Miss Lockhart* did not consider his assessment fair. She slapped her mug on the table so hard the crockery rattled. "Do you have any idea how insulting you are? To think a woman is single because she has never been asked, or if she is married she has done so for monetary security?"

He found himself entertained and very, very interested. "Ah, I've touched a nerve. Are you telling me there is a man alive who dared to propose to you?"

"I am not telling you anything." But swept along by her passion, she did. "A man can convey financial security, but whither thou goest, I shall go, and all that rot. A woman has to live where her husband wishes, let him waste her money, watch as he humiliates her with other women, and never say a word."

"Men are not the only ones who break their vows."

"So fidelity is a vow *you* intend to keep?"

Of course he had no intention of keeping that vow when he was forced to make it, and falling into that trap which had so neatly snared his father. "I've supported more women than Madame Beauchard's best corset maker. If I let marriage stop me, think of the poor actresses who would be without a patron."

She wasn't amused. "So nothing about your wife would be sacrosanct, not even her body. Your wife will cherish dreams that you never know about, and even if you did they would be less than a puff of wind to you."

Women had dreams? About *what*? A new pair of shoes? Seeing a rival fail? Dancing with a foreign prince? But Miss Lockhart wasn't speaking of the trivial, and he found himself asking, "What are your dreams?"

"You don't care. Until I spoke, it never occurred to you that a woman could have her dreams."

"That's true, but you are a teacher, and already you have taught me otherwise." Leaning back in his chair, he gazed at her with absolute sincerity, and then said the most powerful words in the universe. "Tell me what you want. I want to know about you."

She had no defense to withstand him. She leaned back, too, and closed her eyes as if she could see her fantasy before her. "I want a house in the country. Just a cottage, with a fence and cat to sit in my lap and a dog to sleep at my feet. A spot of earth for a garden with flowers as well as vegetables, food on the table, and a little leisure time in which to read the books I've not had time to read or just sit . . . in the sunshine."

The candles softened the stark contrast between her white complexion and that hideous rouge. Light and shadow delineated her pale lips, showing them in their fullness. Her thick lashes formed a ruffled half-circle on her skin. When she was talking like this, imagining her perfect life, she looked almost . . . pretty. "That's all?"

"Oh, yes."

"That's simple enough."

"Yes, very simple. And mine."

Careful not to break into her reverie, he quietly placed his mug next to hers. "Why do you want that?"

"That's what I had before—"

She stopped speaking so suddenly he knew what she had been about to say. Moving to the side of her chair, he knelt on the carpet. "Before your father left?"

At the sound of his voice, her eyes flew open and she stared at him in dismay. She *had* been dreaming, he realized, seeing that cottage, those pets, that garden, and imagining a time when she could sit in the sunshine. Her countenance was open and vulnerable, and his instincts were strong. As gently as a whisper he placed his fingertips on her cheek. "There's one dream you didn't mention, and I can make it come true." Slowly, giving her time to turn if she wished, he leaned forward . . . and kissed her.

⌒

JUST THE WAY YOU ARE
Barbara Freethy

NOVEMBER AVON ROMANCE SUPERLEADER

Allison Tucker knew that today's women were supposed to face their ex-husbands in a modern way—cordially, friendly, and with the attitude that you didn't have a care in the world. But every time she looked into Sam's eyes, she still felt a longing for what might have been if they stayed together—and what could still be . . .

"DID YOU EVER LOVE MOMMY?"

Allison Tucker caught her breath at the simple, heartfelt question that had come from her seven-year-old daughter's lips. She took a step back from the doorway and leaned against the wall, her heart racing in anticipation of the answer. She'd thought she'd explained the separation to her daughter, the reasons why Mommy and Daddy couldn't live together any-more, but apparently Kelly still had some questions, and this time it was up to Sam to answer.

Alli held her breath as she heard Sam clear his throat, obviously stalling for time. In that second she wished herself a million miles away. She hadn't meant to eavesdrop, but when she'd arrived to pick Kelly up after her weekend with her father, she had been caught by the cozy scene in the family room. Even now she could see Sam sprawled in the brown leather reclining chair looking endearingly handsome in his faded blue jeans and navy blue rugby shirt. Kelly was on his lap, her blond hair a mess in mismatched braids, her clothes exactly the same as Sam's, faded blue jeans and a navy blue t-shirt. Kelly adored dressing like her father.

"Did I show you the picture of Mommy when she dressed up like a giant pumpkin for the Halloween dance?" Sam asked.

They were looking at a yearbook, Alli realized with dismay. She'd hidden them away years ago because there weren't just pictures of Sam and Alli in the yearbook, there were other people in there, too, people she didn't want Kelly to know anything about? Why on earth had Sam dragged out the yearbook now?

"Did you, Daddy? Did you ever love Mommy?" Kelly persisted.

Answer the question, Sam. Tell her you never really loved me, that you only married me because I was pregnant.

Alli held her breath, waiting for Sam's answer, knowing the bitter truth, but wondering, hopelessly, impossibly wondering . . .

"I love your mother very much—for giving me you," Sam replied.

Alli closed her eyes against a rush of emotion. It wasn't an answer, but an evasion. She didn't know why she felt even the tiniest bit of surprise. Sam would never admit to loving her. She couldn't remember ever hearing those three simple words cross his lips, not even after Kelly's birth, after the long hours of labor and frantic minutes of delivery.

He hadn't said the words then. Or later in the days and weeks and years that followed, not even when they made love, when they shared a passion that was perhaps the only honest part of their relationship.

Alli clenched her fists, wanting to feel anger, not pain. She'd spent more than half of her entire twenty-six years of life in love with Sam Tucker, but he didn't love her.

～

THE VISCOUNT
WHO LOVED ME
Julia Quinn

DECEMBER AVON ROMANCE SUPERLEADER

If there's one place a proper young lady should not be, it's in an unmarried gentleman's private study . . . crouched under his desk, desperate to escape discovery. Yet that's exactly where (and in what position) Kate Sheffield finds herself. Even worse, Anthony Bridgerton has brought a potential paramour back with him, and Kate is forced to wait out the entire encounter . . .

ANTHONY KNEW HE HAD TO BE A FOOL. HERE HE WAS, pouring a glass of whiskey for Maria Rosso, one of the few women of his acquaintance who knew how to appreciate both a fine whiskey and the devilish intoxication that followed, and all he could smell was the damned lilies-and-soap scent of Kate Sheffield. He knew she was in the house—he was half ready to kill his mother for inviting her to the musicale—but this was ridiculous.

And then he saw Kate.

Under his desk.

It was impossible.

Surely this was a nightmare. Surely if he closed his eyes and opened them again, she'd be gone.

He blinked. She was still there.

Kate Sheffield, the most maddening, irritating, diabolical woman in all England, was crouching like a frog under his desk.

"Maria," he said smoothly, moving forward toward the desk until he was stepping on Kate's hand. He didn't step hard, but he heard her wince.

This gave him immense satisfaction.

"Maria," he repeated, "I have suddenly remembered an urgent matter of business that must be dealt with immediately."

"This very night?" she asked, sounding dubious.

"I'm afraid so. *Euf!*"

Maria blinked. "Did you just grunt?"

"No," Anthony lied, trying not to choke on the word. Kate had removed her glove and wrapped her hand around his knee, digging her nails straight through his breeches and into his skin. Hard.

At least he hoped it was her nails. It could have been her teeth.

Maria's eyes were curious. "Anthony, is there an animal under your desk?"

Anthony let out a bark of laughter. "You could say that."

Kate let go of his leg, and her fist came down on his foot.

Anthony took advantage of his release to step quickly out from behind the desk. "Would I be unforgivably rude," he asked, striding to Maria's side and taking her arm, "if I merely walked you to the door and not back to the music room?"

She laughed, a low, sultry sound that should have seduced him. "I am a grown woman, my lord. I believe I can manage the short distance."

She floated out, and Anthony shut the door with a decisive click. "You," he boomed, eliminating the distance to the desk in four long strides. "Show yourself."

When Kate didn't scramble out quickly enough, he reached down, clamped his hand around her upper arm, and hauled her to her feet.

"It was an accident," she said, grabbing onto the edge of the desk for support.

"Funny how those words seem to emerge from your mouth with startling frequency."

"It's true!" she gulped. He had stepped forward and was now very, very close. "I was sitting in the hall," she said, her voice sounding crackly and hoarse, "and I heard you coming. I was just trying to avoid you."

"And so you invaded my private office?"

"I didn't know it was your office. I—" Kate sucked in her breath. He'd moved even closer, his crisp, wide lapels now only inches from the bodice of her dress. She knew his proximity was deliberate, that he sought to intimidate rather than seduce, but that didn't do anything to quell the frantic beating of her heart.

"I think perhaps you did know that this was my office," he murmured, letting his forefinger trail down the side of her cheek. "Perhaps you did not seek to avoid me at all."

Kate's lips parted, but she couldn't have uttered a word if her life had depended on it. She breathed when he paused, stopped when he moved. She had no doubt that her heart was beating in time to his pulse.

"Maybe," he whispered, so close now that his breath kissed her lips, "you desired something else altogether."

ELIZABETH LOWELL

THE NEW YORK TIMES *BESTSELLING AUTHOR*

"A law unto herself in the world of romance!"

Amanda Quick

LOVER IN THE ROUGH
76760-0/$6.99 US/$8.99 Can

FORGET ME NOT   76759-7/$6.99 US/$8.99 Can

A WOMAN WITHOUT LIES
76764-3/$6.99 US/$8.99 Can

DESERT RAIN   76762-7/$6.50 US/$8.50 Can

WHERE THE HEART IS
76763-5/$6.99 US/$9.99 Can

TO THE ENDS OF THE EARTH
76758-9/$6.99 US/$8.99 Can

REMEMBER SUMMER   76761-9/$6.99 US/$8.99 Can

AMBER BEACH   77584-0/$6.99 US/$8.99 Can

JADE ISLAND   78987-6/$7.50 US/$9.99 Can

PEARL COVE   78988-4/$7.50 US/$9.99 Can

And coming soon in hardcover

MIDNIGHT IN RUBY BAYOU

Available wherever books are sold or please call 1-800-331-3761 to order.
EL 0400

New York Times Bestselling Author
SAMANTHA JAMES

Award-winning, *New York Times* bestselling
author Samantha James weaves unforgettable
tales of romance and enchantment—following
bold and reckless hearts to the breathtaking
places where the truest love must ultimately lead.

GABRIEL'S BRIDE
77547-6/$4.99 US/$5.99 Can

A PROMISE GIVEN
78608-7/$5.99 US/$7.99 Can

EVERY WISH FULFILLED
78607-9/$5.99 US/$7.99 Can

JUST ONE KISS
77549-2/$5.99 US/$7.99 Can

MY LORD CONQUEROR
77548-4/$5.99 US/$7.99 Can

ONE MOONLIT NIGHT
78609-5/$5.99 US/$7.99 Can

And coming soon
HIS WICKED PROMISE
80587-1/$6.50 US/$8.99 Can

Available wherever books are sold or please call 1-800-331-3761
to order.   SJ 0400